"A PAGE-TURNER."
—*Pittsburgh Post-Gazette*

"[A] sly whodunit . . . A surprise finish . . . [Brown] succeeds in conjuring a world in which prey are meant to survive the chase and foxes are knowing collaborators (with hunters and hounds) in the rarefied rituals that define the sport."
—*People*

"Set in a small town in the Virginia Blue Ridge Mountains, the meticulously structured work could be a sociology thesis on the rarefied world of the fox hunt."
—*Los Angeles Times*

"[Outfoxed] will appeal mainly to devoted fans of her animal-centric Sneaky Pie novels. . . . Brown, herself a dedicated Virginia foxhunter, clearly knows her fascinating terrain, as well as her steely, charismatic protagonist."
—*Publishers Weekly*

"Bestselling author Brown places her newest intrigue in the middle of Virginia fox-hunting country. . . . Anyone interested in fox hunting will be pleased. . . . Brown fans and animal lovers will also enjoy."
—*Library Journal*

OUTFOXED

Rita Mae Brown

BALLANTINE BOOKS • NEW YORK

A Ballantine Book
Published by The Ballantine Publishing Group
Copyright © 1999 by American Artists, Inc.

www.randomhouse.com

Library of Congress Catalog Card Number: 00-108945

ISBN 0-345-42819-6

Manufactured in the United States of America

First Mass Market Edition: December 2000

10   9   8   7   6   5   4   3   2   1

CHAPTER 1

On October twelfth, silhouetted against a bloodred sunset, a cloaked figure carrying a scythe was seen by three people. A gray fox also observed the reaper.

A stiff breeze kicked up from the west, sending a sudden swirl of fallen, golden leaves spiraling upward. When they fell to earth the figure was gone.

"Did you see that?" Jane Arnold, known as "Sister Jane," asked.

"See what?" the rugged man next to her replied.

"On Hangman's Ridge, I swear I saw the Grim Reaper." She pointed to her left, the deep green ridge rising softly from the meadows, a lone, massive tree commanding the middle of it.

"Sister"—Shaker Crown put his hands on his hips, shaking his head—"dipping into the flask again."

"Balls." She smiled at him.

It was an alluring smile and one that still carried a sensual message to men that even her seventy years couldn't erase.

"No, ma'am, I didn't see anything. Tell you what I do see. Fontaine Buruss hasn't kept his word."

"Damn him." Jane briskly walked along the grassy farm path to a three-board fence up ahead.

A coop, a jump resembling a chicken coop, was smashed to pieces.

"Lucky no cows are out." Shaker took off his lad's cap,

1

running his fingers through his auburn curls. "Fontaine." He shrugged. No other words were necessary.

"There are days when I think I'm a candidate for sainthood," she said, laughing.

Shaker put his arm around her small waist. "You know, boss, I say that to myself every day."

"Devil." She hugged him in return. "Well, let's stop the gap. Come back tomorrow morning and fix it right." She glanced toward the west. "Much as I love fall, I mourn the fading light."

"Yes ma'am." He vaulted over the splintered wood, heading for a dense forest at the edge of the pasture.

Within minutes Shaker returned, dragging a tree branch with a diameter the size of a strong man's forearm.

Jane put her hand on the fence post and swung over the destroyed jump, both feet up in the air at once. She'd broken a few bones over the years, felt the arthritis, but a life of hard physical labor kept her young. If she'd wanted to vault the coop like Shaker, a man thirty years her junior, she could have.

"Bullhead." She chided him because he didn't ask for help and the tree branch, blown down in yesterday's storm, was still heavy with sap.

The two kicked out the broken boards in the coop, placed them in the middle, then maneuvered the tree branch over the top of the coop.

"That will hold them tonight. Glad it's your fence line." He rubbed the sap off his hands.

"Me, too. Otherwise we'd be out here until midnight. Feels like a storm coming up, too."

"Yesterday's was bad enough."

"It's been strange weather."

"You say that every year."

"No, I don't," she contradicted him as they turned for home.

They'd parked the farm truck at the edge of Hangman's

Ridge. With the wind in their faces picking up, the truck seemed far away. Once inside the old GMC, Sister shivered.

"Someone walked over my grave."

Shaker gave her a sharp look. "Don't say that."

"It's an expression."

"I don't like it."

She burrowed down in her seat as he drove. She wanted to say more about whatever she'd seen on the top of Hangman's Ridge but thought she'd better shut up. They pulled into the kennel just as a weary Doug Kinser walked in, a gorgeous hound trailing behind him.

"Archie!" Sister's voice carried reproach as she stepped out of the truck.

"That's not like Arch." Shaker stared hard at Archie, who stared sweetly back.

"Good work, Doug," Sister complimented the young man, a man so incredibly beautiful that Zeus would have made him a cupbearer on Mount Olympus.

As Douglas led Archie, the hound, to the male side of the kennel, he said, "Sitting in front of a fox den. He wouldn't budge. He was pretty funny. He knows to come when he's called, but it's hard to fault a hound who hunts and dens his fox."

Sister walked over to Archie, one of her favorites. "Arch, did you try to dig that fox out?"

"No. I was waiting him out," a determined Archie answered.

"Softhearted women ruin good packs of hounds," Shaker said.

"So do hard-hearted men. Especially bullheaded ones. Good night."

"Night, boss." Shaker tipped his cap to her as she set off on the half-mile walk to her house. He knew better than to offer her a ride. He walked into the central section of the foxhound kennel, the feeding room. The housing for the hounds was built around this square and neatly divided in half by a concrete wall. Males to the left. Bitches to the right. Outbuildings off this core kennel housed sick hounds, segregated for their own good. Another building was the nursery, a place for bitches or gyps, as they were known, to birth and raise their puppies.

"Where was he this time?"

"Sitting down on the other side of Hangman's Ridge. Just sitting there looking up at the hanging tree."

"On the ridge or at the bottom?"

"At the bottom."

"See any tracks?"

"No."

"See anything on the ridge?"

"Uh"—Doug lowered his eyes, a brief flash of embarrassment—"yeah. Someone up there with an old scythe over their shoulder. Couldn't see their face. Had on a cloak, kind of, with a hood."

"Like Death?"

"Well—like the drawings, I guess. I called Archie to me and bent down to check him over and when I stood up, whoever it was was gone."

Shaker opened the heavy metal gate, turning Archie into the sleeping area where the other dog hounds, burrowed in straw, raised their heads then lowered them. They'd hunted hard that day and were curled up for the night. "Sister said she saw him, too."

An audible sigh of relief escaped Doug's lips.

"Thought you were hallucinating?" Shaker laughed.

"Was pretty weird."

"Certainly sounds like it. I didn't see a thing. Now I wished I'd seen him or whoever."

"Gave me the creeps."

Shaker glanced around the kennel. Everything was in order. "Let's clean the tack. I hate getting up in the morning to dirty tack."

About a quarter of a mile on the north side of Hangman's Ridge, running parallel to it, was Soldier Road, so named because during the Revolutionary War, the recruits hurried down the road to gather at the town square.

Along that road, at sunset, Fontaine Buruss was driving his sleek Jaguar back into town. He'd conveniently forgotten that he'd promised to repair the coop he'd banged up during the morning's hunt. His mind was focused on meeting a lady for mutual pleasure. If he timed it exactly right, he'd be home in time for dinner.

A cloaked figure, scythe on his shoulder, beckoned to him as he drove along the ridge. With his right hand he waved Fontaine toward him.

Fontaine slowed, then sped up.

When he reached his affairette of the month, the beautiful and much younger Cody Jean Franklin, the first thing he said to her was, "That goddamned Crawford Howard tried to scare me today. First he ran me into a coop on Sister Jane's land"— he paused, remembering he'd not fixed it—"and then the silly ass, dressed as the angel of death, waved me to him from Hangman's Ridge."

"How do you know it was Crawford Howard?"

"Who else would do that? He hates me. What did he think he'd do? Scare me to death?"

"Did you see his face?" Cody sensibly asked.

"No, the hood was over the face but it was Crawford all right. I'd bet my life on it." He started to fume and was ready to say he'd get even with that Yankee son of a bitch but then he noticed the time, considered his purpose in being there. "I brought you a present." He reached into his tweed coat pocket, retrieving two small packages.

She opened the larger package. A Navy SEAL watch with

a rubber wristband and a yellow face was inside. "Thank you, Fontaine. I can sure use this." The other package, a tiny glass vial of cocaine, she put on the coffee table.

He wrapped his arms around her and kissed her. She kissed him back. He knew he'd make dinner right on time.

Carrying a bobwhite in his mouth, Butch, the patriarch of the gray fox clan, crawled into his burrow, dropping the freshly killed ground bird.

He, too, had been by Hangman's Ridge, right along the fence line but in the woods. He'd watched Sister Jane and Shaker. He thought Archie was on the other side of the ridge. He'd observed the usually reliable hound get fixated at the red fox den that morning. In fact, he'd had an enjoyable morning watching the Jefferson Hunt get turned around backward while chasing three different red foxes. Better the reds than himself. He had hunting to do and he'd been out too late that night anyway. He should have been in his den by the time he heard the huntsman's horn. Still, the sight of all those humans bouncing around, falling off puce-faced, was too good to pass up. He sat on a moss-covered boulder by the creek and watched. He saw Fontaine, headed off by Crawford Howard, crash into the jump. Fontaine shook his fist at Crawford, who rode off as though nothing had happened. Then he had the delightful prospect of watching Fontaine, who had no sense of direction, ride around in circles in the forest. He only found the others because the hunt doubled back.

His mate and two half-grown children tore into the bobwhite. He'd eaten so much corn while hunting that he couldn't stomach another bite.

Inky, his black daughter, a wing under her paw, smiled. She was a most unusual creature and not just because of her color. She was smarter than the rest of the family and there were times when that intelligence was unsettling.

"The reds were out in full force today. I suppose they felt

it their duty to humiliate the Jefferson Hunt," Butch said, laughing.

"They usually do," his mate, Mary Vey, replied.

"Three hit the ground today. Not a bad day at all. And I saw Death on the way home."

"Someone killed hunting?" Comet, his strong son, asked.

"No, it's been years since that's happened. On Hangman's Ridge, the Reaper stood in the sunset, right by the hanging tree where I suppose he's claimed plenty of men in the past. He wasn't looking my way, so I think I'm safe."

"Anyone else see him?" Comet wondered.

"Sister Jane did. I saw her look straight at him and I expect that tenacious hound, sounded like Archie, on the other side of the ridge saw him, too. Don't know who else if anyone."

"I wonder if she really saw him?" Mary Vey, hearing a rustle at the main entrance, sniffed. The badger from over in the hollow was passing by.

"Oh, she saw him. The question is, did it register? Humans discount anything that doesn't fit into their version of reality," he said. *"But Sister, well, I expect Sister really saw him and knows she saw him."*

"I wonder if her time has come."

That night as Sister Jane drew the down comforter around her—her cat, Golliwog, on her left side; her Doberman, Raleigh, on her right—she wondered the same thing.

CHAPTER 2

"Crashed it all to hell. Slid off his horse, then stood there sputtering, shaking his fist at me. What an inspiring sight." Crawford Howard sucked on his briarwood Dunhill pipe as he gleefully recounted his run-in, literally, with Fontaine Buruss.

"So that's why he was so behind." Bobby Franklin, who looked like a defrocked friar, picked up an ice-cold shrimp, dipping it in sauce. Bobby was president of Jefferson Hunt, which put him in charge of organizing events, of politicking. Jane Arnold, as master, was in charge of everything connected to hunting. The master also made up any financial shortfalls.

"He's been campaigning nonstop behind my back and I damned well won't have it." Crawford calmly ate a shrimp himself.

"Craw, this is political. Of course he's campaigning behind your back and you might wish to start pressing the flesh yourself, and I don't mean just handing out money. You need to talk to people. Make them feel important and most especially important to you."

Crawford stopped chewing. He'd put on twenty pounds since youth, but he was in good shape. Medium height, blue eyes, and a pleasant voice, he was not an unattractive man. He wisely treated his receding hairline as a fact of nature and cut his hair very short, which always makes a man look better in

8

such circumstances. He sported a carefully trimmed short beard and mustache. And he was rich, disgustingly rich.

"I've shoveled money into the Jefferson Hunt Club for years. I should think that would signify the importance I attach to the club." He reached for his iced tea. His gold ring bearing the family crest reflected the dim light.

"You've been a contributor any master would pray for." Bobby paused, thinking about the sacrifices Sister Jane had made to keep the club going when her husband died unexpectedly ten years ago. "But people . . . you need to make people feel important. Fontaine is awfully good at that."

"Useless blowhard. They can't keep him in mattresses or mistresses."

"And he's Virginia born and bred."

"Not that again." Crawford put his glass down.

Bobby, also from the soil of the great, grand, and even haughty state of Virginia, declined to explain further. Crawford was in no mood to consider that the place of his birth was a drawback to his cherished goal, to become joint-master of the local hunt, a goal that in England often led to the House of Commons, if a man was clever. In America the initials M.F.H. behind a man's name or a woman's defined a form of power almost feudal in its scope even to those who didn't ride to hounds. Not to know that M.F.H. meant "Master of Foxhounds" signified that a person was beyond the pale, especially in Virginia and Maryland, still intense rivals over anything to do with horses, hounds, or foxes.

Crawford, after taking a deep breath, continued: "Bobby, only old people care about bloodlines. What matters is a vision for the future and the future is development. I understand that better than Fontaine. I'm a businessman. He couldn't find a dollar bill if it was taped to the bottom of his boot. And his trust fund is heading south." Crawford said this with satisfaction. "He can't carry the burden of a mastership."

"If people financially back him, he can."

Crawford froze. This idea had not once entered his mind. "Never!"

"Why do you think he's working as hard as he is, Crawford? For God's sake, you'd better wake up. You don't have this mastership in the bag."

"It's up to Sister Jane." Crawford felt Sister Jane comprehended money. And he was correct.

"Sister Jane will decide what's best for this club but she can't ignore the wishes of the members, and if there's a huge groundswell for Fontaine, you're in trouble." Bobby deplored the fact that Sister Jane had to find a joint-master, but she wanted to ensure the club's future and she heard the clock ticking. Healthy and vibrant as she was, she couldn't live forever.

Crawford, sobered by this unwelcome news, appetite fading, pushed his iced shrimp away from him.

The waitress at the country club quietly came to his side. "Were they not up to your standard, Mr. Howard?"

"No. They were fine."

"Might I bring you something else?"

"A cup of black coffee and a shot of Springbank, '58."

The country club, old and elegant, kept casks of fine single malts in the cellar. They also maintained special bourbons from Kentucky, small batches brewed by master brewers, for the discriminating palate. "Bobby, allow me to treat you to the best scotch in the world."

"No thanks, Craw, I've got to work late tonight. Princess and I have ten thousand copies of a four-color brochure to finish."

Princess was Princess Beanbag, Bobby's nickname for his wife, Betty, also a partner in business. Their print shop didn't make them rich but it paid the bills and had put one wayward daughter, Cody Jean, through the University of Virginia. Jennifer, the other daughter, was in public high school.

"You're a hardworking man. How do you stay so fat?" Crawford laughed at Bobby, who was as round as he was tall.

"Good genes." Bobby motioned for the waitress to return. "I think I'll have a cup of coffee, too, but with cream, please."

"Certainly." She left and soon returned with the coffees and the Springbank.

Bobby leaned forward. "Crawford, you know I back your candidacy because I think you can preserve and even extend the territory. You can talk to the developers and get bridle paths, you can talk to landowners and explain easements and conservation issues. I admire that in you. But you have a touch of the Yankee and you can't just go up to people and spout off."

"Bullshit. Virginians are the most direct people I've ever met. You people say the most incredible things to one another, scathing, blistering talk."

"When we know one another well—very well. Until then there is the dance of politeness, Craw, and we speak in code. You think you don't need to learn the code."

"Wastes time. If I go to the gas station, I'm expected to talk for fifteen minutes to the idiot behind the pump. I haven't got that kind of time. I have businesses to run and a big farm to manage."

"No one has time anymore but we make time. Those casual conversations—"

"Casual. Boring. The weather. Who shot John." Crawford used a southern expression, which made Bobby laugh because he didn't get it quite right.

"That's how we knit our community together. It's not about facts, issues, or how smart you are, Crawford. It's about respect for people. Respect."

Crawford shifted in his seat. "Well—"

"A little case in point. When you divorced Marty two years ago you cut her off without a penny. She had to fight through the courts to get any kind of settlement."

"Any man in a divorce does that."

"Some do and some don't. But if you want to present your-self as a community leader, m-m-m"—he wiggled his hand—"better to err on the side of generosity. Look, it's an old divorce lawyer's routine, 'starve the wife' and she'll get so worn down and scared she'll accept far less, but, Craw, you are rich. You could have given her a decent package, walked away, and looked like a prince, especially to women, and brother let me give you the hard facts, women run this show."

"Hunting?"

"Life."

He smirked. "The hell they do."

"I can't believe you've lived here for seven years and you haven't figured that out about the South and especially Virginia."

"You have a"—he considered his words—"dynamic wife. You can't extrapolate from your experience. Generalization."

"Okay. Let's say I'm wrong. Women are at the back of the bus. By publicly proclaiming Marty wasn't going to get a penny more than you thought she deserved you made plenty of enemies. Trotting around that twenty-year-old model after you dumped Marty hardly helped matters and how long did that last . . . ten minutes? You could have seen her in New York. You didn't have to bring her here. But worst of all, you opened the door for Fontaine to look like a hero."

"Oh that." Crawford's voice sounded deflated.

"That."

When Marty was in distress and couldn't pay the rent on her small apartment because Crawford had thrown her out of the house and she unwisely and meekly left, Fontaine had hired her to be his assistant in his landscape business. Fontaine was a landscape architect and a very good one when he chose to work.

"That." Bobby's tone dropped.

"I should have kept my mouth shut."

"We all have that feeling at one time or another."

"I accused him of sleeping with her." Crawford flared up. "He finds his way up more skirts!"

"But not Marty's. He was too smart for that, even though she is a fine-looking woman. Fine-looking."

Crawford's eyes narrowed; then he dropped his gaze into his shot of Springbank. "Live and learn."

"It's not too late."

"I made restitution. I bought Marty a house."

"Small but pretty. However, you need to mend fences, build bridges, and above all, listen to Sister Jane. She knows more about people and hunting than all of us put together."

The amber color of the scotch caught the light, golden shafts sinking through the Springbank.

"One other little thing." Bobby held his coffee cup up for a refill. "You need to apologize first to Sister Jane for heading Fontaine into that coop. You need to offer to rebuild it."

"That's Fontaine's job."

"Yes, it is, but do you want this goddamned mastership or not?"

"All right. All right." He quieted while the waitress refilled Bobby's cup. "What else?" He watched her hips swing as she walked back to the kitchen.

"You need to apologize to Fontaine. A public apology would be best."

"I will not."

"Then I suggest you watch your back because Fontaine will get even."

CHAPTER 3

At five-thirty in the morning the phone rang in Sister Jane's kitchen.

She picked up the phone, hearing a groan of suffering on the other end.

"Arrgh. Umm. Aah." The speaker repeated herself, the pain more intense.

"Betty Franklin," Sister simply said.

"Oh, my dear, did you hear me groan? I feel just terrible."

"And it's fifty-three degrees with a soft rain." Sister described the weather that October 14.

"Aah." Betty groaned again for effect.

"Are you whipping in today or are you auditioning for the American Academy of Dramatic Arts?"

"You are a heartless bitch."

"Suffering's good for you, Betty. Tests the spirit. Enlarges the heart. Sharpens the mind."

"I'm about as wonderful as I can stand. Even my husband says I'm wonderful."

"Your husband has imagination." Sister laughed. "But just so I know what to say at your eulogy, tell me, exactly what are you dying from today?"

"Arthritis in my lower spine, in my toes, in my fingers, and my stomach lining is irritated, although not my bowel, thank heaven. Cody's up to no good but I don't know with whom, and Jennifer got a D in math. A D! Naturally my mind hurts, too." This was said with uncommon good humor.

"This drizzle will stop by the time we cast hounds."

A long sigh, then, "Six-thirty. Whiskey Ridge."

"Is Bobby going to make it?"

"No, he's got to deliver the brochure today. I worked all night Tuesday so it was his turn last night. Looks good."

"Jennifer?"

"She'll be there."

Jennifer Franklin, their younger daughter, a senior in high school given to surprising mood swings, received science credits for foxhunting. Each week she had to write a three-page paper on what she learned about the environment. She'd written about the great variety of oak trees, the life cycle of the fox, and this week she was concentrating on amphibians preparing for hibernation. Three pages sounded like not much work but it turned out to be time-consuming due to research, although Jennifer discovered that she enjoyed it.

As Sister hung up the phone she checked to see if the lights were on in the stable and the kennel. They were.

"Good men," she thought to herself, for Douglas Kinser and Shaker Crown were already at work.

As professional first whipper-in, meaning Doug was paid, his responsibility was to condition and prepare the master's horses and the huntsman's horses for the hunting season. He also walked out hounds, assisted in their training, and rode forward of the huntsman so he could turn hounds back if need be. It helped if the first whipper-in was intelligent. Douglas was. He could intuit what Shaker was doing even if he was one mile away from the huntsman.

Golliwog reposed on the marble counter, her luxurious tail swaying a bit. Her calico coat, brilliant and gleaming, was a source of no small vanity to the feline. She'd eaten her breakfast and was considering dozing off.

Raleigh, also full, wanted to accompany Sister. He parked by the kitchen door, ears up, alert.

"Catch cold on a day like this," Golly laconically said.

"Lazy."

"Sensible." Golly rolled over, showing Raleigh her back. She disliked being contradicted.

Sister allowed her members great latitude in dress during cubbing, but she herself remained impeccably turned out. She wore mustard-colored breeches, brown field boots with a ribbed rubber sole, useful on a day like this, a shirt and man's tie, an old but beautifully cut tweed jacket, and a brown cap, tails down. She opened the door and Raleigh dashed out with her.

Golly lifted her head, watching them trot to the barn. *"Silly. Neither one has sense enough to come in from the rain and Sister wastes time hunting foxes. I wouldn't give you a nickel for the whole race of foxes. Liars and thieves, every single one of them."* Having expressed her opinion, she closed her eyes in contentment.

Sister ducked under the stable overhang and shook off the water, as did Raleigh. She walked into the center aisle of the barn, the soft light from the incandescent bulbs casting a glow over the horses and Douglas, too.

Raleigh joyfully raced up and down the center aisle, informing the horses of his presence. They weren't impressed. They liked Raleigh, but this morning he was just too bouncy.

"Ma'am. You might wear your long Barbour today. Don't want you getting the shivers before opening hunt."

"Douglas, you'll make someone a wonderful mother someday." She laughed at him but went into the tack room and grabbed her coat along with a pair of string gloves. She loved Douglas. Teasing him made them both happy. He'd grown from a skinny kid with green eyes, beat up just about every day at school, into a broad-shouldered, curly-haired, beautiful young man with bronze skin. Douglas's mother was white and his father black. He took the best from both.

Sister's son, Raymond, died in a freak harvesting accident in 1974. He was fourteen years old and there wasn't a day when she didn't hear his voice, remember his infectious smile, and wish he was with her.

She spoke rarely of her son. One lives with one's losses. The shock of it and then the subsequent grief had kept her numb for a year and then after that she was flat. She couldn't think of another word but "flat." Three years passed before she thought there might be joy in life but three things sustained her during those three years: her husband, Big Raymond; her friends; and her foxhunting. The former two provided love, the latter, structure and a sense of something far greater than human endeavor.

What was odd about Ray Junior's death was it occurred in a year of the black fox. When Big Ray died in 1991, there was also a black fox. He made mention of it, gasping for breath with emphysema.

"Janie, black fox years are watershed years for us. Mother—"

He couldn't finish his sentence but the black fox superstition was one of his mother's cherished beliefs, right up there with transubstantiation. She said that great upheavals or the death of a family member were always heralded by a black fox. Mother Arnold declared that her grandmother, in her prime during the War between the States, swore that in 1860 the whole state of Virginia was full of black foxes. People had never seen so many.

Sister knew there was a black fox kit, half-grown, in the den near Broad Creek, running through her property. Given the apparition she'd seen the day before yesterday and this fact, she couldn't suppress an involuntary shiver.

"I told you you'd get the shivers. Put a sweater on."

"I'm not cold. But you know, Doug, I saw the damnedest thing and I can't get it out of my mind. When Shaker and I walked back to the coop that Fontaine obliterated, I thought I saw the Grim Reaper on Hangman's Ridge right by that haunted tree. Of course, in retrospect I realize I was probably hallucinating, I was so hungry, but still, the man was as clear as day and I looked away and looked back and he was gone."

"Me, too."

"You, too, what?" She sat on a tack trunk for a moment as Douglas exchanged the regular English leather reins for rubber ones.

"When I tracked down Archie, he was staring right up at the ridge and I saw whatever it was, too. I told Shaker. Don't think he believed me."

"Didn't believe me either."

He held the reins, the bridle hanging from the tack hook. "It's a bad sign, Sister."

"I know, but for whom?"

He shrugged. "Not us, I hope."

She smiled. "You're young. You'll live a long, good life."

"You seem young." He laughed.

"Flattery, young man, will get you everywhere." She stood up, slapped her knees as she rose, then called out to her horse, Lafayette, standing patiently in his stall.

"Lafayette, it's going to be slick as an eel today."

"I can handle it," he bragged. *"I can handle anything."*

She smiled as he whinnied, walking into his stall to rub his ears and chat with him.

"Blowhard." Rickyroo, a hot thoroughbred in the adjoining stall, snorted.

Both Lafayette and Rickyroo were thoroughbreds but Lafayette at nine showed more common sense than Rickyroo at five, although Ricky would probably be a pistol at nine, still.

"Do you want to take the field or whip today?" Doug asked her.

"Take the field. After what happened Tuesday, I think I'd better be right there. Not that Bobby Franklin isn't a good field master—he is. We're lucky to have him on Tuesdays. Anyway, he was ahead, as he should have been, right behind the hounds, so this little contretemps happened behind him. No one was riding tail that day either." It was common practice to have a staff person or trusted person ride at the rear of the field to pick up stragglers, loose horses, loose people.

"I heard that Fontaine is spending money in every store owned by a club member."

"Fontaine is one of the most consistently underrated men you'll ever meet. That's the pity of it. He could have amounted to something."

"Being master of Jefferson Hunt amounts to something."

"Yes, it does, but I meant out there in the world. He's a good-looking man, so talented in his field, but the money he inherited made a bum out of him in a way. Pulled his fangs."

"Seems to do that to people."

"I'm beginning to think if you want to destroy your children, let them inherit a lot of money."

"Not my problem." Douglas laughed.

"Money brings tremendous responsibility and worry. People think if they have a lot of money they won't have any troubles. Well, any problem that can be fixed by money isn't a problem." She smiled. "Who knows, maybe you'll wind up rich."

Doug threw a white saddle pad on Lafayette. "I learn something from you every day. I'm going to remember that."

"Scrape and save now. Learn everything you can from everybody. I promise you, you'll use every single bit of it in this life." She walked outside Lafayette's stall, took her saddle and saddle pad off the saddle rack, and put them on his back. "I don't know what's gotten into me. I'm dispensing advice like a sob sister. You know, I think that damned whatever I saw and you saw has gotten under my skin. I'm afraid, Doug. You know I believe in fate, but it's something else. Something vague."

"I feel it, too."

"Oh, well," she sighed, "it's going to be a wild morning. They'll be popping off like toast and blaming me for going out on such a day."

"Not like the old days."

"No. The days of a master inviting only certain people to ride during cubbing season—long gone. You've got to invite them all, which makes it a holy horror because most of those folks haven't a clue as to what we're doing or why. Furthermore, I am considering cutting their tongues out. Actually, they've gotten much better about babbling in the hunt field. I'm being a crank."

"No, just being a master." He laughed.

Cubbing, a six-week to two-month period before formal hunting, existed to teach young hounds the whys and wherefores of hunting. It also served the same purpose for green horses and now, against most masters' better judgment, green people. The most interesting part of cubbing, though, was it also taught the young foxes what was expected of them, how hounds ran, the calls of the horn, and where to look for cover if they couldn't get back to their home den.

As older hounds brought along the young ones, so older foxes passed on their tricks to their children.

Douglas and Sister faced each other, checking out their gear.

"Ready?" he asked.

"Ready as I'll ever be."

CHAPTER 4

As the drizzle turned into a steady rain Sister had ample time to repent her enthusiasm. The hack to the other side of Whiskey Ridge, twenty minutes, soaked her back because she hadn't fastened tight the collar of her raincoat.

Carefully, Sister, Shaker, and Doug crossed Soldier Road, picking up the gravel road leading to the abandoned tobacco barn where they would first cast hounds.

The hounds, anchored by Cora, a mature female, behaved beautifully. Sister worried that the cooler temperature might encourage the young hounds to consider unplanned excursions but they didn't. Even Dragon, by nature wild and flashy, kept to the middle of the pack.

The few trailers parked by the side of the road testified to the fact that only the diehards would cub on this early morning.

Betty Franklin huddled in her trailer with Outlaw, her dependable, handsome quarter horse.

Jennifer, in the trailer tack room, called out, "Mom, I can't find my heavy socks."

"They're hanging on the end of my nose," Betty replied.

"Oh, Mom," Jennifer grumbled.

Betty heard her rummaging around. So did Jennifer's horse, Magellan.

"That kid can't get organized. We go through this every time." Magellan sighed.

"It's because they wear clothes. They can never find them. Really, they should go naked," Outlaw said.

"They'd get pretty cold." Magellan laughed. *"And it's bad enough to see some of them fully clothed. I'm not sure I could stand seeing all that hairless flesh."*

"Found them!" A note of triumph blared from Jennifer.

"Where were they?" Betty asked.

"In the bottom of the feed bucket."

"That's an excellent place for them, my dear."

Jennifer chose not to reply.

The staff and hounds gathered at the tobacco barn, black in the rain, as Betty and Jennifer emerged.

The only other people there were Marty Howard and Cody Jean Franklin.

Cody, on her own now, had bought an ancient two-horse trailer, paint peeling, and an equally ancient truck but both were serviceable. She made it to the meets on time. And she was glad to see her mother and sister.

Marty, borrowing Fontaine's aluminum rig, not only wore a dark brown oilskin raincoat, she wore brown Gore-Tex pants as well, neatly tucked into her high rubber boots.

"Sister, I know this isn't proper but . . ."

Sister waved her off. "It's cubbing and it's raining and let me know if the pants work." To herself she thought that Marty would be like an olive in a Greek salad; the material was too slick. "Since there are so few of us and aren't we surprised," Sister laughed, "if Cody or Jennifer would like to whip, you are certainly invited to do so."

"Yay." Jennifer trotted over to Shaker for her orders.

"I'll stay with you," Cody said, for she often whipped-in and thought she'd enjoy riding with the master.

Douglas tipped his hat to the ladies, paused a second longer in Cody's direction, and then moved a hundred yards to the north, as Shaker directed him to do. Shaker placed Jennifer behind him and Betty to his right.

"Ma'am." Shaker, proper even in the rain, cradled his hat in his lap. A huntsman shouldn't put his cap on his head until the master gives the signal to cast hounds.

"Oh, Shaker. I'm sorry. Of course we can move off."

He nodded at the master, clapped his hat on his wet auburn curls, and said to his hounds, "Hounds ready?"

"Yes!" came the tumultuous reply.

"All right then, let's be off." Shaker didn't blow his horn. As long as the hounds could hear his voice he kept his horn in his coat front between the second and third buttons. Besides, Sister loathed a noisy huntsman and whips. The quickest way to draw a reprimand from her was to blather.

The hounds moved ahead of Shaker. They lingered at the tobacco barn for an instant, a rich source of fox scent but it was fading fast.

"Come along now."

Obediently they trotted across the meadow, slick to the edge of the woods. He urged them into the covert as he waited outside.

"He's been here!" Dragon triumphantly barked.

Archie, older and pessimistic by nature, therefore the perfect anchor hound, sharply said, *"Of course he's been here, you twit. But he was here at three this morning. Before you run a cold scent look for a fresh one."*

"Besides, you've picked this up under a rotted log, Dragon. It will be washed away within two paces," Cora, ever steady, gently said.

"Cora, can we really do anything today?" Diana, a gorgeous female, first-year entry, inquired of the leader.

Cora lifted her nose a moment. *"Chances are we won't get much. Pick up and put down kind of day. Scent for twenty yards and then nothing, but we must try. A good hound always tries."*

Diana put her sensitive nose down, moving away from the rotted log.

As they moved slowly, their tails, called sterns, were held upright.

Douglas, a bit ahead, peered down over the western side of Whiskey Ridge to the creek below, swollen with rain, high and swiftly rolling. Crossing it would be difficult.

Jennifer, inexperienced, impatient, pushed the hounds up too much from the rear.

Sister and Cody rode up to her. Cody was on Motorboat, happy to be out.

"Jennifer, let them work. They aren't strung out." Sister pointed to the pack carefully making good the ground, working well together.

"I'm sorry."

"Honey, that's how we learn." Sister stopped and waited as Jennifer moved on at a walk. She listened intently, hearing only the patter of raindrops on leaves beginning to turn colors. She heard Lafayette's and Motorboat's breathing.

Cody, a fine rider, sat the thoroughbred–quarter horse cross with that grace so peculiar to her. She knew better than to talk when hounds were cast.

Sister turned to her and smiled as if to say, "That kind of day and I'm glad you're here."

Sister especially enjoyed the people who turned out regardless of conditions. Over the years they'd become her family, since her blood relations and her two Raymonds had died.

Archie, deeper in the woods, conferred with Cora: *"Distinguishable but . . . ?"*

"It's all we've got and most likely all we're going to get. You do the honors." Cora confirmed his thoughts.

Archie lifted his head, wiggled his tail a bit. *"Come along."*

"Old line," Cora added in her distinctive contralto.

The other hounds called out in turn and then together, loping along behind Cora and Archie, who moved forward. If scent had been hot, Archie would have taken his usual position a bit like a safety in football, a defensive position. A hot scent even a puppy can find and make good but a scent such as this, fading fast yet distinguishable on the moss and underbrush, demanded a professional.

Archie and Cora worked side by side, running a few steps, then slowing to check and double-check. It would never do to overrun such a pathetic little trail.

Dragon, bored with the pace, decided he could do better off on the right. Besides, maybe he'd pick up something more potent. He had no sooner shot off about two hundred yards than a loud crack pierced the beating rain.

"Leave it!" Betty commanded, flicking her whip out one more time for effect. The crack worked like magic. It usually wasn't necessary to touch the hound.

He scooted back to the pack.

"Settle, boy, because if you don't, you're going to get yourself in trouble and some of us, too," Cora growled at him.

Dragon said nothing but ran alongside Dasher, his litter mate, who showed promise but could be easily influenced by his brother.

"Dragon, come up with me." Archie curled his lip slightly.

A cowed Dragon did as he was told. The work was difficult and patience wasn't one of his virtues, but Archie had grabbed him by the neck, throwing him down hard in the kennels after Tuesday's hunt. He feared Archie, as would any hound with a grain of sense.

Sister and Cody trotted through the woods, the hounds in sight but well in front of them. Sister picked up the pace and soon was right behind Jennifer, who was right behind the hounds.

The hounds swung out in a big circle. Moving back to the tobacco barn and then picking up speed, they shot across Soldier Road and onto the low, broad, and long meadow between the two ridges. The great tree, enshrouded as though in a silver winding sheet, commanded Hangman's Ridge.

They popped over a coop in the fence line and then headed toward the coop that Sister and Shaker had repaired—Fontaine's coop, as they now thought of it. Once over that obstacle they continued at a trot through the thick woods.

The hounds moved faster.

"Fools." Butch heard the hounds in the distance from the safety of his den.

"Should I give them a run?"

"Just because they're dumb enough to get soaked doesn't mean you should." Butch scowled at his son, Comet.

"But they have to go out," Inky half said, half questioned. *"It's their job."*

"Which is exactly why we aren't domesticated. Domestication is for weak hearts. You can't do what you want when you want; you have to do what the human tells you. I hear, though, that the food is quite good."

"And good medical benefits, too," his wife, Mary Vey, added. She paused a moment. *"They're getting closer."*

"Following my old trail. Well, let's give them something to talk about back in the kennel. Damned if I want them digging out our main entrance." He grabbed a fresh chicken wing, feathers still on. *"Comet, get the rest."*

The two males, mouths full of pieces of chicken, walked out the oval entrance to their den.

"Want me to drop them?"

"Throw them all around." Butch dropped bones, feathers, a cock's comb, and a neck in a wide semicircle around the den entrance.

They casually sauntered back into their snug quarters with four escape routes, one of which hung over Broad Creek, as hounds drew closer.

The pack in full cry charged upon Butch's den within seven minutes.

"Chicken!" Dragon squealed as he grabbed the feathered wing.

"My favorite," yelped another hound.

Archie, with difficulty, resisted the temptation to grab a piece of chicken. He headed instead to the den opening, cocked his head to listen.

Cora joined him. *"I know they're in there and they'll burst out laughing the minute we leave."*

"You're right," Butch sang out to taunt her.

Archie turned to exhort the rest of the pack to start digging even though he knew he was sitting over tunnels and other escape routes. But it was too late. Shaker Crown was upon them.

"Leave it!" he bellowed. He then blew three successive short and sharp toots on his horn, which was his signal that he wanted his whips in immediately. Jennifer came up from behind, Douglas galloped up, and Betty rode in from her position.

Without a word, the mother and younger daughter dismounted, rushing toward the hounds as Sister and Cody trotted up. They, too, dismounted, each human grabbing a hound and pulling the chicken out of its mouth or even reaching into the mouth to pry out the bones.

They knew that chicken bones could splinter in a hound's intestine.

Fifteen minutes of frantic work removed the danger.

Humans and hounds, muddy, stared at one another.

Shaker, voice low and stern, chastised them: "How could you? Archie and Cora were the only two hounds doing their job." He turned on his heel and mounted up. The hounds, heads hanging, were both mortified and enraged, since they could hear the tittering in the den.

Sister walked over to the den. "Gray. This den has been occupied by grays since I first hunted this territory as a child. Maybe I ought to come back out here and drop them a fixture card."

"They know the schedule." Betty laughed.

Douglas swung onto the saddle. "They do know."

"I expect they do." Sister turned to Lafayette, leading him to a log. She stepped on the log, then lifted up lightly as everyone mounted up. "Well, let's call it a day."

Shaker quietly said, "Come along, hounds."

As the small band rode away, Diana, drawn by an overpowering curiosity, snuck back to the den.

"I'll get her," Doug volunteered.

"Don't rate her, Doug. She's going for the fox and she's young," Shaker ordered.

"I won't." Doug knew better than to crank on a young hound, but he cheerfully took the advice. Some people couldn't stand to be told what they already knew but Douglas was an easygoing fellow.

Diana scurried to the den opening, spread her front paws far apart, and stuck her head down the entrance as far as it would go. To her surprise, Inky was coming out to see the pack leave. They touched noses.

This surprised Diana. She jumped back and sat down blinking. Inky did the same thing. Then the smallish black fox crept up closer to the entrance to get a better look at the hound.

The two looked at each other. Then Inky, hearing Douglas, ducked back in.

"Diana. Come along," he sang out to her.

She hurried to him but thought to herself, *"They're like us. They're dogs."* She'd only smelled fox. She'd never seen one before.

Douglas soon joined the others, the rain beating down on them in sheets.

"Thought you said this would clear up," Betty, riding next to Sister, complained.

"I thought it would."

"You say that every time the weather gets filthy. 'Oh, it will pass.'" Betty mimicked Sister's voice, an amber alto.

"It does pass."

"In two days or two weeks." Betty laughed.

Cody rode over to Douglas. They were on the hounds' left. Jennifer was on the right as Sister and Betty now brought up the rear.

"Hi," Cody said.

"Hi," he replied.

They rode along, water spilling over their cap brims.

"You aren't very talkative."

"I think you're making a big mistake," he replied.

CHAPTER 5

The world was wrapped in silver-gray. Fontaine couldn't see the town square from his office window at Mountain Landscapes, the rain was so heavy.

Marty Howard buzzed him. "Mr. Buruss, Mrs. Arnold is here to see you."

"I'll be right there." Surprised, he pressed the disconnect button on his intercom, stood up, and checked himself in the mirror. He straightened his charcoal-gray tie with the small fuchsia squares; then he strode into the small well-appointed reception room, beaming, hand outstretched. "Sister, what a pleasure to see you on such a wicked day."

She smiled. "You're a fair-weather foxhunter."

"I certainly was today. Come on in." He winked at Marty, her blond hair in a long braid down her back. "Bring Sister a steaming cup of coffee."

"We were just discussing that. We were also discussing you giving me Tuesday mornings off so I can hunt. I'll work late Wednesdays," Marty said, happy to have Sister standing there.

"Two against one. Not fair." Fontaine, black hair razor cut to perfection, tan despite the season, wagged his finger at his good-looking secretary. Each time he thought of the distress he caused Crawford Howard, he laughed silently. Fontaine lightly cupped Sister's elbow, leading her into his office, a hymn to eclecticism.

She sat on the burgundy leather sofa. "Fontaine, I'll get to the point."

"You usually do, Mother Superior."

"First, you didn't fix the coop you smashed." She held up her hand as he started to apologize. "I know what happened there. But you wrecked it. You fix it. Those are the rules. Now as to the situation that caused it, talk to me."

The rainy weather affected his energy. He got up to pace on the other side of a coffee table inlaid with granite. He thought moving around would wake him up. "Chalk and cheese. Simple as that."

"I understand that." Marty lightly knocked on the door, bringing in half-coffee, half-cream, Sister's favorite midday drink. "Oh, thank you, Marty. By the way, I think Cochise is going very well. You've worked wonders with that stinker," she said, referring to Marty's horse.

"He just needed time. He's only six, you know."

"Yes. They learn at different rates of speed, just as we do."

"Whoops, there's the phone." Marty hurried out of the room, closing the door behind her.

"Let's stay on line, Fontaine." She used a foxhunting phrase referring to keeping on one line of scent.

He finally sat across from her in a leather chair, a burgundy that glowed against the taupe walls filled with exquisite hunting prints in old gold frames. Fontaine's family had left him the prints. "I can't abide that man. I'd use stronger language but not in the presence of a lady, a grand lady." He smiled, his even teeth a testament to good genetics.

She gratefully swallowed her coffee, the warmth chasing the chill she'd taken that morning. Then she put the mug down, composed herself, and said, "Yankees are what they are. However, he contributes to the hunt. He contributes to every charity in town, even the AIDS foundation, and most of our friends won't give them a penny. He rubs my fur the wrong way, too. He's loud, given to voicing many opinions, and he divorced one of the best women God has ever put on this earth. For nothing, I might add, but then you know all that. The truth is—we need him." She drew in a deep breath, which seemed harder than usual, the air was so heavy. "For all his faults, I think his heart is in the right place, except for the episode with Marty."

Fontaine weighed his words. "I can only address what I see. He uses money like a club or a wedge, depending on the circumstances. He pours money into Jefferson Hunt because he thinks he'll soon be joint-master." Fontaine, being a Virginian, could not say that he himself wanted to be joint-master. That would have been social suicide. He had to wait for Sister to bring up the subject and she had remained ominously silent for the last three years. He knew that she knew that he wanted the job.

"That's obvious. Another problem."

"You are the master. You've been the master for forty-some years. I grew up hunting behind you, Sister. You know I will support you whatever."

"I do know that. It's one of the reasons I'm here. I remember you walking out puppies when you were no bigger than they were. You know hunting even if you are a wimp when the weather turns a little, oh, damp. But a few words. Take a couple of lessons. You're getting sloppy in the saddle."

Fontaine, vain about his riding ability, blushed. "I hadn't realized—"

"No more on the subject. Just do it. Next, hound walk at least once a week."

"I will definitely make time."

"Money. Do you have anything left?"

He grinned. "Not much. I'm not a businessman, Sister. I'm just not."

"I know." Sympathy played on her even, delicate features. "We live in a time where money is the only value for most people. It wasn't that way when I was young and that isn't the nostalgia of an old woman. The golden calf is the true god now. I hate it and I can't do anything about it. Some would say you've squandered your inheritance but you gave to friends, to family. You were not and are not an unfeeling man."

Not expecting this, he quietly said, "Thank you, Sister."

"And I appreciate that you haven't drawn out Crawford in public despite your antipathy. You can be hotheaded."

"I can't promise I won't deck him."

"Well—who knows what tomorrow will bring. Fontaine, I'm seventy—"

He interrupted. "And beautiful. Truly, Sister."

"You do have a way with women." She lowered her eyes, then raised them, a gesture that had drawn men to her since she was a child. "I can no longer put off preparing for the future of the hunt without me. I hope I can hunt as long as Ginny Moss of Moore County Hounds, still whipping-in at ninety, but nonetheless, I must do something I have never wanted to do: I must take a joint-master." Fontaine held his breath as she continued. "You are one of us. You are known throughout the state by other masters. You've hunted with other hunts in other states. You've participated in many Masters of Fox-hounds Association functions. You've chaired committees on public land use. You've made connections in Richmond and in Baltimore, too. You're politically astute, as was your mother, god rest her soul. You have a good sense of what it takes to keep a hunt going although believe me, you never know until you're master. But Fontaine, you also have drawbacks. You are a philanderer of the first order." She again held up her hand. "I'm not judging. You know what Raymond used to say, 'Men have balls. They have to use them.' That's when I brought out the frying pan. At any rate, that caused problems. Messy problems. And you have little money to throw into the pot. Am I right?"

He gulped. "Yes, ma'am."

"Now I must ask you something directly. I am sorry to do this but circumstances compel me. Have you had or are you having an affair with Marty Howard?"

Relieved, he said, "No."

Her black eyebrows rose. "Why?"

He laughed. "Chemistry. And no matter what you may think of me, Sister, it wouldn't have been sporting. She was devastated during the separation and divorce."

"I believe you. Thousands wouldn't." She laughed with him.

"I deserve that."

"Sorrel"—she named Fontaine's wife—"is an unusually tolerant woman."

"Oh, Sister, we married too young. She's my best friend. We have an arrangement. Rather European. I would not end my marriage for anything in the world. I value her and I love her. Can you—?"

He didn't finish because she knew the next word was "understand." She finished her coffee, then simply stated, "Of course I understand. It's eminently civilized. And you have two small children to consider. As long as you and Sorrel"—she accented the "el," which was the proper way to pronounce the name—"can bring stability and comfort to one another, I applaud you. I am only telling you it is something one must consider. You may be rational about such liaisons but that doesn't mean the women will be when things have run their course. Or their husbands if they find out. There's no point in mincing words. Too much is at stake, Fontaine."

"Ma'am?"

"You should be my joint-master but I must consider everything."

His face drained of color, then grew flushed. "Yes. I do understand." His heart was beating wildly and he told himself it was a pastime. Why should he care so much? But he did. To be joint-master, serving with Sister Jane, would be a crowning achievement for Fontaine.

"Here's the hard news. I need you and I need Crawford Howard. Each has what the other lacks. If I chose two joint-masters, could you swallow your distaste and work with him?"

"I don't know."

"Well, you're honest."

"I would be proud to be your joint-master. I would give it everything I've got. You know how much I love hunting."

"You didn't love it this morning."

"You're right. I was a wuss. A wimp. A candyass. But I do love hunting."

"I know you do." She softened. "You know our history. You know the struggles we've had to breed the kind of hound suitable for our territory. You've seen the ups and the downs for much of your life. That continuity is vital for the club, especially now that we've tipped over into the twenty-first century. I still can't get used to saying it or writing the year."

"Me neither."

"I ask you to keep this to yourself no matter how much you want to discuss it."

"Have you spoken to Crawford?"

"No, I have not. I will do so this week and then I have to sit down and make a decision. By opening hunt."

"November sixth."

"Three weeks away and it still feels like opening night on Broadway." She beamed. "But I must. The club needs time to adjust to the joint-masters. We need those transition years while I'm still strong."

"May it always be so," he fervently prayed.

"I can't live forever, Fontaine, but I'd like to. Keep this under your hat. I will come back to you. Depending on Crawford's response, we may need to sit down together, the three of us. Fontaine"—she reached for his hand—"think this through. I need you. Loyalties are already dividing concerning you and Crawford. We need a united club. That's another reason why I must make this decision now."

"Sister, I promise I'll think about this. And I'll think about my own feelings toward Crawford. I'm not perfect but I can change."

She squeezed his hand, then rose to leave.

CHAPTER 6

The winds shifted from the south, bringing in even more moisture, but at least the rains scaled back to steady precipitation instead of a deluge.

Landowners called asking Sister Jane not to chop up their fields, so she canceled Saturday's cubbing. The landowners had more to fear from the trailers churning up the fields than from the horses.

She hated to cancel any hunt but decided not to grumble. She walked down to the kennels to play with the puppies.

Shaker joined her. Puppies were like people. The more you put into them, the more you got from them, the big difference being that puppies were more fun.

Sister and Shaker had worked together for twenty-two years as master and huntsman. They'd become so accustomed to each other, so relaxed when together, they could and did say anything to each other.

Neither was given to gusts of emotion. Both were dedicated to hounds and country life.

Each knew the other's virtues, faults, and secrets, and as is the way with old friends, each knew something about the other hidden from them. Sister knew that Shaker, for all his physical toughness, feared women deep down. He simply thought women were difficult, Sister, his best friend, excluded. Shaker needed love but he didn't know how to find it.

And Shaker knew that Sister's surface amiability masked a steely determination born of rank competitiveness. She didn't know that about herself, could never see that she had to best her older brother, a career officer, killed in Vietnam.

Each had endured the ups and downs of the other's marriage, secret affairs.

When Raymond Junior died, Shaker proved as considerate and strong as Raymond Senior. The bond forged in that sorrow would never be broken.

These two would be best friends until death do us part—united by time, temperament, and foxhunting.

"Good litter." Shaker rubbed a little fellow, turned over to display a fat belly.

"Bywaters blood." She mentioned a Virginian hound bloodline developed by Burrell Frank Bywaters (1848–1922). The Bywaters family, after the War between the States, used those hounds who had survived that violent upheaval to breed a strain of American foxhound with nose, brains, drive, and cry. Hugh Bywaters (1872–1952) continued the tradition, as did other family members.

"That and a touch of Exmoor Landseer." He smiled, naming a fine hound born in 1986 from England's Exmoor hunt. Shaker studied bloodlines. It was his job but also his passion.

"Good litter. Good year."

"Hope so."

"Douglas seems a bit down. Do you know what's wrong?"

"Woman trouble."

"What woman?"

Shaker reached for another puppy. "Same one."

"Oh no." Sister sighed. "I thought that was all over."

"If she could let go of the shot glass—" Shaker shrugged.

"In the blood. Bobby's brother. Drove himself right into a tree the day he graduated from high school. Drunk as a skunk."

"Bobby can put it away when he wants to. . . . He can hold his liquor, though."

"True. Old Man Franklin loved his bottle, too. A lot of things pass in the blood." She held a bright tricolor puppy in her lap. "Good and bad."

"Girl's beautiful."

"Her sister, too. Course Betty was a great beauty when she was young. She's put on a pound or two. Says it fills out the wrinkles." Sister smiled, for she loved Betty.

"I guess." A light red stubble shone on his chin.

"If any of us approached romance rationally, it would never happen and that would be the end of the human race."

"Wouldn't be such a bad thing." He smiled sardonically. "I married one woman and woke up with another." He referred to his dreary marriage, which had ended many years ago, although the scars remained visible.

"For all our faults humans are marginally amusing and sporadically talented. I don't think any of these beautiful puppies will paint *Night Watch*."

They sat in silence in the puppy wing of the kennel. The grown hounds were asleep in the adult wing, so it was quiet except for the patter of rain.

Sister spoke again: "I met with Fontaine Buruss."

"Thought you might."

"Time."

"Naw." He shook his head.

"I said that at sixty but it truly is time at seventy. We need a smooth transfer of power here over the next couple of years."

"Won't be smooth with Fontaine."

"There are precious few candidates. At least the man knows hunting enough to know what he doesn't know."

"He's an empty-headed peacock."

"Don't hold back." She laughed.

"He is. Cock of the walk. Doesn't know a damn thing about hounds." Since Shaker's whole life was hounds, that was his basis for assessing other foxhunters.

"But you do. One of my conditions, should I choose him, is he either stays out of the kennel or he shuts up and learns."

"But he can't learn. He's too interested in how he looks."

She knew there was a lot of truth in Shaker's assessment. Men judged other men differently than women judged men. They were harsher. "Crawford Howard."

"If that goddamned Yankee winds up as joint-master, I'm leaving. He knows less than Fontaine and he can't ride a hair of that horse of his."

"Fortunately, the horse is a saint. But if he were joint-master with me, he wouldn't bother you."

"The sight of him would turn my stomach. He thinks he's a bleeding genius because he built strip malls in Indiana and Iowa. He made money and that's all he's done."

"He plays the stock market and makes more. We need money."

"That's a fact."

"What if I made them both joint-masters? There's a strong current of support for Fontaine in the club. I can't ignore that, nor can I ignore our financial dilemma. We need a business-man. We need someone who can think ahead. Crawford has that ability, Shaker. I can't see my way out of this. I might have to make them both joint-masters."

Shaker reached down, putting another puppy in Sister's lap. "They'll kill each other."

CHAPTER 7

The Garage, an after-hours club in an abandoned garage, drew a young crowd on Saturday night. The music was good, the drinks were watered, and drugs were sold in the parking lot.

Bored, Doug sat at a small round table wondering why he bothered to go out. He'd downed two martinis and knew, given the weather, that drinking a third and driving those twisty country roads home wouldn't be the smartest choice. He left money on the table and walked for the door just as a wet Cody Jean Franklin dashed in.

"Doug. Don't go. I just got here."

"I can see that."

"Have I ever told you what beautiful green eyes you have?"

"In first grade."

"Buy me a drink?"

"No."

She tossed her long black hair. "Why are you so pissed at me."

"One word: Fontaine."

"That? Don't be silly."

"You're sleeping with him, Cody. I know you."

"Maybe you just think you do. I could care less about Fontaine and I'm not sleeping with him."

He grabbed her forearm, his grip tight. "Don't lie to me."

Coolly she said, "Let go."

He released her arm as though it were on fire, brushed by her, and walked outside.

Livid, she ran after him.

Doug had opened the door of his truck by the time she reached him. They were both soaked.

She slammed him against the side of the truck and kissed him hard. He put his hands on her shoulders, intending to push her away, but instead he kissed her back.

"Cody, don't do me like this."

She whispered in his ear, "Dougie, life's full of secrets. Some are even worth keeping. Trust me." She kissed him again. "Let's go to your place."

"Where's your car?"

"Jen dropped me off. I saw your truck."

He leaned his forehead against her forehead, flesh cool in the wet night. "Don't lie to me, Cody. I'm taking you home."

"Great. You can stay at my place."

"I'm taking you home. Period." He unlocked his truck. They both got in, the seats wet from their drenched jeans. "As long as you're fucking around—"

She flared up. "I'm not fucking around."

"Let me finish." He turned on the motor and the heat. "As long as you're doing drugs I'm not getting involved."

"But we are involved."

"Were. We broke up Memorial Day. One gram of coke and half a bottle of Absolut. Christ, I'm amazed that you lived."

She slunk down in the seat, staring out the window.

CHAPTER 8

By Sunday the streams, creeks, and rivers hovered danger-
ously near their banks. The rain slowed to a drizzle. The sun,
trying to break through the clouds, cast an ethereal glow over
the morning.

Crawford Howard worried about the water as he crossed the
arching stone bridge leading out of his property. A hurricane in
'97 washed away the bridge and he'd rebuilt it to the tune of
seventy-five thousand dollars. Stonemasons commanded exor-
bitant fees, especially in collaboration with engineers. They
vowed the bridge would withstand everything except a hurricane of Force 5, the worst of the worst. Crawford had no desire
to find out if that was true. The water, boiling and muddy
underneath the bridge, appeared to mock human planning.

The arched bridge with its large keystone provided a
symbol for Crawford. Opposing forces, lined up against one
another, held everything in place, made the bridge strong. It
reminded him of Elizabeth I's statecraft, playing the great
continental powers off one another while England grew
stronger. He admired farsighted people. Bismarck was another favorite, as was Peter the Great, although Peter was a
touch too emotional for Crawford, who considered himself
supremely rational. It was one of the reasons he was an
Episcopalian. One should worship in a civil and controlled
manner. Evangelism was for the unwashed.

Then, too, the power in most towns gathered at the Episcopal church. A spillover might be Lutheran or one or two might even be Catholic, always regarded with slight suspicion, of course. Lutherans were also suspicious because of the manner in which they'd broken from the Church of Rome. Crawford thought Luther might have tried more negotiation and less passionate denunciation. He could see no reason why Lutherans weren't members of the Anglican Church. After all, it was English whereas the Catholic Church was Roman. That would never do. Too much color and incense for Crawford. Besides which, the Italians perfected corruption and ill-advised business practices.

Crawford made no secret of being an Anglophile in everything except cars. Anyone worth their salt was.

He pulled into the parking lot of Saint Luke's, secure in leaving his Mercedes surrounded by other Mercedes, BMWs, Audis, and Volvos. His ex-wife's flame-red Grand Wagoneer stood out like a sore thumb. He grimaced, then cut his motor and reached down for his umbrella. He hadn't yet put the parking brake on, so the car drifted a bit before he realized it. He pressed the brake, irritated at his loss of focus. He turned the motor on and backed properly into the parking place. He locked the car and walked confidently into the church. He sat next to Marty, who smiled reflexively as he nodded to her.

The first year of their divorce he avoided her, sitting on the other side of the church, but he thought of himself as a proper gentleman, so as time passed he moved closer to his ex-wife each week until finally he was sitting beside her. Loath to admit the guilt and loneliness he felt, he couched his behavior in terms of friendship and civility.

The sermon by Reverend Thigpin, a young, swarthy man, intrigued Crawford because he'd chosen as his text Christ's admonition about a rich man entering heaven.

Reading from Luke, chapter eighteen, verses twenty-two

through twenty-five, where Jesus is speaking to a rich man, Reverend Thigpin's deep voice filled the old building: " 'There is still one thing lacking: sell everything you have and distribute unto the poor, and you will have riches in heaven; and come, follow me.' At these words his heart sank; for he was a very rich man. Then Jesus said, 'How hard it is for the wealthy to enter the kingdom of God! It is easier for a camel to go through the eye of a needle than for a rich man to enter the kingdom of God.' " Reverend Thigpin surveyed his congregation as he took a deep breath. "Are we to divest ourselves of all our worldly goods? Let's look at this in another fashion. At the time this text was written the gulf between rich and poor was cavernous. There was no strong middle class as we know it. Life was brutal, nasty, and short, to paraphrase Hobbes." Reverend Thigpin could use such references. Episcopalians went to college. They may not have read Thomas Hobbes but they knew who he was.

As Crawford listened to the sermon, he admired the young man's audacity in speaking thus in the lion's den. And he agreed with Thigpin's conclusions. We must read the Bible in historical context. We must cherish the message of forgiveness and redemption.

As to wealth, if one shares, one is doing one's duty. After all, in ancient Judaea there were no relief agencies. No one today led such a wretched life as the maimed and poor of that time. And what would happen if people of means chose poverty? There would be even more mouths to feed. The choice was to use one's wealth in a structured, moral manner.

Crawford liked that. He was going to remember that phrase, "structured, moral manner."

When the service ended he leaned over. "May I take you to breakfast?"

Marty studied her fingernail polish, then replied, "The club?"

"Yes."

Within fifteen minutes they were seated at Crawford's favorite table by the large fireplace, cherry logs crackling, each drinking a robust coffee.

"You know, Marty, time teaches us all and it has taught me that I allowed my lawyers to manipulate my complex feelings over our parting. I've spoken to Adrian"—he mentioned the director of the country club—"and I have purchased a full membership in your name. Now you can golf without those long waits at the public course."

Her lovely light brown eyes opened wide. "Crawford."

He lowered his voice. "Perhaps you would tee off with me from time to time, although I will never be as good a golfer as you. Used to frustrate me, Martha." He leaned forward. "I have been foolishly competitive and controlling. Then I turned forty and I don't know what happened exactly. Male menopause and all that but it was more. Some kind of primal fear. Didn't you feel it when you turned forty?"

"No, but I only just did."

"I thought women feared age more than men."

"Depends on the woman. Crawford, this is a generous gift. I'll regard it as a thoughtful birthday present."

"I sent you a dozen roses for your birthday. I almost sent forty but then I thought, 'Maybe not.'"

"How's the farm?" She changed the subject.

"Good, although I'm afraid the water will jump the banks again. If that bridge goes down, I'm building a suspension bridge out of steel girders."

"You'll rebuild what is already there because it's utterly perfect. You have an incredible eye." She laughed low. "Your strip malls look prettier than anyone else's."

"Do you ever regret leaving Indiana and moving here with me?"

"No. It's magical here. I only regret our marriage blew up like a grenade."

"My fault."

"I'd like to think that but maybe I've had to learn a few things myself. I thought I was inadequate. Then I thought you were inadequate. I'm not using the words I used at the time." He tipped his head to one side as she continued. "I was raised to believe my task was to complete you and that you would complete me. But I lived through you. When we were young that must have made you feel quite manly, I suppose. But as we jostled along in years, it must have been a burden. And face it, the sex wears off. No one wants to admit it. God knows, the bookstores are filled with remedies about how to keep the fire in your marriage. Perhaps some people can, but we didn't. I understand your chorus girl." Using the words "chorus girl" was the only hint she gave of a trace of bitterness. "So you see, it wasn't exactly your fault. You acted on your feelings. I didn't."

"You were bored, too?" He felt so incredibly relieved that she wasn't swinging the wronged-and-superior-woman cudgel.

"Constricted." Her hand reached for her throat.

They stopped the conversation while the waitress, the same one he usually had at the club, brought her eggs and his waffles. She refilled their coffee cups, then retreated.

"I went into therapy, you know."

"I did, too." She giggled. "I'm still going."

"Me, too. No one knows but you. Doesn't look good for a man to be, well, you know."

"I know." She told the truth. The double standard cut both ways.

"You won't rat on me?"

"No."

"Martha, do you think we could date? Get to know one another again on a better footing?"

She lifted her eyes to his. "Crawford, I never stopped loving you. I stopped trusting you. Perhaps we should take it slow."

"Tuesday nights?"

"Why don't we hunt together in the morning first, provided you don't run Fontaine into any more jumps."

A sly smile betrayed his glee. "Still mad, is he?"

"Fontaine has an endless capacity for revenge. Underneath that priapic exterior lies something darker than I realized."

"He has to one-up every other man he meets. Like you once said to me, it's 'testosterone poisoning.' I have a fair amount of the stuff myself." He poured more maple syrup on his waffles, which were so light they might have flown away.

She leaned closer. "Maybe it's a deep anger because he'll never be the man his grandfather was. People say Nathaniel Buruss crushed people underfoot."

"It's hard to become rich in business without crushing others. I thought that was a good sermon. Thigpin is quite good. When Tom Farley retired I worried for Saint Luke's but I think Thigpin is tough, good tough."

"Me, too. Back to Fontaine. I mean it. Don't run him into another jump. He's a pretty good rider. You were lucky this time but I'd stay behind him in the hunt field if I were you."

"I hate that you work for him."

"I'm learning a lot and much as you dislike him, he's been very good to me. Only good to me and a gentleman . . . and I'd like to open my own landscaping business someday. I really love it."

"The only reason he's a gentleman to you is I'd kill him if he weren't."

"Craw, in the beginning you didn't care. You were happy to be rid of me and he truly helped me through that awful first year. It was awful. If I learned nothing else, I learned that divorce lawyers have everything to gain by fanning the flames. They don't want to settle. They don't want people to work it out. My lawyer was as reprehensible as your lawyer, except he preyed on my being a woman. He was 'taking care' of me and I fell for it."

"A plague on both their houses. I should have given you all

the money I paid that bastard. Well, it's over. We're going to go on. I'm a different man, Martha. I truly am."

"Parts of the old one were quite wonderful, you know." She smiled flirtatiously and suddenly looked like the beautiful Kappa Kappa Gamma he'd met at Indiana University all those years ago.

He smiled magnanimously. "I owe you a great deal. You believed in me when I was young, and I wouldn't be foxhunting had it not been for you. You got me up on a horse and I will always be grateful for that."

"At first I didn't know if you'd stick it out. If you'd learn to ride. When you did, well, I think it made me love you more than I could ever imagine. You did it for me."

"Yes." He folded his hands together. "Now I can't imagine not hunting. I've put a lot of myself into the club, you know. I hope it pays off."

Crawford couldn't give to give. There had to be a payback.

"Sister visited Fontaine. . . ." Realizing she might be betraying a confidence, she quickly shut up.

Crawford tensed. "There's no reason for her to visit him unless it's about the mastership."

Fumbling, Martha finally squealed, "Maybe not. He has to fix the coop he smashed."

"He didn't say?"

"No."

"How long was she there?"

"Oh, twenty minutes."

He cracked his knuckles. "Damn! Fontaine is such a lightweight."

"Well, we were kind of talking about that. There's this part of Fontaine that wants to prove he's not. He's been cooking up some business deal he won't discuss. I only know it because I see the name Gordon Smith penciled in on his daybook occasionally." Gordon Smith was a commercial contractor building large office buildings in northern Virginia, especially around Dulles airport. Wealthy, highly intelligent, and driven, he lived in Upperville. "I also saw Peter Wheeler's name penciled in last week."

"Fontaine doesn't know the first thing about commercial real estate." He thought a moment. "Why would Gordon Smith waste his time with Fontaine? Peter Wheeler, though, that is bad news. I'd better get over there to see him."

"Don't underestimate Fontaine."

He grimaced, then smiled indulgently. "You're fond of him. He protected you when I was at my worst. I suppose I should be grateful to him. I'm not sure I've evolved that much. Just once I'd like to knock his fucking block off. I want to hear his teeth rattle across the floor."

"That's graphic."

"Sorry." He drained his cup. "I can't help it. I hate that bastard."

"And you want to be joint-master."

Downcast, he said, "Sister hasn't paid a call to me."

"Sister is full of surprises."

CHAPTER 9

Sister was full of surprises. She walked out into the Sunday drizzle just as Cody Jean Franklin pulled into the kennels. Cody was furious about Doug dumping her at her door. She'd had a whole night to get even more angry.

"Cody," Sister called out, Raleigh at her heels.

Cody turned, her baseball cap low over her eyes. She

pushed the cap back. "Good morning. You must have gone to church early this morning."

"Six-thirty service. I get claustrophobic sitting there with the eight o'clock rush. Where are you working now?"

"Freelancing. I catch a ride in the mornings and work at Shear Power in the afternoons. I quit waiting on tables."

"I didn't know you could cut hair."

"I'm the receptionist."

"Cody, what's wrong with you?" Sister bore down. "Learn the print business. Your parents spent their whole lives building that business. It hasn't made them rich but they paid for their home and sent you to college, and Jennifer will go, too."

"Jennifer can run the business." Cody feared Sister, but then most people did have a touch of fear about the dynamic old lady. "I'm not cut out for that."

"Well, what are you cut out for? You're twenty-five. You can't just do nothing."

"Not quite twenty-five."

"Don't quibble. You know exactly what I mean."

"Yes, ma'am."

"You must have a special interest."

"Horses."

Sister whistled to Raleigh, who had walked on ahead. He hurried back. "Hard way to make a living but if you love it, truly love it, then do it. You've only got one life and you spend most of it working. Do what you love. I did."

"You had Mr. Arnold." Cody showed some backbone.

"I didn't start life with Raymond. I taught geology at Mary Baldwin College. Of course, I graduated with a degree in English but they needed a geology teacher so I learned. Funny, it's helped me so much in hunting. Anyway, I worked. I taught even after Raymond and I were married. That was long before your time. I stopped when I had the baby. So there. Find something you like and stop wasting your life."

"I wish I knew. You make it sound so easy."

"It is easy. You're waiting for someone to live your life for you, Cody."

"I'm not. I'm a little, uh, rudderless right now."

"I'm talking to you because no one else will."

"Guess they're talking behind my back."

"This is a small town. The time to worry is when they're not talking about you."

Cody laughed. "That's one way to look at it."

"There's a rabbit over there." Raleigh could see it hop off in the drizzle.

Sister put her hand on the sleek black head. "I don't have any cookies." She returned her attention to Cody. "I'm glad you came out to help with the hounds."

Cody pretended she was there for hound walk. "They need to go out."

"Missed a day hunting. Do you know last year I only canceled twice. Twice. And here it is cubbing and I've already canceled once."

"The weather is—" Cody shrugged.

"Have your parents talked to you? About direction, I mean."

"Dad huffs. Mother is sympathetic."

"I see."

"I don't want to leave here. There's more opportunities in Richmond but I love it here by the mountains. I'd rather bump along than move there or go down to Charlotte."

"Charlotte is totally unrecognizable to me." Sister recalled the small textile town in North Carolina from her youth. "Here I've peppered you with questions but I haven't provided any answers. Can't, you know. Has to come from you."

"Well, when Jennifer gets out of college I think we'll start our own business. Maybe if she really takes over Mom and Dad's business I could work with her. I'm hoping—" She broke her train of thought and couldn't quite get back to it.

"Will you go out Tuesday?"

"I'm trying a new horse for Fontaine. Could be a rodeo show." Cody pulled her cap down again.

"Ride in the back of the field, then."

"Yes, ma'am."

"And Cody . . ."

"Ma'am?"

"You can't drown your sorrows. They know how to swim."

CHAPTER 10

Chickens amused Peter Wheeler. He'd built a sturdy chicken coop with a pitched roof, bought steel broody boxes, and built little ladders for them to perch on when not nestled in the boxes.

He fed them in the mornings, then returned at sundown to count heads, refill the water bucket, pluck eggs from the boxes.

Long ago he ran cattle, kept a few sheep, had hundreds of chickens, and grew hay as well. He'd always kept four horses, since he loved hunting.

Children found their way to Peter. Doug Kinser wound up there. The Lungrun children would come after school, as they desperately needed a happy atmosphere. Children walked over from surrounding farms or hitched rides out from town.

Age wore him down. In his eighties now, Peter had only the chickens left and a well-built harrier named Rooster.

He'd sold his business, a tractor dealership, for quite a bit of money, so his declining years were not attended by that poverty sadly common among the elderly.

He stooped a bit but still had thick wavy white hair plus all his teeth.

Often "his kids" would drive down the country road to visit him. He'd go into town on Wednesdays to see old friends.

Like many old people, he looked forward to chatting with anyone who dropped in.

He heard a truck rumble up to the house.

"Hey," a familiar voice called out.

"In the henhouse," he answered.

The door pushed open; Sister hugged him. "You love these damn chickens." She leaned over. "Hi there, Rooster."

"Hi." He wagged his tail.

"Imelda, here"—he lifted up a plump chicken—"has turned into my best layer." He gave Sister the egg basket.

"Wish it would stop raining."

"Has been wet." He handed her about a dozen eggs as he walked down the broody boxes. "I've got plenty. You take those home."

"Thanks." She reached in, feeling the warm brown eggs. "Peter, has Fontaine contacted you?"

"Wants to buy the place. Crawford, too. The numbers go up and up."

"Fontaine doesn't have money anymore. Don't let him carry you fast."

"Do I look like a fool?"

"No. In fact, you look quite handsome."

"Bullshit. Fontaine says he has investors. Crawford has cold hard cash. Both say they want to save the farm from developers. I say they're both liars of the first water. What do you say?"

"Suspicious."

"And then some."

"Good money?"

"Yes. Crawford started at one-point-five million and is up

to two-point-seven. Fontaine says to give him until November and he'll come up with three million."

"Jesus."

"For a nature conservancy. I asked for papers, contracts, conservation easements. Crawford had them. Now, sugar pie, they look good, but any decent lawyer will spot the loopholes. Sounds like Wheeler's Mill Estates to me." He laughed.

"That's a lot of money."

"I'm too goddamned old to enjoy it but I like the action. Used to love to make deals in my youth—my sixties and seventies."

"Do they know they're competing?"

"They do." He laughed louder. "Lord, it's fun. Those two boys hate each other." He wrapped his arm around her. "Come on to the house. You look peaked, honey."

"I was scared you might sell."

"Come on."

They went inside, drank a little sherry, and laughed at all the things people know about one another and their community when they've lived together a long time.

She checked her watch. "I'd better head out."

"Janie, I still love you. I want you to know that."

"I love you, too."

"Ever wonder what would have happened if we could have married?"

"I'd be feeding chickens." She laughed, then said, "Life's strange."

"It is that."

The fleeting image of the Grim Reaper jolted Sister. She said, "Peter, if I had to do it all over again I wouldn't change a thing. You know when Ray Junior died I thought God was punishing me for our affair. Then time passed and I thought differently."

"God doesn't punish us for love. Only people do that."

"Well, I loved you. I'll always love you. I guess I was a good wife but not a faithful one."

"You were a good wife. I just wish I'd found you before Ray did. I never hated him. He was too good a man. He had his Achilles' heel. We all do. But he was a good man."

"You, too."

"I guess we took what we could. Maybe that's all anyone can do." His voice grew stronger. "My time is coming. I feel well enough but I know my time is coming. I wanted you to know I love you."

She kissed him good-bye and cried the whole way home.

CHAPTER 11

The rain finally stopped Sunday night. The grays emerged from their den, making straight for the cornfield on the east side of Hangman's Ridge. The year, rich in gleanings, kept everyone happy.

In a few weeks the young would disperse to find their own territory, their own mates. Males might travel as far as 150 miles. Females usually remained closer to their place of birth.

Butch and Mary Vey had a small litter this year, only four. One little gray male had been carried away by a large hawk its first time out of the den. The other was sickly and died. Inky and Comet, half-grown, stayed healthy. Both parents taught them how to hunt, what to hunt, how to dump hounds, how to cross the road. In preparation for leaving home they now hunted on their own.

Inky traveled to the edge of the cornfield. She'd eaten so

much corn, she sat down. A rustling through the corn, not the light wind, made her crouch low.

A huge male red fox appeared, saw Inky, and said, *"Oh, it's you."* Without further conversation he moved on.

Inky sat up and blinked. The red fox, *Vulpes vulpes,* as he preferred to be called, felt the gray inferior. This particular male, Target, had an especially splashy white tip on his tail. He was easily recognizable to humans, too. He'd been around for years.

Target's entire family, four kits, also half-grown, were out hunting, as well as his mate, his sister, and her mate. The reds— a numerous, querulous clan—kept themselves busy, so they rarely spoke to anyone else. They feared no one, not even the bobcats, mountain lions, and bears, quite numerous in central Virginia, since the Blue Ridge Mountains provided food and safety.

As to foxhunters and their hounds, not only did the reds have no fear, they delighted in exhausting and then maiming their foe. Few sounds were as lovely to a red's ears as the sound of a human breaking bones.

If the hounds picked up a gray fox, the reds generally ignored the chase, concentrating on sunning themselves or going into their den and sleeping.

The grays could take care of themselves. They ran in smaller circles than the reds, some of whom might run straight for miles. Grays also perfected a figure eight, a maneuver incorporating sharp turns and practiced dives into other creatures' dens. This confused the hounds and infuriated the animal receiving the unexpected caller. However, there was little choice but to entertain the gray until the hounds were called off by the huntsman and cast in another direction. Since the grays were smaller than the red fox, they could squeeze into all manner of hiding places. They also climbed trees, a trick the reds thought much too catlike. Reds intensely disliked cats, who competed for the same game but who also sassed them.

The grays weren't overfond of cats but a feline insult was shrugged off. The reds, proud of their position, felt most animals owed them obeisance.

Inky learned these things from her parents and from experience. She looked overhead as Athena, the large owl, silently glided by. Athena, a deadly hunter, would swoop down, talons outstretched, before her prey knew what hit them.

Inky didn't fear Athena. The owl was civil. Since the fox, red and gray, has no natural enemies, they didn't need to worry about anyone wishing to eat them. Only the small kits were game, and that was usually for hawks or vultures. In droughts or hard times the vultures became aggressive, even attacking newborn calves.

Athena's nemesis was St. Just, the king of the crows. They rarely saw one another, since the crow was a daytime creature, but if he caught sight of Athena, St. Just would harass her even though she was four times his size.

The person St. Just hated above all others was Target. The big red had killed St. Just's mate, eating her with a flourish.

Inky sat there, the moist earth filled with enticing messages. October kept all creatures busy. The bears would soon hibernate, so they were eating everything they could. The squirrels gathered more and more nuts, often forgetting where they stashed them. Everyone prepared for winter. Even the humans cut firewood, put up storm windows, and changed the antifreeze in their cars.

Although it was early, Inky considered going home to sleep. However, she thought an apple might be nice for dessert even though she was full. She nosed out of the corn, sniffed the wind, then headed at a ground-eating trot up to the top of Hangman's Ridge. From this spot she could see most of the valley. Even Whiskey Ridge, running parallel to the north, was a bit lower. The criminals hanged from the oak tree could have been seen from below. This must have proved a potent warning. The last hanging occurred in 1875, when Gilliam Norris was strung up. He'd killed his entire family—mother, father, two sisters, and a brother—with a service revolver. When the sheriff came to arrest him, Gilliam shot him, too. Took fifteen men, including the sheriff from the next county, to bring Gilliam in. People said he'd lost his mind in the war.

Inky heard that story, passed from generation to generation. The first victim of the tree was Lawrence Pollard in 1702. An intrepid man, an explorer and founder of towns, Lawrence indulged in land speculation, as did many colonists. He was selling acreage in the Shenandoah Valley, the deal went bust, and Lawrence's investors strung him up without judge or jury.

From her vantage point Inky could see the Arnold farm, the barn and kennels and the understated two-story brick house painted white with Charleston-green shutters surrounded by oaks and maples of enormous size. At the edge of the expansive lawn was a small apple orchard. Peach and pear trees were around the house for decoration as much as for fruit. The orchard, though, was laid out in neat rows.

Inky swooped down the ridge, ran across a downed log over Broad Creek, and was happily in the middle of the orchard in fifteen minutes.

Raleigh, whom she knew by sight, was in the house. Golliwog, however, was in the orchard.

"I'll tell the hounds you're here."

"They can't get out," Inky replied.

"They can make a helluva racket. The humans will get up."

"I'll be gone by that time, they'll be in a bad mood, and you're the one that has to listen to them," Inky sensibly said. *"I only want one apple. I'm not going to poach your game."*

Golly arched her long eyebrows. *"How can you eat fruit?"*

"It's good."

The cat shook herself. *"Well, get your apple and get out."*

Inky snatched a small, sweet apple that had just fallen, then darted out of the orchard, passing the kennel on her way home. The hounds were snoring.

She stopped, apple in her mouth. She put the apple down for a moment and turned. Golly had climbed up into one of the apple trees at the edge of the orchard. She'd heard that the house cat was smart and no friend to foxes. Figuring she was ahead of the game and not wishing further to irritate the calico, Inky picked up the apple. As she walked by the separate runs, Diana, sleeping outside since the rain had stopped, opened one eye, then both eyes, sitting up with a start.

She opened her mouth, but Inky dropped her apple and quickly pleaded, *"Don't. It will set everyone crazy."*

Diana walked to the fence. *"You're the black fox—"*

"You stuck your nose into my den. I've come for an apple and I'll be on my way. I didn't even go near the chicken coop. All's well."

"You know if I were out of here I'd chase you to the James River," Diana bragged.

"Ha. I'd run circles around you and you wouldn't even know it."

Diana cocked her head to one side. *"I love the chase. Do you?"*

"For about fifteen minutes. Then I have better things to do. The reds like it more than we grays, I think."

"This is my first season. I guess I'll find that out." Diana blinked and lowered her head to be closer to the fox. *"I've been doing okay with cubbing, though, and last year, when I was a puppy, Shaker and Sister walked us every day and sometimes they laid down scent to help us. I think I know what to do if I can concentrate. I lose my concentration sometimes."*

"This is my first year, too, so I only know what my parents have told me and cubbing . . . I like cubbing. It was funny when you stuck your nose in the den. My brother wanted to bite you. He's like that." Inky giggled.

"Glad he didn't. My nose is very sensitive."

Golly backed down the apple tree. She sauntered toward the kennel.

"I'd better go. She gave me a fair warning."

Diana pricked up her ears. *"Golliwog can be very fierce. She scares me."*

"You know we will all be leaving our dens in a few weeks. Right about the time of opening hunt. There will be good runs then. You'll have fun. My dad says opening hunt is like a three-ring circus. I'm going to climb a tree and watch."

"Where will you go?"

"Already found my place. On the other side of Broad Creek. There's so much corn and game, my father said it's all right to live close. He said if hard times come then I might have to push on."

"I'm nervous about opening hunt," Diana confessed.

"Stay away from the people. And if you're on Target, the huge red with lots of white tip, be real careful. He's very smart. My father says he's incredibly smart but cruel. Target will try to lead you to your death. His son, Reynard, can be cruel, too." Diana shuddered so Inky added, *"Stick to a hound that knows what she's doing. You'll be safe then."*

"Thank you."

"I'll wave if you go by." Inky giggled again, then picked up her apple and skedaddled, for Golly was bearing down on her, picking up speed.

The imposing calico stopped. *"Diana, you're loose as ashes. You can't believe one word from a fox's mouth."*

Diana dropped her head. *"Yes, ma'am."*

Satisfied that she had imparted wisdom as well as put that lower life-form, the hound, in her place, Golly strolled, tail swaying to and fro, back to the main house. The night was too damp for her. She was going in the house to snuggle up next to Sister, who was sound asleep. She might clean off her muddy paws and then again she might not. Walking across the old

Persian carpets so prized by Sister would get the mud off fast
enough.

CHAPTER 12

A stiff tiger trap, cut logs shining in the morning mist, like giant's teeth, slowed Dragon for a moment as he scrambled
over, the pack ahead of him. The tiger trap jump, like a coop
but with vertical logs, often backed off riders. Sidetracked by
an unfamiliar smell, Dragon snapped to when he heard Cora's
authoritative call.

Twenty couple hounds, forty individuals, had been carried
in their special trailer to Beveridge Hundred, an old plantation five miles west of Sister's house as the crow flies.

But today it wasn't the crow flying, it was the hounds. Shaker
cast them in the classic triangle cast. Sending hounds on their
mission was truly like a fisherman casting his net. Hence, the
term "cast." Most huntsmen threw their hounds straight into the
wind, figuring the scent would carry and they'd be off in a hurry.
That was a better idea for flat country than for the hills, ravines,
pastures, and deep creeks of Jefferson Hunt territory. Shaker
liked to give his hounds about fifteen minutes to settle; then he'd
cut the corner and move up the side of the triangle into the wind.
He planned his hunt and hunted his plan, always dividing the
territory to be hunted into a series of triangles.

The pack struck quickly, running straight. Their quarry ran
perhaps seven to ten minutes ahead. The scent held on the
still-wet earth. The light shone scarlet as the sun's rim loomed
over the horizon.

Shaker doubled his blasts as he plunged into a stand of black birches, shot out into the thirty-acre hay field just as hounds crossed over the middle of the cut field.

Sister galloped about fifty yards behind Shaker. He soared over the tiger trap; Sister and Lafayette easily cleared the big jump. Cody made it, as did Fontaine, who kept his eyes glued to Cody's perfect butt in the saddle.

Gunsmoke, Fontaine's half-bred, thought the horse Cody was trying for Fontaine, Keepsake, a rangy thoroughbred, was doing great so far. But then thoroughbreds always did better when the field was moving fast.

Marty, Crawford, and finally Bobby safely landed in the hay field.

Three visitors from Bull Run Hunt kept up with the small Tuesday group.

At the edge of the hay field the hounds split. Cora headed left toward The Rocks, an outcropping of boulders, while Archie headed right through double-lined rows of cedars into another hay field.

"Archie, two foxes. Stick with me," Cora called, her bel canto lilt floating over the mists still not rising.

This brought Archie's head up.

Dragon shot his mouth off. *"This scent is hot."*

"Yes it is, son, but if the fox can split us, we'll wind up in East Jesus, the whips will be going in two directions, and each fox can further mislead us. We're on Target. They're on Aunt Netty." Archie knew his foxes by the patterns they ran. *"Reds."*

"I'm not leaving this scent," Dragon howled, nose to the ground. *"Cora's an old bitch, anyway."*

"Good way to get drafted out, you fool." Archie turned, flat out now, belly low to the ground, tail stretched out behind him as he streaked for Cora.

Without hesitation the other hounds, including Diana on her first flaming run, followed Archie. He cut across the hay field, crawled under the old wire cow fence, catapulting over the sunken farm road worn down by three hundred years of use. With one bound he was over the loose stone wall, heading, flying, flashing down to The Rocks.

Moving in the opposite direction, Dragon touched the earth with his nose, bawled for all he was worth, and charged into a smaller pasture. Hay rolled in large round bales dotted the verdant expanse.

"Moron!" a taunting voice called.

Dragon jerked his head up. Sitting on top of the hay round were Target and Reynard, magnificent, shining, as red as the scarlet sunrise.

"I'll tear you to shreds!" Dragon bared his fangs, bouncing toward father and son.

"You fierce beast." Target, falsetto-voiced, mocked him, while Reynard watched the older, wiser fox sucker in the hound.

When Dragon was two strides from the hay round, Target casually jumped down, darting into a burrow in the bale. Reynard followed. His tail flicked into this makeshift den just as Target skidded around the bale.

Growling, saliva dripping, Dragon bumped into the bale as his hind end gave out under him from the force of his sharp turn. His head nearly hit the ground, his two front legs splayed out. He was eyeball to eyeball with a mature copperhead still drowsy and not amused.

Like lightning the snake struck, sinking her fangs, almost as large as Dragon's, into his left cheek. He shook his head but she didn't let go until she'd released her venom to the last drop.

"Oh, God, it hurts," Dragon screamed as the snake finally let go.

"Moron." Target laughed as Dragon, weeping, tried to outrun the pain. At least he had sense enough to go for the sound of the hounds, maybe a mile off by now.

Hounds, horses, huntsman were stymied at The Rocks, water spilling down over the sides in a gentle waterfall.

Aunt Netty, on a ledge behind the waterfall, cleaned her claws embedded with mud. She'd run over the rocks leading up to the small waterfall. Her scent would last for only a few moments on the rock but the morning was damp, the mists were low, and the hounds were close. To be safe she ducked behind the water. She didn't mind getting a little wet. She knew her scent had been wiped out by the waterfall.

Cora, a trifle overweight, panted. *"Aunt Netty works her magic act."*

In the distance they could hear Bobby Franklin, who'd fallen far behind, talk to his horse, Oreo. "Not so fast. Not so fast. I hate running on rock!"

"Stop worrying, you fat pig," the horse replied. *"My sense of balance is better than yours."*

"Everyone in one piece?" Sister laughingly asked.

"Is it always like this?" one of the visitors asked.

"Sure," Fontaine lied, winking.

A rustling noise coming through the woods captured their attention. Dragon joined them in a few moments. He shook his head, he cried, he rolled over.

Shaker dismounted as Sister held his reins. "Snakebite," he tersely informed her.

"His head will blow up like a pumpkin," Cody said.

"Killed my Jack Russell. Remember Darth Vader?" Fontaine said that, which, under the circumstances, was not a helpful recollection.

Crawford, hoping for brownie points, dismounted from Czapaka. He walked over to Shaker, who didn't look up but kept his gaze on Dragon.

"I can throw the hound over my saddle."

"No need," Shaker replied evenly.

"He's better off walking back." Douglas Kinser had ridden in from his outpost.

"Sister, do you mind if I have Doug walk Dragon back?"

"No. Betty's out on your left. Can you get by with one whip?"

"Two's better."

"I'll go." Cody smiled.

"No, you won't. I haven't bought that horse yet, and who knows what you'll get into. It's already been a wild morning," Fontaine commanded.

"I'll whip. I'm not the best rider in the world but I can do it. I know most of the hounds by sight," Marty volunteered.

"Good."

"Fine." Shaker seconded Sister. "You take the right. Three blasts, short and high of equal duration, means come in to me. You know the other signals?"

"Well, Shaker, if I don't you all can come out and find me. Just don't leave me out until sundown."

Crawford, jealous of Marty for the chance to whip, mounted up. He smiled at her but was secretly miserable that he wasn't a strong enough rider to whip. And he hadn't a clue as to how to rate hounds. He thought all a whip had to do was ride hard. In Crawford's case, ignorance was bliss. How he longed to say at some fancy Virginia party, "Oh, yes, I whip-in at Jefferson Hunt." It would be even more delicious to drop the information into a cocktail party in Manhattan. They'd think it had something to do with sexual practices. He'd then get to fire off a double entendre or two, after which he could declaim about foxhunting.

As it was, Crawford could have used Velcro in his saddle.

"Sister?" Shaker worked closely with his master. She'd carried the horn in her youth when the then huntsman died unexpectedly and violently in a bar fight Saturday night. She had a great eye for terrain and a good sense of casting hounds. Not a professional huntsman by a long shot, but she was no slouch either.

She inhaled deeply, the heavy air filling her lungs. "Warming fast."

"Northern edge of the woods?" He swung gracefully up in the saddle.

"Good idea."

As the hounds packed in and trotted to the next cast Diana whispered, *"Is Dragon in trouble?"*

Dasher, her litter mate, as was Dragon, whispered back, *"If not with the people then with the snake. Boy, is he going to be sick."*

Jefferson Hunt named their hounds using the first letter of the bitch's name. Dasher, Dragon, and Diana had been born to Delia, an old lady now retired to laze in the sun.

"If that copperhead hadn't bit him, I would have!" Archie exclaimed.

Shaker stared down at Arch. "What are you talking about?"

"Sorry," the steady fellow apologized. Wouldn't do for him to be accused of babbling.

"How do you know it was a copperhead?" Dasher whispered.

"Head already getting fat. A nonpoisonous snake would have left two fang marks and that's about it."

"Rattler," Cora quietly said.

"He'd be dead by now." Archie tried not to gloat.

At the northern edge Shaker pushed the hounds toward the hay field. They picked up a fading scent moving at a trot. The next hour the hounds worked diligently with a few small bursts as their reward.

Sister lifted hounds and they happily walked back to the trailers.

"Bobby, dear, we could hear you all the way down to The Rocks," his wife chided him.

"Oh." His face reddened.

Behind them Crawford rode in silence, Fontaine behind him. Fontaine was studying Czapaka intently, especially his hindquarters. Confirmation, the way a horse is put together, reveals a lot about the horse's potential use and longevity of service. Cody observed this.

"Nice horse."

Fontaine turned his head back. Cody drew alongside him so they could speak without shouting. "Yes, he is a nice horse."

"Quick with his hind feet?" Fontaine called up to Crawford, meaning "Does the horse kick?"

With disdain, Crawford, not even turning his head, called back. "No, but I am."

"I'll remember that." Fontaine smiled broadly and benevolently for all to see.

"What's Fontaine up to?" Cody thought to herself.

Walking back to the trailers, Target was a deadly foe.

CHAPTER 13

"Going to be a great year. One of the best. They go in cycles." Lafayette dropped some of his hay, reaching down to snatch it up.

Rickyroo, in the next stall, stuck his nose between the iron stall divider bars. *"We were right behind Aunt Netty."*

"Could you see her?"

"No. She vanished. The usual." Rickyroo picked up his red play ball with a handle. He threw it over his head.

Ricky, full of energy, found things to do, things that were upsetting to the humans. If a bridle hung on the stall door, he'd play with it until he had pulled the reins into his stall; then he'd chew them to pieces.

He tore off other horses' blankets when they were turned out in the field.

He also tore a flap off Cody Jean Franklin's frock coat last year because he felt like it.

The humans called him a handful. The horses thought of him as a joker.

Aztec, a graceful five-year-old light bay, a blaze down her face, said, *"It's not fair. You two go and I stay home."*

"You'll go out in the field, Az. Sister believes in bringing along horses slow," Lafayette counseled her.

"I'm as big as you are."

"And so you are, but I've seen a lot more than you have. The last thing we need is you spooking all over the place with Sister on your back. She's a good rider but she's no spring chicken."

"I'm not going to spook. I hilltopped last year." She referred to the practice of hunting but not taking the jumps.

"Be patient," Rickyroo advised.

"You're not," Aztec grumbled.

"I know what I'm doing." He threw the ball at the bars between them.

Golliwog strolled in during the conversation, Raleigh behind her. *"If you knew what you were doing, you wouldn't be playing with that stupid ball."*

"Raleigh plays with balls," came the retort from the dark bay.

"My point exactly." Golliwog sat down on a hay bale, picked the tip of her tail up with her paw, and began grooming.

Raleigh, an exceedingly good-natured dog, said, *"Golly, you're such a snot."*

"Cats," was all Lafayette said.

"You're jealous. You're all jealous. You have to work for a living whereas I simply exist to be beautiful and catch the occasional offensive mouse."

"You're doing a piss-poor job of it." Aztec laughed.

"Oh, really?" Golly dropped her tail. *"Do you have any idea how many places there are for mice to hide? Shall I list them, grass-eater, eyes-on-the-side-of-your-head, big fat flat teeth, no-good . . . !"*

"We're scared." Lafayette reached for more hay in his hayrack.

"I could scratch your eyes out if I wanted to. You're lucky that I like you—basically."

"Golly, cool it." The sleek Doberman nudged the cat. *"We all know that you are the most beautiful, the smartest cat that ever lived. Even smarter than Dick Whittington's cat."*

Having heard what she wanted to hear, Golly's mood instantly improved. *"Say, I heard Dragon got nailed."*

"Archie told me on the way home that the little shit had it coming," Lafayette said. *"When Archie realized they'd split and told his group to catch up with Cora, Dragon refused. He even called Cora an old bitch. Archie's furious."*

"She should have drafted him out when he was a puppy. He was beautiful but he was rotten even then. I told her but she missed it. The problem with Sister is it takes her too long to figure these things out. I knew that puppy's attitude was wrong. Outrageous." Raleigh stood on his hind legs to peer into Lafayette's stall.

"But you're a dog. Dogs know about one another. Same with us." Lafayette nodded to his stablemates. *"We know if a horse will work into the program long before Sister or Douglas knows. It's the nature of things."*

"I suppose, but I'd like to save her the trouble." Raleigh loved Sister with all his heart and soul.

"Humans need trouble. Makes them think they're living." Golliwog laughed.

"Cynic," Raleigh returned to the cat.

"Means 'dog' in Greek, you know." Golly adored showing off.

"It does?" Aztec was surprised.

"Yes. Diogenes lived like a dog. Really, he lived in a hovel and wore rags but he was brilliant. He questioned everything, especially authority. He upset the rich, obviously. They called him a dog. They called the people who followed him dogs. Stuck."

"How do you know all this?" Aztec asked, her deep-brown eyes filled with admiration.

"I read whatever Sister is reading. I sit on her shoulder or on the pillow behind her shoulders. She reads all the time."

"I don't understand the appeal of books." Ricky tossed his ball again.

"Big surprise." Lafayette snorted in jest.

"I'll tell you about books." Golly stretched fore and aft, then sat down quite regally, prepared to declaim. *"It's the best way to enjoy an uninterrupted conversation with the best human minds from any century, from most any country. Superior as we are to humans, imagine if we wrote books. You might know what Man O' War learned and thought. I could learn from the cats of ancient Egypt. It truly is our one great failing. We don't record our experiences."*

"We're too busy living them." Raleigh laughed.

"There is that." Golly smiled and purred. She did love Raleigh quite a bit.

The slam of a truck door diverted their attention. The cat and dog walked to the open barn doors. The sun had just set and soon a light frost like thin icing would blanket the ground.

"Doug and Cody," Raleigh said.

"That started up again?" Rickyroo paid little attention to human couplings and uncouplings.

"How could Doug pick such a loser, even if she is pretty?" Golly returned to her hay bale by the side of the aisle, set up for the morning feeding.

"On again, off again." Lafayette's stall dutch door opened on the other side of the barn from Doug's cottage.

"I don't want her to hurt Doug again." Raleigh's ears swept back.

"Of course she will. She'll hurt everybody, including herself, but there's one thing I'll say for Cody . . . if she gets somebody in trouble, she gets right in there with him."

"What's the worst that can happen? She gets pregnant," Ricky said.

"There's lots worse than that. People commit suicide over love and really dumb stuff," Raleigh replied.

"Well, it doesn't affect us." Ricky felt the whole thing was silly.

"The hell it doesn't." Golly spoke forcefully. *"Everything they do affects us."*

CHAPTER 14

Later that night three short knocks brought Cody to the front door of her small house. She opened the door.

"Hi, Sis." Jennifer leaned against the doorjamb, the hall light framing her hair like a halo.

"Jen, get in here." Cody clamped her hand around Jennifer's wrist, pulling her inside and shutting the door behind her. "You asshole."

Jennifer, unperturbed, unsteadily walked for the couch and dropped onto it. "Shut up."

"What'd you take?"

"Nothing."

"Don't jam me." Cody bent over Jennifer to check out her pupils.

"Couldn't go home."

Cody picked up the phone. "Hi, Mom. Jen's with me. She's going to spend the night."

"What about her clothes for school?" Betty asked.

"She can wear mine. She needs help writing her history report."

"Well . . ." Betty's voice faded. Then she said, "All right."

Cody hung up the phone. "Don't do this."

"You do."

She bent over Jennifer. It was like looking into her own face. "Because I'm weak. I don't want to do it. I don't even want to drink a beer. Something happens and I just do."

"Yeah, well, me, too."

"No one's got a gun to your head. Stay off the stuff. I've wasted the last five years and I'll never get them back and I'm trying to get straight. Hear?"

Jennifer nodded. "Everything is so fast."

Cody sat next to her sister, patting her knee. "Yeah. And everything is so clear. Cocaine. I'm a genius on coke until I come off."

"Black." Jennifer rocked a bit.

"Heading down?"

"Yeah. There's got to be something to cut that, I mean cut the down. I heard speedballs do it." She mentioned a potent cocktail of cocaine and heroin.

"That'll kill you if you get the mix wrong," Cody replied.

"Got anything?"

"No."

"You wouldn't give it to me if you had," Jennifer flared.

"If it would soften the drop, I would. I've been on that ride, little sis."

"What am I gonna do?" Jennifer cried.

"Feel like shit. There's nothing I can do."

Desperation contorted Jennifer's beautiful features. "You gotta help me."

"I am. I'm letting you stay here." Cody sighed. This would be a long night. "Where'd you get the stuff?"

"Easy to get."

"That's not what I asked."

Jennifer laughed. "Why the hell do you care? You get it where you can get it. I can buy it at school—lots of places."

"Jen, you're gonna stop if I have to lock you up and throw away the key. I'm not gonna let you screw around and fuck up like I have."

"Yeah, yeah." Jennifer just wanted her racing heart to slow down and the black clouds to disperse.

CHAPTER 15

The night promised a light frost. Sister Jane made the rounds before turning in for the night. She checked Dragon, head swollen but beginning to feel better. She said good night to the rest of the hounds, hearing a few good nights in return.

She walked back over the brick path to the stable. The horses slept in perfect contentment.

With Raleigh at her heels, she walked in her back door, removed her barn coat and scarf, draping them over the Shaker pegs. Then she slipped her feet out of the green wellies.

She clicked off the lights in the kitchen, the hall, and the front parlor. Then she climbed the front stairs to her bedroom. Two windows, the glass handblown, looked over an impressive walnut tree. Beautiful though it was, the sound of dropping walnuts on a tin roof could waken the dead during the fall.

Golly, already on one pillow, opened an eye, then shut it when Sister and Raleigh entered the room. An old sheepskin rested at the foot of the bed. Raleigh jumped up, circled three times, finally dropping like a stone.

"You weigh more than I do," Sister teased him.

"Close," Raleigh replied.

A chill settled in the room. Built in 1707, the house was a marvelous example of early American architecture. Insulation was horsehair in the walls, some of which also had lathing. Years ago when Ray was still alive they'd blown fluffy insulation down the exterior walls and it helped cut the cold. Materials had advanced since then, and she often thought of just ripping out the walls from the interior and putting up those fat rolls of pink insulation with numbers like R-30.

The expense halted that pipe dream, as did the total disruption to her life. Bad enough to be disrupted at forty but by seventy her tolerance had diminished proportionately.

She hopped out of bed, slipped on a sweatshirt, and hopped back in.

She picked up Arthur Schnitzler's *The Way into the Open,* published in 1908. There was a line in the novel she appreciated, "the bereavements of everyday life." She read a bit, then put it down. Neurotic, edgy Vienna displeased her tonight.

She reached for George Washington's foxhunting diaries, which had been compiled for her by an old friend who worked at Mount Vernon. The good general had kept diaries, notes, letters from the age of fourteen on.

She read a few lines about hounds losing a line on a windy day. Then she put that down, too. Normally she loved reading Washington's foxhunting observations. He was a highly intelligent man and a forthright one about hunting. But she needed relief from hunting. Right now it was causing as much headache as joy.

She opened a slim red volume of Washington's *Rules of*

Civility and Decent Behavior in Company and Conversation.
These notes, written in 1746, when the general was fourteen,
were, he hoped, going to be engraved on his brain. The physical act of writing pinned the words in the mind as well as on
the page. But for the young, tall youth, the main purpose was
mastery over himself.

She read out loud to Golly and Raleigh: "In the presence of
others sing not to yourself with a humming noise, nor drum
with your fingers or feet." She paused. "Well, that leaves Kyle
Dawson out of polite society."

"Sister, you haven't seen Kyle Dawson in years," Raleigh
reminded her.

She peeped over the book, speaking to the animals. "Here's
one for you. Number thirteen. Ready? 'Kill no vermin as
fleas, lice, ticks & c in sight of others; if you see any filth
or thick spittle, put your foot dexterously upon it; if it be
upon the clothes of your companions, put it off privately; and
if it be upon our own clothes, return thanks to him who put
it off.' "

"I don't have fleas." Golly rolled over, reaching high into
the air with her left paw.

"Liar." Raleigh lifted his head.

"That got a response." Sister turned the page. The phone
rang. No one close to Sister called after nine-thirty in the evening. It was now ten. "Hello."

"Hello, is this Mrs. Raymond Arnold?"

"Yes."

The deep male voice replied, "This is Dr. Walter Lungrun.
I was hoping I could cub with you this Thursday."

"Are you a member of another hunt, Mr. Lungrun?"

"No, ma'am, I'm not. I've just returned to the area to do
my residency."

"Ah, well, come on ours anyway. You'll have to sign a waiver
and release form saying you know this sport is dangerous and
if you break your neck so be it."

"Yes, ma'am."

"It will be good to have a doctor in the field. What's your specialty?"

"Neurosurgery."

Sister glanced at the silver-framed photograph of Raymond in his army uniform that rested on her night table. "Lungrun. From Louisa County?"

"Yes. I left to go to Cornell and then to NYU School of Medicine."

"So you're smart, Dr. Lungrun." Her voice lightened.

"Smart enough to call you." He was light in return.

"Well then, I'll see you at seven-thirty at the Mill Ruins."

"I look forward to it."

"Good-bye, Dr. Lungrun."

"Good-bye, Mrs. Arnold."

She hung up the phone, folded her hands over her chest. "How extraordinary."

CHAPTER 16

"Why do I have to do it? I don't see why," Jennifer, just a shade shorter than her older sister, argued.

"Because I said so." Cody slipped her arm through her sister's arm. "Come on."

However, before they were out the door an irate Betty was pounding up the front steps. "Just where do you think you're going?" She pointed at Cody. "You were supposed to take her to school."

Betty pushed both her daughters through the door, slamming it behind her.

"Mom, I can explain," Cody started.

"In a minute." Betty held up her hands for silence, turned her bright blue eyes on her youngest. "Well, miss?"

"I got tired so I crashed with Cody."

"And I just won the lottery." Betty was having none of it.

With a slow step the young women moved toward the sofa. There'd be no getting out of this.

However, Cody tried. "Mom, why is Dad supporting Crawford Howard for the joint-mastership? Crawford doesn't know anything about hunting."

"Since when have you been interested in the politics of the Jefferson Hunt?" Betty plopped onto the chair facing the sofa.

"Curious."

"Yeah." Jennifer picked up the theme.

"Crawford will put the club on a financially secure base. Right now that's crucial. Sister knows enough about hunting for ten masters. What we need is money or an angel."

"Crawford could write checks."

"Cody, no one is going to write out thirty to fifty thousand dollars a year above and beyond the annual budget simply to help the club. That kind of commitment demands a joint-M.F.H. behind his name."

"Fontaine is a better choice." Cody brushed back her black hair, which had fallen in her eyes.

"Fontaine can't keep his dick in his pants." Jennifer sniggered.

"Mom, they carry on like that in Washington all the time. If presidents can do it, why not Fontaine?"

"This is Virginia, not Washington." Betty's jaw jutted out.

Her girls stared at her. There was no rejoinder. Another quiet sigh escaped them.

"Cody and I overslept. It's my fault. I didn't set the alarm like I said I would," Jennifer explained.

"Lame." Betty crossed her arms over her impressive chest.

Cody thought to herself that a lame excuse was better than no excuse, but the weight of the lies, at first so gossamer thin, bent her shoulders. She'd lied about herself since high school and now she was lying for Jennifer. While these fabrications might solve the problem temporarily, they only seemed to worsen it long term. Cody knew the only reason she was still acceptable at Jefferson Hunt was that she could ride. Her beauty attracted men. Her problems eventually repelled them, except for Doug. She studied her sister. In Cody's eyes, Jennifer was more beautiful than herself. Where her hair was black, Jennifer's was a rich seal brown and her light-coffee-colored eyes made her so warm, approachable. Cody's eyes were beginning to betray hard living.

"Mom, I'll go to the principal. This is my fault." Cody squared her shoulders.

"That's noble of you. However, we aren't leaving this room until I get the truth. And if I don't, Jennifer, you are coming home with me and you're grounded, and I mean grounded for the next month. No allowance. No parties. No hunting. Zip."

"Mom!"

"That's right, *Mom*," Betty shouted.

"I didn't feel good, so I came here. It was closer than home." Jennifer stretched out her long legs, crossing them at the ankles.

Betty wordlessly looked to Cody, who finally said, "She was—"

"High." Betty cut in. "Do you think I'm blind? Jennifer, we went through this last summer. You promised you'd stop but"—she weighed her words—"that's proved beyond your powers."

"Mom, it wasn't so bad. I mean this is the only time since

June. Since last time. Really. I just felt like it. I was stupid. It won't happen again."

"What amazes me is that you are seventeen years old and you can find dope or whatever you call it these days and the police can't. We're beyond apologies, Jennifer. We're going into a treatment program."

"No." Jennifer's face turned crimson.

"And if you know what's good for you, Cody, you'll cough up the money and go in, too."

Cody pinched her lips together.

"You can't do this to me!" Jennifer jumped up, towering over her medium-sized mother.

Betty rose but Jennifer pushed her back onto the chair.

Cody shot from the sofa, grabbing Jennifer. "Don't touch Mom, Jen."

"She's a fucking saint?" Jennifer snarled.

"She's our mother and she's a lot closer to it than we'll ever be. Don't touch her."

"Fine." Jennifer hauled off and socked Cody instead.

Cody, bigger, stronger, and smarter, ducked the next punch, stepped inside a roundhouse swing, and with the back edge of her hand chopped Jennifer hard in the throat. Both of Jennifer's hands went for her throat. She choked and Cody grabbed the back of her collar, dragging her to the sofa.

Looming over the coughing girl, Cody said, "You're going to treatment."

Betty never imagined her younger daughter would attack her. The corroding effect of drugs even when one wasn't on them shocked her. She would have died herself before lifting a hand against her own mother.

Jennifer started bawling. She choked a few times, then snarled at Cody. "You hurt me."

"You hurt yourself," Cody fired back. "Mom, how much is the treatment program?"

"I don't know. Central Virginia Hospital has an outpatient

program. I hear it's good. Cody, we can't afford to send you. You've been out on your own and you need to do this for yourself."

Jennifer bellowed, "What am I going to say to my friends? I'm in drug rehab. Mom, this will ruin me. I won't have any friends."

"Then they aren't really your friends." Betty raised her voice. "And I'm not worried about your friends. I'm worried about you."

"You can't tell me what to do." A flash of defiance illuminated Jennifer's eyes.

"As long as you're under my roof, you'll do as I say. We're going to Central Virginia."

"Now?" Jennifer's voice dropped, betraying fear.

"Now. Cody?"

"I'm coming."

CHAPTER 17

At five-thirty in the morning the frost covered the ground like a silver net. The few leaves underfoot would soon give way to blankets of maple, oak, hickory, gum, sycamore, and poplar. Fall, a bit late this year, was about a week away from peak color. Flaming red edging the green of the maples stood out against the dawn light, as did the yellow oak leaves.

Shaker divided hounds in the kennel. Those who would be hunting that day were placed in a draw run. Excited to be chosen, they tormented those left behind with boasts of how good the day's hunt would be.

Hounds remaining in the kennel were deemed unfit or unready for many reasons. A bitch going into season would be put in the hot bitch pen until her estrus passed. A hound footsore from Tuesday's hunt would be left in the kennel. A hound having difficulty mastering his or her job would be held back lest he or she distract the other hounds from their task. Hounds under two years or a year and a half, depending on development, would be left in the puppy runs. Dragon languished in sick bay. Although he was recovering rapidly, his left eye was swollen shut.

Shaker patiently explained to his charges the reasons for their missing the party. He double-checked everyone, making certain plenty of fresh water was available and that they had eaten their breakfast.

The hounds to hunt wouldn't get breakfast until their return. Full hounds run slow or sit down and throw up. No one minded delaying breakfast if it meant they'd hunt. They pricked their ears, waved their tails, hopped around in circles.

"All right. Settle. Settle now. It's another hour before you go on the party wagon." Shaker called the hound van the party wagon. "No point in wearing yourself out before the party starts."

He had backed up the hound van to the draw run the night before. He had only to open the door into the draw run and the hounds would race down the chute to the opened door of the van. This saved time because without a draw run a few hounds, overexcited, would zoom past the van.

He walked outside the kennel to light his pipe. Shaker wouldn't smoke near his hounds. Their noses were so sensitive that smoke bothered them. He wanted those noses sharp for the hunt.

He read somewhere that dogs in general hear six times better than humans and that a human has about five million scent receptors whereas a hound has over twenty-two million. Whatever the numbers, hounds heard and smelled more than a human could imagine. He thought about that sometimes, about how dull our world would seem to a creature with broader, sharper senses.

What must it be like to see through the eagle's eye or the owl's?

What he saw was the gray giving way to the first streak of pale pink. The clear sky promised a spectacular day, but not for hunting. Those raw days when the smoke from the chimneys hangs low, those are good hunting days. Today scent would evaporate rapidly. However, there was no wind, hardly even a lick of breeze. That would help. He'd have to drop hounds on a line fast and hope for a burst. Whatever line they'd get wouldn't last too long unless, of course, the fox moved along the creek bed.

He sucked contentedly on his briar pipe, a Dunhill of great antiquity given him by his father. Lights were on in Sister's kitchen. No doubt she was already on the phone with a member who needed to know right that moment what Sister Jane thought about wearing Prince of Wales spurs or could the member show up in a running martingale, even though it was improper?

Shaker knew he had not the patience to be a master nor the money. He'd worked his way up to being huntsman, getting the horn when he was thirty-one, no small accomplishment. In his mid-forties, he had no money other than what he earned and that wasn't much. His benefits, housing, truck, standing in the community pleased him, but most of all he loved what he did. He loved it more than money, more than anything. In the end even more than his ex-wife, who when he turned forty bedeviled him to think about his future, take a job where he could make some good money. Sheila never understood him but then maybe he didn't understand her. Women seemed to need security more than he did. He asked for a fine day's hunting, each hound on the line, and he lived one day at a time.

He could hear Doug in the stable. Having a good professional first whipper-in made the huntsman's life much easier. Shaker's horse would be tacked up and loaded on the van. He could rely on Doug to get ahead of the hounds, an assignment that took a brave and good rider.

Although young, Doug would carry the horn someday. Shaker had known Doug since he was in grade school. He'd come to the kennel and tag after Shaker and Sister Jane like a hound puppy. There wasn't much love or stability in Doug's childhood. He found both at the kennel.

The back door opened and closed. Sister Jane, dressed except for the barn coat she was wearing, waved good morning.

Raleigh ran ahead. *"What a day."*

"Morning, big guy." Shaker ran his palm over the glossy black head.

Sister beamed, breathing in deeply. "If we can't get up a fox, we'll have a perfect trail ride. Not that you won't find a fox." She winked.

"I'm beginning to think the fox finds us."

"There is that."

"And who had called this morning, ass over tit?"

"Only Ronnie Haslip. He can't find his tweed jacket. I told him the day would warm up fast. He can ride in his shirt and vest. For whatever reason that seemed to satisfy him. He said he'd called everyone but couldn't find an extra coat and he'd go straight up to Warrenton to Horse Country and buy a coat after the hunt. He worries more than his mother and she was world-class." Sister Jane laughed. "Oh, the Franklin girls are in rehab."

"Heard yesterday."

"As Raymond would say, 'The shit has hit the Franklin fan.' " She admired the lacy pattern of the frost. "Wouldn't he just love today. He took credit for every bright, low-humidity day we had."

"Direct line to Great God Almighty."

"That's what he said." Sister laughed, remembering her husband's sacrilegious streak. Raymond liked nothing better than pouncing on someone who touted the Bible. She herself thought one worshiped best outdoors. "Do you ever miss Sheila on a day like today?"

Accustomed to her sudden direct hits, the curly-haired man shook his head. "No."

"Not even on a full moon?"

"Well"—he smiled—"maybe then."

"Good." She smiled triumphantly. "It won't do for a man to be too independent of women."

"I have you."

"Ha. My solemn vow is to fuss at you. Think of it as marriage without the benefits."

"Long as I can fuss back." He patted her on the back.

"Deal." She leaned into him. She'd known Shaker nearly as long as she had known Raymond. She knew his virtues and his faults. She loved him for himself as well as for his talent.

"Rodeo?"

"Yep."

They turned to enter the kennel, to load up the hounds. Doug was already loading the horses.

The phone rang in the kennel.

"Jefferson Hunt." Shaker listened, then handed it to Sister Jane, his hand over the earpiece. "Crawford."

"Hello."

"Sister Jane, might I have a few words with you after the hunt today?"

"Of course, Crawford, but you have to survive it first."

CHAPTER 18

The massive stone ruins of an old mill perched over the fast-running creek. Broad Creek, swift moving and ten yards wide on Sister Jane's property, was twenty to thirty yards wide in places at Wheeler Mill, which was eight miles south of her place. The raceway remained intact two centuries later. The men who built this mill intended for it to last.

As a courtesy to Peter Wheeler, too old to maintain his property, the hunt club, once a year, cleaned the raceway of branches or any other floating debris, bushhogged the trails, and repaired jumps. The stone fences rarely needed fixing, having been constructed in 1730, same as the mill.

The Wheeler line would die with Peter. Speculation as to the disposition of his estate intensified with each passing year.

An early riser, the old man sat on a director's chair in the bed of his truck, having been hoisted up by Walter Lungrun, who'd arrived early.

When Sister saw the young doctor she breathed in sharply. He reminded her of her husband. Walter—tall, blond, wide-shouldered, and square-jawed—was handsome without being pretty, just as Raymond had been.

Upon seeing Sister, Walter walked over, tipping his hat. "Master, good morning."

Shaker stared at him as though seeing a ghost, then returned his attention quickly to the hounds.

Before he could say his name Sister smiled. "Dr. Lungrun, you are most welcome. I'll try and scare up a fox for you. Is this your first hunt?"

"When I was in college and med school I hunted a few times. May I try first flight?"

"You may. If you make an involuntary dismount I'll keep going, you know, but whoever is riding tail today will pick you up."

"I'll try not to embarrass myself." He clapped his black cap back on, tails up.

Only staff could hunt with cap tails down.

Sister surveyed the field. Twenty-five people on Thursday morning at seven. Opening hunt was two weeks away. Each hunt the field swelled as people, presumably in shape, eased back into the routine of foxhunting.

The regulars were out in full force except for Jennifer and Cody Franklin.

"Folks." She motioned for them to ride over to her. A few were frantically searching for the last-minute ties, gloves, and girths back at their trailers. Shaker and Doug had unloaded the hounds, who were being wonderfully well behaved. "First flight with me. Hilltoppers with Fontaine. Will you do us the honors, Fontaine?"

"Of course, Master." He touched his hat with his crop. Much as Fontaine hated missing riding up front, he knew he was being given a position acknowledging hunting sense and better yet, this was done in front of Crawford Howard. Of course, Fontaine's knowledge of the territory didn't mean he possessed the much coveted hound sense. But to lead Hilltoppers, Fontaine didn't need to have it.

"Ralph, will you ride tail?" she asked Raphael Assumptio, known as Ralph, a middle-aged man, strong rider and better yet, competent in a crisis.

"Glad to." He, too, touched his cap with his crop.

"Huntsman."

Shaker, holding his cap in his lap as was proper, nodded, put his cap on, and said, "Hounds ready?"

"You bet!" came the chorus.

Lafayette turned his head. *"Ready to rock and roll?"*

As Sister patted his gray neck, the other horses neighed in anticipation.

Shaker stuck to his plan, dropping the hounds where he thought he'd hit a line along the creek. Flecks of frost clung to the sides of the creek and overtop the banks, but across the pastures the light frost had already transformed into sparkling dew.

He moved along on the farm road paralleling the creek bed. He glanced back, smiling when he saw old Peter Wheeler, hand cupped to his ear, waiting to hear the hounds, which when in full cry were music to his ears.

Peter hadn't long to wait because Dasher called out, *"Over here."*

As this was Dasher's first year, the other hounds weren't quick to honor him. His litter mate Diana respected him, though, and she trotted over, putting her nose to the earth. *"He's been here."*

On hearing both Dasher and Diana, Cora thought she might double-check their work. *"For real. Come on. I say he's fifteen minutes ahead of us."* She touched the earth again. *"Maybe twenty."*

With a burst of speed, the hounds tried to close the gap, but the fox, who'd been hunting, meandered over fallen logs, lingered on stone walls waiting for mice. Once he heard the hounds he doubled back, slipped down the raceway embankment to run along the watercourse. Then he climbed out right at Wheeler Mill, paused to consider what an old man was doing in the back of a pickup truck. He sauntered behind the truck, stopped and sat to stare at Peter, then got up and walked into the mill, where he had a tidy little den with so many exits the hounds couldn't trap him if they put a hound on each visible one. He even had exits running under mighty timber supports.

Peter bellowed for all he was worth, "Yip, yip yooo," giving the rebel yell instead of "holloa" or "tallyho."

Within three minutes the hounds arrived at the truck, then plunged into the raceway, the creek, then back out, since the fox had zigzagged by the creek and then the raceway. It only took the hounds perhaps half a minute before they were all in the mill itself.

Shaker was a minute behind his hounds. He could see Douglas ahead parallel to the creek. He knew no hounds had veered off course.

He hopped off Showboat, his Thursday horse. Showboat calmly stood while Shaker gingerly walked across the low stone wall into the mill. Otherwise he'd have to ride around, and Shaker believed in getting to his hounds as quickly as possible, in this case to reward them for putting their quarry in his den.

Sister and the field galloped up as Shaker bent low to open the oak door into the bottom of the mill.

The hounds sang, *"He's in his den. He's in his pen. We've got him cornered! Mighty hounds are we!"*

Shaker blew triumphant notes on his horn; then he trebled them, which made the hounds dance all around the enormous mill wheels and the smooth areas where the kernels dropped to be bagged up. They leapt over one another, they dug at one of the den openings, they jumped straight up in the air so Shaker would notice them.

"I found the line first," Dasher boasted. The black marking on his head came forward in a widow's peak.

"I was first into the mill," Diana, thrilled at her success, barked.

"We did well as a pack. The youngsters led the way." Cora allowed herself great satisfaction.

"I still think if we'd crossed the raceway instead of moving

alongside it we would have nabbed him," Archie, brow furrowed, flews hanging loose, said.

"Archie, you worry too much." Cora laughed at him.

"There is no perfect hunt, Cora. We can always improve."

"You're right, Arch." She humored him.

Outside Sister Jane rode over to Peter. "Thanks for the view."

"Granddad taught me that yell." Peter felt young again despite his infirmities. "And I tell you, Janie, he walked right up here and stared at me. Insolent he was. Insolent and big, oh, a big fine red dog fox. I've seen him before. Fox everywhere this year but none so big as this boy."

"You're a good whip, Peter."

"Tell you one thing, pretty girl, if there's not foxhunting in heaven, I'm not going." He laughed; his eyes sparkled.

She remembered him when he was younger, when his hair was pitch-black. Peter Wheeler was a handsome man to have in the field or in the bed.

"I hope you won't be going any time soon even though I bet the foxes are grand. Foxes from the great runs in England during the nineteenth century. Now there's a thought."

He beamed at her. "When you were seventeen, I predicted you would be master someday. You had it even then, Jane." He reached in the pocket of his flannel shirt for a cigar, a Macanudo for a mild early-morning smoke. "It's an inborn thing. Can't be taught. Can't be bought."

"Thank you."

"And I'll tell you something else. You're still a fine-looking woman. I'm glad you didn't dye your hair or tie up your face. Looks stupid and fake. Hate to see that on a woman. Silver hair makes you look distinguished. More like a master." He chuckled. "And a word of advice—and that's the great thing about being two years older than God—I can say whatever I damn well please. To hell with the rules, Janie, do as you please. Time's a-wasting." He laughed. "Go seduce some fellow half your age. You can, you know. Here comes Shaker.

Like the cat that ate the canary. And look at those hounds, will you. Just as pleased with themselves as Shaker. My, how I'd love to be on the back of a horse." He was so excited he stood up, energy racing through him.

The field buzzed behind the master, happy to have such a good beginning and happy to have a moment for gossip, pass the flask, take a few furtive puffs on a cigarette, and quickly grind it out on the bottom of a boot. The horses chatted, too.

Sister rode over to Shaker. "Well done."

"Not bad. I'll cast in the other direction, up toward the graveyard."

"Fine."

She turned back to her field, took her place in the front as Crawford edged up behind her. He dearly wanted to ride in the master's pocket, the most coveted position in the field.

Czapaka murmured to Lafayette, *"I'll try not to bump you. He can't hold me, you know, but I don't want to go first. You've got more guts than I do. You go first."*

True, Lafayette did have to negotiate obstacles and terrain first, but Showboat was in front of him on those times when he could see him. That gave him a good idea of the footing. If Showboat and Shaker were out of sight, he used his judgment, which was solid. Lafayette took Sister Jane to the jump. She didn't have to squeeze him over.

"If it gets too bad just dump him," Lafayette advised. Being a thoroughbred, he had no tolerance for someone with bad hands.

They waved good-bye to Peter as they walked north. A yip now and then meant a faint, faint scent lingered, but they crept for about a half hour, arriving at the graveyard, headstones so old the writing had worn down to curves and straight lines. The years still read clear. Those resting within were Wheelers, Jacksons, and Japazaws, descended from an Indian leader of the last half of the seventeenth century, the first half of the eighteenth. It was always a source of pride and defiance among the Wheelers, Jacksons, and Japazaws that they claimed their blood. Many a settler denied sexual congress with the native peoples, much less married them.

Archie walked through the open wrought-iron gate, twelve feet high with a scroll at the top. *"Half hour."*

Cora joined him. *"Let's make certain."*

They deliberately walked through the graveyard, feathers scattered behind a large monument. A bobwhite had provided a feast for their fox.

"There's another one." Archie sniffed a crossing scent. *"About the same time."*

"Arch, I'll go to the edge of the graveyard with this one and you go to the edge with the other. Let's come back and compare. If we leave the graveyard, the whips will come in thinking we've split but I don't know which line is better."

"Okay." Archie moved north.

Cora moved south, taking the pack with her before some young one got impatient, although Dragon's disgrace seemed to have sunk in.

Within a few minutes the pack was at the southern edge of the graveyard, which opened onto a rolling fifty-acre pasture. Archie halted at the northern end, cut over about ten years ago. A border of mature trees had been left around the graveyard.

Cora called out, *"It's about the same. The scent."*

"Same here," Archie replied. *"But if we go into the cutover we have a better chance of staying with it. The scent will surely be dissipated on the pasture."* Archie knew the territory better than anyone.

"Come on, kids." Cora swung the pack around. They fell in behind Archie, slipped through the wrought iron, and headed into the tangles.

The young ones had been trained to go into rough country during their hound walks but this was the real thing.

A lovely young bitch hesitated.

"Get your butt in there," Archie growled. *"You don't want Shaker to push you in."*

She scooted in.

Douglas up ahead viewed, letting out a holler.

Shaker didn't bother his hounds. They were working well; they needed no encouragement. To speak to them would bring their heads up. Besides which the hounds could hear Douglas better than he could. They knew what it meant.

The field followed along a farm road. The brush, thick, inhibited horses going in after the hounds. They covered a lot of ground at a steady trot. The cutover acres gave way to a bog. The road, higher, got them through. Sister saw hounds on both sides of the bog, in a line, moving forward, working hard because there couldn't have been much to go on in that mess. Once out of the bog they fanned out, picking up the scent on the moss at the bottom of a fiddle oak.

"Fading fast." Cora urged the others, *"Try to keep your head down more, youngsters, even though it will slow you down. It's so easy to overrun the line in these conditions."*

Once out of the bog they entered a high meadow; a cool wind caught them on the spine of the meadow. The hounds dipped their heads under it, although Dasher would stick his nose up. True, he got wind of heavy scent, but it wasn't fox.

"Don't even think about it," Archie snapped.

Dasher dropped his head obediently, even though the deer scent sorely vexed him.

Diana stopped at the highest point looking to the east. There, sunning herself on a rock, was a luxurious vixen, gray. She had little interest in the proceedings.

"Look."

Archie stopped to see the fox. *"She's not the hunted fox. But oh, this is tempting."*

The pack came to a halt. Sister, too, saw the sunbathing vixen.

She paused, waiting for her hounds, and Crawford, the damned fool, bellowed, "Tallyho."

This brought a chorus of tallyhos behind her. The hounds all brought their heads up. Shaker stopped; the hounds stopped, then turned. The gray fox, disgusted, shot off her rock. The hounds picked up the scent, red-hot, and ran full speed ahead.

Sister squeezed Lafayette. They roared over the meadow, cleared the four slip-rail fence into the next meadow, and approached a trick drop jump at the edge of that. The slope on the other side was mossy, which meant horses slipped. The drop wasn't all that steep; it was the footing. Of course, the horses collected themselves in no time. It was the people that didn't.

Sister gracefully leapt over, barely leaning back in the saddle. She stayed over Lafayette's center of gravity regardless of the jump.

Crawford kicked Czapaka too hard. The horse had no intention of refusing but then over the jump Crawford looked down, panicked, and snatched the seventeen-hand fellow in the mouth, infuriating him. Czapaka skidded, Crawford hung up on his neck, and as the horse brought his hind end up under him, he let out a serious buck. Crawford was launched into space. Having relieved himself of the lump on his back, Czapaka turned around and jumped back over the jump, which brought Walter Lungrun to grief as he was approaching the jump. On the other side Czapaka galloped back toward the trailers, which in his estimation were three miles back.

Walter and Crawford picked themselves up simultaneously on both sides of the jump.

"Goddamn him! Goddamn that brute," Crawford screeched as the field receded from view.

Ralph cleared the jump, having ascertained that Walter was fine. "Crawford, you in one piece?"

"Yes, goddammit!"

"Know your way back to the trailer?"

"Yes, goddammit." Crawford was linguistically stuck.

Walter's horse, an old hunter named Clemson, wise in the ways of the sport, stood still. It was neither his fault nor Walter's that they parted company. Czapaka, crazed with freedom, crashed into them on their approach. Walter was already in his two-point position and the big Holsteiner knocked Clemson, a 16.1-hand appendix quarter horse, nearly off his feet.

Walter, not the best rider, was nonetheless a caring one. He checked Clemson's legs, walked him, reins over his head, to make sure the old fellow wasn't banged up.

"I'm fine. I can't abide warm-bloods. Dumb-bloods!" Clemson said.

Walter patted him on the neck, then swung up into the saddle. A hair under six feet, Walter looked much taller because of his terrific build. He slipped his feet in the stirrups.

"Ready?" Clemson asked, and was squeezed lightly in return.

They cleared the upright in good order as a still-cursing Crawford walked down to the eight-foot gate and struggled with the rusted chain and latch. This brought forth a torrent of verbal abuse.

Walter hid his laughter and trotted to catch up. He saw no reason to fly like a bat out of hell, since he could hear hoof-beats ahead.

Just as Walter found the group, Fontaine and the hill-toppers found Crawford, walking across the high meadow.

"It's a glorious morning for a walk, Mr. Howard."

"Shut up, Fontaine."

"All in a day's sport."

"I'll see your ass on the ground before the season's over." Crawford slapped his own thigh with his crop.

"Ah well, your ass is there now and buddy, there's so much of it." Fontaine laughed, riding on. The hilltoppers followed, suppressing giggles.

It never occurred to Crawford that not one of the hill-toppers asked if he was all right.

By the time he reached the trailers his feet hurt as much as his pride. Czapaka stood at the trailer as though an angel of reason. If Peter Wheeler weren't still on the truck bed, Crawford would have taken the crop to Czapaka. Which wouldn't have been a good idea no matter the horse but most especially Czapaka, who never forgot and never forgave.

"Horse's all a lather," Peter called out.

"Yes, he was a bad boy." Crawford tried to be sociable. He was glad that Martha worked Thursdays. He would have hated to have her see his debacle. Fontaine would tell her in lurid detail the minute he got back to the office.

He loaded up his horse and drove off, waving good-bye to Peter.

When Crawford drove out, Sister Jane and the field had pulled up two meadows beyond the high meadow. The fox disappeared. No den was in sight. No stream to wash away scent. Not even cow patties to foul scent.

The hounds worked the ground but they couldn't find even a sliver of hope.

"Let's call it a day," Sister advised Shaker, who was standing beside her.

"Cagey devil."

"Related to my reds. Must be. They're too smart to be foreign foxes."

She did recognize foxes. She made scent stations, kept track of litters in the spring, threw out dead chickens given her by farmers. The chickens were shot full of wormer, which helped to keep the parasite loads down.

Sister was proud of her healthy foxes.

As they turned back for the trailers, Shaker blew in Douglas and Betty Franklin. The morning proved better than he thought it would. He was happy. Sister was happy. The hounds were happy. Only Crawford was unhappy, and that was his own damn fault.

Once at the trailers, the hounds loaded, Betty broke out her hamper basket, as did other members. These impromptu breakfasts, sitting on the ground, delighted everyone.

Hunting port made the rounds, as well as iced tea. Sister kept a cooler full of soft drinks in her trailer.

After she'd made sure the hounds and horses were fine, she sat down, leaning against Betty's trailer.

"I ought to get you a director's chair." Betty handed her a saddle pad to sit on.

"I ought to get one myself. Too many things to do," Sister replied.

"Dr. Lungrun, come on over here and feed your face." Betty waved him over and he gratefully accepted.

Everyone talked, laughed about Crawford, asked questions of Walter, praised the hounds.

"Tabor Lungrun?" Bobby Franklin asked him.

"My father."

"Ah. We're glad to have you with us and hope you'll come back out."

"Dr. Lungrun, join us."

He smiled at Sister Jane, finding her the most beautiful older woman he had ever seen. "I need two sponsors, do I not?"

"I can't sponsor you because I'm the master."

Bobby held out his hand and shook Walter's. "I'd be happy to sponsor you, Doctor. My pleasure."

Fontaine, quick to curry favor with Sister Jane, held out his glass. "Me, too. Your father was a good man ruined by a not so good one. We'd be pleased to have a Lungrun in the fold."

The only reason Fontaine brought up that unhappy episode was so that no one would forget it. Small worry. No one in Virginia ever forgot anything. Misdeeds from 1626 were recounted with as much relish as if they'd happened yesterday.

But Fontaine, who knew better than to point out another man's misery, also wanted that joint-mastership. Since it was Crawford Howard who'd destroyed Walter's father in what Crawford said was a bad business deal and others said was calculated greed, Fontaine wanted everyone to remember right that moment.

"I'd be happy to ride with Jefferson Hunt." Walter bowed his head a moment. "Mrs. Arnold, I apologize for calling you after nine-thirty. I've been informed that you go to bed early."

"Beauty sleep," Betty teased her.

"Then I need to be comatose." Sister laughed at herself.

"Hear. Hear. A beautiful woman need not disparage herself." Fontaine held up his glass and the men drank to the master, who rather enjoyed it.

As the group broke up, Douglas sought out Betty.

"Mrs. Franklin, I thought Cody was hunting today?"

She liked Douglas and often wondered why he bothered with Cody, who treated all men badly. "Douglas, both of my girls are in a drug rehab program. They must stay at the hospital for a week and then they'll be back with us but still part of the program on an outpatient basis."

Bobby, in the trailer tack room, stuck his head out the door. "Betty, people don't have to know that."

"They know already. About drugs. We were the last to know." She turned to Douglas. "Because we didn't want to know, I'm afraid. Anyway, they're both doing something about it."

"Is Cody allowed to see people?"

"Not this first week. After that, as I said, she'll be out. You knew. I mean you knew about the drugs?"

He nodded that he did.

Bobby stepped down with an oomph. His knees hurt from carting around all that weight. "Guess there are no secrets in this club."

"You don't have to answer this, but do you take drugs?"

"No. I'll drink sometimes but I can pretty well keep a lid on it."

"Thank you for being honest with me." Betty touched his shoulder.

On the way home Bobby fumed first about that conversation but then about Fontaine. "He's going to tear this club apart. He's going to undo all the good that Sister and Raymond built over the years. He didn't have to bring that up about Tabor Lungrun. We all know why he brought it up."

"The young people don't remember."

"They'll know now. They'll ask and the whole thing will be like fresh paint."

"It was murky."

"Murky. It was business, Princess. Crawford put up the money and Tabor put up the work. They went into the cattle business together twenty years ago. The market crashed. Tabor lost everything. Crawford could take it as a tax write-off. That's not dishonest."

"Buying Tabor's farm at a bargain basement price is dicey."

"Business, Princess, business. The Lungruns never had much anyway. He had to sell the farm to keep the family going."

"Well, he loved that farm. He'd worked and scratched and scrimped. You know the Lungruns are made fun of in these parts, poor whites. He pulled himself up and then was brought down. Crawford could have floated him a loan or helped. No. He took advantage of him."

"Crawford is from Indiana. He doesn't think like we do. To him it was a matter of numbers."

"That poor man loved every blade of grass on that farm. Luckily he didn't live to see Crawford sell it eight years later at an enormous profit. No, by that time he'd shot himself, the poor bastard."

Bobby softened somewhat. "Terrible thing. Leaving those little kids with no father."

"And Libby Lungrun about killed herself working two jobs. She did kill herself. I think cancer can be brought on by worry."

"Honey, you read too many books about that stuff." He exhaled as they turned into their small farm entrance. "She was something to look at, Libby Olson." He called her by her maiden name.

Betty cast him a sly glance. "Yes."

"When a man stops looking he's dead."

"Just so you don't punish me for the same thing. That son of hers could have stepped right out of a movie. The old movies when they were all handsome."

"Guess he could."

As they pulled in front of the small, neat barn Betty said, "Bobby, you ought to reconsider supporting Crawford. It's not going to work."

"Well, it's not going to work with Fontaine either!" He tried to change the subject. "Walter's made something of himself. Lost track of him after he graduated from high school."

"I'm warning you. This is going to blow up in your face. We have enough trouble as it is with two girls in the hospital and everyone in the county buying laser printers. Let's tend to our own business. Jane will do what's right."

"Sister Jane doesn't have many choices."

"Crawford isn't one of them!" Betty slammed the truck door hard and stomped to the back of the trailer. She let the ramp down with a thud, narrowly missing her foot.

CHAPTER 19

Sister Jane and Douglas stood up, groaning. Without thinking about it they mirrored each other, putting their hands in the small of their backs.

She laughed when she saw him. "You're too young to ache."

"Bending over like that really gets me."

They'd examined each hound that hunted that morning. When hounds came off the party wagon they walked back into the draw run and then each hound was pulled out, paws inspected, everything checked, and then sent back to their various kennel runs. The only way to properly do this was to bend over or kneel down. If you knelt down, your knees hurt. If you bent over, your back hurt. They alternated pains.

Shaker slipped on arriving back at the kennel, going down hard. He must have clenched his jaw with special force because he cracked a back tooth and part of the filling fell out. He would have finished his kennel chores despite his discomfort but Sister forced him to get right back in the farm truck and hurry to the dentist. She believed the farther away a pain was from your head the less it hurt.

"We deserve a reward. Come on. I'll make you a fried-egg sandwich."

Doug happily trailed after her. They walked into the kitchen, where Golly had tossed bell peppers on the floor.

"Now why would she want to do that?"

"Meanness," Raleigh answered.

Douglas bent over, handing one to Sister. "She's bitten holes in this one."

"I wonder if I could get a video of that? You know that TV show, home videos or pet videos. Whatever. Golly can just start earning her keep here."

From the next room a strong meow was heard. *"I do earn my keep."*

Smiling, Sister Jane tiptoed to the swinging door between the kitchen and the pantry, which then opened onto a huge dining room with a fireplace so gigantic a person could stand up straight in it. On the middle shelf of the pantry, nestled in the dish towels, reposed the calico.

"Aha."

"Got bored."

"Imagine what would have happened if I'd done that," Raleigh, still in the kitchen, complained.

"What would have happened is you would have drooled over everything and then stepped on a pepper and squashed it. I merely sank my fangs in. A simple test for freshness."

Golly's jabber amused Sister, who reached down into a square basket, retrieving fresh eggs. "I'm making fried-egg sandwiches. If you care to join us, I'll fry you an egg."

"I'll come if you fry bacon." Golly rolled over to show her tum-tum.

Sister walked back in. "She's talking a whole row."

"Cats are funny."

As she greased the skillet, Sister chatted and then asked, "Did you know about Cody's drug problems?"

A silence followed. Then Doug said, "I did."

"Don't worry. You aren't betraying a confidence. Betty called me yesterday and told me both girls are at rehab or in rehab. I wonder what's correct? Anyway . . . Bobby's not much help. He's pretending it's like a broken leg."

"Mrs. Franklin told me this morning."

"But you knew about the drugs, I mean?"

"Well, I did, sort of. Cody goes on and off. I wasn't sure about Jennifer. I don't see her except when we're hunting and usually she's fine then."

"Yes. I had no idea. I wonder what else I miss." She buttered the whole wheat bread as the bacon sizzled.

Golly graced them with her presence, entering with a flourish as the bacon was flipped out of the pan.

"Don't even think about stealing my bacon." Raleigh frowned.

"I'll do as I please and if you value your eyes, you'll do as I please." She cackled.

Sister tore up a strip of bacon in small pieces, putting it on the counter for Golly. She gave Raleigh a whole strip when he sat. Then she put plates on the table.

"Drugs are all around." Doug opened his sandwich to put pickles on the egg.

"I guess they are"—she sat opposite him—"if you know where to look."

They both looked at the door because they heard a car drive into the driveway.

"Let's hope it's UPS so we can eat in peace."

It wasn't. It was Crawford Howard in his big-ass Mercedes, the V-12, the top of the top.

He knocked on the back door, then charged on through the mudroom into the kitchen. Most old friends walked in on Sister Jane, although she'd never considered Crawford an old friend.

"I'm sorry. I'll come back."

"Would you like a fried-egg sandwich?"

"No. I've already had my lunch. Thank you."

"Sit down. A Coke?"

"I'll get it." He opened the refrigerator door, pulled out a Coke, got a glass of ice, and sat down.

Sister winked at Doug when Crawford's back was turned. "Doug, stay a few minutes after feeding tonight."

"Sure."

Crawford sat heavily in the chair. He'd had a face-lift, a good one. He'd gotten some fat sucked off his middle, too. While it improved his appearance it didn't much improve his personality. "Doug, I'm glad you're here. I'll pay you twenty dollars a ride if you'll work with my horse. I'll board him here. Sister, what's full board?"

"Four hundred. Field board is two-fifty for hunt members."

"The Haslips get five hundred."

"I know, but we do try to limit ourselves to members, giving them a discount."

"Can't think like that, Sister. Business means whatever the market will bear. You've got to make hay while the sun shines."

"I'll consider it." Sister remained noncommittal.

"I'd be happy to work with Czapaka. He's a talented horse." Doug wiped his mouth with a napkin, rose, and carried his plate and glass to the sink. He washed them off, putting them in the drying rack. Sister hated dishwashers. Pretty much she hated most appliances. "Well, I'll be working the greenies if you need me."

Sister, wishing she could go with him to ride the young horses, waved as he left by the back door.

Crawford hunched over the table. "I'll get to the point." Being a Yankee, Crawford felt this was the superior approach, the waste-no-time approach. He never gave a thought to the fact that spending time with someone shouldn't be wasting time. "I have money. I have contacts. I have vision. I want to help the club. If you appoint me joint-master I will expect to contribute fifty thousand a year plus whatever overruns we have. You are the senior master. I can't hope to know what you know about hunting and hounds but I can learn."

This was a generous offer from an ungenerous man, in

most respects. She placed both hands around her cool glass. "I appreciate your financial acumen. Just keeping the territory open costs us roughly twenty thousand a year, as you know. And you do have vision. I have a lot to think about, Crawford, and I'd like to make a decision before the season is over."

"I thought you wanted to make a decision by opening hunt?"

"That's two weeks away and I'm on the horns of a dilemma. I do truly appreciate your special skills but there is strong support in the club for Fontaine Buruss."

"Yes, I know." Crawford's jaw clenched.

"He's a foxhunting man." Which was to say he was better qualified in many ways than Crawford, although Sister would never be so crude.

"He's also an irresponsible person. His sexual peccadilloes alone will—well, you know. His latest is Cody Franklin and I'm not so certain he doesn't give her drugs. Supply her."

This startled Sister. She wondered if Douglas knew. "That's a disturbing accusation."

"I've hired detectives."

"You what?"

He nodded, grinning. "Oh, yes. I take the reputation of this club seriously. There's a century of history in Jefferson Hunt. We must protect that."

"Can you prove this about Fontaine?"

"I think I can. I also know he's been in meetings with Gordon Smith, the developer around Dulles airport. Now, I ask myself what would someone of Smith's stature want with Fontaine? To develop."

"Does he?"

"I called him and he said the talks were merely preliminary. Smith said he was interested in developing along the Route Twenty-nine corridor. He's not interested in gobbling up hunting fixtures. He was plain about that but then he's a hunting man, too. I think Fontaine is doing this to make himself look good. He doesn't really have much to offer Mr. Smith."

"He has contacts. He knows everyone."

"Well . . ."

"Can you prove this about the drugs?"

"By opening hunt, Sister, I think I can prove a lot of things."

"I hope you're wrong. I truly hope you're wrong."

Crawford dimly realized he'd upset Sister. He thought the news would be disturbing and put him in a good light. Now he wasn't so sure.

"We can't have someone like that as a joint-master."

"No, we can't, Crawford, but you can't hang a man without evidence. I beseech you not to discuss this—"

He jumped in. "Of course I won't. Fontaine would get wind of it; then I can't nail him."

"Do you intend to turn this over to the sheriff?"

"Yes. I do. Absolutely."

"I see."

CHAPTER 20

A light wind kicked up at twilight and by seven o'clock had some bite to it. Sister, walking to the stable, turned back and grabbed the blue barn coat with the blanket lining. With Raleigh at her heels, she caught up with Doug on his way back to his cottage.

"Sorry I couldn't get back to you until now. It's been pandemonium. The caterer lost the menu. Had to go over the entire thing. Marty Howard called to ask if she could come by tomorrow regarding her ex. Betty Franklin called to say she disavows herself from Bobby's support of Crawford. My sister called to say she thought she should have Mother's china for the next year. I'd had it long enough and would I ship it to Sutton Place. I swear, Manhattan isn't far enough away. I think I'll suggest that Kay spend the next year in Paris. God, what a pain in the ass she is. Oh and the load of pearock we ordered for the walkways was delivered to the Haslips instead and they think they'll keep it. Fortunately, they paid the bill." She suddenly smiled brightly. "And how was your day?"

"Pretty good. Aztec jumped a whole course today. I think you should hunt her Saturday. The jumps have settled in at Rumble Bars." He mentioned Saturday's fixture. "She'll do fine."

"Why not? Lafayette can stay home and loll about. Sorry to dump my worries on you. It's been that kind of day."

"I still don't see why you hire a caterer for opening hunt. The members can feed everyone. You do enough."

"No. The members host breakfasts throughout the season. It's fitting that I should host the first one."

"I guess." Douglas was always thinking of ways to save Sister money. As far as he was concerned people could bring their own drinks and sandwiches.

"What'd you think of Crawford?"

"Barreling up the driveway?" His green eyes noticed a cobweb on the stall bars. He attacked it immediately. "Spider intelligence."

"Huh?"

"They come where the flies are."

"Fortunately, there aren't many of them." She loved fall and winter for that reason as well as others. "Crawford."

"If you need the money that badly, okay. If there's any other way to steer this ship into the future—do it. I'm sure that Attila the Hun was more offensive but you know, Attila's dead."

"M-m-m." She walked with him to the end of the aisle.

They rolled back the tall double doors, stepped outside, rolled them back.

He shivered. "That came up fast." Looked at the treetops. "Out of the northwest, too. No point standing out here. Come on."

Once inside his two-story cottage, Sister sat by the fireside. Doug quickly built a fire, throwing on a walnut log, which released a warm aroma. He took good care of the cottage. The heart-pine floors shone. The old Persian carpet Sister had given him fit perfectly in the living room, as did an old leather sofa facing two wing chairs with a simple coffee table between, a square one.

A flintlock with a powder horn hung over the fireplace. A cow horn, a true Virginia hunting horn, hung on a peg next to a nineteenth-century hand-colored hunting print. A white buffalo-plaid blanket was folded over the back of the leather sofa.

Spare, clean, yet inviting, Doug had a way of pulling things together that Sister Jane envied. She'd had to pay Colfax-Fowler to decorate her house back in the sixties and she'd updated it about every seven years since then. Sister never pretended to be aesthetically attuned but she had sense enough to follow those who were. Raymond evinced more interest in these things than she did.

Doug had absorbed a lot from Raymond not only in the way he arranged his cottage but in how he dressed. With an uncanny sense of color, he could pick the exact right tie, the correct fold of pocket handkerchief, the right break of the trousers over the shoe.

When Ray died Sister gave Douglas his clothing, generously paying to have everything altered for Doug, who was Ray's height but thinner. Ray's clothes were so classic that they looked as good today as the day he'd bought them. As Shaker was a short man, none of Ray's clothes would fit him so she gave the huntsman Ray's beautiful gold watch and his saddle.

"Coffee?"

"No. Too late for me."

"Where's Raleigh?"

"Asleep in the hall. He didn't hear me go out. I won't take up much of your time. You work all day. You don't need your nights—"

"I like having you here."

"Thank you."

"Sure you don't want anything?"

"No. Before Crawford barged in I wanted to ask you if you're still in love with her. It's none of my business and yet it is. If I can help you in any way, you know I will."

"I know that." He sat opposite her in the big wing chair. "Summer, well—let me start again. When she ended the relationship in May, it hurt. But I learned a lot about myself. I can't blame her. Then last weekend she ran into me on purpose and well, we're talking again."

"Yes."

"So I don't know where I am."

"But you know where she is."

"Physically, yes."

Sister drummed her fingers on the arm of the sofa. "These are hard habits to break. Usually the person is broken instead. I hope she makes it. But you can't get yourself in a relationship where you're worrying about her all the time."

"I know. I'm glad she went in voluntarily."

"She's a beautiful woman."

He sighed. "That makes it harder."

"Funny how we get turned around by looks. My mother said, 'You can't judge a book by its cover.' She was right but I fell for Raymond because he was big, blond, and handsome. But in those days you couldn't just jump into bed together or live together. The courtship process was definite. As I got to know him I discovered he was quite a lovely man. Well, I don't need a trip down memory lane and neither do you. If I can help you in any way, I will."

"I know."

She rose and he rose with her. "You know the people who sell these damned drugs should be shot. Either that or we legalize them. We have years of dolorous evidence to prove that what we're doing now doesn't work."

"That's for sure." He walked her to the door. "Wasn't it something to see Walter Lungrun? He was in high school when I was in junior high. Went to all the football games. All-state. I loved to watch him. I think he could have made pro even though he went to an Ivy League school. He's grown up, though. Something's different."

"Yes. I suppose facing life and death every day grows up most everybody."

"I'd kill Crawford if I were Walter."

She smiled at Douglas. "I don't know if I would, but I'd take pleasure in long, slow suffering."

They both laughed as she hopped out the door into the biting wind. She hurried to her back door, opened it, and hung up her coat.

Golliwog sauntered into the mudroom. *"You're late and I'm hungry."*

CHAPTER 21

To prove their dedication both Fontaine and Crawford hunted Saturday morning in filthy conditions. The wind cut them to ribbons; a light rain stinging like needles irritated them.

Although she didn't expect much, Sister thought the worst that could happen was they'd have a good hound walk. Keeping hounds fit tended to keep the people fit, too.

To her surprise Walter Lungrun was out. The small field kept close together, spending the first half of the early morning jumping ditches, fording swollen creeks, and hunching down in their jackets to stay warm.

Finally hounds hit above a freshly trimmed oat field, cut much too late. The run was short but intense. Sister decided to stop on a good note.

They rode back toward the west, the sharp wind smack in their faces. Combating the elements occupied Fontaine and Crawford.

Dragon, back in the pack, behaved impeccably.

Sister Jane patted Aztec on the neck. She behaved like a lady; no jump fazed her.

A howl ahead of them brought every hound head up.

"What's that?" Dasher asked.

"Mountain lion," Cora answered. *"And I'm as happy to chase one as a fox. As long as I don't chase deer, I think I'm in the right."* She glanced up at Shaker, who was trying to decide what to do.

109

He didn't want to send his hounds up until he knew exactly what was there. If it was a mountain lion, the scent of it might send some horses into a frenzy. Also, Sister was on a young horse. The horse had a fine mind but still, she was green.

He raised his horn to his lips, then brought it down again. "Sister, let me go ahead. You'll hear the horn if we can hunt home."

This was a code between them. No point in telling the field you're worried about them.

"Fine. Doug should be up there."

"He's ahead to the right a bit. Betty's behind us." Shaker chirped to the pack; they eagerly trotted ahead of him. He was a huntsman who wanted his hounds in front of him always. Some didn't but Shaker did.

The young entry, curious, surged ahead of Cora.

"Not so fast," the strike hound ordered them.

"We'll stop when we get around the corner." The three D young hounds plunged forward, the trees bending overhead, the light in the forest failing as the clouds lowered.

They stopped cold. Inky, crouched low but fangs bared, kept her paw on a plump rabbit she'd killed. Circling her was a half-grown mountain lion.

Diana growled, charging forward. *"Leave her!"*

The mountain lion, startled, backed off. Dasher and Dragon remained frozen to the spot, which gave Diana enough time to tell Inky, *"Go home. Fast. I'll get the pack on the big cat. Foul your scent any way you can because there are experienced hounds behind us. My brothers don't know much."*

Inky shot away to the right, scampering over dripping moss and pine needles, skidding down a bank and plunging into a narrow drainage ditch. She paddled in the water for forty yards, then clambered out. The water trick would gain her time but a hound like Cora or Archie would work that opposite bank. They knew the water trick and they were close. Very close. She prayed that Diana could set them on the lion and she wondered that she was foolish enough to square off against the cat. However, it infuriated her that she'd worked hard to bring down that rabbit and the sluggard wanted to steal her dinner.

Diana, rooted to the spot, the rabbit between her paws, shouted for her litter mates: *"Follow me!"*

They barreled down, putting their noses to the ground as Diana deftly steered them onto the mountain lion's tracks. The scent, stronger than Inky's, was easy to follow. Within minutes the whole pack was behind them with only Archie holding his ground bellowing, *"The fox went this way."*

Even Cora, a rock of a hound, ignored him. She reasoned that they could get up a fox any day but a mountain lion, so close, well, why not?

Shaker, up behind them now, watched a smallish bitch pick up the rabbit, running with the prize in her mouth. He peered at the mixed-up tracks, thought he saw one fox pawprint, dainty, but he clearly saw the cat pawprints. He plunged into the woods, knowing that Douglas would be ahead of him. A dirt road bounded the forest two miles away. Doug had to get there before the hounds did even though it was sparsely traveled.

Sister listened for the horn. When she heard the double notes she trotted and quickly found the spot and the tracks. She saw Shaker's scarlet coat disappear into the darkening woods, heard him encourage his hounds with another double blast. She couldn't take her tiny field in there. She pushed Aztec into a canter, hoping to reach the edge of the woods and turn left. Blessed with fabulous ears, as long as she could hear her hounds she could follow. She knew she was onto a big cat. How and where the beast would run was anybody's guess.

They reached the small pasture, picked up the sunken farm road, and headed toward the state road. She could hear Fontaine and Crawford jockeying for position behind her, since there was now room. A flash of buckskin on her left in the woods told her Betty had headed into the fray using an old deer trail. All hounds were on. Betty had no one to push up, so she could move out and she was heedless of her kneecaps. Outlaw, Betty's mount, would take good care of her and that confidence radiated from both horse and rider.

Aztec flicked her ears back and forth. The scent of mountain lion puzzled and frightened her a bit. The two riders behind her moving up irritated her. She felt Sister's right hand stroke her from her poll down to her withers as they flew along and she thought to herself, *"It's okay. Sister would never ask me to do anything that would hurt me."* She focused again on the road.

Sister held her hand up like a right-hand-turn signal. "Hold hard!"

Crawford bumped into Fontaine, who turned around and cursed. "Hold your horse, fool."

Sister, without turning her head, rebuked them by saying, "Gentlemen."

Martha and Walter, the only other two in the field, sat still behind the two rivals, whose shoulders had tensed up.

"They're to your left, Master," Crawford prattled.

"I know that." Sister wanted to say, "You flaming asshole. What I don't know is if they're turning."

Before she could say or think anything, the half-grown mountain lion blew past them on the other side of the state road. She was running low and if one wasn't concentrating, she resembled a German shepherd.

"Oh my god. Oh my god." Crawford pointed.

Fontaine, cooler, called in a singsong voice, "Tally-lion."

Since the hounds were still a ways off, he could holler without bringing their heads up. Otherwise he would have turned his horse's head in the direction the lion was heading, taken off his cap, and held it at the end of his arm, also in that direction. This way he would alert staff without disturbing the hounds. As any experienced foxhunter knows, the quarry you see may not be the hunted fox. It's imperative to keep hounds on the hunted fox or, in this case, lion.

Sister calmly waited for Douglas to pass, then the hounds, in good order, then Shaker, a big grin on his face. She fell in right behind her huntsman, perhaps twenty yards behind him.

Shaker pressed to the hog's-back jump, big logs built to create a rounded obstacle almost like a huge lobster trap. The huntsman shot over. Aztec eyed the jump. She hadn't seen one like that. Then she felt Sister squeeze and thought, *"What the hell. It looks like fun."*

If Aztec had sucked back then, Czapaka would have quit for sure and Crawford would have taken the jump but the horse wouldn't have. Czapaka, edging ahead of Gunpowder and an inflamed Fontaine, jumped the hog's back in good form. Walter and Clemson cleared, as did Martha and Cochise.

Behind them they heard Betty and Outlaw. They sailed over, then ran alongside the small field until Betty drew parallel with Sister.

"Some pumpkins," Sister called out.

"Tell you what." Betty laughed, the rain slashing at her face.

The hounds picked up speed. The humans and horses flew over the pasture. The footing got slick. They headed into a small wooded border between two properties, jumped a rising creek, and with three strides more jumped a slip-rail fence dividing two properties and then into more woods.

Sister halted. Shaker and Douglas, hounds at their feet, stared up at a massive rock outcropping, black in the rain. On top of it the mountain lion looked down at them. She'd had enough. She never did grab the rabbit, the cause of all this, and she'd had just about enough trouble for one day. Let one hound try to climb up to her and she intended to break its neck.

St. Just, the king of the crows, who had been shadowing them, perched in a poplar, leaves yellow.

"Leave it!" Shaker commanded.

"I'm not afraid!" Dragon, in frustration, yelped.

"Haven't you learned anything?" Archie said in disgust.

"Obey!" Cora commanded.

Dragon shut up, glowering.

Hearing Sister, Shaker cupped his hand to his mouth. "Hold there, Sister."

She pulled up. They could all see the lion on the rocks.

The hounds bunched up, following Shaker. Betty rode under the mountain lion's snarl.

"I don't like you either," Outlaw sassed.

Instead of going in front of the pack, Douglas made sure that Betty got out safely and every hound was out. Then he and Rickyroo trotted away as the big cat let out a spine-tingling roar. Spooked Rickyroo.

"I wouldn't have missed this day for anything in the world," Martha said.

"Me neither." Walter took off his cap, wiping his brow. Chilly as it was, the run and the fear made him sweat.

"Staff, please," Sister called out.

The little field moved over so Shaker, the hounds, Doug, and Betty could ride through. Hounds always had the right of way, with staff next. Field members turned their horses around so they faced the staff. One never turned a horse's butt toward a passing staff member.

"Ma'am?" Shaker drew alongside of Sister, his horn tucked between the top two buttons of his jacket.

"A leisurely trail ride back to the trailers, I think."

"Good." He wiped his hands on his britches. The reins were slippery. "It's been years since we ran a cat."

"She'll have a tale to tell her friends and so will we."

Flying alongside the hounds, St. Just cawed, *"Not bad for cubbing."*

"Where have you been?" Cora inquired. She liked St. Just, who often acted as aerial reconnaissance for the hounds—so

great was her hatred of Target, in particular, and red foxes in general.

Most crows disliked foxes but ever since Target had killed St. Just's mate this dislike had turned into a vendetta.

"I've been preparing my nest for winter. Going to be a cold winter."

The humans noticed the crow flying overhead, then peeling off. While they couldn't understand what was communicated, the staff members knew if scent was bad and crows were circling and cawing, often hounds would find a line.

The sky deepened to gunmetal gray. Sister remembered the Reaper on Hangman's Ridge. She didn't know why that incident popped into her head.

They rode toward the trailers visible now at Foxglove Farm.

Walter rode up alongside the master. "Is it always like this?"

"Sure." She smiled.

CHAPTER 22

Candles floated across the carp pond, which pleased Fontaine but not the carp. Although the evening remained as rainy as the day, the candles, housed in small lanterns in clever boats, kept their flames. Fontaine's house, built in 1819, exuded serene Federal appeal. Over the years a wing was added here or there but the successive owners never lost the simplicity of design so central to the Federal period. The carp pond anchored the back left corner of his spring garden, mulched and tidied for the coming winter. The fall gardens shouted color from zinnias, mums, holly bushes, and shiny-leafed bay bushes. The sudden turn in the weather meant those loud colors had perhaps a day or two before they faded, giving way to the silvers, grays, beiges, and whites of that most stringent season.

The foliage, nearing its peak, offered a contrast to the rain. If tomorrow proved as clear as the weatherman promised, the giant oak in the front lawn would be an orange almost neon in brightness.

Sorrel Buruss, on the board of the historical society, had arranged this dinner party. Fontaine, unlike many men, loved preparing for a party. So many house chores, piling up over the weeks then months, were accomplished in the frantic rush to get everything shipshape before guests arrived.

Thirty people, black-tie, laughed, reached for canapés off silver serving trays, enjoyed Cristal champagne as opposed to the cheap champagnes so often foisted off on guests at these dos.

Sister chatted with the president of the university. The Franklins made a point of introducing Walter Lungrun to the movers and shakers of the community. Walter had been away for almost ten years. His family, being poor, was not social so he needed to meet people. Also, in those ten years, many new people had moved into the area. Fontaine invited him at the last minute, which gave him as much pleasure as he took in not inviting Crawford.

Given the people attending this soiree, Crawford seethed but he was plotting his parry even as the assembled were shepherded into the dining room, a phenomenal shade of cerise with linen-white trim. Only Sorrel could have thought of such a color, which in the glow of the candelabra and wall sconces was fabulous. Sorrel believed anyone having a dinner party using electric lighting was an infidel.

The Heart Fund dinner and dance, headed by Crawford, would trump this, or at least Crawford Howard hoped it would.

He'd hired the best dance orchestra in the country and was transporting all of them to Virginia at his own expense. The Heart Fund would have been better served had he just given the medical charity the forty thousand dollars he would spend on the orchestra. But then these fund-raisers were about far more than raising money for the charity.

Sister Jane sat at Fontaine's right and the president of the university sat at Sorrel's right. Even if Fontaine hadn't wanted to be joint-master, the seating arrangement would have been the same. The president, powerful as he was, was transient. Sister Jane was permanent.

Sister observed Sorrel shining in a turquoise sheath dress, one shoulder exposed. The color, set off by the dining room walls, made Sorrel the center of attraction.

She probably would have been regardless, for she possessed a seemingly effortless elegance and a ladylike sense of decorum. Sorrel's blond hair carried a few streaks of gray, which somehow made her even more appealing. Even Sorrel must bow to the vulnerability of age.

Sister had bowed to it emotionally years ago but she wouldn't give an inch physically.

Sorrel, a Richmond girl, could have married many a fine fellow but Fontaine, carefree, bursting with obvious masculinity, won her heart. That he still held it said a great deal about his wife's perseverance as well as Fontaine's own qualities, which perhaps he shared only with her. She knew about the other women. She didn't always know who they were but she knew. Since she viewed passion as a danger and not a delight, Sorrel had little desire to retaliate. As long as appearances were maintained, the children protected, she closed her eyes.

Fontaine's foolishness with money caused her much more concern. But tonight none of that was apparent.

A harpist played after dinner. Real Cuban cigars, not fakes, were offered to the gentlemen in the smoking room. The ladies retired to a drawing room, relieved of the burden of supporting male egos.

The men felt the same way, although they wouldn't have put it in terms of supporting female egos, only that paying court to women was tiring. That rigid law of southern life, women must be flattered, could try a man's patience as well as his imagination.

Fontaine racked up the balls on the pool table. Bobby, Walter, and the university president reached for their cues. The other men sat along the park benches against the wall, waiting for their turn. Four fellows dealt cards over the inlaid-wood card table, the monogrammed chips in neat stacks by each player's right hand.

Bobby won the toss and broke. Brightly colored balls ricocheted everywhere. He socked away one, two, and three but just missed putting the fourth ball in the pocket. Walter took over, bending his muscular frame. As Fontaine watched the young man fire away he was glad he hadn't bet more than five dollars on this game. Walter was too good.

Fontaine leaned into Bobby as they observed Walter's deft touch.

"Why are you supporting Crawford?"

Knowing he hadn't told anyone but his wife as well as hinting to Sister, Bobby nonetheless knew that his lunch with Crawford at the club had to have been reported.

"The money."

"I'm hardly a pauper."

Bobby felt a tightness across his huge chest. Tiptoeing around Fontaine's financial history he said, "Of course not."

"Crawford Howard will alienate everyone in the club sooner or later."

"I fear that," Bobby honestly answered.

"Then why in bloody hell are you supporting him?" He kept his voice low, a light voice for such a butch-looking man.

"He knows how to generate money."

"Off other people's hides." Fontaine displayed the aristocrat's disdain for trade.

"I'm afraid that's true, too, but half the fortunes in this room were made off other people's hides. That they were done so long ago simply sanitizes them," Bobby shrewdly said, shifting his weight from one foot to the other.

Walter finished out the game. "Guess I had a lucky run."

Each player handed him five dollars.

"More than luck." The president smiled. "I don't know if I can afford another game."

"You break." Fontaine picked the smooth balls out of the pocket.

"How much?" The president brushed his sandy hair from his forehead.

"Five dollars," Fontaine said, then remembered his guests who were sitting. "Bobby and I will bow out. Ronnie, Ralph, up next? Ready?"

"Sure," they said.

Fontaine walked over to the bar, pouring himself a brandy and one for Bobby. Not a true drinker, Fontaine would sip socially. He'd snorted two lines of good cocaine after dinner. Retiring to his own bathroom away from everyone, he quickly inhaled his stimulant of choice. A touch of booze after that put him in a mellow yet quite clearheaded state. He could take or leave drugs. He knew most people couldn't. He genuinely liked coke but he watched himself. He'd seen men ruin careers and families thanks to the white powder.

"Bobby, I give you a lot of business and I bring you a lot of business."

Bobby's bushy eyebrows shot upward. Crawford was a cornucopia of business, too. "You do and I am grateful."

"We've known each other all our lives. I can't believe you'd do this to me."

"I'm not doing anything to you. I'm trying to . . ."

He didn't finish because Walter joined them, having just won the game in record time. "May I?"

"Of course. Brandy?"

"No thanks. Soda water."

"Not a drinking man?" Bobby mildly asked, knowing that Walter's father sure was.

"No, not much. Seeing the insides of alcoholics cured me of any desire to be a drinking man. That . . . and Dad." Walter smiled.

"You must hate Crawford Howard." Fontaine, wanting Bobby to hear this, asked.

"I do," came the swift reply.

"How old were you when all that happened? Twelve? Fifteen? Time goes by so fast." Fontaine swilled the deep golden amber liquid in the glass.

"Fifteen." Walter leaned his arm on the bar, putting his foot on the brass footrail.

"Painful." Bobby lifted the brandy to his lips.

"It was but, Mr. Franklin . . ."

"Call me Bobby."

"Thank you. I will if you'll dispense with Dr. Lungrun." He nodded. "Anyway, I learned. I learned self-reliance. I learned I wasn't the center of the universe. Mom needed help and I learned to put the family first. As much as I hate Crawford Howard, in a sense, he made a man out of me."

"You made a man out of you." Fontaine placed his glass on the countertop. "Plenty of other young men would have escaped somehow—booze, drugs, women, you name it."

"Why did you come back?" Bobby was genuinely curious.

"I love this place. I came back for Mom. It's what she wanted."

Neither Fontaine nor Bobby could think of what to say until finally Fontaine said, "We're glad of that."

Harry Xavier, having cleaned up at the card table, stood,

shoving money in his pocket. "Dr. Lungrun, you young pup. I'll take you on at the pool table."

The men crowded around. Xavier's skills had emptied many a wallet.

Back in the drawing room the ladies surprised themselves with their vehemence. It began innocently enough with Betty Franklin mentioning Peter Wheeler "hunting" from the back of his pickup.

The disposition of his property, on everyone's mind, provoked the heated exchange.

Tinsley Wetherford Papandros declared that Peter should have settled his estate years ago. In his decrepit condition he could fall prey to whoever offered the most money.

Isabel Rogers, a tawny beauty, backed up Tinsley, saying the least he could have done was put the land in conservation easements.

Betty replied that was all very well for a rich person to say. Isabel was rich, but if Peter had done that he would have devalued his land. Only someone who wanted to farm would buy it.

"Devalue the land? What about the environment!" Lisa Bredell nearly shouted. She was president of the Blue Ridge Conservation Council. "There isn't going to be anything left for our grandchildren."

"Don't overstate your case," Sister dryly said.

Lisa wheeled on Sister. "You of all people should know what I'm talking about. There won't be any land for your precious hunting."

"Don't talk to Sister like that," Betty firmly said.

"She's not God," Lisa popped off. The champagne loosened her tongue.

"She is on the hunt field." Sorrel laughed, hoping to restore harmony.

"It's primitive," Lisa, not a Virginian, stated.

"We don't kill the fox." Betty felt hot anger rising in her throat.

"How do you know? You all will say anything so you can charge over the countryside shouting 'tallyho' or whatever you shout."

"Of course we know," Sister, fighting back her own anger, said. "If the hounds killed a fox, they'd be covered with blood. The pieces of the fox would be there for us to see. You overestimate human intelligence, Lisa. The fox is smarter than we are, than the hounds, than the horses."

"Certainly smarter than Fontaine." Sorrel laughed and most of the ladies laughed with her.

"Back in the late seventies the sport began to change. Not that we could catch the fox but we tried. Now we'll call off the hounds," Betty reported.

"How?" Lisa's lower lip jutted out in stubborn disbelief.

"The horn. Hounds are taught to obey the commands the same as cavalry officers obeyed the bugle." Sister, unless in hunting company, did not discuss her passion at social events. However, Lisa, Tinsley, and Isabel were not convinced.

Sorrel passed around small chocolate cookies. "Ladies, go to opening hunt. See for yourself."

"When is that?" Tinsley asked.

"First Saturday in November. There's a wonderful breakfast afterward. You'll enjoy it." Sister smiled although she felt like slapping their faces.

"All right," Lisa said, half-defensively.

"Will Peter Wheeler be there?" Isabel inquired.

"He hasn't missed opening hunt since he returned from World War Two. Or at least that's what he tells me." Betty laughed. "That was before my time."

Sister, knowing what Isabel was after, which was to woo Peter into signing a conservation easement, said, "He's an old man. He doesn't know how to use a computer. He doesn't want to. He doesn't have an answering machine. He figures if it's important, you'll drop by. He doesn't own a fax, a video machine, and he doesn't have a satellite dish either. He's a country man who loves country ways. He knows more about the environment than all of us put together but Peter isn't going to sign anything that limits his options."

"But it's to protect the environment!" Isabel protested.

"For you. Not for him." Sister plainly stated the truth, which, as always, is hard to swallow.

Before Isabel could further hector Sister and Betty, Sorrel reached for her elbow. "Come on, I want to show you that fabric."

Isabel hesitated, then stood up.

"Tinsley and Lisa, join us."

A command is a command no matter how nicely put. The two placed their small plates on the coffee table, falling in behind Sorrel and Isabel.

"Ladies, we won't be long," Sorrel called over her shoulder.

"Take your time," Betty said, a hint of malice in her voice.

Sister leaned over to Betty. "How are the girls?"

"I don't know. We aren't supposed to communicate. Part of the program. I pick them up Tuesday evening."

"I pray for them. It's about all I can do."

"Me, too. I've had to relinquish my ideal of the omnipotent mother. I thought I could bind all wounds, create all happiness." She sighed deeply. "I liked it when they were small. I really was the most important person in their world."

"It's a bit like getting fired, isn't it?" Sister said.

"It is. Well," Betty waved her hand. "I don't want to talk about it. There's nothing I can do at this point. But before I forget it, I want to go on record." She whispered into Sister's ear, "I am not in agreement with Bobby. I do not support Crawford. Absolutely not."

"What are you girls whispering about?" Kitty English, an attractive middle-aged woman, crossed the room.

"You." Sister laughed.

"Me? What have I done?"

"Best basketball coach the university has ever had. Better than the men." Betty adored women's basketball.

"And I want to know where you bought those shoes. Just enough heel to look spiffy but not enough to break your neck." Sister admired the low heels.

"Oh, that." Kitty plunked herself down on the sofa and they merrily chattered away about shoes, high heels versus low heels versus total rebellion against fashion—always said, never practiced. They talked about basketball and lacrosse, the endorsement deals of professional athletes, and how many of them wind up in court for violence. They decried the lack of any good women's clothing store in town. All three of them hated driving to Washington, D.C., which wasn't that good for women's clothing anyway, and Richmond, which was a fashion joke. They agreed one had to go to New York City, but who could afford it? Then Kitty shared her secret: Charlotte, North Carolina. Five hours by car and two really wonderful women's stores.

By the time Sorrel returned with her environmental trio, high spirits had been restored.

CHAPTER 23

The long corridor between both halves of the new wing of Central Virginia Hospital, lined with large square windows, let in the light. The old part of the hospital, built in the thirties out of brick, although renovated, was dark and depressing by contrast.

Having been in the operating room since seven that morning, Walter was glad to see natural light. He loved his work although at times the sheer intensity of operating drained him. He started med school thinking he would become a surgeon but discovered neurosurgery fascinated him. The hardwiring of the human body, an astonishing edifice, amazed him and not the least because nerves could regenerate. Without his being fully aware of it at the time, regeneration was a necessity in his own life.

Dr. Thesalonia Zacks, young and pretty, called Tandy by her friends, met Walter and they walked to the small cafeteria on that side of the hospital.

One black coffee and a turkey sandwich later, Walter was feeling better.

"Don't know why, but all the research indicates people addicted to drugs, alcohol, even cigarettes"—Tandy emphasized "even"—"don't feel pleasure to the level of most of us. The substance enhances pleasure for them, whether it's nicotine or whiskey or even sugar. The old saw is it passes in families and it does but we still can't explain why, say, child A of an addicted parent does not become an addict whereas child B does. The truth is we are on first base with research and that's because for decades, for centuries, medicine viewed alcoholism or drug addiction as a personal failing."

"No one puts a gun to anyone's head and says, 'You will smoke a cigarette today.' There is an element of choice."

"Yes, but there again—to what level—we don't know. Walter, I have had patients tell me they had their first drink at age twelve and knew they had to have more. Often they didn't even like the taste."

"How did you become interested in this?"

"My mother. Alcoholic."

"My father."

Their eyes met, a sense of understanding between them. "Is he still alive?"

"No. He killed himself when I was fifteen. He'd lost everything in a bad business deal. He drank more and more until he disappeared down that bottle. Death may have been the easy part for Dad."

"I'm sorry."

"What about your mother?" he asked.

"She's still alive. My father left her. My two brothers refuse to have anything to do with her. She's a binge drinker. She can stay dry for six months, eight months, and then she'll buy six bottles of vodka, lock herself in the house, and drink until she's wiped them out." She held up her cup for more coffee. "Of course, this stuff is addictive, too. I read somewhere that Voltaire drank sixty cups of coffee a day."

"If it would make me as intelligent as he was, I might try it." Walter accepted a refill, too. "The Franklin girls are being released today. Right?"

"Right."

"How do you think they'll do?"

"They have as good a chance as any. The parents are supportive. The mother more so than the father. He's not hostile but he still doesn't get it. Betty said she'd spoken to you."

"Yes, at Fontaine Buruss's party. She asked me to check in. I'm glad I did. Your program is impressive."

"It is and it isn't." She leaned back in her seat to stretch out her long legs. "I don't like treating drugs with drugs. In some cases it's the only treatment we have. Especially heroin users. My personal feeling is we substitute one dependency for another but if we don't use what little we have available to us they often backslide. You know the story." She appraised Walter. He was more handsome than she remembered from passing him in the halls. "Fortunately, that's not the problem for Cody and Jennifer. Cody has a longer history of abuse, obviously. She's burned more bridges behind her and has more messes to clean up. Jennifer's rebelling and the drugs are mixed in with that so-o attractive stage of life. How does anyone survive adolescence? I didn't smile from age eight to twenty because of my braces."

"Good orthodontist."

She laughed. "Thank you. Do you know Cody and Jennifer well?"

"No. I know Betty and Bobby somewhat. I grew up near here. Kids don't pay much attention to older people. I've started foxhunting and that's how I've come into contact with the Franklins again."

"The girls are very beautiful."

"Pretty is as pretty does."

"Men don't usually say that."

"Then you're talking to the wrong men."

"Not now."

He laughed. "Keep talking."

"Really. My experience with men is that they are completely undone by looks. That's why Cody has gotten away with her addiction as long as she has. There's always a man to rescue her. Only makes it worse, of course."

"I'd rather look at a pretty woman than not, but maybe I've seen enough in my life to know that if there isn't more, it's never going to work. You know?" He leaned forward. "One of the most fascinating and beautiful women I know is seventy years old. She walks into a room and you can't look at anyone else. She's electrifying and on a horse she truly is the goddess of the hunt."

"Jane Arnold." Tandy smiled. "Yes, Cody and Jennifer have mentioned her. She scares them half to death. I'd like to see her."

"Opening hunt is the first Saturday in November. Ten o'clock at Sister Jane's place, Roughneck Farm. If you'd like to come, I'll call Sister Jane."

"I can't ride."

"Don't have to. Come and enjoy the spectacle and then eat all that good food."

"Thank you. I don't have my Filofax with me but if I'm free I'll call you. I'd like to see a hunt."

"Before I forget. Do you know where the girls get their drugs?"

"If I did, I'd tell the sheriff. Even in rehab people protect their sources. Talk about misplaced loyalty but . . . There's something more going on. Cody's not protecting a dealer boyfriend. I don't know what it is. I just know there's something more."

CHAPTER 24

"You people make me sick." Alice Ramy shook her finger in Sister Jane's face. "You think you can do whatever you please. A bunch of rich idiots!"

"Alice, show me the hound."

Without a reply the disgruntled Alice, as wide as she was tall, waddled out to her chicken coop. The plump bodies of chickens lay about inside and outside the coop.

Rooster, Peter's harrier, rested amid the carnage.

"I locked the gate. I'm not touching him. You take that damn hound out of here and you pay me for my chickens!"

Sister opened the gate. "Hey, Rooster."

The harrier pricked his ears. *"I've been framed!"*

Sister quietly approached and petted him. "It's Peter Wheeler's hound. He's bred to run rabbits, small game."

Alice grumbled. "I'll call the animal control officer."

"Don't do that. I'll take him to Peter."

"Thank you. I didn't kill these chickens but I'd like to eat one. I'm afraid of that harpy, though."

"He ought to be shot!"

"Alice, if this hound had killed these chickens, he'd have eaten at least one. Have you counted your dead?"

Alice quickly counted the two roosters and seven hens.

A cluck from under the henhouse gave hope to all.

Sister knelt down. "The rest are here."

Alice couldn't kneel down. "How many?"

"One, two, three, uh, some are hiding behind the others but I'd say you have eight. No roosters, though." Sister stood up, brushing off her knees and her hands. "Let me take this big Rooster home."

"Good. He can kill Peter's chickens!"

Sister accepted Alice Ramy's choleric nature. She was a woman only happy when airing a complaint, some terrible thing that had happened to her. Her narcissism was such that she even shied away from the disasters of others, their short-comings. She concentrated solely on her own dramas. Sister patted the harrier on the head, then walked around the inside of the pen. "Here you go, Alice." She pointed to a shallow tunnel dug under the wire.

Alice thumped over. "That's how he did it."

"Look at the size of this hound. Look at the size of the tunnel. And look at these tracks." Sister pointed to clear fox prints.

"Dog. I told you."

Sister knelt down again. "Hey, sweetie, give me your paw."

"Give it to you. Wouldn't give it to that bitch. I was on the trail of that fox. Aunt Netty. I'd know Aunt Netty anywhere. By the time I got here, Aunt Netty had had her jubilation."

Sister pushed the paw into the dirt right next to the fox print. "See the difference?"

"Yes." Alice shut her mouth like a carp.

"This hound couldn't have shimmied under the wire. My

guess is he was on the fox but far behind. It's a good day for scent."

"What am I going to do with all these dead chickens?" Alice chose not to apologize, since she could never be wrong. She simply accepted that the fox had killed the chickens but that didn't mean she was wrong.

"Give you fifty cents apiece."

"Two dollars apiece."

"Fine." Sister reached in her jeans pocket, counted out eighteen dollars, handed them to Alice. Then she picked up the chickens, tossing them in the back of the truck. Alice threw in the two dead roosters.

"I'll shoot that fox if I see him."

"Put a thin strip of concrete on the outside of your chicken coop or even a hot-wire. Might work. But don't shoot a fox, Alice. It's unsporting. If the fox comes back, I'll replace your chickens. Just don't kill him."

"Maybe."

"When the scared chickens come out, I'm willing to bet you another ten dollars that you're missing a chicken. Fox carted it off."

"What I want to know is why was this hound sitting in the middle of the chicken yard?"

"I just got here!"

"My hunch is, like I said, scent was good so he could have been a half a mile or even a mile behind the fox. Be easy to keep on the line today. By the time Rooster got here the fox was gone and as luck would have it, you walked out just then."

"You can't trust people. You'd say anything to cover a precious hound of yours or Peter Wheeler's. All you foxhunters stick together."

Sister whistled softly to Rooster, who followed her. "Can't trust some people, Alice. Let me know if the fox comes back."

"I could pee on her leg," the harrier offered, but Sister trotted him out of there, putting him next to her in the truck. She wanted to get to Hangman's Ridge before anyone saw the dead chickens in the back of the truck. No point in wasting good chickens. She'd strategically place them throughout that fixture after filling them full of ivermectin, a wormer.

By the time she reached Peter's, she and Rooster were good friends. She honked the horn. Peter opened the back door. "Hey, Pete. Rooster was in the middle of Alice Ramy's chicken pen. It's confusing calling him Rooster in the middle of roosters."

He slowly walked out, saw the dead chickens. "Guess these chickens won't be crossing the road. Alice Ramy's a good five miles from here. Rooster, what are you doing?"

"Fox killed her chickens. She blamed your hound, who doesn't have a drop of blood on him. God, she's a miserable bitch."

"Yeah," the dog agreed.

"Guess I'd better keep an eye on you, buddy." Peter clapped his hands and Rooster jumped out of the truck when Sister opened the door. "Come on in for a drink."

"Thanks. I'll take a rain check. I want to put out these chickens."

"Good idea." He turned for the house. "I forgot to ask you the other day. . . . When I go, will you take care of Rooster and my chickens?"

"Yes. I wish you'd stop talking about dying."

"Well, I feel just fine but I need to put my house in order. I've lived a long time. I'm damned grateful but it may be worth dying to get away from Crawford Howard." He then related how Crawford had dropped by, giving him the hard sell. Sister didn't get the chickens out until sundown.

CHAPTER 25

Aunt Netty ducked into Target's den, as hers was a half mile farther on. She'd carried her booty long enough.

"A feast!" Charlene sank her fangs into a limp wing.

"You should have seen Alice Ramy, the sow," Aunt Netty crowed in triumph. *"If I were bigger I'd break her neck, too."*

Reynard, Charlie, Grace, and Patsy ate in respectful silence as the adults discussed corn, oats, and mice.

"The gleanings are especially good down by Whiskey Ridge," Target said.

"It's good everywhere. A perfect year. Oats, rye, corn, barley, fat mice, fatter rabbits." Aunt Netty lived to eat. *"Even my useless husband mentioned it the other day."*

"I haven't seen Uncle Yancy since July," Charlene noted.

"I hardly see him myself, which I consider a benefit," his wife remarked. *"He's spent most of the summer down at Wheeler Mill studying the wheels and the raceway. He likes to talk to the foxes down there, reds, you know. Yancy feels that he can prove all mammals descend from a great prehistoric fox. He says birds come from flying reptiles, so we have nothing in common with them, but all mammals come from the original fox."*

"Even humans?" Reynard wondered.

"Yes. They're more closely related to us than we'd like, but better to be close to a human than an armadillo, I suppose."

Grace, the image of her mother, put her paw on a piece of

flesh because Charlie was inching toward her. *"Does that mean we'll build machines?"*

"I don't follow, dear." Aunt Netty, full, stretched out on her side.

"If we're related to humans will we build machines like they do?" Grace slapped her brother, who put his nose too close to her portion of chicken.

"Gracious, no. Machines dull your senses. We'd never be so foolish." Netty laughed. *"That's what's wrong with them. They get further and further away from nature. Yancy says there was a time when they had better eyes and ears than they do now. He said once humans could even smell game. If they keep on the way they're going, they'll even lose their sense of direction. Yancy says millions of them live in cubicles stacked on top of one another. Seems impossible but he says he's seen it on television."*

"Where does he watch television?" The patriarch of this family joined the conversation.

"Doug Kinser. Yancy sits on the window ledge and watches the eleven o'clock news."

"Why bother? It's only about them." Charlene shrugged.

"Yancy says you never know when they're going to do something stupid like build a dam. Affect all of us. Even St. Just."

"I'll snap his neck yet." Target's eyes lit up. *"He's worthless."*

"Worthless but smart. He won't be satisfied until he sees you dead." Aunt Netty lifted her head. *"Children, take the chicken outside. Help your mother clean up this den."*

Patsy, the quiet one, whispered, *"Dad, how can a blackbird kill a fox?"*

"Can't." Target swished his tail around.

"He can lead the hounds to you, Target. Pride goeth before a fall," Netty warned.

"I'll get him before he gets me."

As the young foxes gathered up the debris of their meal,

Aunt Netty scolded: *"What are you all doing here, anyway? You should be in your own dens."* Her speech was clipped. *"Charlene, you spoil these children. Why, the grays are already in their new homes, even that little black thing. She has a pretty face. She'll need it with that black coat."*

"Who cares what the grays do?" Reynard, parroting his father, said.

"I do. They aren't stupid, you know." Netty, who'd seen a lot in her day, couldn't help but sound superior. *"They've taken the good new dens near the cornfields. Makes it that much harder for you. You should have found a place last week."*

"I'll chase one out and take his den," Reynard bragged.

"I wouldn't be so sure of that." Aunt Netty had no time for youthful folly. *"Opening hunt is not but ten days away. You'd better get yourself situated."*

"We can dust those guys." Charlie, the good-natured son, laughed.

"And so you can but what if you duck in a den and find Comet there? He's a young gray but he's tough, very tough, just like his father. You'll have a fight on your paws and hounds at your heels. Prepare now." Having imparted enough wisdom for one day, Netty closed her eyes, curling her tail around her nose.

Charlie picked up a drumstick; Reynard, some feathers. Grace batted the neck around and Patsy picked up the backbone. They walked outside, scattering the bones. The sun filtered through the trees.

"Why do they start formal hunting in early November?" Grace asked.

"Because we're looking for dens. They'll get better runs. That's what Mom says," Charlie answered.

"It's because there's frost on the ground. Usually. The first frost comes around the middle of October but some years not

until later. By November the frost is here until April. Scent holds," Patsy said.

"Maybe it's both things." Grace walked toward the creek. She liked to watch the fish. She'd seen bear catch them and she thought if a dumb bear could do it, she could do it.

Reynard dashed by her. Charlie ran after him. Patsy bumped into Grace just to hear her squeal. A perfect October day was meant for play. They could worry about hunting later.

CHAPTER 26

The last label peeled off the sheet of paper was smacked onto the envelopes. Formal invitations to opening hunt had already been mailed the first of October. This mailing was the fixture cards.

Fixture cards listed the time and place of each hunt. Often at the top of a fixture card was printed the phrase "Hounds will meet."

Scheduling fixtures drove many a master to drink. Even with the fixtures scheduled, last-minute changes wreaked havoc. A hard rain might prompt a farmer to request no one ride over his fields and with good reason. A crop of winter wheat could get cut up or the slipping and sliding of trailers could turn a pasture into brown waves, which, when frozen, were hell to negotiate.

The ladies of a hunting club usually did the mailings. Gentlemen built fences. Both genders cleared trails. However, as those lines blurred, the new order was whoever could do the job, did it.

The ladies, gathered in Sister's living room, laughed, gossiped, teased one another.

Golly sorted the mail. Raleigh slept by the fireplace.

A knock on the front door brought Sister to her feet.

Crawford asked to come in. The ladies said hello.

"Perfect timing." He smiled. "I'll take the fixture cards and run them through my postage meter."

"Why thank you, Crawford," Sister said.

"Martha wasn't here, was she?"

"No," Betty Franklin, sitting cross-legged on the floor, remarked. "She got tied up at work. Called about an hour ago."

"Oh." He wanted to say something but whatever it was it stuck in his throat.

"A libation?" Sister reached for his jacket.

"No. I'll do this right now and drop them at the main post office. Oh, I forgot to tell you, thirty coop flats with top boards will be dropped over at Rumble Bars tomorrow. Had the lumber yard knock them together."

There were many ways to build coops but if the sides were built, then carried to the site, they could be leaned against one another, braced, a top board put on, and then painted. It saved time building the flats off-site.

"Crawford, that's wonderful." Sister was pleased. He allowed himself a smile. "When we know how the fox runs we can put up more. This is a good beginning. What a wonderful surprise. Are you sure you wouldn't like a drink?"

"No. No. I really need to go." He picked up the cards all in their envelopes in cartons according to zip codes. Out he went.

"H-m-m," was all Betty Franklin said.

Before that subject could warm up, Sister deftly said, "Did I tell you girls the caterer called this morning and said I'd better switch from spoon bread to corn bread? I mean how can you have a hunt breakfast without spoon bread, ham biscuits, gravy—well, I'll make us hungry. Anyway, he said there are now so many Yankees in Virginia that every time he makes spoon bread there's a dreadful mess."

"What does he mean, a dreadful mess?" Georgia Vann asked.

"Yankees pick it up with their fingers. They think it's undercooked corn bread." Sister emitted tinkling laughter.

"No!" Betty howled.

"I can't believe that. How can you not know how to eat spoon bread? I mean, it's called spoon bread." Lottie Fisher shook her head, then laughed.

"That's what he said." Sister laughed more.

"The hell with the Yankees." Lottie waved the rebel flag figuratively.

"You know, we give foxhunting clinics in the beginning of cubbing. Maybe we should run a hunt breakfast clinic or a southern cooking demonstration," Betty merrily suggested.

"As long as you organize it," Sister said.

"Spoken like a true master." Betty giggled some more.

"Isn't it glorious to be superior to Federals?" Georgia teased.

"Like Crawford." Lottie had to get back to that. "I wonder what he's about? I mean, I heard he's trying to win back Martha. If I were her, I'd slap him right in the face."

"She did that already," Betty dryly said.

"Shotgun," Georgia laconically said as she reached for a piece of pound cake with fresh vanilla icing dribbled over it.

"He's not worth going to jail over." Betty thought the pound cake looked pretty good, too. This was her third piece.

"Maybe he's learned something," Sister said. "More coffee? Drinks?"

"You sit. You threw this together after hound walk. You must be tired by now." Georgia got up, walked over to the gleaming silver coffeepot, and poured into the cups handed her.

"If I had a nickel for every time I wanted to shoot Bobby Franklin, I'd be rich." Betty laughed at herself. "Who knows what Crawford and Martha have to work out together. It's hard for a middle-aged woman to make it alone. Let's not forget that, girls."

A quiet murmur rippled across the gathering.

"Sister, you know I can't keep my mouth shut. Are you really going to make Crawford a joint-master? You must know the club's abuzz with speculation." Georgia blushed.

"I don't know. Crawford and Fontaine have a lot to offer."

"And a lot to sidestep." Lottie hated Crawford. She thought he was a rich oaf who tried to buy his way into everything. He didn't belong here.

As they batted pros and cons back and forth, as well as Martha Howard's future, Sister listened. She thought to herself, if only Raymond Junior had lived. He'd be old enough now to assume the responsibilities of a joint-master. She'd always dreamed of that. She snapped out of her reverie. "Don't question the will of God," she said to herself, then said to the ladies, "I really do appreciate your concern for the hunt."

"Not just the hunt, Sister Jane, we appreciate you. Can't you go along for one more year as sole master? Surely something will turn up or resolve itself," Lottie inquired earnestly, her soft brown hair framing her square face.

"I've said that for the last five years."

"You're stronger than we are. Wait five more." Betty echoed what the others were thinking.

"I don't know. There's a black young vixen on the farm. You know everything happens in the black fox years."

The ladies knew the black fox legend. "That doesn't mean it's going to happen to you," each said in her own way.

"Well—I hope not." She was tempted to tell them about the lone figure on Hangman's Ridge but decided that would be between her and Doug Kinser. "But let's change the subject to something more cheerful or challenging. Can you imagine Crawford Howard without his clothes on?"

CHAPTER 27

The old office in the center of town exuded a sepulchral air. The sturdy white Doric columns, the large iron doors boasted of public wealth, solidness, and civic duty. Built in 1926 on a flood tide of government spending and public speculation, the post office, like the country that spawned it, witnessed the subsequent depression, another world war and three smaller ones, more economic booms and busts.

When the post office was being built, slabs of granite lying along Main Street, men came to the post office wearing coats and hats. If it was summer, they wore jaunty straw boaters. In the winter, fedoras and borsalinos predominated. Ladies festooned in hat, gloves, purse, and shoes dyed to match sashayed onto the black marble floors. The very colors the ladies wore announced their feelings about the day and about themselves. Farmers, some still driving teams, would tie up at the gray iron balustrade designed for that purpose. Wearing overalls and straw hats in the warm weather, they'd stride into the halls cheerfully greeting everyone, stopping to talk about that riveting subject: the weather.

As Crawford Howard pushed open the heavy doors with his back he harbored none of these memories. A post office was simply a post office to him, not a community statement. But it remained a federal building and therefore a citizen trust. An American can enter a post office at any time of night or day to deposit mail in the shining brass slots, to open their own large or small mailbox with their key.

People didn't dress to go downtown anymore. They barely pulled themselves together, properly groomed, to attend church. The South and especially Virginia practiced a dress code much stricter than that of the rest of America but even here in the bosom of courtliness standards were falling. Many wore jeans and T-shirts. Businessmen still paid attention to their furnishings, as did those ladies who were hoping to catch a businessman's eye. But even their standards of dress were lower than just thirty years before.

Crawford reached the slots and slid the mail in. One brass slot was marked with the town's zip code, another was marked VIRGINIA, and a third was marked OUT OF TOWN but it may well have read OFF THE WALL. Virginians, without making noise about it, quietly, calmly, considerately believed any activity of importance took place within the state's borders. From the Potomac to the Dan River, from the Atlantic to the early steep folds of the Alleghenies shared with its rebellious sister, West Virginia, this was the center of the universe.

Even Crawford, as he methodically tossed the mail in the slots, listening for the satisfying soft thunk on the other side as it hit a mail basket, even he who knew the world had adopted this point of view. What was Nairobi, London, New York compared to Charlottesville, Fredericksburg, or the dowager herself, great fusty Richmond? Crawford, a direct and active man, hardly realized the seductiveness of the area. When he repaired here with Martha, flush with the first fortune he'd made, he came for the beauty of the place and because it was an hour by air to New York City, only fifteen minutes more by air to Atlanta. Washington, D.C., was a half hour by air or an hour and a half by car if no state troopers prowled the corridors to that corrupted seat of power. He certainly did not move to central Virginia for the people. He made fun of them, decrying them as parochial, falsely genteel, and silently racist.

When Virginia elected Douglas Wilder, the first black governor in the history of the United States, he questioned his stand on Virginia's racism. The more he thought about it, the more he decided Virginians were no more racist than New Yorkers.

As the years rolled along he would travel out of state and find himself irritated by the lack of grace in random encounters. He began to fume about the manner in which people drove in Boston and once in Los Angeles he upbraided a man at a business meeting for not wearing a suit and tie. He told the young man that he was being disrespectful to the other men at the meeting. One should always consider the effects of one's dress and demeanor on others.

This is not to say that Crawford Howard, born and bred in the hurly-burly of Indianapolis, that gritty competitor to massive Chicago, had become a Virginian. This is only to say that the state of Virginia, her siren song sweet and strong since 1607, had filtered into Crawford's ears.

He began to tip his hat to ladies even if only a baseball cap. He smiled at older women and told them they were alluring. Before telling a male competitor how wrong the competitor was, Crawford might even say something like "Have you considered this . . . ?"

The natives first ignored him. In their eyes he was a rich barbarian. Over time, his good qualities—vision, responsibility, and determination—won praise from some. He cared far too much about money and talked about it and business far too much but he had come a long way.

Fontaine Buruss, of course, would never give him credit for smoothing over his rough edges. There were those who agreed with Fontaine but they were often the same people who, if living in England, would not speak to you if you couldn't trace your lineage back to William the Conqueror. William and his men had a lot to answer for.

As Crawford picked up the now empty carton, he walked

under the cream-colored swinging bowls of light, lamps hanging by heavy chain; he passed the long tables whose red marble tops contrasted richly with the black marble floor. He paused for a moment to consider whether the drunk sleeping on a marble bench in the corner was still alive. He was and Crawford pushed open the door, walking down the cascade of broad steps to his Mercedes.

He cruised by Martha's apartment. He told himself he was curious. Then he motored by Fontaine's office. The light was on. A bead of sweat appeared at his left temple even though the temperature was now fifty-four degrees. He parked in the lot across from Fontaine's office. The sweat rolled down to his chin. He wiped it off, walked into the lobby, and knocked on the door.

"Who is it?" Martha's voice called out.

"Your beau." He liked the sound of that.

He heard a muffled exchange. "Come in," Martha said.

Fontaine and Martha, bending over a drafting table, stood up to greet him.

"Hello," Fontaine coolly said.

"Hello," Crawford replied to equal degree.

"Did I get the date wrong? Were we supposed to have dinner tonight?" Martha hastily reached for her daybook.

"No, no, I was dropping off fixture cards at the post office and I don't know . . . drove by and saw the light on." He smiled.

"We're trying to come up with something English but not too rigid for the Haslips' new garden. See." She pointed to designs.

A moment of silence followed. "We might as well start fresh in the morning," Fontaine said warmly to Martha.

"Fine."

"A nightcap?" Crawford asked hopefully.

"Sure," she replied, a quiet look of happiness on her face.

This infuriated Fontaine, who rolled a second set of plans,

popping them into a heavy cardboard tube. Half sounding playful and half in warning he said, "Watch out for him, Martha."

Crawford, face suddenly bright red, replied through clenched teeth, "This is no affair of yours."

"You were a damn fool to let her go in the first place. If I weren't married, I would have asked her out myself."

"Since when has that stopped you!"

Fontaine gave his reply, a straight right to the jaw. Crawford, not being a boxing man, crumpled.

Martha knelt down as he shook his head, then scrambled up. He did not offer to return the blow. Crawford recognized his physical limitations. He was four inches shorter than Fontaine and about ten years older. No amount of elective surgery could turn back the clock.

"Come on, Crawford." She tried to move him toward the door.

He held his jaw with his hand. Hurt like hell but he managed to hiss, "I'll dance on your grave!"

CHAPTER 28

Bridles, broken down, stripped, and dipped, hung overhead on tack hooks, which resembled grappling hooks. Underneath, a plastic bucket caught the dripping oil.

Sister and Doug sat on low three-legged stools, buckets of clear rinse water and buckets of washing water between their feet. With a toothbrush in hand they scrubbed each steel bit until it shone. They ran their fingers over the bits, searching for pitting. Korean steel bits pitted quickly. They weren't worth the money paid for them. German bits were good but nothing compared to English steel. The English from the nineteenth century onward excelled in creating a smooth, perfectly balanced bit with superior steel, no cheap alloys. The expense, initially steep, panned out over time, for the bit lasted generations.

This held true for English vegetable-dyed leather, too. In order to speed the process most tanners chrome-dyed their leather. Vegetable dyes couldn't get the consistency of color—Havana brown, tan, or black—that chrome could but the vegetable dye imparted a soft sheen to the leather as well as being better for the leather itself.

Sister, not a wealthy woman but a comfortable one, refused to cut corners on tack or anything relating to the care of her horses. Since she spent little on herself it all worked out.

She had splurged by putting a gas stove in the tack room. Fake logs inside it glowed red and it looked just like an old wood-burning stove. Threw out lots of heat, so much so that usually she had to crack a window.

The day, perfect for cleaning tack, was raw. The temperature, in the low fifties, sounded good but the light rain sent a chill right through you. She was glad she had bought the gas stove.

With only six days until opening hunt, she and Doug worked to make sure each piece of tack was spotless, boots were shined to perfection, pants, coats, hats, everything was dry-cleaned or brushed.

The hounds, too, were subjected to beauty treatments. The central room in the kennel was heated, with a large drain in the middle of the floor. Hounds were taken out of their runs to be scrubbed and have their nails clipped and ears cleaned, and were then allowed to dry off on the benches in the central room before being taken to their runs again.

The runs, scrubbed down each morning with an expensive power washer, were kept scrupulously clean.

As Shaker worked in the kennels, Sister and Doug merrily chattered away.

"Someone's coming," Raleigh announced as he heard a car a quarter of a mile away. *"I'll go to the door."*

"Don't bother. It will be some hunt club member half-hysterical because he or she has lost their boots and they want to know if they can wear field boots. It's always something." Golliwog rolled over, turning her head to the side, very coy.

Raleigh jumped to his feet as the silver Jaguar rolled down to the stable. Fontaine dashed toward the tack room. He wasn't wearing a raincoat.

Once inside the tack room, he shook himself slightly.

"Please," Golly complained as a raindrop landed on her.

Raleigh circled three times and lay down on the sheepskin thrown in the corner.

"Sit down." Sister pointed to a tattered wing chair.

"Thank you. Getting everything ready. I knew you'd be here. I didn't even bother going to the house. How are you, Doug?"

"Fine. Can I get you coffee or anything?" Doug inquired.

A small refrigerator and kitchenette were in the corner.

"No. No." Fontaine couldn't ask Doug to leave. After all, both he and Sister were working and he did barge in without calling first. "I'm here to tell you that I had an unfortunate experience with Crawford last night." He paused; then his tone relaxed. "Unfortunate. Hell, the man really wanted his ass kicked bad. He walked into the office at about nine-thirty. Martha and I were working late. He was sniffing around Martha, as you know that's sort of on again, and anyway he accused me of impropriety, not just with Martha but with every female since Cleopatra. I passed my hand over his jaw." Fontaine broke into a grin, an appealing crooked grin.

"In other words, you wouldn't serve with Crawford if Christ Almighty told you to." Sister had to laugh.

"Well—yes."

Doug laughed, too, although he suspected Fontaine had been chasing Cody despite her protests. She'd finished her intensive rehab and was home but she hadn't called him yet. He wondered if she was okay. Then he wondered if he was okay.

"I appreciate you coming out here on a rainy day to tell me."

"I'm sorry I can't accommodate you, Sister. And I found out he's been trying to get Peter Wheeler's land. He offered him life estate."

"That's no surprise." Sister knew Crawford would try that.

"He intends to develop it."

"That's what he says about you." Sister shouldn't have blurted that out but there it was.

"Never. That's a hunt fixture. If the damned development keeps up we'll be in the middle of West Virginia riding mountain goats."

"You called Gordon Smith." She figured she might as well show her hand.

"I did." He was surprised that she knew. "I called him to ask if he could help me put together a syndicate to preserve the Wheeler place. He's only interested in commercial real estate, not residential, and the Wheeler place had no commercial application. I was direct about that. He was helpful. I'd only met him a few times at political fund-raisers but he really was helpful. The impediment, as you know, is this conservation easement clause."

"I got an earful of that the other night. I assume some members of a syndicate want it and others don't."

"Correct." He watched the oil drip into the bucket. "I'd better go home and do the same. Saturday will be here before I know it." He asked Doug if he had heard from Cody.

"No." Doug wanted to say, "Have you?" but kept his mouth shut.

"Betty called to say she's pleased. She thinks both girls

profited from the experience, which I gather was tearful, expensive, and rigorous," Sister said.

"So they say." Fontaine sounded noncommittal. He stood up. "I'd better get rolling."

"This will all work out somehow but I'd avoid Crawford in the hunt field if I were you."

"No problem. He'll pop off Czapaka in the first hour. Even if they made a saddle with a Velcro seat and he wore Velcro pants he'd part company with that horse. Beautiful horse. Oh well, overmounted again."

"Men tend to do that." Sister let fly a small barb. "In all respects."

Fontaine laughed. "Oh, but the fun of it." He walked out into the rain and sprinted to the Jaguar.

"Full of himself," Raleigh observed.

"God's gift, he thinks. Going to seed, I think," Golly commented.

"How long before we hear from Crawford?" Sister smiled as she put a bit into the clear rinse water.

"Um-m, by supper."

"Wanna bet?"

"How much?" Doug, graceful hands, reached over and flipped a girth off a saddle rack.

"A dollar."

"I'll take that bet. What do you think?"

"He'll call or be here within two hours."

Doug glanced at the wall clock, a cat with a tail for a pendulum, its eyes rolling in time with the tail. "By three. Okay. You can give me that dollar now."

"Ha." She scrubbed an eggbutt-jointed snaffle. "I can feel waves of distrust and disgust coming off your body around Fontaine. Is this a guy thing because the ladies preen when they see him coming?"

"I don't know if it's a guy thing. I flat out can't abide him.

He's pompous, racist in a sly way, and he doesn't give a shit about anybody or anything other than his own pleasures."

"Well, that's about as much as I've ever heard you say about anybody—ever. What else?"

"He treats me like a servant. I may work for you, Sister, but I'm not his slave. Fontaine wants to hear not 'Master' but 'Massa.' No shit."

"I suppose there is that in him. It's all smoothed over, of course." She reached into the bucket, scrubbing under the water. "It's Cody. I can't prove anything but it's the way he looks at her."

"Damn him!"

"I can understand Crawford's anger, too, but I know Martha didn't have anything to do with Fontaine on that level. He was enjoying playing the savior too much to spoil it. Besides, he has too many other women to service. Why in the world would Cody fool around with him . . . if she has?"

"I don't know if she has." Doug laid the girth across his knees, scrubbing the underside. "At first I thought maybe he leaned on her, using her parents. He does a lot of business at Franklin Press. Maybe he threatened to take business elsewhere. She feels guilty about what she's put her parents through over the years. I thought, okay, maybe that's it."

"You don't now?"

"No."

"It can't be a sexual attraction." Sister was incredulous. "She's not that dumb even if he is handsome."

"No. He has a hold on her."

"You think she has slept with him then?"

A sickly look passed over Doug's handsome features. "Yeah."

"Oh, Doug, I hope not but if she has, maybe it's over."

"I don't know."

"Do you think she loves you?"

"I don't know." His voice dropped.

"Steady on. Whatever is supposed to happen will happen and even if she brings you pain this will lead to the right woman. Maybe not to Cody but to the right woman." His stricken face brought a swell of sympathy. "Doug, I didn't know you cared that much. I hope she is the one, truly. If she's the one you want then I hope it works out."

"Thanks, boss." He smiled weakly. "You like her, don't you?"

"I love her. I've known her since the day she was born but I'm afraid for her. She's been a handful since birth. Betty said she kicked like a mule in the womb. I don't know what to tell you, Doug. It seems there's something inside Cody that drives her on like Juno's fly biting Europa." She didn't need to explain mythology to Doug. He loved the Greek myths.

"Maybe people are born like that."

"I don't know but I do know you can't try to satisfy her or anybody. You take care of yourself. You can't fix Cody."

"I hope that's what rehab was about."

"I do, too."

"Car!" Raleigh informed them.

"Crawford." Golly rolled onto her other side.

When Crawford strode through the door Sister couldn't help but laugh as Doug shook his head.

"How'd you know it would be Crawford?" Raleigh asked in amazement.

"Cats know everything."

CHAPTER 29

Crawford, narrow-eyed, waited for an invitation from the silver-haired master to sit down. Once he heard that he unzipped his raincoat, the latest, most expensive Gore-Tex model, hanging it on a coatrack by the door.

"Crawford, hand me that sponge as long as you're standing up?" Sister asked.

He handed her a long, natural sponge before easing himself into the chair Fontaine had just vacated. "Knees. Football."

Sister pointed to her entire body. "Bones. Life."

Doug laughed.

"Just wait." Sister waggled her forefinger at him.

"I hurt now."

"Where?"

"Where I broke my shoulder blade."

"Okay. That counts. You can join the aches-and-pains club." She dipped the fresh sponge into the clear rinse water. "Crawford, I'm all ears."

"I'm sure you are. I passed Fontaine on Soldier Road. That mouth of his is an inexhaustible motor. He is a person entirely lacking in self-control." Crawford realized he was going on in the wrong vein. He crossed his arms over his chest. "What did he say?"

"He had words with you, etc. . . ." Crawford glanced from Sister to Doug and before he could say anything she added,

150

"He's not going to repeat what you say." She paused and with a malicious little grin said, "But I might."

At that moment, too self-important, brimming with wounded pride, Crawford sputtered, "I don't care who you tell. He's damned lucky I didn't call the sheriff."

The blow to his jaw, turning an interesting shade of reddish blue, bore testimony to Fontaine's aim.

"Did you ice it down?" Doug politely asked.

"Yes. He caught me off guard. If he'd given me fair warning I could have defended myself," said the man who couldn't. Crawford, reared in suburban luxury, had never been in a fistfight in his life.

"Fontaine was born with an unfortunate infirmity of temper." A wry smile played over Sister's lips as she dipped the clean sponge in a white jar labeled SADDLE BUTTER. A friend sent Sister the tack conditioner from out west and she found it the best stuff she'd ever used.

"What do you mean?"

Crawford evidenced little appreciation for the subtleties of the English language.

"Hothead. Fontaine's always been a hothead."

"Oh."

Sister held out the brow band at arm's length. "Doug, we dipped this at the beginning of the summer. It still looks good. I'll just wipe it down with the butter."

He reached over, rubbing the leather between thumb and forefinger. "Yes. Fine."

Sister pointed to the tack dripping oil into the bucket. "I need a couple of warmish days before opening hunt or I'm going to soak up all that oil on my breeches. I should have done this at the beginning of September but I never found the time. Time speeds by me like light." She put the plain, flat hunting bridle back together as she talked.

The deep rich brown of the English leather bore no adornment, no lines cut into the sides, no raised portions, just excellent flat leather. An old friend had made her this bridle before he died. It was his last gift to her—that and a lifetime of friendship. As her hands flew over the supple yet strong leather, she felt the edges which he had minutely beveled.

"Sister, I'll cut to the chase." Crawford liked to use expressions he heard bandied about in his business. These were generally sports allusions or sexual allusions designed to make the speaker appear manly and in control. Usually whoever mouthed such stuff was neither, although Crawford was, in a business sense anyway. "I believe Fontaine should be removed from Jefferson Hunt."

"He has committed no crime which reflects badly upon the hunt."

"Not true. He simply hasn't been caught. He is an adulterer and he's violent."

"Oh, Crawford." Sister wrapped the thin chin strap around the bridle in a figure eight. "There'd be no one left were those the criteria. You yourself would fail the test."

"I never went to bed with Tiffany. Not until I separated from Martha. You may not believe me but it's the truth."

The drip, drip of the oil punctuated the silence as Sister thought of a neutral response. "That showed admirable restraint. However, I can't toss people out of the hunt for being human. Sexual escapades are a common and often amusing human frailty. Besides, Crawford, we have to have something to talk about, otherwise conversation descends to the weather or worse, politics."

"You are a tolerant woman."

Before he could continue she shot back, "Masters need to be."

"Why? Your word is law."

"My word is law until each year when the board of governors of the club elects their master."

"As long as you live, you'll be elected master. You know that."

"Crawford, if I could afford a private pack I would have one. Believe me. A subscription pack is an invitation for endless political maneuvering and there's enough maneuvering being a master as it is. Dealing with landowners, for example. Making certain one complies with all Masters of Foxhounds rulings and bylaws. And remember, the MFHA sits in Leesburg. We, in Virginia and Maryland, are right under their noses. You do it right or you get the boot."

"But you can still remove a member."

"No, I can't. Only the master of a private pack can remove someone from the roster. I can remove a member from the field."

"You could petition the board." He glowered, which made him look like a middle-aged child angry about having to go to bed.

"No. Fontaine has endangered no one in the field. He has shown respect to master and staff. Whatever his quarrel with you, it's between the two of you."

"But it's over the joint-mastership!" Crawford exploded.

"No." Her voice was firm. "The joint-mastership allows you two to compete openly. You're like oil and water. And kindly remember, I do not have to appoint a joint-master."

"You can't appoint one. You have to ask the board's approval." With that statement Crawford betrayed the fact that he would use the bylaws of the club not only to dislodge Fontaine but to try and force himself on Sister if he gained enough board support. If he could remove Sister he would, but he knew that was impossible. Crawford hadn't a clue as to what Sister did as master other than she was responsible for hiring and firing staff and maintaining territory. He wanted a position of power and respect in this community. It took him a while but he learned that money wasn't enough in Virginia. It helped but it wasn't enough. He wanted to lord it over people. What better position than joint-master? And when Sister went to her reward he had enough money to bribe everyone. He'd be sole master.

Crawford had half learned his lesson about money. The other half would come back to haunt him, namely that even poor people can't always be bribed. Many Virginians still believed in honor, quaint as that concept might be in the twenty-first century.

"You are exactly right. But I don't have to recommend anyone."

"The board can suggest you take a joint-master."

"They can but they won't," she replied with the confidence of a person who knows how things get done.

"You've got to end this impasse. What if you died during opening hunt?"

"I'd die happy."

"But the club would be thrown into chaos. You need an understudy—an understudy with a fat checkbook. I can supply this club with a great many things, including building a separate kennel for the half-grown hounds. I know you don't like to turn them out with the big boys and the puppy kennel gets overcrowded."

Her patience wearing thin, Sister stood up, putting her hands in the small of her back. "Crawford. If you are that rich, if you love hunting as much as you say you do, if you love Jefferson Hunt as much as you say you do, you know what— you'd spend the money for the love of the sport. We'd name the goddamn kennel after you."

As Sister rarely swore to someone not close to her, Doug's eyes widened, his shoulders stiffened. He knew that Crawford didn't know she was really, truly pissed off.

He snarled. "Only a fool spends money without getting something out of it."

"Which proves my point. You don't love foxhunting as much as you love being important. You want joint-M.F.H. behind your name. It's a bargain for you, Crawford. To be a master, to be a huntsman, to be a whipper-in, you have to love it. You have to eat, sleep, and breathe hunting, knowing all the while that most people don't understand what you're doing or why you're doing it. People outside of Virginia, I mean."

"Maryland," Doug laconically added.

"Well, yes. And parts of Pennsylvania." Sister was loath to credit anyone north of the Mason-Dixon line.

"Red Rock, Nevada." Doug, his green eyes alight, smiled.

"Doug, I know that. Anyway, Crawford, Americans live in cities now. The old ways are lost to them. They think we ride about shooting fox with guns. They think we're all rich snobs. They haven't a clue. So you have to love it because you aren't going to get respect outside of Virginia." She glanced at Doug. "And a few other important spots."

"I know that. I don't need a lecture on the reality of foxhunting."

Doug stood up. "You need one on manners, Mr. Howard. It won't do to worrit Sister." He used the old form of "worry."

Crawford cut him off. "If you want to mix with white people, then you ought to learn how to use the King's English. Don't say birfday. Birthday. Ask not ax. You people can't learn to talk."

"Crawford. That's quite enough." Sister, enraged, choked out the words.

Doug, who cared little what a wimp thought of him, growled like one of the hounds. "Mr. Howard, if you trouble Sister anymore, I'll decorate the other side of your jaw and for the record, if you become joint-master I will resign as first whipper-in."

"I wouldn't have you anyway." Crawford looked to Sister. "Damned half-breed doesn't know his place. You dote on him. You dote on him as though he were your son. It's understandable but he's not your son."

"Crawford"—her tone deepened, her speech slowed—"I

will overlook your desire to be master in any way you can manage. Ambition is a curious thing. I cannot overlook your attitude and insult to Doug. And you're absolutely right, he is like a son to me. Now I suggest you leave us. I also suggest you take the opportunity to review this conversation. Furthermore, however you feel about Fontaine, Doug, and myself, I expect you to behave like a gentleman at opening hunt. Good day, sir."

"Get your ass outta here." Raleigh, an imposing presence, stood next to Sister, his mouth slightly ajar.

Crawford snatched his expensive rain gear off the coat-rack, slamming the door on his way out.

"Really." Golly fluffed her fur, then stood up, stretched, turned in a circle, and lay down again.

As Crawford started his motor, Sister sat back down, then stood up again, tossing the bucket of wash water down the industrial sink, filling it again.

"Money and the demons it incubates," was all she said as she and Doug returned to their task.

CHAPTER 30

Along with the steady rain, charcoal clouds obscured the mountains, pressing down into the dark green pastures. The tops of ancient oaks, walnuts, and hickories were tangled in the low clouds. Overtop the rivers and creeks the mists hung thick but there the color was bright silver. Occasionally a patch of clearness would appear and the flash of red maple or orange oak was startling.

As Fontaine turned back toward town, his silver Jaguar, swallowed in the rain and mist, was almost invisible save for his headlights. He laughed to himself as he passed Crawford Howard on his way to Sister Jane's. Crawford's Mercedes, a metallic deep red, would be hard to miss even in the thickest fog. Crawford, hands gripping the wheel, eyes intent on his side of the road, neither waved nor acknowledged Fontaine, a breach of manners in the country.

Fontaine laughed to himself as he pulled over to the one-story white store at the crossroads. Low-pressure systems made him sleepy. If he ate chocolate or something loaded with sugar, he could usually keep from nodding out.

ROGER'S CORNER, a long rectangular sign proclaimed on top of the roof. Two lights aimed at the sign illuminated the rain and clouds more than the sign.

Fontaine liked Roger's Corner, especially the worn wooden floors, the ornate black-and-gold cash register.

"Hey, bro," Roger, amiable, called out from behind the counter. "Cuts to the bone, don't it?"

"Makes me tired." Fontaine scooped up Moon Pies, Yankee Doodles, and a small round coffee cake. "Your coffee potable today or do I need a sledgehammer to break it up?"

"Ha ha," Roger dryly replied as he poured him a cup of strong, good coffee, not café au lait or anything fancy, just wake-you-up coffee.

Roger had inherited the store from Roger Senior. Both were attractive men, lean and long-jawed.

Fontaine drank the coffee as he leaned against the counter. The cellophane wrapper on the coffee cake crinkled as Fontaine opened it. "Every time I go to New York City I buy these coffee cakes made by Drake's. Can't get them down here. I mean these are okay but those little Drake's things are the best. I love the crumbs on top."

"Never been there."

"Gotta go, buddy, gotta go."

"If Yankees will stay on their side of the Mason-Dixon line, I'll stay on mine," Roger joked.

"There is that. Hey, Cody been by here?"

"No. Thought she was in rehab. Betty stopped by last week. Told me. Both kids." He shook his head, for it was too confusing.

"People are gonna do what they're gonna do." He polished off the coffee cake. "Maybe those places give folks some understanding." He beamed. "If it feels good, they'll do it again."

"That's just it, though, isn't it? Feels good when you're doing it and feels bad when you're not."

"Life's just one big hangover." He held out his cup for a refill.

"Had a few of those." Roger laughed.

"Coming to opening hunt?"

Roger, a foot follower, enthusiastically said, "Best breakfast of the year."

"Muffin hound."

"I do my share of running. Tell you who did blow through here . . . Crawford. Not twenty minutes ago. He asked me what my annual take was." Roger laughed. "I said, 'Why do you want to know?' and he said, 'I'd like to buy this place.' I don't know what to make of that guy."

"Would you sell it?"

"I don't know." He shrugged. "Man's gotta work at something."

"If he gives you a fair price, you can work at something else. But that man's a snake."

"You know, he might be." Roger, like a bartender, tried to stay out of other people's disagreements and personality clashes. "When I first met him I thought he couldn't pull piss out of a boot if the directions were on the heel. I was wrong. He's smart enough but he's not—what am I trying to say?"

"No practical knowledge. Couldn't start up a chain saw if his life depended on it."

"Kinda."

The small pile of cellophane, white wrappers, and napkins diverted Fontaine's attention. "Did I eat all that?"

"Yep."

He sighed. "Better go straight to the gym. See you, bud."

However, he didn't head for the gym. He headed for Cody's place, taking the precaution of parking his car behind old holly bushes.

He knocked on the door, rain funneling off his cowboy hat like a downspout.

Hairbrush in hand, she opened the door. "Fontaine, what are you doing here?"

He stepped inside. "You look as wet as I do."

A towel wrapped around her head looked like a fuzzy turban. Her white bathrobe was worn thin at the elbows.

"I've got an appointment."

"Why didn't you call me?" Fontaine didn't unzip his raincoat.

"I needed time to think."

"I thought that's what you were doing in rehab."

"I did. I needed time to think in my own place." She stuffed her hairbrush in her pocket. "I need to change a lot of things, break a lot of habits." She took a deep breath. "I can't see you anymore. I guess this is as good a time as any to end it."

"Why don't you settle back in before you make sweeping decisions," he smoothly replied, his voice pleasant, seductive.

"I need to be clear. Look, you'll always have a mistress somewhere. It's your nature. For all I know you've got two or three stashed in Richmond or Washington. I don't know. You're a player."

"Only you," he lied.

While he chased skirts with a kind of predictable boredom, he liked Cody. He liked any woman that could ride well, hold her liquor, and make love with abandon.

"I can't do it." Her lips compressed.

"Anyone else?"

"That's not the point."

"Yeah," he said sarcastically.

"One other thing, Fontaine, and I mean this. You stay away from my sister."

His eyes opened; he took a half step back involuntarily. "I resent that."

"I know you."

"Nobody knows anybody." He turned on his heel and left, far more upset than he imagined he would be.

Cody locked the door behind him, sat on the edge of the twin bed that served as a sofa, pushed against the wall, embroidered pillows everywhere. Love didn't enter into this decision. She'd never loved Fontaine. He was fun, spent money like water. His approach to life was "Do it now." There was a kind of wisdom to that, since you only have the moment you're in, but Fontaine never gave much thought to the future. Again, that was part of his charm.

Cody was realizing she had to think a great deal about her future. She'd seen too many human shipwrecks at forty and fifty and sixty in rehab. Seeing and hearing the old druggies and drunks knocked sense into her head far more than the counseling sessions with the doctors.

She had to get some training, find a decent job, and forget going out at night to the bars until she could handle it—or maybe forever. What was there about the soft wash of neon light over a polished bar that made her reach for a vodka martini or sneak into the back for a toot? Night seemed to absolve her of tomorrow but then tomorrow would come. Wasted, the sunrise rarely gave her hope. A panic would set in. She'd snort another line until there wasn't anything left except the shakes and a black hole into which she'd tumble.

She wasn't going down that rabbit hole again.

Tears ran down her face. She knew better than to take up with Fontaine in the first place. She thought she could forget

Doug. She did for a while. Maybe she'd treated him badly last spring before he got fed up with her boozing and coking. That way she felt in control. Junk him before he'd junk her.

She'd thought a lot about him in rehab, too. She dreaded the apologies she needed to make. She knew her mother and father would forgive her. She knew Doug would forgive her, too. In his way, he already had but she had to sit down, face-to-face, and truly apologize. She thought after opening hunt she might have the courage.

She rubbed her hair with the towel, tossed it toward the bathroom, shook her head. She brushed out her long sable hair.

"Hell." She reached for the phone, dialing Doug's number. The answering machine came on. "Doug, I bet you're at the stable. I know this is an intense week. Why don't I take you to dinner after opening hunt? Bye."

CHAPTER 31

The last week before opening hunt kept everyone frantically busy. Turnout for cubbing was heavy and people who should have been legging up their horses starting in July thought that two shots of cubbing would do it.

Shadbellies for the ladies, weaselbellies or cutaways for the gentlemen, frock coats, Meltons, were brushed out and hung on the line or brought back from the dry cleaner. Caps were knocked off with a small wisk brush as were top hats and the always charming derbies. Spurs submitted to rigorous polishing. Shirts and stock ties were ironed, buttons wiped clean, on the coats. Stock tie pins dangled in open buttonholes, where they wouldn't be lost in the nervousness of preparation. The last thing a hunter did was to fasten that stock pin horizontally across the tie.

Ties would be four-in-hand or just flipped over in a cascade of white. Not a hint of yellow or gray for opening hunt; those ties had to be white, white, white.

Garters—and many still used them, as was correct—were also polished. They'd be just above the boot line and if a lady or gentleman wore the old buttoned pants, the garter would be between the third and fourth button.

Breeches, whipcord or the newer materials, were checked along the seams, the suede knee patches checked, too.

The one item everyone appreciated most and talked about the least was a good pair of underpants. Anything with a raised seam eventually rubbed your leg raw. A few underpants were even padded on the crotch to protect that sensitive area from damage. Of course, if they were riding properly, the next generation should be safe.

Vests also dotted clotheslines. The fortunate few wore white vests handed down from the nineteenth century and the most proper attire for the High Holy Days of hunting: opening hunt, Thanksgiving hunt, Christmas hunt, and New Year's hunt.

Most people wore a canary vest. Tattersalls were used during formal hunting but not during the holiest of holies, although a few hunts demanded tattersall in the hunt club colors. A vest in the hunt's colors was also proper, although few wore them because they needed to be specially made.

Jefferson Hunt, formed by veterans of the Revolutionary War, had Continental blue with a buff piping for its colors. A hunter could earn his or her colors only in the field. No amount of good deeds or financial support could buy colors. They were not given lightly and they were given only at Thanksgiving hunt.

Winning your colors meant a gentleman was entitled to wear a scarlet frock with three buttons. A master rode with four buttons, five if the master carried the horn. A gentleman could also wear a scarlet weaselbelly, which is a coat with tails, with a top hat, colors on the collar. This was the most elegant of all outfits, although a black cutaway or tails might also lay that claim. There was something about a man in tails and top hat, scarlet or black, that proved irresistible to women.

The gentleman with colors was also entitled to wear a contrasting cuff on the top of his black boots. Ideally this cuff would be champagne-colored but that, too, was proving hard to find since World War I. A tan top was now acceptable, although the champagne was coveted and those men who cared paid leather craftsmen or leather buyers to find them the exact right color with the right toughness to withstand the rigors of the hunt. A few men would wear mahogany tops, which were certainly acceptable but actually more proper for coaching.

A woman with colors wore a black coat, frock, Melton or shadbelly, tails, with the colors on the collar. The tops of her boots could be black patent leather.

Both genders also wore the special hunt button if awarded colors. For the Jefferson Hunt it was a simple intertwined JH.

Not only were the clothes being aired out, polished to a mirror shine, inspected and inspected yet again, but the horses were going to the beauty parlor. Braiders, paid plenty, showed up at barns at dawn to weave tight little braids, always on the right side of the neck, yarn the color of the mane woven into them. An even number of braids for a gelding, an odd number for mares was the rule. Many members braided their horse's manes but as they aged and those fingers hurt on a frosty morning, they engaged braiders. Often the top of the tail had a braid laid into it, a nice touch. Staff might even braid the entire tail and then fold it up, since they traversed rough country. The last thing a whipper-in wanted was his or her horse's tail dragging thorns or vines. On regular formal days staff executed a mud tail, a simpler version of the braided, folded-up tail.

The night before the hunt, the horses would be washed in special shampoos, some even concocted for the horse's color. People might put a little Dippity-Do on the manes. The next morning the animals would be brushed down with brushes and then crisscrossed with rubbing cloths until they literally gleamed. Hooves would be painted black or, if white, painted with a clear hoof paint, a mixture that wasn't like house paint but filled with emollients as well as color. The old adage "No hoof, no horse" was as true today as it was in Xenophon's day.

The hunters with experience packed a gear bag for themselves and one for their horse. In their gear bag they folded an extra stock tie, extra stock pins, safety pins to help keep the stock tie in perfect position, Vetrap, extra socks, rawhide strings for last-minute tack repair. A pair of white string gloves would be in the gear bag and those would be put under the saddle billets, one on each side, before mounting up. A second pair of formal gloves, ideally deep mustard but tan was acceptable, since deep mustard was hard to come by, was also in the bag—just in case. Gloves seemed to walk away. Hair nets, the color of a lady's hair, were in the gear bags and if a single gentleman was smart, he'd put a few different-colored hair nets in his own gear bag.

Few things impress a lady more than a single man who has thought of something particular only to women. Fontaine always carried a box of tampons in his trailer. This earned him more than the normal gratitude.

Then there was the question of flasks. Gentlemen could carry a large flask on the left front side of their saddle, above their knee. These expensive heavy handblown flasks with silver tops created instant popularity in the hunt field. Hunting flask recipes were as zealously guarded as four-star-restaurant specials. Invariably, later in the season, one club would issue a challenge to the others as to which person had the best flask contents. Judging this contest was hotly contested itself. Whereas a master might pull out his or her hair trying to find volunteers for fence building, no master ever had to work to find judges for the flask contest.

The contest would take place after that day's hunt. This meant beds in stables, homes, even horse trailers would be thoughtfully provided.

Ladies, too, could carry a flask but theirs was a small rectangular affair, also handblown, nestled in a square case that also contained a sandwich tin. The smallness of their flask in no way detracted from the lethal contents. Ladies, too, entered the flask contests.

In the old days, masters might spot-check the sandwich tins just like a Corinthian class at a horse show. The sandwich had to be chicken, no mayonnaise, on white bread, crusts trimmed off.

Today few masters were that fierce.

No makeup was allowed on a lady, although lipstick finally triumphed by the 1970s. Small pearl stud earrings were acceptable but most women had learned the hard way not to wear anything in their ears.

Sister Jane, a lenient soul during cubbing, put the fear of God into her field for opening hunt. Years ago she dismissed a very popular lady member for wearing overlarge earrings and too much rouge. She also dismissed a gentleman for having a running martingale on his horse—only a standing one would do. The running martingale's further strap divides after passing through the neck strap. The standing martingale had one thick further strap and this was the only proper hunting martingale. Naturally both people were humiliated and furious even though Sister did not single them out verbally but rode up to them and whispered in their ears. The gentleman finally forgave her, since he realized a running martingale could cause harm to the horse and rider even if stops were correctly placed on the tack. Flying through rough and close territory it would be possible for a stop to be torn off or bent in such a way that the rings of the running martingale could flip over a full cheek bit. The chances seemed remote but after a person had hunted for a few decades, he or she had seen a lot of things that could have been prevented with forethought, things that seemed irritating or silly to the novitiate.

The lady, of course, never forgave Sister and harrumphed off to another less strict hunt where she lambasted Sister until that master finally told her it was imprudent to criticize a master to another master.

But every person preparing for opening hunt knew Sister had a sharp eye for turnout as well as territory. Proper turnout is a sign of respect for the master and the landowners.

The hounds, too, prepared for the great day. Anticipation built. Arguments flared. Young entries feared they wouldn't be called out on this day because the huntsman or the master felt they might fumble the ball. Old hounds counseled the younger ones, often repeating themselves, which only further upset the younger ones, who couldn't absorb any more information thanks to the tension.

The horses loved the constant grooming. Since they had to follow hounds, the burden of proof was not on them. The excitement rippled through the stable but there was little anxiety with it. A green horse might fret but the tried-and-true hunters believed the foot followers came out to see them. Good manners kept them from saying this to the hounds but every hunting horse believed this and acted accordingly, which caused a snipe and a snip from a few hounds on the great day.

The staff horses affected a world-weariness laced with pride. Being a master's horse meant one had acquired special knowledge plus one was bold. Lafayette oozed confidence and leadership. The huntsman's horse also swaggered and the whipper-in horses bordered on belligerent. These paragons would trot or walk by the field horses and bid them hello, a hello bursting with egotism.

The foxes, too, prepared for opening hunt. Since 1782, hunters had gathered on Hangman's Ridge by the oak tree. When the private packs coalesced into a subscription pack they continued meeting there.

The foxes, knowing this, often slept in on that day. But over the years they learned that Sister Jane and Shaker Crown treated them fairly: no earthmen to dig up their dens, no Jack Russells for the same purpose, no traps, and help for foxes in times of trouble. During the winter of the three blizzards in the mid-1990s, Sister, Shaker, and Doug fought their way through the snows to feed their foxes within a two-mile radius of the kennel. Once the roads were plowed they also drove to the other fixtures and pushed their way through the snows to put out corn, grain, and dog food for all their foxes.

The foxes attributed this to Sister and she was a good master, but the times had changed drastically in America. Few hunts had ever used earthmen or Jack Russells as they were used in England, although hunts in poultry-raising counties did in the old days. Trapping a fox and carrying him to another territory, called dropping a bagged fox, was made illegal by the Masters of Foxhounds Association. Apart from being cruel, it was a serious offense because such a fox could spread disease. The practice could result in a hunt being excommunicated from the MFHA. That meant no other hunt could draft hounds to the excommunicated hunt. No other hunt could enjoy a joint meet with them. No member of a recognized hunt could hunt with them.

Sister believed strongly in sporting chance. The foxes knew that and in gratitude for her work during the year of the blizzards they mapped out their routes for opening hunt to ensure that Sister and the Jefferson Hunt always had a rip-roaring opener. This was one of the few times when the reds and the grays cooperated.

This year they determined to move straight away east for four miles, working in relays, then curve northwest and finally come back to the ridge. They figured this ought to take two and a half hours. They agreed on their checks, too, those places where they'd disguise their scent. Given the importance of the occasion, they demanded that too young or slower foxes stay in, or within fifty yards of, their dens.

They did not want a nonparticipating fox to mess up their route.

Butch would tell his children, *"It's not the hounds you fear on opening hunt; it's the humans!"*

CHAPTER 32

Thursday night as Cody was pulling socks out of her drawer, tossing them all over the bed, a knock at her door disturbed her.

Irritated at the interruption, she opened the door.

"Found her two miles from Roger's Corner." Doug had his arm linked through Jennifer's.

She was too out of it to protest.

"Oh God!" Cody's face fell. "Bring her inside."

As Doug propelled Jennifer to the twin bed–sofa, he whispered, "Should you call your mother?"

"Eventually, yes. Right now, no." She picked up the phone and dialed Dr. Tandy Zacks. After ten minutes of paging, she finally got Dr. Zacks on the phone. She told her what had happened.

"Bring her to me."

Cody and Doug were surprised to find Walter Lungrun at

the rehab clinic but they were soon glad of his presence. As Jennifer began to be more aware of her surroundings she pitched a major, hateful fit. It took the muscle power of both Walter and Doug to restrain her.

After two hours of pure hell, Cody sat down and sobbed. She was struggling for her own sobriety. She didn't know if she had the strength to struggle for Jennifer's.

Walter sat with her on one side; Doug was on the other. Dr. Zacks and two other doctors were in another room with Jennifer, who alternated between snarls and sobs.

"Cody, you've done all you can do. Let Dr. Zacks call your mother. Jennifer is a minor and we must notify your parents. My advice to you is to go home or go somewhere where people will support you. Go somewhere safe." He put his large hand on her shoulder while looking at Douglas.

"Mom's going to need support herself," Cody said, crying.

"She is. We'll do what we can."

"Dad doesn't get it. I should be here."

"Cody, you've been through enough. You don't need any more upset. Go on now. If we need you or your mother needs you, you'll hear from us."

"She'll be with me." Doug scribbled down his number for Walter. "Top one's the house. Bottom is the barn."

Still crying, Cody walked out with Doug. She looked over her shoulder and Walter made a pushing-away motion with the back of his hands.

"Oh God, Doug, I'm afraid she isn't going to make it."

"But you are." He wrapped his arm around her waist. "Only Jennifer can save Jennifer. Come on. Let's pick up your tack and I'll help you clean it."

"Already done."

"Chinese food? We can take it home and be by the phone."

"Okay." She wiped away the tears, then reached in her coat pocket for a tissue. "Did she say why she was wandering around out there?"

"She wasn't verbal."

"Her car!"

"When it shows up maybe we'll know where she was."

It did show up, right at Bobby and Betty's house.

Jennifer refused to tell who she met or where they went. Mostly she was still screaming obscenities at everyone, especially her mother and father.

When Betty called Cody later she told her she was all right. Cody should stay where she was.

That night Cody curled up in bed with Doug. Snuggled in his arms she finally fell into a sound sleep.

CHAPTER 33

The first frost usually came around the middle of October. The silvering would melt within an hour of sunup and many nights the temperature still didn't dip low enough for frost. By November the frosts were steadier.

Sister Jane brought her unwieldy potted ficus tree inside by mid-October, along with two potted Russian junipers, which could withstand the cold, but she'd grown fond of them and thought them decorative. The other potted plants—hibiscus, tiny rosebuds, portulaca, tulips in hopes of spring—had all been covered with a thin layer of straw with about an inch and a half of mulch over that. On the northwest corner of the garden and the back patio she constructed burlap windbreakers. What they lacked in aesthetic appeal they made up in effectiveness. Sister vowed that one day she would figure out an attractive system to protect those plants.

The ficus tree, emphatically healthy, nearly touched the twelve-foot ceiling. The trunk was thick as a strong man's arm.

Golly lounged in the branches, feeling quite warm toward Sister for providing her with a tree. If in a good mood, she'd swing from limb to limb like a monkey.

If Raleigh offended her, Golly would pull the mulch out of the Russian junipers, scattering it about the floor. Sister would scold the dog, to the cat's malicious delight.

It was the Friday before Saturday's opening hunt. Everything that could be done was done.

Sister's shadbelly, worn on the big days, hung on the old wire mannequin. Sister was one of those people who had to lay her clothes out the night before. Wardrobe decisions and mornings didn't mix. The cleaned coat hung over the white vest, her great-grandfather's cut down to fit her, and that was buttoned over a perfect Irish linen hunting shirt she'd picked up at Hunt Country. Her stock tie, same material as the shirt, was draped over the shoulder of the mannequin. The simple gold stock pin was pinned through the bottom coat buttonhole. Her top hat, the true ladies' top hat, which gracefully curved in toward the brim, hat cord attached, rested on the wire head. Her boots, with a cedar insert to keep them firm, sat under the wire form, the knee-length socks stuffed inside along with a sheer pair of white silk socks in case it was really cold the next morning. Her spurs sat on top of the socks, simple hammerheads. Her mustard gloves, butter-soft, were folded and in her hat. Her father's pocket watch was in the bottom left vest pocket. A thin, unadorned braided belt, Continental blue, was already threaded through the dark canary breeches laid out on top of the blanket chest, her thin cotton underpants half in, half out of the front pocket.

A small linen handkerchief, an O embroidered on it, was neatly folded into the top vest pocket, left. The O stood for Overdorf, her maiden name. In the right lower vest pocket was a small, sharp penknife. The upper pocket carried ten Motrin in a tiny plastic bag just in case the weather got really raw and her myriad battle scars and breaks talked back. Although hunt staff were not allowed to carry a flask on their saddle, Sister, as the master, could carry one and she used her grandfather's flask. Since she was the master the masculine bit of tack was acceptable, as was scarlet, which she chose not to wear, although younger lady masters were doing it. Sister could never get used to the sight of a woman in scarlet although she thought it was handsome.

Usually she filled her flask with iced tea but today she filled it with hunting port. A small silver flask, a bold roman A in the center, was slipped inside her left shadbelly pocket. This carried straight Scotch, Famous Grouse. She rarely used it but sometimes a member of the field needed restoration.

She read down her checklist. The only thing she didn't have was a stirrup leather, used as a belt. For opening hunt she didn't want that peeping out from under her shadbelly, although her vest points should cover it. She thought it a good idea to carry an extra stirrup leather. Her couple straps, used to collect hounds if needs be, were already attached to her saddle, as was her pistol case, the Ruger .22 inside, filled with birdshot. Used only in extremes to ward off a bolting hound, the sight of it often upset nonhunters. Better a butt full of birdshot than a hound running in front of a car.

Usually she carried a .38 under her jacket or on the small of her back. She'd only had to use it once when a dying deer, hideously injured, front leg blown mostly out of the socket, crossed her path. She was glad to deliver the coup de grâce. Wearing a shadbelly left no room for the .38 but Shaker, Doug, and Betty would have theirs under their coats.

She walked downstairs, her footfalls reverberating throughout the house. No radio or TV was ever turned on unless she wanted the news. She detested noise of any kind save the cry of her hounds.

A small cooler squatted on the kitchen table. A checklist was beside that: two bottled waters and two Cokes and a sandwich. Sister could never eat at a hunt breakfast because no one ever gave her time. She was crowded from the minute she walked in the room. Self-preservation taught her to pack a cooler and eat in the trailer before going in to the breakfast. Since hunting people knew not to bother a master who was gathering hounds, she could usually eat.

"Ham or chicken?" Raleigh asked. *"Ham will make you thirsty."*

She sliced a loaf of fresh pumpernickel, buttered two thick slices, slapped on chicken, tossed pieces to Raleigh, and tore smaller pieces for Golly, who happily shinnied down the ficus tree.

The phone rang.

"Hello."

"Back at you," Betty Franklin said.

"Ready?"

"Had to let my britches out a notch. Clearly I've failed at my diet and"—she tried to make her voice light—"I've failed as a mother. Jennifer went back to rehab last night for an impromptu visit and I apologize for not being at hound walk."

"You left a message—"

"I did but I didn't tell you why I wasn't there. Anyway, I sat there for four and a half hours while she cursed, cried, kicked. Oh yes, kicked. Bobby lasted thirty minutes. He couldn't take it. I told him to go work late."

"I'm sorry."

"Is Cody still there?"

"I saw her at the kennels this morning."

"Cody, thank God, had the sense to call rehab and hustle her down there. Doug found Jen a couple of miles from Roger's Corner. Did I tell you that?"

"No."

"Did he tell you that?"

"No. He wouldn't unless it was necessary."

"He's a good boy. Or man. I keep seeing that little boy with the big green eyes. Jane—I don't know what to do."

"Honey, I'm just sorry. I wish I could tell you what to do. Is she at rehab now?"

"No. She's home in her room. Dr. Zacks, who I like a lot, by the way, said let's try her on an outpatient basis. If it doesn't work, back she goes."

"This is going to cost a fortune."

"So far, a week's stay cost $6,280. Counseling is $120 a session and she'll need to go in at least twice a week. Once a day all next week and then twice a week. One hates to focus on the money but it is a factor."

"Are there statistics about the success rate of this kind of thing?"

"Yes. They aren't impressive. Over half the patients relapse. Dr. Zacks believes the Alcoholics Anonymous and the Narcotics Anonymous help tremendously if people will commit to it. Jennifer is so young. How many seventeen-year-olds will be sitting in a Narcotics Anonymous meeting?"

"I often wonder if Raymond would have—"

"Ray. No. He would have gotten drunk with his fraternity brothers when he got to college. He would have smoked a little weed but Ray was a happy kid. That boy was like sunshine. Jennifer came out of the womb unhappy, honestly."

"They come into this world ready-made. Betty, want to have a slumber party? Come on over."

"I'd love it but I'd better stay here. Bobby can hardly speak to Jennifer. She's got his number. If he corrects her, she blames him. If he doesn't pay attention to her, she says he doesn't care. Right now he's guilty and useless."

"It's harder for men."

"Some men. I'm not making excuses for him based on gender. You know, I'm getting to the point where I'm not making excuses for anybody and I don't want to hear any either. God-dammit, Jane, we are each responsible for our own lives. That's it. No passing the buck. If Helen Keller, blind and deaf, could make something out of her life, I don't want to hear this shit about being a victim. Jennifer Franklin is not a victim no matter how much she wants to be. Right now she's a spoiled, rotten brat and I'd like to knock the stuffing out of her."

"Good."

"Good?"

"Betty, if you're mad you'll do something. If you're sad you'll bawl and sit on your ass. And you're right, Jennifer has no excuse for her behavior."

"I wish I'd known the signs. I could have caught Cody earlier. I was so obtuse."

"Drugs aren't part of your life."

"Well, I was born in 1952. It's hard not to have some awareness of drugs but I was never part of that scene. You were lucky. You missed it."

"Because I'm older than dirt." Sister laughed at herself.

"You'll never be old. God, here I've dumped my troubles at your door and right before the big day. I'm sorry."

"Opening hunt will take care of itself. This is a little more important."

"I can't make up my mind whether to let her hunt or make her stay home. It's one of the only two things that make her happy."

"What's the other one?"

"Sex."

"Oh dear," Sister blurted out.

"I say 'Oh shit.' They're all doing it. I mean at that age I thought about it but I didn't *do* it. So we've drawn blood to test for AIDS and other unsavory consequences. She had the sense to use contraceptives. Foam. She used foam because she didn't want to go with me to the doctor to get the Pill or to get some other kind of contraceptive. She thought it would upset me. Well, it would have but not as much as not knowing. Bobby can't even talk about the sex. He gets red in the face and stammers."

"Do you know who she's sleeping with?"

"I need a calculator. She hasn't restricted herself to boys either. Jennifer is freely distributing her favors."

"Is she afraid she's gay?"

"Hell, no. She thinks it's cool. Oh, she doesn't know what she is."

"The first thing is to get her off drugs. If she's going to spend her life as a bisexual harlot at least she can be a sober one. If you want my opinion about hunting, I say let her do it. Plus as long as she's riding, she's not in bed with someone. If it makes her happy, that's one step in the right direction."

"Maybe you're right. I'll tell Bobby what you said."

"What did Dr. Zacks say?"

"We didn't even get to hunting. We were too busy dodging the karate kid. She's quick, too, I can tell you. Oh, I forgot to mention that Walter Lungrun was there when I got to rehab. He helped Cody and Doug when Jennifer blew up. He's a commanding man when he needs to be. You know, this is the damnedest thing—he reminds me so much of Big Ray."

"Me, too." Sister smiled. "A quiet, take-charge kind of man."

"But he even looks like Ray when he was young."

"Betty, enjoy Bobby while you have him, warts and all."

A silence followed. Then Betty replied, "You're right. I know you miss both your Rays every day."

"You cope with the loss, the physical loss, and you even learn to be thankful for the time you did have but, Betty, there are days when I would give anything, anything, to hear my husband's laughter or for Junior to open the back door, throw his books on the floor, and bellow, 'Mom, where are you?' "

A sigh followed. "I will try to cherish Bobby and Jennifer but right now it's not easy."

"Well, think of this. Two months ago, two weeks ago you might not have given a nickel for Cody but look how she's trying. People can change if they want to."

"You're right. You're right. You know if I didn't have Outlaw, if I didn't have hunting, I think I would have unraveled at the seams a long time ago. And I have you."

"Thanks."

"All right, Madam Master, I'm going to make sure my husband and my youngest daughter are ready for tomorrow and I'll say a little prayer that it's a three-fox day. Good night, Jane."

"Good night, Betty." Sister hung up the phone. She sat on the kitchen floor as Raleigh trotted over.

"Me, me, me!" Raleigh begged as he rolled over.

Sister scratched his tummy.

"A little to the left." Raleigh giggled.

"I would bite, as in sink my fangs to the hilt, anyone who rubbed my stomach. First destruction. Then Death!" Golly bragged as she quickly filched another piece of chicken from the table.

The phone rang again.

"Bag it," Raleigh suggested.

Irritated, Sister nonetheless rose to pick up the offending instrument. "Jane Arnold."

"Sister, this is Crawford Howard."

"Yes, Crawford. How are you tonight?"

"Fine, thank you. I called to apologize for losing my temper. I'm sorry."

"Me, too."

"I also wanted to tell you, since everyone gossips—I wanted you to hear from me that I am dating my ex-wife with the hope of reconciliation." He spoke rapidly.

"Well, I hope it works out for both of you." Sister remained furious at Crawford's insults to Doug.

"It's awkward with Martha working for Fontaine, which was my fault. Totally."

"Avoid him tomorrow." She almost added "and me."

"If he knows what's good for him, he will avoid me." Crawford abruptly changed subjects. "Have you come to a conclusion about taking on a joint-master?"

"I have and I will bring this matter before the board, which, as you know, meets next Wednesday."

"The ninth?"

"I don't have my calendar in front of me but I think it is the ninth. Anyway, it's always the second Wednesday in the month."

"Right. I'll be there." Crawford cherished being a member of the board of governors. "Watched the weather report?"

"No. I think I'll trust my senses," she said.

"Ought to be a good day. Overcast. Cool. Ought to be a real Jefferson Hunt day." He was dying to pry her decision out of her.

"Crawford, you have deeply offended me. Your treatment of Doug was despicable." She decided it was better to let him have it than hold in her anger. Besides, he was too dense to know how angry she really was. "You did right in calling me to apologize but I know how badly you want to be joint-master. I'm not fooled. I don't think you are truly repentant. You had best apologize to Doug and if you don't really think about what you've done, if you don't understand, if you do it again, I will throw you out of this club so fast you won't know what hit you—and don't think you can buy off the board of governors. Good night."

Agitated, unable to go directly to sleep, Sister picked up Washington's diary.

The acquisition of his own pack in 1768 provoked him to keep track of its progress.

She read entries, enjoying his economy of language and his abbreviations, old spellings.

"Went huntg being joined by Mrs. Washington in her ex-cellent scarlet habit along with Mr. Peake, Wm Triplet and Harrison Manley. Rode Blueskin. Billy on Chinklin.

"After a chace of five hours dogs were worsted. Billy sorely tried."

Billy Lee was Washington's huntsman, carrying a large French hunting horn on his back. The two men cherished a friendship and the general visited the stables and kennel each morning and again in the evening.

She read six pages, her eye resting on this entry: "Hunted a black fox twenty miles. He returns to his den fresh. Seventh time on this jet fox. Billy has given up declaring this black fox came from The Nether World. He swears he will never hunt him again."

She finally fell asleep, the diary on her chest, to dream of riding with George Washington, M.F.H.

CHAPTER 34

The weatherman had lied. A thin band of pale pink deepened to salmon, then scarlet, over frost-covered fields, washing them in dawn's hope. The rim of the sun peeped over the horizon illuminating maples, oaks, hickories, black gums, syca-mores, beeches, black birches, dogwoods, willows, all the great varieties of the deciduous trees of the piedmont, garbed in rich colors.

This would be a perfect early November day, crisp, clear, leaves still on the trees, pumpkins still being plucked in a few southern-exposure fields, drying cornstalks tied in stocks in other fields. Acorn, walnuts, chinquapins, beechnuts dropped, rat-a-tat, onto fields, outbuildings, cars.

Diana, Dasher, and Dragon, bursting with excitement, stood outside the kennel. The experienced hounds slept soundly inside, not even lifting their heads when the three litter mates walked through the magnetic flap door. The tin roof on the equipment shed shone with the coating of frost. A light breeze from the northwest rustled the leaves.

"I hope this is a good day," Diana whispered.

"Me, too," Dasher echoed.

"I'll be leading the pack. Of course it will be a good day," Dragon bragged.

"You can't be the strike hound. You don't know enough. Stay behind Cora." Piqued by his egotistical brother, Dasher grumbled.

"Cora's too slow."

"No, she's not. She doesn't pop into fifth gear until she's sure. You just run flat out with your mouth running, too. If you overrun scent, you don't know it until it's too late, Dragon. I'd think by now you would have learned your lesson."

Turning his well-proportioned head to face his brother, Dragon replied, *"The snake could have bitten anybody. It just happened to bite me."*

"Target knew a sucker when he saw one." Dasher longed for the day when he would see the flashy bold red. *"And Reynard saw him do it to you, which means all the foxes know you for what you are."*

"Dachshund." Dragon threw the worst insult he could think of at his brother.

"At least that's a hound. You've got the brain of a Jack Russell," Dasher replied with gleeful malice.

Dragon bared his fangs.

"Chill." Diana bared her own formidable fangs. *"If you two get in a fight, you'll sit right here in the kennel. Neither*

*one of you is thinking too clearly. If you can't get along, then
shut up."*

"He started it." Dragon pouted.

"Did not."

"Did too."

*"I'll grab you by the ruff, throw you down, and sit on you!
Now leave it. I mean it."*

The brothers respected their sister even if they did not respect each other. Snarling under his breath, Dragon pranced
back into the kennel.

Dasher sat down next to Diana. They both stared at the sun,
clear of the horizon now.

"About time for Shaker and Doug," Diana remarked.

"Lights on at Doug's." He lifted his black nose, sniffing the
wind. *"Deer."*

*"Strong. Just watch. If Dragon can't get up a fox, he'll go
off again. I know it."* She thought a moment. *"But I have to
give him credit. He really doesn't go off on deer. He just finds
another fox. He's so hardheaded."*

Dasher stood up as Doug emerged from his cottage. *"Cubbing was one thing, Sis, but opening hunt, all those people
looking at us . . ."*

"Shaker won't take any hound he doesn't think can handle it."

"Can't believe he's taking Dragon."

*"He's been good the last two cub hunts and he's handsome.
People like to look at handsome hounds."* She heard the front
door of the kennel open as Doug entered. *"Let's go back in."*

On the far side of Hangman's Ridge, the western corner
where the fence line divides the woods from the fields, Target
preened in his den. The purpose of opening hunt was for all
creatures to see and admire him. He had to admit that he had
never looked better nor had Charlene, although her brush was
a tad thin.

His children, finally in their own dens, had their marching

orders. Yesterday morning he told Reynard to stay over by Whiskey Ridge, since his largest son might let his ego interfere with prudent judgment. He couched this in terms of saving himself for Thanksgiving hunt, when Reynard could be the star. He'd discussed the day with Butch, who agreed not to mislead hounds. This would be a day for the reds to shine.

"Wonder why Butch was so cooperative?" Charlene was suspicious.

Target puffed out his white chest. *"Can't cut the mustard."*

"The original plan was we'd share the day. We'd start and they'd finish."

"He was glad to bow out, my dear. He's lazy as sin and probably, although he wouldn't admit it, he knows he's not in our league. He'll have other hunts."

"M-m-m," was all Charlene said.

Aunt Netty, Uncle Yancy, Charlie, Grace, and Patsy each knew the plan. Within a half hour they'd leave home to go to their various destinations.

The plan was for Target to start the day. A cornfield was in the bottomland on Sister Jane's side of Hangman's Ridge.

Shaker would surely cast there. It was easy and a mere quarter mile from the top of the ridge, where the field would gather. Target would trot out the back side of the corn so everyone could see him; then he'd run around the base of the ridge leading them north-northeast. He'd jump over the coop that Fontaine had smashed so again everyone could admire him. After two miles he'd drop into the creek and slip into Aunt Netty's den; one opening was in the creek bed. Aunt Netty would cross onto the other side of the creek after she walked over the last fifty yards of Target's tracks. She would veer into the creek, making certain to walk across the large fallen tree. The hounds would go to the tree trunk and not the den. As soon as Aunt Netty was sure they'd picked up her scent she was to run through the woods into the meadows on the back side. Her run would be about two and a half miles, since Netty was the fastest fox around. The tricky part would be stopping short of Soldier Road, doubling back on her own tracks, then heading back toward Hangman's Ridge in a large loop. She would only double on her own tracks for two hundred yards, maybe three hundred, depending on how fast the hounds were behind her. At the abandoned moonshine still she would jump into the burrow in the middle of the still and Grace, almost as fast as Netty, would take over. Being young, Grace was only to run a half mile back into the cornfield where the cast was first made. Then Uncle Yancy, deep in experience, would fly out of the field, up, straight up the ridge and straight to the hanging tree. He'd wait a bit, then run down the ridge on the other side, stopping at the tree line if the hounds were too close. A lovely old gopher hole was right at the fence post and Yancy had connected it underground to the base of a walnut. Yancy, shrewd, had so many entrances and exits, some almost impossible to see, that he could sit in there with three hundred hounds outside. They'd never figure it all out.

About one hundred yards from that point, Patsy was to lead the field back to Sister's house. The interesting part about this section of the run was that hounds and horses would have been moving along, in some places at speed, for a good five miles. That ought to separate the wheat from the chaff. But this section would test the intelligence of the hounds. They'd be charged up. They'd lose the scent. Uncle Yancy had asked a skunk friend to spray about ten yards from his fence post entrance. That would confuse hounds. Skunk scent would cover fox scent and just about any other scent. So the hounds would need to cast themselves, searching for the line. Even if a few managed to push through the stinging skunk scent to the fence post entrance, they couldn't do much about it. Digging wouldn't bring them much, plus the entrance would be covered in skunk scent, too. Yancy made sure of that.

It might take the pack ten to fifteen minutes to pick up the new line thanks to the little traps he had laid for them. This would be quite a test. It would help him understand how good the pack was this year. After all, even though Americans no longer hunted to kill, a fox couldn't be too careful and the American foxhound was blindingly fast, much faster than the English foxhound. What if Shaker blew them back and the hounds didn't return to him? That damned young hound chasing Target got his comeuppance but what if he'd been on one of the young foxes? They might not have been so clever. It was one thing to be born bright; experience still counted for much.

He was pleased with the battle plan that they'd all worked on. It would thin out the ranks of all the creatures, especially the humans.

He expected many a good laugh as the woods and fields became littered with humans taking an involuntary dismount.

Patsy, a bright red, would show herself at Sister's front door and then disappear. A large earth had been dug under Sister's front porch. Even if the hounds could get under the porch, they'd wreck the boxwoods and Shaker would have to call them off.

The reds, for years, had been digging earths all around the house and the outbuildings and down by the strong running creek at the bottom of the back field.

They liked to observe the hounds and the staff. One needed to study one's quarry.

Over at Butch's den, the whole family had gathered.

"Why did you agree to that? Why give the reds all the fun?" Comet was furious.

"I said we wouldn't interfere with their program." Butch licked his front paw. *"I didn't say we couldn't go out and watch. Besides, there's a whole hunt season before us. Who knows, we might need Target's cooperation."*

"Let the reds do all the work. We can learn this pack from them," their mother advised.

"But you've known this hunt forever," Comet whined. *"What's to learn? We should be out there."*

"Box of rocks." Butch cuffed his son. *"Hounds grow old and die. Young ones take their place. The pack changes like seasons. Sister Jane can breed for more speed, too. And never underestimate a hound. They're intelligent. Not as intelligent as we are but intelligent. Climb a tree where the coop is, the smashed coop. You can see the pack coming from the cornfield across the pastures over the coop and into the woods. We'll find out how fast they find, if Cora is still the strike hound and if Archie is still the anchor."*

"You go. I'm going to Netty's den," he mouthed off. *"Let's see how they work in water but if I feel like it, maybe I'll just mislead all of them."*

"You do and you'll be one dead fox," Buster spat. *"Not only will the reds not help you if needs be, I won't either."*

"The reds are a bunch of snots."

"Hey, I didn't say I liked them. But there are times when we need one another. You do as I say!"

Inky, silent, would do as her father told her. She was anxious to see how Diana did on her big day. She hoped her friend would be impressive because she'd heard that hounds could get drafted out. They weren't always bad hounds but they didn't fit in with that pack. She liked Diana and was very grateful for the hound's help. She didn't tell anyone. She knew better.

The grays left their den, the distance to the cornfield and pasture being about a mile and a half.

"Dad," Inky whispered as they reached a large rock outcropping, *"when's the last time a fox died?"*

"Hunting?"

"Uh-huh."

"Six years ago an old red, Herschel, got shingles. Gave the hounds a heck of a chase and then when he reached his den he sat on the outside of it. He knew he had to die, you see, so

he chose a swift death. He was a brave fox, Herschel, and he didn't deserve to get shingles. For a red, I liked him fine."

A huge shape overhead startled them, so silent was the approach. Athena, the two-foot owl, was returning to her nest after a successful night.

"You'll miss opening hunt," Comet called up to her.

She circled them and said in a low chortle, *"To ride well is the mark of a gentleman. To ride too well is the mark of a misspent life."* Then she vanished as silently as she'd appeared.

CHAPTER 35

Raleigh and Golly sat side by side at the kitchen window. Hounds, sterns up, eyes bright, walked behind Shaker. Doug, riding Rickyroo, walked in front of the hounds at a leisurely pace. Betty Franklin and Outlaw took the left flank. Cody took the right. Jennifer, a good rider, rode with her father, which pleased him.

As they rode off, light streaming in from the east, Golly said, *"I'm glad I'm not a pack animal."*

"Me, too," came the dry reply.

Golly, sitting on the window ledge and therefore eye to eye with the handsome Doberman, replied by curling her upper lip and emitting the smallest of hisses. Raleigh just laughed.

An old farm road snaked up to the top of Hangman's Ridge. The pack reached this ten minutes after leaving the kennels. At the foot of the ridge, in the flat meadow once used for growing soybeans, trailers were bumper to bumper. People came from neighboring hunts wearing the individual colors of their hunts. Each rider from another hunt had called Sister to request permission to wear their hunt's distinctive colors. Sister always gave that permission although some masters did not. In that case riders had to wear black coats and boots with no cuffs.

People came to follow on foot. It was going to be a big day thanks in part to the gorgeous weather—good for humans, not so good for scent.

As Sister rode by, men tipped their caps, top hats, and derbies. Ladies called out, "Good morning, Master," as was proper. Ground followers also doffed their hats or waved. Lisa Bredell, Tinsley Wetherford Papandros, Isabel Rogers all mingled around, dying to find something to bitch and moan about. Each woman wore the perfect outdoor ensemble. Peter Wheeler sat on his truck like an elderly, beloved pasha holding court. When the hunt climbed the ridge his best friend, Granby Vann, a distant relative of Georgia Vann's, hunting in a frock today, would drive Peter up. From the vantage point of the ridge they would be able to see much of the hunt. Most of the foot followers would stay high also.

Each horse, braided, hooves painted, tail plaited, felt the excitement. Their coats, especially the chestnuts', caught the morning light, a thousand copper sparkles, whereas the dark grays gleamed like black diamonds. Dappled grays, flea-bitten grays, light grays, almost white, vied with blood bays, light bays, seal browns, and a few paints as to who was the best-looking horse that morning.

Children, barely able to breathe with anticipation, mounted their ponies. Adults heaved themselves up, the older and wiser ones bringing mounting blocks. Once up, a friend on the ground gave their boots a last-minute flick of the towel.

On they rode, up the hill, a pageant timeless in beauty, a passion older than the walls of Troy.

"Hold up," Shaker gently spoke to his hounds.

Thirty couple, tricolor, medium-height American hounds

carrying sculpted heads looked up at the huntsman and then back to the master.

"What beautiful children," Sister said, beaming.

As the humans gathered round the hanging tree, Sister counted heads: 92 mounted and perhaps 130 on the ground. She couldn't be sure, as more were climbing the hill. Thank god she'd ordered twelve cases of champagne for the breakfast, plus the usual bar. She laughed to herself because some of these people would rush to the bar with a siphon. How they lived to middle age or beyond amazed her.

Walter Lungrun was perfectly turned out. She smiled at him and he tipped his cap.

Fontaine wore a black weaselbelly, since he knew Sister loved the look. His white cords were set off even more by the rich, black coat. His top hat, smoothed and brushed, suited him.

Crawford wore a scarlet swallowtail with a white vest and his top hat was also perfect, with a scarlet cord attached to his coat. Men would kill for that scarlet cord, as they searched years for them. Most had to make do with a black hat cord, which strictly speaking was not proper. There was Crawford, his hat cord correctly in place, his boots direct from Lobb in London, costing him somewhere between $5,000 and $6,000, depending on the exchange rate. Everyone else got along with Dehners or Vogels, not cheap but at least under $1,000. But there was Crawford in the best boots money could buy in the world. His gloves, handmade by a glover also in London, were composed of more than thirty pieces of leather, matched, stitched so that he couldn't feel the seams. No one in America even knew how to make such gloves anymore. His breeches, his shirt, his stock tie—all bespoke his wealth and, in his favor, his taste.

Martha, wearing a deep navy frock coat made by hand in Hospital, Ireland, surely was the best turned out of the ladies. Like her ex, everything on her body had been made expressly for her. Ravishing, she smiled both because she knew she looked good and because Crawford was courting her as though they were young again.

Once Peter Wheeler was in place, Sister stood in her stirrups. "Gather round." As they moved up closer she looked at each person, acknowledging their presence. "Ladies and gentlemen, thank you for being here today. This is the one hundred and twenty-first time that the Jefferson Hunt has gone out, save for 1917 and 1918. We are thankful to be here yet again. I know of no sport as exciting. I know of no people quite as brave, occasionally foolish, and always gallant as foxhunters. The words 'gallant,' 'glory,' and 'honor' seem to have disappeared from our language and certainly from our behavior. Foxhunters may be the only people left who understand and live by those words. We are the last humans to practice chivalry. Therefore we wish our quarry a good day and may we never catch him. We wish our hounds a good day's sport and we thank our horses for their spirit and their patience with us. I wish each of you a splendid day, a day you will forever remember with happiness and pride." She paused. "Hilltoppers ride with Bobby Franklin. Field, come with me. Huntsman." She nodded to Shaker, who placed his cap on his head, ribbons streaming down, as were Sister's.

"Hounds ready?" Shaker asked.

"Yes!"

Smiling, Shaker rode down the side path of the ridge to the cornfield.

Crawford's horse, Czapaka, hopped around a bit, as did others.

"I am the best-looking horse here," Czapaka bragged.

"Shut up, asshole," Cochise, Martha's tough leopard Appaloosa, ordered.

Clemson, not the prettiest of horses but one of the wisest, Walter on board, simply said, *"You have yet to finish a hunt the way you started it, buddy."*

The humans chattered, too, until they reached the bottom of the ridge, the cornfield beckoning.

The field halted. Doug was already on the far side, the north side of the cornfield. Betty took the left side but farther away, halfway up the ridge on the trail. Cody stayed in the meadows but was near the fence line.

"He's in there." Shaker's voice encouraged the hounds. He lifted the horn, blowing a few notes.

"Yahoo!" Dragon plunged right in.

"You're still wet behind the ears. You stay behind me," Cora growled as she sped past him, the drying corn leaves rattling as she brushed them.

No sooner were all the hounds in the corn than Target trotted out the north side. Doug saw him, removed his cap, and pointed his cap and Rickyroo in the direction that the enormous red was traveling.

Not satisfied with being viewed by the first whip, Target moved away from the corn and brazenly sat down in the field.

A child in the rear of the field screamed, "The fox." His mother, mortified, reached down, putting her hand over his mouth. "Sh-h-h. He's too close to tallyho."

By now the field had spied him. Happy with this, Target trotted away until Cora burst out of the other side of the cornfield, her lovely voice booming.

Archie, anchoring and still in the corn, replied, *"I'm behind. Go on, Cora."*

"It's him. It's him." Dasher was so excited, his nostrils full of hot, fresh fox scent, that he yipped like a puppy.

Target, about two hundred yards ahead of the strike hound, put on the afterburners. He scorched the meadow, jumped Fontaine's coop, to the thrill of the field and the foot followers on the ridge. Then he ran hard through the woods.

The field followed Sister, surprised at the fast pace, for she didn't think scent would be good but then she didn't think they'd jump a fox and stay so close either.

Lafayette, smooth and always balanced, arced over Fontaine's coop. Most everyone made it and those few who didn't cursed under their breath, rode to the rear, and hoped to boot their horses over. Everyone did but one poor little lady, a picture of frustration. She gave up and joined Bobby Franklin as he leaned over to flip up the kiwi gate latch.

The music carried up to the ridge. Peter Wheeler stood on the back of his pickup and kept repeating, "Can you beat that? Can you beat that? Biggest damn red I ever saw in my life!"

Sitting atop the hanging tree, St. Just also watched everything. Usually he flew low over the red fox, cawing loudly for the hounds to close the gap. His jet-black feathers shone iridescent, his deep-yellow beak opened and closed, revealing his tongue, but he made little noise.

Target charged straight for Aunt Netty's den. He lingered a bit too long in the field, showing off, and he needed to widen the gap between himself and Cora. He glanced back, seeing Dragon running neck and neck with Cora.

"I hate that hound," he thought to himself, wishing the snake had killed Dragon.

Target ran through a rotted log knowing that would slow Cora and Dragon for a moment. Dasher, Diana, and other hounds were only a few paces behind the lead hounds.

This gave him just enough time to warn Aunt Netty as she reposed on the log fallen across the creek.

"Netty, go on now. They're too close!"

She scrambled up the other side of the bank and headed off at a burning clip. Target ran halfway across the log, then jumped into the water. This was a slight variation on the plan but the only way to keep the hounds from the mouth of the den. He swam down the creek, then climbed up the bank into the opening.

As planned, the hounds, noses to the ground, streaked across the fallen log.

Blinding speed had served the slender, cagey Netty all her days. She put further distance between herself and the hounds as she zigzagged through the woods, emerging onto the back meadows still deep green.

A sizable hog's-back jump punctuated the fence line, an old three-rail. Shaker cleared it right behind his hounds. Sister, fifty yards behind her huntsman, also sailed over.

As they thundered through the fields she heard hooves moving up too fast behind her.

Lafayette put back his ears. He slightly turned his head. *"Bug off,"* he warned Czapaka.

Crawford couldn't hold the big Holsteiner.

Just as Czapaka's nose drew even with Lafayette's, Sister unleashed her whip, which she'd switched to her left hand. The thong and cracker snapped right in front of Czapaka's nose. The warm-blood, startled, half reared, then stopped dead. Crawford slammed up on his neck, then slid off to the side as the entire field passed him.

Bunky Jenkins, riding tail this day, perceived that Crawford was fine. He didn't stop to help him, which only made Crawford even more furious.

With reluctance, Martha turned back. He mounted up and then they had to fly to catch up because the pace accelerated. An upright jump, four logs stacked on top of the other, guarded the other side of the field. Cochise popped over and Czapaka with a whip and a spur followed.

They reached the back of the field. Fontaine had moved up right in Sister's pocket, the most prestigious place in the field. Crawford choked on his fury.

Aunt Netty burst out from the woods, ran almost to Soldier Road, and then doubled back on her own tracks. Those people on the top of Hangman's Ridge could see her as she doubled, then sped off first south, then zigzagged north as she headed toward the ridge. Then she veered back again. She knew the hounds were a quarter mile behind. She was pleased with herself.

Grace waited at the still.

"They're in fine fettle today, Grace. Go now."

"Cora first?" Grace had been told to fear Cora's speed.

"And that arrogant young entry, Dragon. He's fast. Very fast but fortunately he's not very bright. Go on."

Grace trotted toward the old farm path, then picked up her speed.

Cora stopped at the still. *"Aunt Netty, I know you're in there."*

"Go to the right. You'll pick up Grace's scent. We'll make this a good day for Sister. After that, it's business as usual."

"To ground! To ground!" Dragon lifted his head back as he ran up and almost over Cora.

"Forget it." Cora moved to the right.

"But I've put a fox to ground!" Dragon wanted to be a star.

"Scent is tough today, you fool. It's warmed up. There's a light breeze. The ground is drying out. Don't spoil the plan."

"I put a fox to ground," he bellowed.

Lightning fast before the other hounds joined them, Cora leapt up and turned sideways like a marlin on a line. She crashed into Dragon. He hit the ground with a thud, the wind knocked out of him. Then Cora seized him by the throat and shook him. She dropped him and ran to the right, picking up Grace's scent.

"Over here. Over here."

The rest of the pack followed her as Dragon, choking, stood up, shook himself, coughed, then sullenly hitched up with the rest of the pack.

Sister and Lafayette leapt over a fallen tree trunk as a shortcut to the farm road. She'd heard Cora and then the pack turn. As she glanced behind her she saw her field strung out, the attrition rate rising.

"Stay with the hounds," she thought to herself, and wondered when she'd had this long a run, this fast.

Grace ran back over Target's evaporated scent, making a semicircle. She flew over Fontaine's coop, not knowing the grays were in the trees watching her. She ran straight into the cornfield and then in a change of plan, because she was young and got confused, she blasted out the back of the cornfield with Uncle Yancy.

"What do I do?"

"Stay with me. There's no den up here, Grace. You'll have to run with me. You okay?"

"I'm not tired. I've only covered a half mile."

Grace and Yancy skirted the fence line into the woods, a deep ravine in the far distance. Just to make life interesting, totally confuse the humans, they ran two large, loopy figure eights in the woods. The humans would think they were on grays until someone caught sight of them.

Lottie Fisher's horse stumbled. Fontaine, who happened to be looking back, pulled up Gunpowder. Lottie, quite good-looking, brushed herself off as she checked her horse.

"You need company?" Fontaine reined in Gunpowder, lightly dismounting and removing his top hat. "Gets so lonesome in these woods."

She blushed. "Thank you. I'm fine. He's fine, too." She patted the gelding's sleek neck.

"How about a leg up, then?" He cupped his hand under her right leg. "One, two, three." He pushed her up into the saddle.

Then he swung up on Gunpowder, top hat back on his head.

"Thank you so much, Fontaine."

"The pleasure was all mine." He grinned. "Shall we join them?"

Off they galloped on the last loop of the figure eight. The coop up ahead led into the meadow.

Lottie didn't realize Fontaine was not behind her until she

came right up on the rear of the first flight. She didn't think a thing of it.

Together, Grace and Yancy dashed straight up the ridge, right to the hanging tree, dodging the screaming people, some of whom yelled "tallyho" to no avail. They scooted under Peter Wheeler's truck.

Old Peter, on his feet, slapped his thigh with his hat. "Yip, yip yoo." He belted out a rebel yell. "Yip, yip yoo. I never saw anything like this in my life. Two red foxes. Yip, yip yoo. Janie, where in the hell are you?"

Sister had just cleared Fontaine's coop with Georgia Vann now riding in her pocket. But the entire field was feeling the effects of the long run. The staff horses, in fine condition, felt loosened up. But other horses who should have been conditioned but weren't really began to labor, drenched in creamy white sweat.

Crawford stopped at the back of Hangman's Ridge. "He feels lame."

"Looks lame." Martha confirmed his opinion.

"You go on. I'll walk him to the trailers," he instructed.

"Are you sure?"

"Sure. I'll take the shortcut around to the trailers."

"Crawford, you might want to stay in the meadow even though it takes longer. You don't run the risk of fouling scent quite so much."

He glared at her, for he hated to be told what to do. "Fine."

"I'll see you back at the trailers. Hope he's okay." She trotted off. Then, when far enough away from Czapaka, she broke into a canter.

Crawford thought all this talk about fouling scent was bullshit, hunters showing off. He headed straight into the shortcut.

Overhead, St. Just flew low, startling Czapaka.

By the time Sister reached the hanging tree she, as a show of respect, stopped to ask Peter what happened.

"Two! Two, Janie, and two different than the first one you

flushed out of the cornfield. I never! I never!" Then he turned his aged body, pointed with his hat to the direction the two foxes ran, the hounds already on.

"Thank you. You're my best whip." She smiled, squeezed Lafayette, and they were off again.

She leaned back as she cantered, slowly, straight down the ridge. No time to fiddle with the old farm road and bypaths now. A few more people rolled onto the earth with a thud. Loose horses ran about, finally stopping to graze.

At the base of the ridge Sister swooped around, heading toward her house. A zigzag fence was to her left, a few old locust posts from the former fence still in place at the corners. She smelled the skunk as she neared the zigzag. She cleared the zigzag, started into the western woods then stopped. Hounds were all over the place like marbles rolling.

"Hold hard!" she shouted, raising her left arm.

People strained to pull back. They stood there, horses and humans panting like the hounds. The temperature inched into the low sixties. They were burning up and there had been not one check or slowing of pace for one solid hour.

Georgia Vann dropped her feet out of the stirrups, as did Walter Lungrun. They flopped onto their horses' necks to relieve crying muscles. Even Martha, always in great condition, breathed heavily then leaned all the way backward in her saddle to stretch out.

The hounds, eyes watering, circled around one old locust fence post. Uncle Yancy and Grace snuggled down in the den, slowly making their way underground to the walnut, its canopy a cooling covering.

"Stay down. We don't come out until the pack is off Patsy." But as they inched toward the walnut they found Patsy still underground.

"What are you still doing here? You can't go out now. You'd have to be as fast as Netty," Yancy, upset, shouted.

"The pack split, Uncle Yancy," Patsy explained.

"I hear them above us," Grace said.

"Only half. I swear I was at the base of the walnut and I was ready to run but I heard a young hound go off back toward the east. Half the pack went with him."

"If that damn little buster spoiled our plan, I'll run him right out of the forest myself!" Yancy spat.

Sister waited. She heard half her pack. They rarely split and on a day like today such behavior would be quite unusual.

Cora milled around the fence post. *"I can't get through the skunk. Fan out again. Fan out, I tell you!"*

The hounds obeyed.

Diana, timid, said, *"I think I've got something here but it's blood. Is it fox blood?"*

Both Archie and Cora loped right over. They put their noses to the ground, then looked at each other. *"Yes."*

"Follow me!" Cora commanded.

As Sister followed her hounds, running, but running more slowly, since Cora wasn't certain about this just yet, she glanced around for the whips. Betty was off to her left. She could see Outlaw's buckskin coat better than she could see Betty in her black frock. She saw no one on the right nor did she see Shaker. She couldn't remember when they'd parted company. The pace, killing, would begin to tell on the older hounds.

As the field rode off, Grace, Yancy, and Patsy, one by one, crept out of the hole. They put their noses to the earth like hounds.

"Cora said blood." Uncle Yancy frowned.

They continued moving on in a line.

"Here," Patsy said.

The other two ran over, noses to the ground.

Yancy grimly picked his head up. *"It is blood. Fox blood."*

"What do we do?" Patsy worried.

"Should we follow them at a safe distance?" Grace asked.

"No. Wait until we hear the hounds go back to the kennel.

We're close enough that we can hear. Then we follow this trail ourselves."

Sister pushed on. The hounds, baffled again at a creek, milled about. She counted heads. Only fifteen people were left out of the forty-one that had ridden first flight. She wondered how many hilltoppers were left. She hadn't seen Bobby Franklin since the hog's-back jump at the high meadow. Even Fontaine was out of the run and she couldn't remember when he'd dropped back.

She couldn't worry about who was where now. Hounds picked up the scent again about thirty paces downstream. She found a crossing and over they went. As she stayed close behind she glanced at the ground, a habit born of tracking on difficult days. She, too, noticed blood. Not buckets of it but a steady drip, drip.

She reached the high meadow, took an in-and-out on the western side, then cantered across the meadow. She pulled up before the hog's back.

Doug and Shaker dismounted and held up their hands. She saw a horse on the ground and then a human.

"Stay here. Martha, you're in charge. Don't anyone move."

Crawford had just reached the last of the field. He, too, pulled up, Czapaka now sound as a dollar.

The hounds sat in the meadow. Some of them were lying down.

Sister dismounted. Gunsmoke, on his side, was barely breathing. Fontaine, face down, wasn't breathing at all.

"He has no pulse," Shaker simply said.

Sister didn't bother to ask him if he'd called 911 on the tiny hand-held he carried. She knew that would be the first thing Shaker did.

"Doug, help me turn him over. Shaker, how long have you been here?"

"About one minute and a half."

She and Doug rolled Fontaine over. No mark was on him

save one hole on the left side of his chest. He was emphatically dead.

"Better call the sheriff."

He flipped open the phone and dialed 911 again. As he gave precise directions to the sheriff's department, Sister and Doug walked over to Gunsmoke. She felt his pulse. She checked his gums, which weren't white. She pointed to a mark across his throat. She felt to see if his windpipe was broken.

Then she walked back to Lafayette and got her flask out of its case. She knelt down by Gunsmoke's head, pouring port into her hand. She rubbed it over his lips. His eyes opened.

"He's got the wind knocked out of him and he's scared. We've got to get him up. Doug, give me your whip."

She stepped back and cracked her whip, stinging the lovely animal on the flank.

"Oww!" He struggled up.

"Sorry, Gunsmoke." She ran her hand along his neck, pressing her ear to his neck, low. "He's all right, I think."

She hadn't realized that she was shaking slightly. She cupped her hands to her mouth. "Martha, take the field home and start eating breakfast. Now!"

Martha, smart, knew Sister needed everyone out of there before people panicked. She waved and turned the diminished band home.

Sister bit her lip. "Did you see anything or anybody?"

"No," Shaker replied.

"No, but I heard a shot about fifteen minutes ago. I thought it was another whip," Doug replied.

Betty rode out of the woods, beheld the spectacle. "Oh my God. What happened?"

"We don't know."

"Is he dead?"

"Yes," Shaker said.

Betty, too, dismounted. She viewed the corpse with horror, her hand flying to her mouth as she realized he'd been murdered.

A whining drew Sister's attention. Dragon walked up, dropping a dead red fox at her feet. The fox, too, had been shot. It was Reynard, Target's son. A rope was still wrapped around his hind paws.

Sister patted Dragon on the head. The humans scarcely knew what to say.

As Gunsmoke caught his breath he shook a little bit.

Lafayette asked, *"Did you see anything?"*

"No. I took the hog's back and I hit something. I don't remember anything." He cast his big brown eyes at his dead rider. *"He was a strong rider, you know. Never gave a false signal."*

"I'm sorry." Lafayette sympathized. If it had been Sister, he would have been crushed with sadness.

"Yeah." Gunsmoke hung his head.

"I told you I'd get the fox," Dragon bragged as he rejoined the pack. The other hounds stared at him, not daring to speak under the circumstances.

They all heard the sirens on Soldier Road. As the ambulance and patrol car turned onto the farm road the noise grew louder.

Overhead St. Just cawed and circled once. Vengeance was sweet.

CHAPTER 36

Three blasts on the horn brought Cody to the hog's-back jump. Cody arrived in about five minutes' time, bringing Sally, an older hound who had slowed due to the pace.

Shocked, the sheriff was there, as was an ambulance.

She remained silent. After brief questioning the whips were released to take hounds back to the kennel.

Sister Jane and Shaker remained behind. The sheriff, new to the area, had been recruited nationally from a list of qualified candidates. The county department, swept clean with a new broom, certainly increased in efficiency. However, Benjamin Sidell, secure in his knowledge and training as only an Ohio man can be, was surprised by murder in this most Virginian of pastimes.

"Mrs. Arnold, can you think of anyone who might want to kill the victim?" Ben had asked the other obvious questions establishing everyone's whereabouts.

"Sheriff, any one of us collects enemies in life but no, I can't think of anyone who'd trip over the line," she truthfully answered.

Shaker stepped up to stand next to Sister. He watched the hounds following Doug in good order as Betty led back Gunsmoke. When Ben turned his gaze directly to Shaker, the curly-haired, broad-shouldered man simply shrugged. "Good-looking. Bad at business. Bad with women."

"Some life." The young sheriff allowed himself a wry smile.

"Will you notify his wife and children? They should be at the University of Virginia football game today. You might try there," Sister Jane thoughtfully informed Ben.

"Thank you, I'll go there myself." He ran his hand over his slick hair, good haircut. "Was Mr. Buruss a good friend of yours?"

"I knew him all of his life. Yes, he was a friend, although I'm not sure I would depend on him. It's difficult to think about it right now, Sheriff. Did I like him? Yes. He was a most charming man even when he was lying to you."

"Ah." The sheriff had discovered Virginia specialized in such fellows. "And you, Mr. Crown?"

"Didn't like him but I could get along with him."

"And why didn't you like him?"

"Empty-headed. Thought he knew hounds. Didn't."

"That's a reason to dislike a man?"

"To me it is."

"Yes, well . . ." The sheriff's voice dropped off. The ambulance crew had loaded Fontaine on the gurney. The wheels clicked as they rolled it the few yards to the ambulance. "Perhaps you could tell me why this dead fox has a rope around its hind legs. Did you shoot it while hunting?"

"No, sir!" Shaker, stung by what to him was an accusation, was vehement.

Sister spoke up. "Sheriff, we don't shoot foxes. That would be unsporting. We chase them. We don't even let the hounds kill one if we can help it."

"So this isn't your fox?"

"No, sir." Shaker's face reddened.

"This is a young male. He's from a litter about one mile from my house. He moved off to find his own den and I've only seen him once since then, which was a few weeks ago.

Males generally travel farther than females to find their own territory, but he remained close."

Ben was incredulous. "You're telling me you *know* this fox?"

"Yes." Sister folded her arms across her chest.

"Course we know our foxes, man. I've been hunting this red family for three decades."

"You can actually recognize them?"

"Can't you tell the difference between dogs?" Sister tried to lower the hostility level between Shaker and the sheriff.

"Sure, but a Lab looks a lot different from a Chihuahua!"

"Foxes vary in size. Their markings, too. You see this fellow is still thinnish because he's young. There's tons of game so he'd only be thin if he were sick or young and as you can see this was a fine, healthy fox. He had only a bit of a white tip on his brush whereas his father has a wide white tip," Sister told the young sheriff.

"What's a brush?"

"The tail," Shaker said as the ambulance's back door closed.

"I see. All right. You know this fox and, I take it, his father."

"Was a fine litter. They all lived." Shaker admired Target and his get. They ran him ragged sometimes.

Sister began to feel exhausted. The shock was seeping in. "Sheriff, the death of a red fox is to be lamented. The death of a good gray, too. We don't want our foxes killed. Whoever killed this beautiful young male no doubt killed Fontaine as well."

"Why do you say that?"

"Because he laid a drag, man!" Shaker exploded.

Before the sheriff could respond Sister quietly added, "Your killer created a scent line, fresh and fresh with blood, too, which would inflame the hounds. This way they would turn away from the hunted fox to this line. The pack split. The killer knew Shaker and I would stay with the pack on the hunted fox.

By the time we got the pack back together the deed would be done."

"You know that, too?"

"Yes." She again spoke in a soothing tone. "But we can be fooled just as you can, Sheriff."

"One more question." He flipped through his notes. "Doug Kinser heard one shot. It would have taken two. The fox is shot, too. Right?"

"Doesn't mean we would have heard that shot. Hounds were giving tongue. The hoofbeats would drown out most noises. It would be easy not to hear a shot," Shaker said with conviction.

"Sheriff, we want to help you find whoever killed Fontaine. But, please, we're tired. Our horses are tired. You know where to find us but let us get our boys back to the stable," she requested. "Let me make a suggestion. Ask a good veterinarian to perform an autopsy on this fox. He may not have been recently killed."

"What?"

"He could have been killed, frozen, thawed when needed."

"Ah." This was a new thought to the sheriff, who let it sink in before asking, "Do you have a list of who hunted today?"

"The field secretary will have a list of caps—those are the fees paid by nonmembers. With a good night's rest I think we can reconstruct who was with us today, mounted and on foot."

"Thank you." Ben smiled, a nice smile. "I apologize for detaining you."

Once back to the stable Doug ran up to help both Sister and Shaker.

"Have Betty and Cody gone into the house?"

"Yes, but they swore they wouldn't say anything until you came home." Doug had already slipped the saddle off a grateful Lafayette.

"Well—they've had the best opening hunt we've ever had

until this. They've had an hour and a half to eat, drink, and make merry. I guess I have to tell them."

"I'll go with you." Shaker thanked Doug for taking care of his horse and the two friends trudged up to the house.

As they walked through the mudroom and into the kitchen the aroma of ham, biscuits, gravy, grits, roasted turkey, and candied yams assailed them.

The caterers continued to replenish the main table and the dessert table.

Sister had braved spoon bread despite the caterer's warnings. Another large tray, perched on a young man's shoulder, was being carried through the swinging doors.

The caterer, Ted, glanced up from his labors. "Ah, Mrs. Arnold, we're down to half the champagne."

"Good." She smiled reflexively, then turned to Shaker, who put his hand quietly on her shoulder.

"Well?" he asked.

"Well, I guess I'm going to have to spoil my own party." She dropped her gaze to the uneven-width heart-pine flooring, then looked up at him. "Here goes."

When she pushed through the swinging doors people at first didn't notice. The packed dining room hummed. The living room, too, was overflowing with people. Many of them knew something had happened to Fontaine but no one as yet had guessed the truth.

Raleigh threaded through the people to be by Sister's right side. Shaker was on her left.

Golly reposed on a bookshelf above all. Rooster, attending with Peter Wheeler, ensconced in a club chair by the fireplace, noticed Sister flinch for a split second.

One by one the parties, hunters, quieted, glasses poised in midair as they turned toward Jane Arnold.

People parted like the Red Sea. Betty moved toward Sister, as did her husband.

"Are you all right?" Betty asked.

"I think so," Sister answered.

Bobby tapped his wineglass with a spoon. People had begun to stop talking. Now they quieted completely.

Shaker staunchly beside her, Sister nodded to her guests, then took a deep, long breath.

"Friends, this opening hunt was one of the best opening hunts we've ever had. May we all remember its glory." She searched for the right words. "It is my duty . . . to inform you, with sorrow, that Fontaine Buruss was killed today. Shaker found him at the hog's back. Fontaine was shot. We know nothing more than that. Please cooperate with Ben Sidell in any way you can and please assist Sorrel and the children in any way you can. Thank you."

A horrified silence enveloped the room. Then a low murmur, like a wind from the west, moved through as it accumulated power.

Hours later the last person, Peter Wheeler, with Rooster, had left. Sister paid the caterer, who cleaned up then left. She'd fed the pets, taken a shower, and called Shaker and Doug to make sure they were doing okay.

When she hung up the phone a longing for Raymond filled her with stale grief. He would know just what to do even in this most improbable of situations. His deep voice would have filled the gathering with authority. He would have handled the sheriff with the correct mixture of assistance and personal power. He would have put his strong arm around her and whispered, "Steady on, girl."

Ray Junior would be in his thirties now. He would have been much like his father.

Like most women of her class and her generation, Jane had motored through life without fully realizing how much her husband had shielded her from the unsavory aspects of life. She was always grateful for his economic acumen but the emotional buffer Ray provided was not clear to her until he was gone.

Golly snuggled on the pillow beside Sister, who tried to read. Raleigh lay at the foot of the bed.

The phone rang.

"Hello," a weary Sister answered.

"Mrs. Arnold, it's Walter Lungrun. I seem to be forever calling you late and I apologize."

"That's all right."

"I hope I will be able to help in some small way. I know the coroner and I will get the report but more importantly, if you'll take me to the place where you found Fontaine I might be able to, well—help."

"Thank you, Walter."

"The earlier the better. Might I meet you at six-thirty in the morning?"

"Of course."

CHAPTER 37

Uncle Yancy, Grace, and Patsy had been the first foxes to the hog's back. Yancy waited until Shaker blew in all the hounds. With a split pack he wisely didn't show his face but as he heard the one hound group swing around, he popped out of the hidden entrance under the big walnut. His nieces followed.

They crept toward the hog's back, not even stopping to hide themselves as the remainder of the field rode on the farm road.

As a few humans stood on the meadow, the hog's back between them and the foxes, Yancy remained in the woods. Although Shaker was there, he didn't trust Dragon, the hound that broke off from Cora and the main pack, taking young entry with him. By then, one o'clock, the scent had risen so that a mounted human could smell it but scent was safely over hounds' heads. Still, why take a chance.

The three reds waited. The ambulance roared down the rutted path. Then came the squad car. They strained to catch part of the conversation. It wasn't until Reynard was hoisted up by the sheriff that they realized their brother, Yancy's nephew, had been murdered.

Yancy raised his head as St. Just circled the meadow. The crow didn't see the foxes. But Yancy knew St. Just was in some way responsible for this dolorous occasion.

Finally the humans, hounds, and horses left. The sheriff put Reynard in a plastic bag, placing him in the back of the squad car.

Patsy ran to find Target and Charlene. She was surprised to discover Butch and his family loping over the meadows to help. The outright killing of a fox outraged all foxes.

Throughout the night under the noctilucent clouds, the foxes moved in circles. Inky, down a ravine about a mile and a half from the hog's back, found a rope—not just any rope but a special rope for bringing down steers at full tilt. The strands, braided, were impregnated with wax.

By the time she returned at sunrise, everyone had gathered again at the jump. The foxes didn't need to see the sun to know it was up despite low Prussian blue clouds.

"I found a rope in the rock ravine. Hoofprints, too."

Buster, who had climbed one of the trees to the side of the hog's-back jump, said, *"Did the humans find the marks on the tree? High. High enough to catch Gunpowder."*

"Yes," Yancy replied. *"The sheriff and his people found the marks on the bark, slight but perceptible. They performed the basics but they missed a lot. They missed the hoofprints along the fence line on the woods side."*

"Could have been one of the whips coming in to fetch

hounds." Target, sorrowful at the loss of his handsome son, could still think clearly.

"Yes, but it could have been his murderer, too," Charlene, eyes filling with tears, added.

"What a pity we were stuck at the walnut tree!" Yancy yipped. *"If nothing else, we could have smelled which horse it was or even caught sight of the killer. That split pack cost us dearly."*

"Clever. One doesn't expect a human to be that clever. Almost foxlike," Butch murmured. *"And you're sure the last time you saw Reynard was day before yesterday?"* he asked Target again.

They'd gone over it again, everything they'd initially said to one another when they gathered at the jump yesterday. Everyone was tired, footsore, and depressed.

The only thing new was the rope.

"I have an idea," Inky said in a low, respectful voice. Her elders turned to her. *"If someone will come with me to the kennel tonight maybe we can talk to some of the hounds and tell them what we've found. Next hunt we can agree to go there."*

"Dumb," was all Grace said.

"You underestimate hounds, Gracie. You'll pay for that someday," Yancy corrected her.

"I'll go with Inky," Aunt Netty volunteered. *"Cora has sense. I can talk to her. I think Archie will listen, too."*

"What if Raleigh's out?" Comet wondered.

"Raleigh's main concern is Sister Jane. It's the damn cat I worry about." Target grimaced.

"She's too spoiled and fat to chase us." Patsy sniffed.

"She's not too fat to scream at the top of her lungs and get the kennel in an uproar," Comet said.

Aunt Netty's tail waved to and fro slightly. *"Well, I'm willing to chance it. Reynard must be avenged. Only a coward shoots a fox and only a cad would use the carcass as a drag."*

"*Hear, hear,*" the others agreed.

"*That Raleigh is fast,*" Charlene warned, "*if he has a mind to chase you.*"

"*The only animal faster than myself is a cheetah,*" Netty boasted.

"*Well, I wasn't thinking of you exactly. I was thinking of Inky. No offense, Inky, but I don't know how fast you are.*"

"*Not as fast as Aunt Netty.*" She called the red "Aunt," which was what all the young animals called her. "*But I can climb a tree if I have to.*"

A low flutter hushed them. Athena glided down, tail used as a brake, to sit on the top railroad tie of the hog's back. "*I'm very sorry,*" she said swiveling her head to the reds. "*St. Just is behind this. Whoever killed Reynard, he led them straight to him.*"

"*Leave St. Just to me.*" Target crouched low, baring his fangs.

The others agreed that they would.

"*When will the hunt meet at this fixture again?*" Comet asked. His gray fur, soft as the clouds, lightened a bit.

"*Not for another two weeks,*" Yancy said. "*The only way the hounds can get to the rope is if someone bolts during hound walk.*"

"*That's a big risk for them. Ratshot in the rear if they keep going.*" Charlene frowned. "*What are we to do?*"

Patsy and Grace said at the same time, "*Bring the rope here.*"

"*No,*" Aunt Netty sharply replied. "*The humans need to find the rope where it was dropped or thrown. That will tell them where the human killer was. They must be led to the rope. As it is, by the time we get them there the tracks could be gone, especially if it rains.*"

"*We need Raleigh.*"

"*Sister, Shaker, and Doug may not follow Raleigh,*" Grace said to Comet, who'd proposed the idea.

"If he goes on hound walk, which he often does, he can help convince the humans. If a hound bolts, even a hound as respected as Cora or Archie, the humans will crack the whip and then finally use ratshot. That's their job. They'll think the pack is going to hell. If Raleigh makes a commotion and the hounds honor him, I think the humans will follow. We have to try it, as it's our only hope." Yancy listened. *"Is it settled then?"*

"Yes. We'll go tonight."

The foxes and Athena silently melted into the forest about an hour before Sister, Shaker, Walter, and Doug emerged on the other side of the meadow. They reached the jump in a few minutes, peering into the woods as a twig crackled.

They combed the scene. The sheriff and his deputies trained in crime detection were good but they weren't hunters or country people.

"There are so many hoofprints here." Walter ran his fingers through his blond hair.

"Let's divide up. Walter and Shaker head south down the fence line, one on either side. Doug and I will head north. Shaker, give a toot, I will, too." Sister always carried an extra horn, a lesson learned when Shaker fell hard from his horse years ago, squashing the bell of his horn.

Twenty minutes later Doug, on the forest side of the fence line, found tracks. "Look."

Sister climbed over the fence, dropped to her hands and knees. "Yes. Could have been a whip coming in. Betty, maybe. These look like number one shoes, smallish feet. Could be Arts." She mentioned the other popular shoe.

"Not a quarter horse. Not round enough." Doug, too, was on his knees. "God, Sister, that's half the horses in the hunt field. There were horses yesterday we'd never seen before."

"I know. I know." She stood up, put the horn to her lips, and let out a steady, one-note blast. The hounds heard it, two and a half miles away. They replied, which sounded faint and far away on this cool, overcast morning. "Good hounds." Sister smiled weakly, for she remained terribly distressed.

Doug leaned against the fence. "You've bred them. They can hold their own against any pack." A touch of pride crept into his light baritone.

Walter and Shaker joined them within seven minutes.

"What took you so long?" Doug asked.

"We were clipping right along." Shaker hunkered down. "Ah. Number one."

"Maybe Arts," Sister said.

"No. Number one." Shaker stood back up. "If only there'd been a bar shoe or a weighted shoe, a little dog to the inside. Number one. Standard. Well. Let's follow it."

"It might not be the killer," Sister calmly said.

"No. But then again it might." Shaker put his head down and followed the tracks over the fallen leaves. The pine needles carpeting the earth nearly threw them off, but they picked up the tracks again once out of the pine stand.

They lost them at the flat-rock outcropping and even though they each took a different direction off the flat rocks, they were soon brought up short by a tremendous thunderclap overhead. With no warning the heavens opened. Cascading heavy rain drenched them to the bone.

By the time the four reached the stable they were all shivering. The tack room, toasty, warmed them as Sister made a fresh pot of coffee on the hot plate. She offered clothing—she'd kept shirts and sweatshirts around for just such a purpose—but the men stood by the gas stove. Slowly they began to thaw out and dry out.

"See the body?" Shaker asked.

"Yes. I went down to the morgue." Walter's eyebrows furrowed for an instant. "The bruises on his left side were apparent. He'd been hit cleanly in the chest. Right through the heart, I would say. Apart from whatever emotions he felt at the fall I'd guess his death was swift. I suppose that's a kind of mercy.

Can't jump to conclusions. I'll have to wait for the coroner's report. Except whoever shot him was a good shot. Dead-on." He realized his pun. "Sorry."

"You know I never liked that son of a bitch, so I can't pretend I'm sorry." Shaker opened a small cigar box, offering the men a smoke.

"I'll take one. I need something soothing." Sister reached in, grabbing a thin cigar.

Shaker cut the end for her with his round cutter, then held a flame. As she inhaled the end glowed scarlet and gold and he said, "Funniest damn thing, though. I would have bet you dollars to doughnuts that Crawford would be murdered. Not Fontaine."

"Countenancing murder, are you?" She closed her eyes gratefully as the mild yet complex tastes reached her tongue and throat.

"No. But Crawford stirs up hornets' nests. Fontaine"—he shrugged—"lightweight."

"A crazed husband?" Doug offered.

"Hell, no. By the time he got at them the husbands were bored." Shaker roared with laughter.

"If you say so." Sister exhaled, knowing what the others did not—that Fontaine had had a fling with Shaker's wife before she left.

"Business?" Walter asked.

"Worthless," Shaker resolutely replied.

"Better find out who he owes money to, then." Doug turned his back toward the stove. His pants stuck to his muscled legs.

"Half the county. I can tell you that." Sister took off her boots, her wet socks, too.

"I can see it now: 'Murder among the hunt set.' 'Galloping revenge.' How about 'Toff goes to ground'?" Shaker smiled slyly and the others couldn't help it; they smiled, too.

"The papers and TV stations will have a field day. Paper ought to be delivered by now." Walter sipped the coffee, glad for its warmth. "I expect there will be a lot of questions at the hospital today."

"Walter, you were kind to come out here this morning."

"Sister Jane, I will help in any way I can."

"Smart killer, I'd say. Drawing off the young entry like that. Had to be a real hunting man." Shaker puffed contentedly.

"He'll forget something, something so small. . . . They always do, you know." Sister half believed what she said. Mostly she hoped it was true.

CHAPTER 38

The morning after Fontaine was killed, while Sister, Shaker, Doug, and Walter investigated the hog's-back jump, Crawford Howard nicked himself shaving. Normally, this slip would have brought forth a torrent of vituperation: at the razor, at the shaving cream, at the lighting, and lastly at himself.

This morning he kept whistling. Fontaine was truly totally dead. He'd called last night to offer his services to Sheriff Sidell and to make certain that swaggering ass, Fontaine Buruss, really was gone, his temperature at least forty degrees below normal. If only that insufferable oaf weren't in the cooler, Crawford would have the merriment of watching him go into rigor mortis. Let the funeral director deal with that.

He wondered how to handle Martha. Sensitive, attached to Fontaine, she would be weepy for days, perhaps weeks. She'd sobbed when Sister made the announcement. Crawford put his arm around her, offering solace.

How he kept himself from gloating even he didn't know. He congratulated himself on his discipline.

Washing the white shaving cream off his face, patting his cheeks dry, he scrutinized himself in the mirror. Thanks to a discreet and gifted plastic surgeon in New York City he looked maybe forty-five, not the fifty-four he was. His hairline had receded a bit but other than that, he looked good. He was getting bored with the mustache and beard. Too artsy. He thought he'd make an appointment at the barber's to get the beard shaved off. He'd softened a bit but he'd put down his money at the gym, arriving four days a week at seven to work with a personal trainer.

He had envied Fontaine, his luxurious mane of hair and his trim waistline. Fontaine kept in splendid condition, burning the calories in bed no doubt.

Ah, but he was dead now. Dead. Dead. Dead. Crawford had never realized what a solid sound that word had. Deadwood. Dead honest. Deadbeat. Dead. He began to enjoy the word. It wasn't far from "deed." Was being dead a deed? Was being dead a state of being, which English seemed to suggest, or was dead no being at all, just a linguistic twist?

Dead.

Well, he wouldn't be dead for many a year. His doctors told him that.

He'd win his ex-wife back. He didn't think of her as an ex but merely as a woman he possessed who had slipped out of his pocket. He loved Martha but he possessed her. A man had to own many things in order to be important and a good-looking woman was one of those things. Children, of course, were optional.

She'd want to stay on at the office until Sorrel Buruss decided what to do with the business. Martha was uncommonly loyal. Then he'd steer her toward home again. A pair of diamond spray earrings from Tiffany would help.

The best thing about Fontaine's untimely demise, untimely

for Fontaine, was that now Crawford would be joint-master of the Jefferson Hunt. Sister really had no choice.

He'd been reading about hounds. He'd wait but in good time he'd suggest an infusion of July blood and perhaps some Dumfriesshire, also. After all, he could read a pedigree as well as any other person. Top line, tail line. How simple.

Joint-master. About time, too.

CHAPTER 39

Given the jolt of the day, Cody spent that night at her parents' home. Bobby spent half the night on one phone line while Betty was on the other.

Cody imagined the county intersected with a series of actual lines and they'd glow when in use. Finally the entire country would be pulsating with talk.

She and Jen sat in the kitchen eating fruit while overhearing Mom and Dad.

"Any ideas?" Cody asked.

"No. He didn't look bad, did he? Asleep except for the hole in his coat. I've never seen a dead person before." Jennifer took the clinical approach. "I was with the field but I could see he didn't look slimy."

"Fresh is better than nonfresh."

Jennifer sang. "The worms crawl in, the worms crawl out, and I'll play pinochle on your snout."

"That's compassionate." Her older sister peeled back an orange, tossing the rind at Jennifer.

"He was old."

"Not as old as Mom and Dad. Early forties, I think."

"Forty is old." Jennifer bit into an apple. "I'll never live to be forty."

"Bullshit. We'll live way beyond that. Don't give me this dying young crap. James Dean. Kurt Cobain. Elvis."

"Elvis was old."

"Forty-two. I don't exactly get Elvis."

"See. You have to be old to get him. Like Nine Inch Nails. Old."

"They're not old."

"Yeah they are. Another decade. What matters is what's happening right this minute. The eternal present."

"Have you been reading self-help books? That doesn't sound like something you'd say, Jennifer."

"The therapy sessions are warping my mind."

"Not enough." She sighed. "So you have no compassion for Fontaine Buruss?"

"All he wanted was for someone to slob his knob. Yuck."

Cody laughed and Jennifer laughed, too. Fontaine, driven by sex, gravitated toward a female as she lurched out of puberty. Maybe he didn't sleep with underage girls and maybe he did—who knew? Or if they did, they weren't talking—but any sign of sexual maturity captivated him. He was handsome. Women are fools for handsome men.

Betty called from the next room, her small office off the kitchen also called the recipe room, since she kept file after file of recipes. "Keep it down. How will it sound in the background if you two are whooping it up?"

"Yes, Mother," they both said.

"Who are you calling now?" Cody asked.

"Aunt Olivia."

"Mom, she lives in Chicago." Jennifer giggled.

"She grew up with Fontaine. She'll want to know."

"Is there anyone you haven't called? What about the bag boy down at Kroger's?" Cody teased her.

"You two are taking this shock rather well." Betty strode out of her office.

"Shit happens." Jennifer burst out laughing again.

Betty's hand flew to the space between her breasts. "Jennifer."

"Mom, it's not like he was my best friend. And he didn't look so bad dead."

She walked across the kitchen floor, her slippers barely making a sound, opened the refrigerator, taking out a soda.

"Better take two. You'll be thirsty from all that talking," Cody advised.

"And what do you think of all this?"

"I don't know." Cody grew somber. "I got along with him." This was an understatement but since her family had no idea of her affair, they couldn't appreciate her approach. "Once you knew what he was, he was easy. That's how I see it."

"And that's how most women saw it." Betty popped open the can. "But murder?"

"Yeah, well." Jennifer suddenly darkened.

"Guess he pissed the wrong person off." Cody tidied up her pile of orange parts.

"What if it wasn't personal? You're assuming it is. What if this is some nutcase who is opposed to hunting?"

"In Virginia. Mom." Jennifer rolled her eyes.

"Pretty farfetched." Cody supported her sister.

"Well, serial killers are around us. This could be some person's sick idea of power. Random killings in the country. It happens. No place is ever safe from that kind of sickness now. People kill to kill."

"Bet he owed somebody money." Jennifer had a pedestrian worldview so at odds with her heavenly beauty.

"He did owe money." Betty sat down with her girls. "Cody, you used to see him at the barn. Weren't you trying out that horse—uh . . ."

"Keepsake."

"That's the one. Ever notice anything off the mark?"

"He didn't talk business with me. If anyone had good reason to kill Fontaine, apart from someone he owed money to, it would be his wife, don't you think?"

"She'd never!" Betty's voice grew loud.

"I didn't say she did, only that she had more reason than anyone. That is, if your soon-to-strike-again serial killer idea is wrong," Cody replied.

"I wouldn't laugh about that. There are serial killers in Virginia. There are too many unsolved murders." Betty raised her voice. "And that's the thing, Cody, that's just the thing. How in the hell did Fontaine get separated from the field to follow a splinter group of the pack? It doesn't make any sense."

CHAPTER 40

November resembles a curveball. Just when you think you know where the ball will go over the plate it shifts on you and you're swinging wind.

The rain morphed into tiny ice bits clicking on windowpanes; cars skidded off roads. Inky and Aunt Netty met at the base of Hangman's Ridge. They trotted to the kennels, a half-mile distance but seeming much farther in the biting weather.

"No hound will show his face in this. They're curled up in deep straw." Netty thought they were spoiled.

When Sister built the main building out of cinder blocks she had dropped fluffy insulation in each row before the next row was laid over it. The result was a structure that hounds couldn't chew to pieces when bored yet one that stayed cool in summer and warm in winter. Then, too, hounds threw off a lot of body heat, making the sleeping quarters toasty.

"We won't need to worry about Raleigh and Golly. They'll be in the big house." Inky squinted through the sleet. *"She takes good care of her pets."*

Aunt Netty said, *"Before you were born and the blizzards hit, she put on her snowshoes and fed us."*

"Don't most masters feed their foxes if the weather is bad?"

"Some do. Some don't. Some believe that a fox has to survive nature's tantrums. Others believe a little help now and then is a good thing." Netty paused. The kennel loomed up ahead. *"Might as well go right up to the chain-link fence and bark."* She trotted up. *"Yoo-hoo. Cora. Archie."*

No one stirred inside.

"Do you mind if I try?" Inky politely asked.

"Go right ahead."

"Diana. Diana, it's Inky."

They heard a few grumbles back in the bitch section of the kennel and then the magnetic door flap went *whap as* Diana, head down, pushed through. The lovely tricolor, lots of black on her saddle, hurried to the fence. She was surprised to see Aunt Netty.

"Diana, this is Aunt Netty."

"Golly," the hound gushed, *"I've been on your line but I never thought I would see you."*

Aunt Netty, pleased, replied, *"I know a trick or two."*

"What are you all doing out on a filthy night like this?"

"Diana, we need your help." Inky came straight to the point. *"Reynard, Netty's nephew, was shot, then used as a drag to split the pack."*

"That's how—" Diana hoped Dragon wouldn't get into more trouble, since he'd led the split faction.

Netty interrupted, her sharp features ablaze, sleet stinging her face. *"We have only one clue."*

"What?"

"A rope left in the ravine to the northeast of the hog's-back jump. This weather will blot out any hoofprints but the rope should still be there. If we help you, do you think you can get the pack to go there on hound walk?"

"The humans will never stand for it. If we bolt, I mean."

"I think I have a way." Netty raised her voice, as the sleet intensified. *"Since Raleigh goes on hound walk you must tell him this plan. His cooperation is the key."*

Diana listened gravely as Netty mapped out her idea to be used on the first clear day.

After the sleek red finished, Diana blinked her eyes. *"I'll talk to the others."*

"Thank you." Inky smiled.

"Diana, has anyone told you you're much like your grandmother, Destry?" Before Diana could answer *"No,"* Netty chortled. *"Now, that was a hound."*

The foxes melted into the darkness as Diana walked back to the kennel. She was young. Who would listen to her? But she hadn't put a paw wrong since cubbing began. She decided to whisper to Cora while the others slept. If Cora listened, it meant two things. First, they might get the humans to the rope. Second, she had earned the respect of the pack's strike hound.

She softly picked her way through the sleeping girls, as Sister called them, to snuggle next to the hard-muscled, lightning-fast Cora.

"Cora," Diana whispered low. *"There's a rope in the ravine. It might have something to do with Fontaine's murder. We need to get the humans to it. Aunt Netty has a plan."*

At the sound of Aunt Netty's name Cora's eyes opened wide. Diana had her full attention.

CHAPTER 41

Puffs of breath rolled out of Sister's, Shaker's, and Doug's mouths like cartoon balloons. Each carried a knob-end whip with a long eight-plaited thong. A twelve-plaited thong existed but it was so expensive, almost two hundred dollars for twelve feet, that few staff members were fortunate enough to own one. At the end of the thong a brightly colored thin popper dangled.

The popper, if one were to be perfectly perfect, should be the same color as the hunt's colors. Made in Italy, woven of silk, long poppers could be ordered from Fennell's Tack Shop in Lexington, Kentucky, for 95 cents. Shorter ones were sold by Horse Country in Warrenton for about $1.25.

In desperation people had been known to use shoelaces for poppers, L.L. Bean duck boot laces proving the most reliable.

The knob-end whips, formed from ash, blackthorn, or even apple wood, were generally used only by staff members for walking hounds. A good knob-end was passed down from generation to generation, as was a good antler-handle formal hunt whip.

The three humans gathered in front of the kennel paid no mind to their knob-ends. Wearing down vests, thermal underwear, and other secrets of keeping warm at sunrise, they discussed who to take and who to leave in the kennel. They were as fooled by the weather, that sudden sharp turndown, as they were stunned by Fontaine's murder.

Raleigh, called aside by Cora, listened intently.

Golly, lounging in the house kitchen, thought Raleigh loony tunes to roar out on a frosty morning, thanks to last night's odd weather. She ate whatever crumbs were scattered on the countertops, then paraded into the pantry, where she jumped onto a shelf, throwing down dish towels until she succeeded in making a nest to her specifications in the remaining red-and-white-striped dish towels. Golly was very particular.

"Let's just take them all, Shaker. They've been penned up a full day because of the weather. Doug can take the right; I'll take the left. If our young group bolts, I think we can get them back. The longer we leave them in the kennel, the rowdier they'll be."

"There is that." He pulled his lad's cap further down on his head. "I've my doubts about this Dragon. Pity he's so handsome."

"Took his father two years to mature and settle down. Don't give up on him yet." She thought to herself that if he didn't learn his lessons she would couple him to Archie. Archie did not suffer fools gladly.

"Ready?" Shaker asked Doug.

"Yes." Doug pulled up his turtleneck.

"Okay, then." Shaker opened the draw run gate and out they ran, invigorated by the cold and filled with purpose.

"I'll go up front." Raleigh danced around.

They walked in good order through the hickory-lined back lane that spilled out onto the low meadows, long grasses mixed with lespedeza, bent over by the frost and last night's battering. As the sun rose each blade reflected its rays, thousands upon thousands of tiny rainbows.

Athena silently flew along the edge of the meadow, then disappeared into the woods.

She landed in the substantial pin oak by Netty's den. *"They've just plowed into the meadow at the bottom of Hangman's Ridge."*

Netty stuck her head out of her front entrance. *"Thank you, Athena. I'll be on my way."*

"You're not telling Target, I take it. Wise. Almost owl-like." A low hoot rumbled from the enormous bird.

"He's too emotional. And if St. Just shadows us—you never know about St. Just—Target might forget our mission."

"I'll rouse Inky."

"I've underestimated grays. She's very bright."

Athena blinked that she agreed, then spread her wings, lifting off, moving quietly between the trees, then tilting upward to skim the tops.

As Netty hurried to her rendezvous spot with Inky, the humans and hounds reached the far edge of the ridge. A curious geological formation, with gneiss and quartz underneath, ancient rocks had been folded into an eight-hundred-foot-high ridge, quite flat on the top but blunt on the northern end as though someone had cut the end off with a cake knife. The other three sides tapered down to the plain. The northern face was a sheer drop.

Hunt staff's intent was to walk around the edges of the large meadow and then go back to the kennel, a distance of around two and a half miles at the most. A brisk beginning to the day for canine and human.

Fontaine's coop, the replaced boards blacker than the faded boards, separated the woods from this meadow.

For a moment the humans didn't notice that Aunt Netty and Inky sat on top of the coop.

Raleigh called out, *"One, two, three!"*

Every hound lifted up his or her head, singing, *"Do you ken John Peel."*

Netty warbled, *"At the break of day."* Then hopped off the coop.

Sister said, "We're foxhunters, aren't we?"

Shaker took off his cap, swinging it once around his head in a circle. "She's in there. She's in there." He gave a little whoop.

The hounds trotted to the coop, each one leaping over. Sister, Shaker, and Doug followed.

Raleigh stayed up with Cora. His blinding speed would be useful if any hound's discipline began to waver. Raleigh would run the hound down, bump him hard, and stand over him. If that didn't work, he'd sink white fangs into a juicy hip. He didn't think it would come to that.

Inky and Netty ran at a steady speed, occasionally glancing over their shoulders. They reached the other side of the woods in fifteen minutes. Cora and Archie were behind them with the humans far in the rear. At the hog's-back jump leading onto the high meadows, the two vixens swerved left, hugging the fence line. The hounds reached it about three minutes later, moving single file along the fence. Even though most of the leaves had come down in the winds and sleet, the undergrowth hadn't died off. The humans fought their way through except for Sister, who trotted along the meadow side of the fence line in case her hounds swerved back out.

Instead they swerved deeper into the woods. She climbed over, fanning back to the left. Sister wasn't as fast on foot as she used to be but her powers of endurance were superb. Shaker stayed as close to his hounds as he could, slipping and sliding on the slick, icy leaves and pine needles. Doug swung out on the right once the hounds cut off the fence line.

They pushed on for another mile, perhaps more. The humans, tired, had slowed to a jog.

Archie yelled out, *"Slow down. Slow down. They're falling behind."*

The pack slowed to a fast walk. Netty and Inky stayed in sight range just ahead.

Dragon bolted but before he passed Cora, Raleigh hit him

so hard he rolled over three times. The Doberman seized the young hound's throat, scaring the crap out of him.

Raleigh let go. *"You'll learn to be a team player or I'll rip your useless throat out."*

Tail between his legs, Dragon circled around to the back of the pack.

Panting, Sister was brought up short at the ravine, a fold in the land but a deep one. The hounds had stopped at the edge, too. The humans caught up just as Inky and Aunt Netty stopped at the rope.

"Here it is! Good job," Netty encouraged Cora. *"We'll leave you here."*

"See you in the hunt field," Cora replied.

Inky looked for Diana, whose tail was up, her nose to the ground, then scampered off in the direction opposite Netty.

As Sister, Shaker, and Doug skidded, slipped, and slid down the ravine, she said, "Never saw anything like that in my life."

"Me neither." Shaker lurched forward, grabbing a tree branch or he would have been pitched head over heels.

"You okay?" Doug asked. He moved down the side diagonally.

"Yes." Shaker prudently decided to descend the way Doug was.

Sister, too, followed suit.

At the bottom of the ravine the hounds patiently waited.

Cora, Archie, and Diana sat around the rope, the other hounds behind them. Raleigh had joined Sister. If she fell, Raleigh thought he could help her up.

Doug reached the spot first. "Here!" He pointed.

Shaker, at last at the bottom, knelt down. "Damn fine rope." He looked up at his employer and friend. "Thinking what I'm thinking?"

"Uh-huh."

"Should we leave it here and bring Sidell out?" Doug sensibly asked.

"No. I'll tell you why. The rain and sleet washed out any prints. We're lucky this is still here—not dragged off by an animal or dragged off by the killer. Sooner or later he'll realize he dropped it."

"I don't think he dropped it." Doug, sweating from the long run, unzipped the front of his jacket. "This ravine is a shortcut back toward Soldier Road. Or up to the high meadow, depending on the direction you're moving. Right?"

"Yeah." Shaker ran his large hand over his chin. Vexed, he hated not having an answer.

"I think our killer came back through here, tossed the rope, and rejoined the hunt. He had to have hidden the rope somewhere in these woods or somewhere close by, cut out of the hunt, picked it up, tied it to the tree, and then when the deed was done, ridden down through here and tossed it."

"He'd have to be a pretty good rider." Shaker held his hand under his jaw as though holding back his words.

Doug took the rope from Sister's hand as she picked it up. "Can't buy a rope like this in Virginia. This is the real deal."

"What do you mean?" Sister asked.

"Belongs to a calf roper or a steer roper. Rodeo. They use special ropes, special twists in the braid. Who would have a rope like this?"

"Nobody in our hunt field rodeos—I mean willingly." Sister had to laugh, because a few people performed unintentional bronc riding out there.

"Let's walk out. Head down farther and climb out the west side. It's easier," Doug suggested, since a massive rock face with an overhang and ledge loomed before them.

"Cora. Archie, D-puppies, and the children. You may be the best pack of hounds in Virginia. You're certainly the only detective pack." Shaker praised his charges.

"Thank you," they cried in unison.

"And you were impressive." Sister petted Raleigh. "Never saw anything like it. The hounds and Raleigh stayed behind those foxes at a steady pace."

"The foxes knew." Shaker's voice rang with conviction.

"Seemed to." Doug shook his head.

As their bodies recovered from the run the cold set in. They zipped up their coats while sliding down in the bottom of the ravine, staying to the west of the creek running through it.

"Whoever did this sure knows the territory," Doug said.

"That eliminates eighty percent of the hunt field." Sister laughed. "They're so busy showing off for one another they don't look where they're going. God help them if they ever have to get back on their own."

"Be easy to slip off. Especially during opening hunt. Clever. Damnably clever."

Doug walked beside Shaker, since the hounds behaved impeccably. "I can't figure out how whoever it is got Fontaine to go with him."

"Fontaine could have stopped to go to the bathroom." Sister thought Fontaine was doing more of that lately, but then men did as they got on in years. He wasn't that old, though.

"He stopped and another fellow stopped with him. Then led him off? That sort of thing?" Shaker breathed out two straight lines of mist from his nostrils.

"Partly. But Fontaine would come back to the main group. He wouldn't get sidetracked by the splinter pack."

"We were moving fast that day. His hearing wasn't as good as yours." Doug paused. "Course, no one hears as good as you. You're uncanny . . . part fox." He smiled at Sister. "Sounds bounce around out here. He might have followed the hounds that sounded the closest. He might not have heard the main pack. We really were flying. I mean, people ran out of horse the first hour. I watched them pull out," Doug remarked.

"When did you have time to watch the field?" Shaker grumbled.

"When I reached Soldier Road. We were running so hard I headed straight for the road. I hoped I could turn the pack but they turned on their own. Almost one hundred eighty degrees. But they were heading back before that because I passed riders on the farm road early on. The pace was scorching."

"Maybe Fontaine turned back," Shaker said.

"Gunsmoke. No way." Sister shook her head.

"He'll be fine," Doug said. "Had to call the vet this morning about Trinkle. Asked about Gunsmoke."

Trinkle was a bitch with uterus problems. She was going to have to be spayed, a pity, as she had great bloodlines and was a good hound in her own right.

"Maybe Fontaine stopped to help someone. Someone good-looking," Shaker added.

"That's the best theory yet," Sister agreed. "And if he or whoever stopped in the woods, they wouldn't be that easy to see. For one thing he wore that gorgeous black weaselbelly with the white vest. Made for him in Ireland. God, he always was one of the best-turned-out men in the hunt field. If he'd been in scarlet, he might not have slipped away so easily."

"Huh." Shaker was considering all this as they climbed upward.

"If you want to kill someone and you don't want to get caught, I guess you plan for years or you plan pretty intensely and wait for the wind to blow in your favor. I don't know if things had turned out differently, if the young entry hadn't bolted onto that drag, that Fontaine would be alive. But whoever did it was waiting. The drag was brilliant. If it didn't work, he would have tried later. Maybe something in the hunt field. Maybe something somewhere else. This strikes me as planned but still trusting to luck. That's what I'm trying to say."

"Sister, what you're trying to say is our killer is one bold son of a bitch." Shaker, breathing hard, was relieved to finally reach the top of the ravine.

They were at the back side of the meadows surrounding Hangman's Ridge. The ridge was a quarter of a mile in front of them to the west. They'd made a lopsided semicircle around it. Soldier Road was to their right, the bridge spanning the ravine and the creek immediately behind them. This early in the morning, the roads icy, there was no traffic.

"Only a mile back home." Shaker smiled, as he intended to stay in the meadow. The walking would be much easier.

"I suppose Ben Sidell will question everyone that hunted. Someone is bound to have seen Fontaine stop."

"Maybe," Doug answered Sister.

"You know last hunt season I noticed he'd stop to relieve himself. Maybe he was getting prostate problems. I suppose they can occur at about any time."

"Wouldn't know." Doug laughed.

"You will." Shaker laughed right back. "Then they go up in there with a Roto-Rooter."

"Ah, the indignities of age." She laughed along with them.

"But not there, Sister, not there." Shaker laughed even harder.

"Honey, that's where your indignities begin."

They laughed the whole way back to the kennel, keeping in this vein.

Later when Sister walked back in the kitchen, Raleigh, who knew where lazy Golly would be, snuck up on her and blew in her ear.

"P-s-s-t," she spat.

"Scares the pee right out of me." Raleigh giggled, then told the cat everything as Sister called the sheriff.

"You knew about this. You left me knowing what the foxes and the hounds were going to do?" The cat was desolate.

"You snooze, you lose."

"I'll get you for this, Raleigh Arnold. I'll get you if it's the last thing I do!"

CHAPTER 42

That same evening the clouds lifted, creating an odd sight: dark cumulus, Prussian blue overhead, with a thin band of turquoise twilight underneath.

Everyone on the farm was behind on their chores because of the long hound walk and the sheriff coming to pick up the rope. He asked questions about everything, which they expected. No doubt he would check today's reports with Saturday's, searching for discrepancies or new information. No one could accuse him of not being thorough.

Just as Sister and Doug were bedding down the horses they heard a trailer rumble down the drive.

Raleigh hurried outside, leaving Golly inside. He let out a perfunctory bark, then shut up. Golly was so upset at missing events she spent the remainder of the day following Raleigh around, to his amusement, not to hers.

"I'll see who it is." Sister slid back the heavy metal stall door, a mesh to allow cooling breezes in the summer.

In winter Doug or Sister could throw on an extra blanket. Keeping a horse cool in summer's oppressive heat proved far more difficult than keeping them warm in winter.

The thin band of turquoise above the mountains slowly turned purple.

Sorrel Buruss cut the motor on the Chevy dually truck and

stepped out into the cool air. "Sister, will you take Gunpowder and Keepsake? I should have called but I don't know. I can't seem to keep anything straight in my head and I know Fontaine would want the horses well cared for and used. They'll sit around in the barn and that's not right."

"Sorrel." Sister put her arm around the pretty woman's shoulders. "I'll give them the best of care. We'll hunt them and when you've had time to think things through if you want to sell them, I will."

"I'd like to donate them to the hunt." Her lower lip trembled.

"Let's wait and see how much money you have left when all is said and done. Okay?"

Sorrel, a well-groomed woman even in grief, cried. She couldn't speak.

"Doug can unload. Come on. Let me get you a cup of coffee or a drink if it's too late for coffee. All right?" As Sorrel nodded her agreement, Sister walked back into the stable. "Doug, will you unload Gunsmoke and Keepsake? We'll be caring for them for a while."

"Sure."

Once in Sister's kitchen, the fire roaring in the huge fireplace, Sorrel relaxed a little. "The funeral is tomorrow and I couldn't stand one more deeply sympathetic condolence. One more person at the door. God, I must be awful. The kids are at Mom's. They're upset but at the same time kind of excited, all the food, flowers, people."

"I often wonder what stays with them. The telling detail. I don't know. I remember a great deal from my childhood and yet when my brother was alive he'd recall the same event not so much in contradiction but with a different emphasis. It used to make me wonder about my mind."

"I gave up on my mind a long time ago." Sorrel half smiled, grateful to be out of the gloom of her own home. "I apologize for just dropping in on you. I could have called. . . . I just went to the barn and pulled those guys out of their stalls. At least I remembered their halters and lead. I have moments when I can't remember anything. I'm moving but I'm not functioning. Does that make sense?"

"Yes." Sister offered her some cookies, then sat down herself.

Raleigh reposed by the fireplace. Golly sat on the kitchen counter.

"I don't know how I'm going to get through tomorrow."

"You will."

"How did you do it? Twice."

"I told myself that the men in my life wouldn't take kindly to a wife or a mother who fell apart in front of God and everybody."

"I guess we just go on—I mean, I don't even know why I'm here. I mean here as in alive. I don't seem to have a purpose. I never did. I had a purpose as a wife and a mother but I can't see anything. I—"

"Sorrel, maybe we don't have a purpose. Maybe we're here to just live. But whatever, right now you go through the motions. The substance of your life may be revealed later."

"You have a purpose." Sorrel's face was so innocent and so open.

"To live."

"You have the hunt club."

Sister smiled. "Yes. I doubt that philosophers or even those people eager to live your life for you would find that much of a purpose but I have Nature, I love God's creation, and this is a way to appreciate it."

"You've lived a fabulous life."

"Well, let's just say I may not have done much good in this life but I haven't done much harm either." She smiled, pushing another cookie at Sorrel. "Eat. I know it's hard but if you don't your blood sugar will go haywire and you'll feel like you're on a roller coaster. I've got some nice cold chicken.

How about a chicken sandwich with lettuce, pumpernickel bread?"

"Yeah!" Golly shouted.

Sister sternly eyed the calico.

"I don't think so, thank you. Board . . . What do I owe you?"

"Nothing. Really."

"Sister Jane, can you think of anyone who would kill Fontaine?"

After a considerable pause Sister said, "I can think of plenty of people who might want to kill him but none who would."

"He lived every single second while he was here." Sorrel smiled ruefully. "I adjusted. I guess you could say my flame didn't burn as bright as Fontaine's."

"No. Your flame burns steadily. It has to, Sorrel; you're a mother. Men can leave. They can leave us flat out. They can die. They can run off with other women or they can show up on their thirty-seventh birthday and declare they want to climb Mount Everest before they're forty. We're tied to the earth. Once the children are grown I suppose we can do those things, too, but how do you break a lifetime of holding back?"

"I never thought of it that way."

"I think a lot. I'm alone much of the time or I'm doing chores. My mind is always on an adventure." She picked up a cookie, putting it in Sorrel's hand. "Okay. You don't have to eat it but look at it. I'm making a sandwich even if you won't eat it. Take it with you."

"There's enough food in my house to keep a brigade full."

"Then I'm making one for myself."

As the older woman buttered the bread she chatted and listened.

Doug knocked on the back door, then came inside. "Horses are fine, Mrs. Buruss. I've turned your trailer around."

"Thank you."

"It's a great trailer," he said admiringly.

"Only the best. You know how he was."

"I'm sorry. I don't know what else to say." His handsome face radiated honesty.

"There isn't anything else you can say. Thank you, Doug."

"Did Sister tell you? We found the rope. We think it's the rope."

Sister turned her silver head to face Doug. "I was getting to that."

Both Sister and Doug explained how they'd found the rope, where they'd found the rope, and what it looked like.

"Sounds like Fontaine's King's rope."

CHAPTER 43

Four hundred and sixty people crammed into the pre-Revolutionary Episcopal Church. Built in 1749, laid brick with white lintels, the unadorned structure sheltered by ancient spruces and hickories exuded an inviting presence. It didn't take a particularly active imagination to envision colonists tying up their horses, doffing their tricornes, or adjusting their Sunday hats if female, to cross the threshold into the vestry.

Every member of Jefferson Hunt attended, many genuinely sorrowful. Crawford, not at all sorrowful, escorted Martha. He walked to the grave site in the churchyard as well, just to make sure the walnut casket would be lowered into the ground.

Martha, keeping her misery in check, wiped her eyes from time to time. Crawford kept his eyes down much of the time.

The Franklins sat together. Jennifer held a lace handkerchief to her eyes, not to dab tears but to hide the laughter. Dean Offendahl, one of her high school boyfriends, in the choir, would wink at her. Betty, outraged, headed straight for Dean once the service was over. A funeral might be a good place to fall in love but it wasn't a good place to flirt. Jennifer, unaware of her mother's mission, walked with Cody and Bobby to chat with Sister, Doug, and Shaker. Together they walked out to the parking lot, a light northerly wind mussing everyone's hair.

They stopped out of respect as the funeral director ushered Sorrel and the kids into the black limousine. Fontaine's sister from Morgantown, West Virginia, and her family followed in the next black limo.

"She's holding up remarkably well," Betty quietly remarked.

"You'd think she'd be glad to get rid of him," Cody said in a low voice.

Doug firmly said, "Cody."

She shrugged.

Sister walked over next to her. "If love were logical, you would be one hundred percent correct but love isn't logical. If it were, no one in their right mind would marry. For all his faults, she loved him. She loved him from the day she met him in college."

"I'm sorry. I didn't mean to be rude."

"I suspect you have mixed emotions yourself."

This terse sentence from Sister cut to the bone. Cody wondered if Sister knew about her affair. Unlike most people, Sister Jane did not feel compelled to tell people what she knew. A slight chill bumped down Cody's spine.

"Would you like to ride with me?" Doug offered, hoping for the chance to talk to Cody alone before the gathering at the Buruss home.

Cody agreed and once the door was closed she blurted out, "God, I'd give anything for a drink right now."

"No."

"I won't, I won't. But funerals make me shaky."

"Cody, did you ever notice a special rope in Fontaine's stable?"

"What do you mean?"

"From out west. King's ropes, I think. Stiff. Used to rope steers and calves."

"No."

"Think hard. Maybe he hung it in the tack room or inside his trailer. You'd notice it, as it's different from the stuff you buy at the co-op."

"No. I'd show up three times a week, saddle up Keepsake, and that was that. In and out."

CHAPTER 44

Alone in bed that night, Sister scribbled on a yellow legal pad. She was reconstructing everything she could remember from the time she first saw Fontaine until he vanished. Next to her was her red leather-bound hunt diary. After each hunt she wrote the events in her diary. Reading about hunts years later delighted her.

She and Raymond used to sit in bed together writing in their respective hunt diaries. He'd fuss at her because she'd use a fountain pen and he was afraid she'd spill ink on the sheets. She never did.

Outside the night was crystal clear as only a November night can be.

Golly rested on the pillow next to her. Sister thought of it as Raymond's pillow. Raleigh curled up in front of the fireplace in the bedroom, the aroma of cured hardwoods filling the room.

The more she thought about opening hunt, the more disturbed she became. Why kill Fontaine in the hunt field? Surely it would have been easier to kill him somewhere else.

The risk in killing a human being when near to a hundred mounted followers as well as foot followers bespoke either boldness or frenzy. Granted, the foot followers remained on Hangman's Ridge with Peter Wheeler. Foot followers almost always camped out at the Hangman's Ridge fixture because of the vistas and because they could eat their breakfasts, drink coffee or roped coffee, and catch up with old friends.

The killer knew all this, of course, but what puzzled her was why take such a chance? It was a hell of a chance. Wouldn't it have been easier to lure Fontaine onto a back country road and shoot him? Or poison him?

On one level she was furious, white-hot with rage, that someone would commit a crime in *her* hunt field.

On another level, she was frightened. The swiftness of the murder, the cool appraisal of the situation, and then the lightning strike, pointed to an exceptionally courageous person.

She'd listened to the arguments and theories from friends. It had to be a foxhunter, one who really knew the sport. Well, that was obvious. Others said it was planned but impromptu, which is what she, Shaker, and Doug pieced together once down in the slippery ravine.

Still, there was an element of elegant revenge. The killer picked the hunt field for an emotional charge. The hunt field meant the world to Fontaine but it must also have meant something for the killer or for the killer and Fontaine together.

She also thought it would decimate her hunt field. What a pity, for the season had promised to be a great one, one of those magical seasons that rolls around every fifteen to twenty years.

She'd canceled Tuesday's hunt since the funeral was Wednesday. Tomorrow the regulars would be out. Saturday would tell the tale because it was an especially good fixture, Beveridge Hundred.

She turned out the light but couldn't sleep. Every time she'd turn Golly would grumble. Finally, she clicked on the light to read *Anna Karenina*. Tolstoy was a bit of a hunting man. Not so good a hunting man as Turgenev, Balzac, or Trollope but still she liked reading those authors who understood and appreciated hunting. Then, too, *Anna Karenina*, complex, shifting, profound, never loosened its grip on her, not from the first day she'd picked it up at age seventeen. Of course, then she hated Karenin. Now she understood him perfectly.

In the stable, snug under their blankets, the horses dozed. Gunsmoke woke with a start. He usually lay flat out and snored. He whinnied.

Lafayette awakened. *"Okay?"*

"Yeah. I keep feeling that rope hitting me."

"I wouldn't think to look for a rope over a jump. Not when hounds are running," Lafayette said.

"It was high."

"When did Fontaine leave the field?"

"He pulled off for a toot after helping Lottie Fisher. He'd pull the stuff out of his jacket, sniff, wait a minute, and then rejoin everyone. People thought he was going to the bathroom. Course, sometimes he did."

"No one called him over?"

"Not exactly. He sat for a minute to catch his breath, too. Hard run. Anyway, I saw Rickyroo in the distance. Doug was ahead of the main pack; then I heard the pack split. Off to the right and behind us I heard hoofbeats. Fontaine turned my head away because he started moving toward the main pack. The horse and rider were behind in the woods but moving fast. I wonder if that person beckoned him? He headed

toward the split pack after that. You could really hear them, too. No one called out to him. I hear better than he does. Did. I could hear the horse in front of me but now way ahead—and the woods were thick. Fontaine was following. I'm certain of that."

"*Weird.*" Lafayette's eyes were closing.

"*I remember one thing before I hit that rope. Behind the fence line, back in the woods, a horse snorted.*"

CHAPTER 45

There's a ghoulish streak in humankind. An airplane crashes in a field. People rush to witness the disaster and be horrified by body parts strewn over a mile or so. Traffic slows at a car accident not simply because a police officer demands it but because drivers and passengers can't resist straining to catch sight of blood and maybe even guts.

Perhaps it's a fascination with death or a secret relief that this time it's not you. Whatever, people are strange in a way other animals are not.

More people arrived at the Beveridge Hundred fixture than had gone to opening hunt. Sister, Shaker, Doug, Betty, and Cody were given their .22 revolvers back Friday night, the evening before the hunt. None of them had fired the shot that killed Fontaine. In fact, none of the guns had been fired at all.

Since Fontaine was killed by a .38, Sheriff Sidell had tested Shaker's .38, as well as Betty's and Cody's, since they were carrying that caliber in a holster under their coats. Those guns hadn't been fired either.

After a short acknowledgment of Fontaine's passing, Sister Jane nodded to Shaker, who cast hounds into an old house ruin at the rear of the big house. Beveridge Hundred, one of the first plantations built after Europeans pushed into the piedmont, had weathered the fluctuations of finance and wars over the centuries. Outbuildings crumbled during bad times, some were rebuilt during the good times, but the big house was kept running come hell or high water—and both had come to Beveridge Hundred.

Hounds poked around the old outbuilding, fanning out until Diana said, *"Here."*

As she was a young hound, normally other hounds would wait for a tried-and-true hound to second the find but Diana had earned the respect of Cora and Archie. They honored her find and within minutes the hounds, huntsman, whips, and field rolled over the sweeping river-bottom meadows of the three-hundred-year-old estate.

The fox executed a large, loopy figure eight, then ran the same territory again in a circle. Sister figured they were on a gray, a distant relative of Butch and family, no doubt.

The loop became tighter and on the third run, now at speed, the fox ducked under a timbered farm bridge to his den. Hounds raced to the den, dug, howled, and celebrated their prowess. The gray was already at another exit just in case the huntsman didn't call the hounds off.

Shaker dismounted, praised his hounds, and blew triumphantly on his horn.

"I put the fox to ground," Dragon bragged.

"We all put the fox to ground." Archie acidly bumped the younger hound, who stumbled.

"I was first. I am the fastest hound in this pack."

"And the most foolish," Dasher chided his brother.

The argument progressed no further, for the air, sparkling,

and the temperature in the mid-forties suggested another fox might be found if they didn't tarry.

Shaker trotted the pack a quarter of a mile away and then cast them back toward the big house. They picked up a line, then dropped it. Picked another and dropped it. Scenting became spotty until a solid squatty hound stopped in his tracks. *"Hey, what's this?"*

Archie inspected. *"Not deer. I vaguely remember this."*

"Bear," Cora said definitively.

"Ah, well, you know the fox scent is evaporating and I don't recall us ever being given a lecture about bear, now, do you?" Archie had a twinkle in his kind, brown eyes.

"Well, then!" Cora's stern waggled a moment and she was off, the whole pack behind her gleefully chasing a bear, gleefully bending the rules because even hounds need to cut a shine now and then.

Doug rode ahead as first whipper-in. Betty rode on the left and Cody on the right. Territory was wide open, rolling hayfields and corn stubble.

The jumps, mostly post and rail or stacked logs, had sunk over the years so even the most timid negotiated them.

On and on they ran under a climbing November sun, pale gold. A thin line of cedars obscured the next field but they soon charged through that, around the edge of freshly planted winter oats and into a manicured woods. Virginians called cleaned-up woods "parked out."

A roar and a shout from Doug did not halt hounds. Shaker pushed his horse harder while Betty rode into him. Sister realized something was unusual. She held up her hand to stop. Behind her those who couldn't control their horses bumped into those who could, which sent curses into the air, looks of reproach, and a few apologies.

A black bear, displeased at the attention, stood on her hind legs. She would have broken the neck of any hound who jumped her or torn the life right out of any who attacked.

"Scum!" she bellowed.

Diana, not a coward but not a fool, stopped, as did most of the other hounds.

"Leave it!" Doug shouted while struggling to keep Rickyroo under control.

"I'm out of here!" Rickyroo reared up.

Doug hung on for dear life as Betty and Outlaw rode up. Outlaw, a brave fellow, had no desire to stay in close proximity to the bear but he held his ground as Betty cracked her whip.

"I'll kill every damn one of you!" the bear threatened.

"Oh my God." Ricky, utterly terrified, bucked, reared, shimmied sideways, and eventually dislodged Doug, who landed flat on his back.

The bear thought this interesting and she lumbered toward Doug, who rolled over, trying to get to his feet.

Hounds gathered by the fallen whip.

"Back off. Back off. We didn't know we were that close!" Archie snarled.

"By the time I'm finished with you you'll never hunt bear again." Her fangs glistened and she snapped her jaws rapidly open and shut, making a clicking sound.

Shaker pulled his .38 but the bear, on all fours, headed toward Doug and he was afraid to fire. He fired overhead, which frightened the hounds, who associated the sound with stop-this-instant. The hounds moved to Shaker except for Archie, Cora, Diana, and Dragon.

Betty squeezed Outlaw hard and the sturdy quarter horse leapt past the fray and came behind Doug as he managed to get to his feet.

"Back off!" Archie growled as the bear stood up again, ready to swipe the horse.

Doug grabbed Betty's outstretched arm and using Outlaw's motion, he put both feet together and bounced once on the ground to swing up behind Betty.

Diana, Cora, and Dragon circled the bear, hoping to confuse her, but she was intelligent as well as angry. She lunged for the horse burdened by two riders and Archie sprang up, grabbing her paw. Cora, Diana, and Dragon struck from behind. Distracted, the bear forgot about Betty, Doug, and Outlaw. She took her free paw and smashed down on Archie's head. He didn't loosen his grip. She bashed him again then threw him off like an old rag doll.

The three other hounds let go as the bear ran off. Shaker, once certain that Doug and Betty were all right, hurried to his anchor hound.

Archie lay on his side, blood pouring from his mouth.

Cora lifted her head and howled, a cry of pure anguish, for she loved old Archie. The other hounds followed their strike hound.

Shaker knelt down, joined by Doug.

"Oh, Archie." Shaker felt for the hound's pulse.

Tears rolled down Betty's face. She'd had no tears for Fontaine when she rode up on him after being called in by Shaker. Perhaps it was shock or perhaps in her mind Fontaine wasn't worth her tears but Archie was.

Shaker lifted the hound, carrying him back to his horse. Archie's broken neck dangled. Hounds ceased crying and obediently followed the huntsman, although the air was filled with sorrow.

Archie was draped in front of Shaker's saddle. He mounted up, holding the hound with his right hand while he held the reins with his left.

He rode up to Sister, who was about five hundred yards away but in the cleared-out woods. She and the field had witnessed everything.

"Ma'am." He could barely speak.

Sister's eyes clouded. "I think we'll call it a day, Shaker."

A field member offered Doug his horse, which was proper. Anytime a staff member loses a horse, a member of the field should always dismount and offer theirs. Although most old-line foxhunters know this, few do it, since staff ride hard.

"Thanks. I'll walk back to the trailers." Doug touched his cap.

As he walked back, head hanging, Doug wiped away his own tears. It wasn't until Beveridge Hundred came into view that he realized he hadn't seen Cody. She'd been clearly in sight even as they barreled through the line of cedars. He'd lost sight of her at the field of winter oats but then there's no reason one whip should see another.

However, the pack ran tight. He didn't think anyone had straggled off.

He asked around as he passed trailers and people untacking their horses. No, she wasn't back yet.

He walked over to Sister. "Cody's not back."

Sister glanced around. She'd been so distraught over Archie's death she hadn't counted her whips or her field.

"Ask Shaker to blow her in."

Doug walked fast now to the hound trailer. Shaker had placed Archie on the front seat of the truck, a towel under him and an old horse blanket over him. Although the hound was dead Shaker somehow felt he had to be covered.

"Cody's not back. Sister wants you to blow for her."

Shaker strode to a small rise, held the horn to his lips, and blew three long, long blasts. It didn't bring Cody but it brought Jennifer.

"I'll go look for her."

"No. Not with the bear out there," Doug commanded her.

Crawford sensed the problem and willingly pitched in. "Let's unhitch my truck; it's four-wheel drive. I think we can get back there."

"We'd better do it," Shaker grimly agreed, as did Sister, who joined in on the hillock.

As the people turned back, Jennifer stayed on the rise. "Hey, wait!"

Cody, walking arm held against her waist, was leading Motorboat, her chestnut. Jennifer ran out to greet her. Doug followed.

"What happened?" Jennifer took Motorboat's reins.

"Bear ran right by us. Scared the shit out of Motorboat and me, too. I hit the ground." She sheepishly grinned.

"Thank God that's all," Sister whispered to herself.

St. Just, perched on top of the stable weather vane, said nothing. He was making a point of shadowing the hunt.

A silent pack of hounds rode back to the kennels.

Finally Cora said, *"There will never be another Archie."* She paused. *"We must have an anchor hound. It's a hard position to play, kind of like a catcher in baseball. Not much glory. A lot of work and you've got to know the batters."*

No one spoke.

Later as the hounds bedded down, curling up with one another, Cora filled the stillness. Every hound's head lifted as she said, *"Diana. You'll learn as you go."*

CHAPTER 46

A murdered man, a bear, Cody's broken arm, and one fine hound killed . . . Jefferson Hunts were becoming a little too exciting. The next Saturday's hunt would probably find a field clogged with two hundred riders.

Betty Franklin was fine until she got home. Then she suffered a terrible attack of the shakes and Bobby had to give her a shot of brandy to calm her down. Since Betty wasn't a drinking woman it didn't just calm her down, it made her comatose.

Jennifer snuck a drink out of the unlocked liquor cabinet when her father wasn't looking. She, too, retired immediately to bed.

Doug helped Shaker bury Archie in the hound graveyard, a special place surrounded by a wrought-iron fence, a magnificent walnut in the middle.

After that sorrowful duty, he finished up his chores, then hopped in his truck to go to Cody's. She was in surprisingly good spirits. The codeine helped.

Sister sobbed when they put Archie in the ground but then pulled herself together to write up the day's hunt. Her journal, meticulous, kept track of weather, winds, condition of the ground, hounds, horses, casts, and lastly people.

The final line in her strong handwriting read, "What will I do without Archie?" She closed the book, opened the back door, and called for the house pets, both of whom were at the kennel, getting the full story from the hounds.

Golly dashed in first. The night was turning cold and besides her catnip sock beckoned. Raleigh lagged behind but a sharp word from Sister motivated him to hurry in.

Just as she closed the door the phone rang. She picked it up and was not pleased to hear Crawford's voice.

After a few pleasantries, he said, "I have some information that might help the investigation."

"Why tell me?"

He paused a moment, since he expected Sister to be breathless with anticipation. "Uh, because you might best know the approach."

"I see."

"He had come to terms with Peter Wheeler."

"What?"

"Yes, he'd finally gotten the old man to sell but neither one would tell. But the deal hadn't closed because, as you know,

Fontaine was killed. However, the important part is Fontaine never deposited a down payment with his Realtor, who was Donald Vann."

Donald was Georgia's brother-in-law.

"Georgia Vann told you this?"

"I'll get to that." He enjoyed teasing out his news. "Fontaine, as we all know, spent money like water. Anybody's money. He had a silent partner. Donald doesn't know who it was. But the money never made it to Donald. He thinks Fontaine spent it and was frantically trying to find another twenty-five thousand dollars."

"He couldn't have been that foolish." But she knew he could. Her heart sank.

"Find the partner and you might find the killer." A certain smugness crept into Crawford's voice.

"Over twenty-five thousand dollars?"

"If that's your life savings, yes. People kill for less. Maybe he sweet-talked someone out of their money, promising pie in the sky when he would develop Peter Wheeler's."

"I just don't think Fontaine would develop Peter Wheeler's. Besides, it's hardly the place for a shopping center."

"Homes with a hunting theme."

"It was Georgia Vann, then?"

"She hinted, so I tackled Donald."

"I'm sure you did. Well, Crawford, thank you."

"That was quite a hunt today, wasn't it?"

"We lost a great hound. One of the best hounds I've ever known."

"Oh, yes." He'd not given the hound a thought. "By the way, I know with the turn of events you haven't had time to consider the joint-mastership but will you be making an announcement soon?"

"No, I'm putting everything on hold until Fontaine's killer is found. If he's not found, then I'll address this issue at the beginning of next season."

"That long? Is that wise?"

"I think it is."

"Sharing the power now means one season for the joint-master to learn and for people to adjust to him."

"Picking a joint-master under these circumstances would be troubling. And what if, God forbid, I selected Fontaine's killer."

"I did not kill Fontaine nor did I pay to have someone do it. If I were going to kill someone, I certainly wouldn't do it in such a haphazard manner." He caught himself, hastening to add, "But I wouldn't kill anyone. That's what the laws are for, you know."

"I didn't suggest that you killed Fontaine."

"I know what people think."

"I'm glad you do." A touch of acid invaded her voice. "Now let me ask you a question about opening hunt. You nearly passed me. I cracked my whip in front of Czapaka's nose. Do you know why I did that?"

"To keep me from passing you."

"Right. But why do you need to stay behind the field master?"

"I don't know. They don't always do it in England or Ireland. I mean, if you have a horse that can stay with hounds, you just go. I've seen it. I've ridden there." A touch of pride made Crawford smile.

Sister thought to herself, "He must have been strapped to the horse." But she said, "The territory is different in England and Ireland. We have more forests, more of the wild. Maybe it's wild on the Welsh border but you hunted the shires. It's beautiful. Manicured. You can take your own line to almost any hedge or fence. We can't do that for the most part. If you pass the field master in America, you're going to run into hounds. That means you'll ruin the hunt for everybody but most especially hounds."

"I wasn't going to run into hounds." He was defensive and mad now.

"Hell no, Crawford. You were going to run all the way up to Fauquier County." She was so damn mad herself she said, "Good night." And hung up the phone.

Her exhaustion evaporated. Anger hit like a jolt of rich caffeine. She stomped into the den, yanked all the topo maps out of their tubes, and unrolled them on the old drafting table Raymond had bought forty years ago because he said it reminded him of Thomas Jefferson.

The maps kept rolling back up, so she picked up silver hunt cups she'd won in shows over the years, any heavy knick-knack she could find, placing them on the corners of the maps, which she had arranged in order. Within five minutes the entire opening hunt fixture lay before her, as did Golly, loath to miss the sensation of paper underneath her.

"You're right on the ravine, Golly. Move back."

"No."

Sister gently pushed the cat to the edge of the topo maps. Golly swatted her. Sister swatted right back, so Golly turned her back on her but remained on the edge of the maps.

Sister used her hunt journal to double-check the progress of that hunt. With a blue editing pencil she made a dotted line for the cast and subsequent run. Then with a red crayon she made a dotted line where she thought the pack had split and run. It was by guess and by God, since she hadn't been following the splinter group, but it was the best she could do.

"Jesus," she said under her breath.

"He won't help you," an irritated Golly replied.

"Sweet Jesus." Sister traced the red line again. "He was laying the drag as we hunted. I'd thought the drag was laid before, you know, like at four or five in the morning. But look at this ground." She pointed to a large grayish spot representing rock or stone and Golly, herself now interested, looked. "They ran over rock. They had to have run over rock because otherwise Fontaine would have gone all the way over here. See?" She pointed to a path around the rock outcropping. "And that would have taken too long, plus the killer would have exposed himself passing through the meadow. They stayed in the woods and ravine. Had to. Oh, why am I talking to you, Golly? The killer rode hard over bad territory close to the ravine and then curved toward the hog's back. But the killer never jumped the hog's back. I assumed he jumped the jump, tied up the rope, and waited in the meadow. Damn. I should have done this before now. I can't believe I've been so stupid!"

"You were overwrought. Besides, it's a logical assumption. A sensible person would lay the drag with no one around. And a sensible person wouldn't fly over rock." The cat put her paw on Sister's hand.

Sister checked the grandfather clock. "Ten-thirty. Damn. Too late to call Peter Wheeler. I'll call in the morning and then I guess I'd better call Ben Sidell." She sighed deeply, rubbing her forehead with her hand. "This narrows the killer down to a good, good rider who knows our territory." She shook her head. "I'll call Peter Wheeler in the morning. That's a start. You know, Crawford was missing for part of the hunt. Said he thought Czapaka was lame but then discovered he had a stone in his shoe. But I can't believe Crawford could ride that good. Not on the best day of his life."

CHAPTER 47

At seven-thirty the next morning Peter was seated at his kitchen table, Rooster at his knee.

"Woman accuses her sister of stealing her child at birth." He rattled the newspaper. "Says the infant was spirited out of the hospital." He looked over the top of the paper. "Twenty years ago."

Sister laughed, as did Peter. "I guess she just noticed."

"Uh-huh." He laughed again. "Are you going to make me one of your famous Jane Overdorf omelettes? I'll read to you as you work."

"Lazy ass."

"That's right. I'm an old man and entitled to many privileges."

She greased the skillet, chopped cheese, broke six eggs into the skillet. "Crawford must be cracked." She tossed the broken eggshells into the sink.

"Well, only partially. Fontaine did top Crawford's offer. He did promise to bring me cash. I said I wouldn't sell. Think he kept stringing someone along? You know, he had their money, told them he had me in the bag. That kind of thing. I say Crawford is rich enough to pay someone to kill Fontaine for him. That's what I say."

"Do you want onions in your omelette?"

"No. Wouldn't mind a pickle, though."

"In the omelette?"

"Where else?"

"You might like it reposing alongside your golden, fluffy omelette."

"Sounds good." He returned to the newspaper. "Ah, here's one for you. At two o'clock a man wearing a Donald Duck mask robbed First Guaranty Trust in Elkins, West Virginia. The teller said . . ."

She flipped the omelette over as Rooster whined. "Yes." Peter didn't reply. She flipped the omelette onto a plate, turned around to serve him. "Peter. Oh, Peter."

CHAPTER 48

Word of Peter Wheeler's death splashed over the county like a winter squall. The animals spread the word, too.

Inky, on her way back from a night's successful hunt, was told by her brother.

"I relied on his chickens," Comet mournfully said.

A harsh caw overhead silenced them. St. Just landed on a blue spruce branch, his weight dipping the branch downward. He hopped to a larger limb, cocked his head to one side, and sneered, *"The only thing more worthless than a gray fox is a red fox."*

"You'll make a mistake someday. We'll be waiting," Comet challenged him.

"Reynard thought the same thing." St. Just's feathers gleamed blue-black; his long beak shone like patent leather. *"I led the human to his den. I'll see every one of Target's family killed and I'll get Target, too. If you know what's good for you, you won't cooperate with them."*

"Which human?" Inky asked.

"I'll never tell." He tantalizingly dropped to a lower branch almost within reach. *"Wouldn't you just like to break my neck?"*

Comet inched forward; Inky stayed put.

St. Just waited until Comet was within striking distance. Then he lifted off, swooped low over the fox's head, and taunted, *"Death to foxes."*

"There's been enough talk of death." Inky shook herself. *"Archie was killed."*

"Heard." He watched St. Just disappear to the east. *"No raven or blackbird is a friend to foxes but he's evil. I'd enjoy hearing his neck snap."*

"He's smart." She thought a moment. *"Do you think whoever killed Reynard and Fontaine was smart?"*

"No, and we'd be a lot better off if he was. Dumb people are dangerous. Much more dangerous than smart ones."

CHAPTER 49

Face flushed, Crawford leaned over the long table filled with paper samples. "You're a board member. We've got to do something."

"How many other board members have you spoken to?" Bobby, wary, tidied up the paper books.

"Everyone," came the sweeping response.

"What did everyone say?"

"Georgia Vann and Lottie Fisher backed Sister Jane. Isaac Diamond sat on the fence. He said he thought I had a lot to offer but recent events have been too upsetting. Any major decision should be put on hold. Billie Breedlove is out of town and—"

Bobby held up his hand. "I get the picture."

"No, you don't get the picture. Now more than ever members need to know that strong leadership will continue. And we need a sound financial basis. We need an investment portfolio."

Like most businessmen Crawford assumed he could apply business practices to foxhunting but it never quite worked that way—not so much because people were profligate but because any enterprise where Nature is one's partner is fraught with insecurity. Nature doesn't give a damn about profit.

"You can't go head to head with Sister Jane."

"Exactly. That's why I'm trying to go behind her back!"

"Crawford, that will only make matters worse. If the master says she wants to wait a year, then she waits a year."

"She's old. She could pop off at any time." He slapped the table, rattling the pencils.

"Her mother lived to be one hundred and two. Her aunts made it into their nineties and everyone kept their hair, their teeth, and their faculties. You'll die before Sister, especially if you don't calm down."

"Don't talk to me that way."

"For Chrissake, someone's got to tell you how to behave. You can't just stroll into a place and expect everyone to hop to your tune."

"I've been here seven years."

"And you haven't learned a damn thing." Bobby lost his temper. "What you've done for seven years is try to change this entire community to suit you instead of learning how to fit in."

"Fit in? No one gives a straight answer. No one around here seems to be in a hurry to accomplish a damn thing. People accept bizarre behavior and say"—he changed his voice to a fake southern accent—" 'That's jess his way.' No wonder you lost the goddamned war you're always talking about. You're a bunch of idiots!"

"Mr. Howard, this conversation is at an end." Bobby, furious but calm, stood up.

"What the shit? You're too good to hear this. You know it as well as I do. Nothing changes here. You might as well be set in concrete."

"What changes is we can no longer call one another out for duels. Please leave."

"Leave? I didn't say you were stupid."

"You didn't have to."

Betty, who had been in the back office, hurried out. "Bobby."

"Don't worry, honey. We'll take it outside. I won't wreck the place."

Crawford, naturally, would no more fight in the back alley than he would ever learn: When in Rome do as the Romans do.

"That's not why I came out. Peter Wheeler died this morning. Sister was with him. He was reading the newspaper," Betty said.

Bobby's face registered this news. He loved the old man, as did everyone.

"The land! What's going to happen to the land?" Crawford blurted out.

"Get out of here." Bobby put his hand between Crawford's shoulder blades and literally propelled the sputtering man out the front door of the printing shop.

"You can't treat me like this."

"You're lucky I don't knock your teeth out. Get out and stay out."

Crawford, halfway through the door, held his hand out to brace it against shutting. "Don't get high-and-mighty with me. Your oldest daughter is a coke whore and Jennifer's not far behind, you fat pig!"

Fat, he was, but also brutally strong. Bobby smashed his left fist into Crawford's stomach. He followed with a right to the jaw that nearly lifted Crawford off his feet. The tanned, well-dressed man was rocketed out the door, which Bobby slammed and locked.

Betty, hands on hips, said, "Well done."

"Goddamned son of a bitch will probably sue me. Jesus, I could kill him. You were right. You were absolutely right. It would never work. Why I ever supported him . . ."

"It seemed right at the time. How's your hand?"

"Hurts."

"Come on. I'll ice it down."

They heard the big Mercedes's throaty purr. Then the car roared away.

"I'm surprised he didn't call an ambulance. It would have helped his case." Bobby, overcome with rage mingled with grief, put his arm around his wife. "Is that what they call our daughters? Coke whores?"

CHAPTER 50

Walter Lungrun stood over the coroner—towered is more like it, for the county coroner, Gaston B. Marshall, stood five feet five inches in his shoes. Combative, shrewd, and careful, Marshall had the full confidence of the sheriff.

Peter's scalp was pulled down over his face as the tiny saw bit through his skull. Gaston would harvest tissues, peering into the miraculous body, finally stilled. He never lost his respect for the organism although he often had little respect for the soul that had inhabited it.

"Damn good shape for an old man. Usually this generation, liver's shot. Booze fueled social life. Still does, I guess."

As Gaston snipped and clipped, Walter observed with detachment. He had loved Peter but as far as he was concerned Peter had already vanished or gone to the next sphere. He wasn't really sure and wisely kept it to himself. Patients feel more secure if they think their doctor believes in God.

After the autopsy, Gaston scrubbed up.

"Appears natural," Walter said.

"Yes. A heart attack pure and simple. I doubt the pain lasted for longer than a second or two. You saw the left ventricle."

"What's left of it."

"Still, I treat each autopsy as though a murder may have been committed. Keeps me on my toes and we both know there are drugs that can create, if you will, a natural-appearing death. Each time there's a medical advance there's also an advance in murder—for the more intelligent. The less intelligent, the stone, bone stupid will bludgeon, crush a skull with a rock, splatter with a baseball bat. The next level up of the primates prefers a sharp instrument, a slit throat, a stab through the abdominal cavity. A grade above that I'd say that pistols are the preferred weapon. It's when we start dancing with the poisoners that the game changes. And quite often those safecrackers that leave few fingerprints are women."

"I thought women killed less than men."

"Well, I think that's true but I suspect they kill more than we know. We just don't catch them. Remember the famous Alfred Hitchcock episode? Oh, hell, you're too young, Walter, but maybe you saw it on TV as a rerun. You know the one where the husband has been killed with a blunt instrument. The wife is all worry and concern. She had a shank of lamb in the oven and decides not to waste it, so she feeds it to the policemen. Oh God, that's a good one. Killed him with the frozen lamb, don't you see?"

"I have seen that one. Hitchcock was twisted." Walter laughed.

"I wonder. Maybe we all are."

"Gaston, you're in a business where you see the worst. You and Ben Sidell. I guess criminal lawyers do, too. Has to affect your worldview."

"Yes, it does. When you see a five-year-old child whose face has been battered to pulp, she's been strangled, raped, and then the corpse has been abused, you do kind of lose your faith in the goodness of man. Although if anyone could have restored my faith in the goodness of men it would have been Peter Wheeler. A gentle man, a gentleman. He probably saved more children than the Red Cross. Unwanted kids from rich families, unwanted kids from poor families, he'd teach them to ride, teach them to hunt. Today people don't do that anymore, especially men. I guess they're afraid someone will accuse them of being a child molester. Pretty much we've gotten away from taking care of one another."

"We'll not see his like again," Walter agreed. "He was good to me. He was good to everyone."

They strolled down the well-lit corridor to Gaston's office filled with African violets.

"Thank you for allowing me to observe."

Gaston's smile, crooked, was nonetheless appealing. "Just wanted to see if you knew your stuff, kid. Last time I remember you you were staking out the end zone as your private domain." As Walter smiled Gaston continued: "I want you to look at something." He reached under his desk, pulling out a plastic bag. "Just took this out of the cooler."

Walter opened it. Reynard was inside. He carefully removed the fox, stitched up after his autopsy.

Gaston explained, "Ben Sidell was going to give him to Amy Zolotou"—he mentioned the vet—"but I asked that she come here so we could examine him together. You know, very little work has been done on foxes because they're considered vermin. Vets don't know much. . . . I mean they're canids." He used the proper medical term, not "canines." "But they aren't identical to dogs. We have a lot to learn about these little stinkers."

"He's beautiful."

"Healthy. Stomach was full of corn. He'd just eaten. Either heading back to his den or just in it."

"Be awfully hard to bolt a fox from his den unless the killer had a Jack Russell."

"So whoever it was waited for him to return. Sat up in the early-morning hours."

"Upwind. If he'd smelled a human he'd have scampered off. Damn shame." Walter stroked the glossy head.

"He'd been cooled but not frozen. I don't think he was dead more than six to seven hours before he was dragged."

"Have you talked to Jane Arnold?"

"Yes. She said in order for the scent glands to be effective—she said on his pads and by his anus—he'd have to be fresh. If he went into rigor mortis, a hound could smell the fur, of course, but the scent really comes from the pads and especially the anus or urine. I never knew that."

"She'd know. The killer knew, too."

"Put in the refrigerator, I'd say. Then hidden and picked up somewhere during the hunt. Might even have been packed in ice to ensure freshness but not frozen. It's a damned queer thing."

"Does Ben want to keep him for evidence?"

Gaston shook his head. "No. He's got our report. Photos. Amy Zolotou was good, by the way. Good vet. His head and his brush are in pretty good condition, considering he was dragged."

"Do you mind if I take him?"

"No. What are you going to do with him?"

"Go to the taxidermist. Thought he could mount the head and the brush."

"You might not want to identify this fox, Walter."

"I won't." His eyebrows lowered a moment. "But seems a crime to waste a good fox."

"That's one way to look at it." Gaston put Reynard back in the bag. "I'd say that this fellow was my most unusual subject."

CHAPTER 51

The red taillights of Walter Lungrun's car glaring like banshee eyes receded down the driveway. They were the only pinpricks of light in a night raven black.

Sister watched from the mudroom. She was grateful that Walter had stopped by to offer sympathy over Peter's death and to tell her he'd seen the fox's body. He carefully did not mention standing in on Peter's autopsy.

While biologically on schedule, Peter's death certainly was untimely in other respects. She relied on his wisdom, his sense of people.

Raleigh stuck his nose in her hand. *"Don't worry."*

Rooster, brought home from Peter's, was so sad it made her heartsick to see him. Even Golly was nice to him. She'd brought the chickens home, too.

She patted Rooster's head, then flicked her black-and-blue wool scarf off the peg, slipped into a worn but warm olive quilted vest, pulling on a barn coat with a flannel lining over that. She and Raleigh walked out the back door.

The mercury had plummeted into the low twenties. She walked past the stable, the dutch doors shut against the cold. She heard Lafayette snoring, which made her laugh. She'd never met a horse who could make as much noise sleeping as her trusty gray partner.

Two hundred yards away she passed Doug's cottage, the pale straw-colored leaves on the Indian corn attached to the front door rustling in the light wind. She heard laughter within. Cody's car was parked on the other side of Doug's truck. The farm road ran between Doug's cottage and Shaker's bigger old-fashioned Virginia farmhouse on the right, a hundred yards farther down. A single light shone from the up-stairs bedroom, the lace curtains pulled on each side. He was reading Patrick O'Brian sea stories, no doubt. Shaker, like millions of others, loved those tales. And like millions of other men he felt he'd been born in the wrong time. Luckily for Shaker, his work was physical and occasionally danger-ous. Most poor sods chained in front of computer screens could only dream of adventure or they lived for the weekends where they did what men are supposed to do: run, jump, climb, battle the elements and sometimes each other.

She walked under the allée of hickories. The front drive was lined in maples. Much as she adored the intense fall color, she liked this back farm road with the hickories. It had a safe feel and in the summer the leaves formed a canopy over the dirt road. The hickories shorn of their leaves guarded the lane like dark, symmetrical sentinels.

The lane forked. To the left it ran up to the base of Hang-man's Ridge, snaking finally up to the great oak itself. To the right it curved into the hound graveyard.

Sister pushed open the wrought-iron gate, smooth on its hinges. In the middle of the square under the walnut tree reposed a larger-than-life stone statue of a hound running. On the front it read: REST, DEAR FRIENDS. WE WILL HUNT AGAIN SOMEDAY.

On each side of the base, a bronze plaque was bolted and each hound's name was engraved, birth date and death date.

The plaques, representing forty years of Jefferson Hunt hounds, were filled. Newer plaques were affixed to the wrought-iron fence. The last one, bearing three names, had Archie's name freshly carved.

A stone bench under a crabapple tree nestled in one corner. Sister sat down, Raleigh at her feet.

A fat snowflake twirled earthward, soon followed by another and another. The dark sky now had a pinkish cast.

Raleigh leaned shoulder to shoulder with Sister on the bench.

"Orion and Thurman, Bachelor and Button, Laura and Grinch." She sighed. "I was young then and oh that seems so long ago, Raleigh, and yet like yesterday." She read aloud other names. "Yoyo, Chigger, Splash, and Schooner. What good hounds. How lucky I've been in this life to have known such hounds. To be able to stay healthy, to have good friends. I think foxhunters are as nutty as golfers. You can't think about much else, really." The snow dropped thicker and faster. "You know, Raymond wanted to be buried here but his mother wouldn't hear of it. She dragged him to Hollywood in Richmond. He's with his kin and two presidents, John Tyler and I can never remember the other one. He'd rather have been with the hounds. Ray Junior is on the hill. Someday I'll be with him. I think about moving Big Raymond. Once his mother died I guess I could have but then—" She put her arm around the glossy black shoulders. "It seems I should leave well enough alone. I guess they'll plant Peter with his people. They're all up by Monticello. It's funny how families come back together in death. So often they couldn't do it in life but once dead, people who hated one another are laid side by side. If that great day comes and the tombs give up their dead, can you imagine the shock? You pop out of your grave and there's your brother, Fred, who you would happily dispatch all over again. Ha."

"Something's outside the cemetery."

She hugged him closer. "Archie was the best. Brave and true. Diana, Cora, and Dragon didn't back down but poor Archie paid for his courage. If you'd been there, you'd have jumped right in. Raleigh, you're young and may you live a long time. You'll be with me at the end. I promise. Golly, too, spoiled-rotten cat." She smiled, determined not to cry. "I look at this ground and four decades of my life are here. It doesn't seem possible. Losing Archie doesn't seem possible. And Peter Wheeler. If you could have seen Peter in his forties and fifties. What a man. God, what a bizarre time." She shivered, not from the cold. Sniffled. Collected herself and said with quiet determination, "I'm going to lay a trap for our killer. I can't tell a soul and I refuse to kill a fox. I'd like to get the killer for killing the fox as much as for killing Fontaine. Damn him." She paused. "Thanksgiving hunt. If only the foxes will cooperate."

As she said that Inky came out of hiding. *"Don't chase me,"* she said to Raleigh. *"I'll help."*

"I'll tell the hounds."

Sister, startled, blinked. "You."

Inky blinked, then scampered away, leaving perfect fox prints in the gathering snow.

CHAPTER 52

A long polished table left just enough space to squeeze in and out of one's chair. Vin Barber wanted a conference room like the conference rooms the ritzy Charlottesville and Richmond lawyers had. But Vin couldn't get along with a plethora of partners and so kept his practice to himself and his son—more to himself, since his son was an unimpressive specimen.

Vin was, nonetheless, a good lawyer whose specialty was real estate and conservation, the two being allied.

Sitting at the head of the table, his bald head bent over the long legal briefs encased in heavy light-blue paper, spectacles down his nose, Vin could have walked out of a Daumier lithograph, minus the wig and robes, which would have improved his appearance.

Sister sat on his right and Bobby Franklin sat on his left. As president of Jefferson Hunt, Bobby needed to attend the meeting.

Having just heard the last will and testament of Peter H. Wheeler, they were stunned.

"Remarkable!" she exclaimed.

Bobby folded his hands together. "Yes, but can we meet his conditions?"

"I'd damn well try if I were you," Vin, characteristically direct, said.

Bobby leaned across the table toward Sister. "Live to one hundred."

"God willing."

"No joint-masters." Vin put his hands behind his head. "You don't really want one anyway, do you? Even if Crawford wrote big checks, can you imagine talking to him on the phone every twenty minutes? He's high-maintenance. Like to run you wild."

"We can manage without a joint-master but operating expenses don't diminish, as you know. Inflation affects us as well as General Motors." Sister grasped the economics of the club, which is more than some masters. "We'll find a way. But let me be clear: All of Peter Wheeler's estate is held for Jefferson Hunt so long as I live and so long as I don't take a joint-master. And he has left an annual income of fifty thousand dollars a year from his portfolio to maintain the farm."

"Correct."

"That's not the tricky part." Bobby, like most fat people, sweated easily and he was sweating now.

"I know." Sister frowned.

"The tricky part is that once you have passed on, Doug Kinser must be the next master. Jesus, the board will hit the roof."

"Because he's black?" Vin questioned.

"For some, I expect their hemorrhoids will flare up," Sister dryly replied. "But no, the real reason is the board of governors wants to govern. This removes from them the right to elect their master annually. Not so much a problem now but quite the issue when I'm dead and gone."

"Doug would be the first black master in the country. In the world," Bobby thought out loud. "Course, he's only half black."

"People don't see it like that." Vin tapped the eraser end of the pencil against the blue cover. "If you look the tiniest bit black, then you're black."

"Like the old race laws. If you have one percent Negro blood in your veins, you're Negro."

"Virginia had laws like that?" Bobby was appalled.

"Not just Virginia. Many states. Midwestern states. People feared mixing the races." Vin paused. "The idea was like to like, I guess. I remember my grandma saying to me, 'Stick to your own kind.' There's a logic to it," he honestly added. "I can't say that I agree with it but there's a logic to it."

"Bobby, our bylaws state that the master must be elected by the board of governors, who are in turn elected by the membership."

"That's what I'm saying. As long as you live, we don't have a problem."

"We do if I get decrepit."

"You can still be master. You can still control the kennel and the hiring and firing. Someone else can be field master. We don't have a problem. Oh, we'll hear some quibbles about how you should have a joint-master but I can deal with that and so will others," Bobby confidently predicted.

"Do we have to tell the membership of this?"

"Well—" Bobby unfolded his hands, making a tepee out of them.

"No one need know the full contents of this will so long as you enact its provisions," Vin added. "There's enough money annually for you to pay a salary, let's say, put a first whipper-in at the house and he has to care for it. It could be quite comfortable."

"Yes." Sister's mind was roaring along at a mile an hour. "Vin"—she leaned toward him—"I don't mind if this will is read to the membership, but can we wait until after Thanksgiving hunt? It's only two weeks away."

"Of course. We can do anything you say. Do you accept the terms of Peter's will?"

"I do and may God rest his soul. There won't be a day of my life that I don't think of Peter and thank him in my heart." She couldn't finish. She broke down.

Bobby reached in his jacket, bringing out a linen handkerchief with an F embroidered on it. "Here." His eyes watered, too.

She wiped her eyes. "Another question. Peter wishes Doug to succeed me, which really is the best plan—"

Bobby interrupted. "But he has no money."

"We've got a few years left to figure out how to make sure he does have the resources to run the club. There are bigger obstacles. First, we must convince the club that the title of hunt secretary carries almost as much weight as master."

"That's saddling Doug with a hell of a burden," Bobby blurted.

"It may be but it also ensures that those with a big ego and big pocketbook like Crawford might contribute generously if elected as hunt secretary. Look, once this will is read, no one but a bloody fool will try to fiddle with it. We need that land. It's good land, too. We couldn't possibly buy it. Not at today's prices and it's close to a hundred acres. The club will fall in line." She held up her hand. "We'll have to hear this, that, and who shot the cat but they'll fall in. My question to you, Vin, is twofold: What if Doug should predecease me? Secondly, what if Doug were convicted of a felony?"

This got both men's full attention.

Vin cleared his throat. "If Doug predeceases you, then you have the right to name your successor with the stipulation that it be someone Peter taught as a child."

"And would we be within the spirit and scope of Peter's will if, say, Doug committed a felony? I should say was convicted of a felony. Then would I have the right to name a successor? Again, someone who Peter taught."

Flipping up pages of the will, Vin read intently. He cleared his throat again. "I think you would not be in violation of this will."

Bobby, bolt upright now. "You think Doug killed Fontaine?"

"I didn't say that. I'm asking a reasonable question. Personally, I hope Doug does succeed me. He will be a fine master once he gets the hang of it. Don't jump to conclusions."

Of course, they had.

CHAPTER 53

The motor purred as Sister Jane and Bobby Franklin sat in her Durango in the parking lot of Vin Barber's law firm. Over a foot and a half of snow had fallen last night, the temperature stayed low, and the skies threatened more snow.

"Talk to me." She crossed her arms over her chest.

That directive meant tell me everything and I know plenty as it is.

Bobby sighed. "When I thought you were searching for a joint-master I supported Crawford Howard. Let me hasten to add that was a grievous error and I have since repented of my ways."

"In florid fashion, I've heard."

"Uh—yes. Anyway, Fontaine found out—not that I was actively campaigning for Crawford. I'd only verbally committed to his support and I hadn't yet lobbied other board members. Well, Fontaine threatened to take away his business from me and to make sure others shunned my press. As you know, Fontaine did use us for most of his needs. The income from Mountain Landscapes has been steady. Crawford threw me big jobs but I wasn't sure if all of his jobs would outweigh Fontaine's jobs and vice versa. I believed Fontaine's threat. I was between a rock and a hard place."

"Let me get right to the point, Bobby, and I ask this with no malice intended: Did you kill Fontaine?"

"No. I'd much prefer to kill Crawford."

"That seems to be the prevailing mood."

"About me?"

"No, about Fontaine's death. When asked, people say they wonder why Fontaine, or they say exactly as you did. Curious."

Bobby squirmed in his heated seat, the warmth toasting his back. "How do I turn this thing down?"

"Flip it off." She reached over and cut off the heated-seat button. "The warmth in the car is sufficient, although I love these heated seats."

"I carry my own heat with me." He smiled sadly. "Now look, Sister, do you honestly think I would or could kill Fontaine Buruss because he threatened my business?"

"No, but I had to ask. But you could kill him if he threatened or harmed Cody."

Bobby's head rocked back a moment. "Why do you say that?"

"You tell me."

"Rumor."

"Have you asked her?"

"Of course not."

"All right, then, let's look at this from another angle. Do you think Cody had an affair with Fontaine?"

Bobby really squirmed in his seat now. "He was old enough to be her father almost."

"Since when has that stopped a man?"

A sickly pallor flooded Bobby's broad face. "Yeah. Is this relevant?"

"For Chrissake, Bobby, if I didn't think it were, do you think I'd sit here for the sheer pleasure of making you uncomfortable?"

"I know. I know." He gripped the handguard as though the vehicle were moving. "Do I think Cody had an affair with Fontaine?" An agonizing silence followed; then he spoke much too loudly. "Yes. Goddammit. Yes. I could have killed him for that. She's made enough of a hellhole of her life as it is without him digging her in deeper." He caught his breath. "Rehab and therapy. Betty and I have to go once a month along with the kids—I'm finding out stuff I wish I didn't know. Cody would sleep with anyone to get cocaine—more than one at a time. I'm amazed she's alive and not suffering from AIDS. And Jennifer has always worshiped Cody. That was misplaced admiration. I hope we've stopped this before she *really* follows in Cody's footsteps." He wiped his forehead with the palm of his hand. "If they were sons, I'd have thrashed them within an inch of their lives."

She swallowed. "Bobby, we've known one another for a long time. Children go their own way and even if it's the wrong way they have to learn. Cody had sense enough to put herself through rehab. She's looking for a good job. Restaurant work brings her into contact with much of what she needs to avoid. It's going to be difficult for both of your girls but Jennifer has an earlier start on cleaning up. Everyone knows Cody's history here. At least Jennifer's misdeeds are on a smaller scale. Cody's back with Doug and if anyone can help her stay on the straight and narrow—it's him."

"I'm very grateful to him," Bobby mumbled. "I behaved badly this summer. I even rejoiced when they broke up." He stared out the window, tears rolling down his cheeks. "You know, I'm ashamed of myself. I was worried about what people would say."

"Color."

"That didn't help. Money. You know a father likes to see his daughters married to men of means. Right now that seems—superficial."

"It's the way we were raised. And it's not far wrong. Love is potent. Money is omnipotent. No father wants to commit his daughter to a poor man. Have you said anything to Cody about Doug?"

He shook his head. "No."

They sat watching a few isolated flakes fall, presaging more to come.

"Maybe you should talk to Cody."

"That's what Betty says." He turned his face toward hers. "I don't want to upset her. I'm afraid she'll go backward."

"Admitting you were wrong about Doug isn't going to upset her."

"Actually, I was thinking about Fontaine. Asking her."

"I don't know. Done is done."

His voice, barely audible, shook. "I don't know if Jennifer will make it. She's in trouble before Cody was—at her age—or, maybe I see it. . . . I didn't see it with Cody. Jennifer's still under my roof. I don't know what to do."

"Jennifer has your full attention. I suppose negative attention is still better than no attention. She's always been in Cody's shadow. I thank God I passed through adolescence before the words 'self-esteem' were uttered." She sighed.

He brightened, then laughed. "God, it's such bullshit."

The gloom lifted. They sat in silence again.

"Early snow. A long winter, I think."

"I love winter." He smiled. "Always loved Peter Wheeler's Christmas tree. It will be lonely without him. They don't make them like that anymore. People don't have time for one another anymore."

"We do."

"The club. It's an obsession that keeps us together . . . but yes, we're lucky that way. Except for Fontaine's murder. I still can't get over that. During the damned hunt." He slapped his leg.

"I never thought I'd be facing anything like this."

He checked his watch. "I'm glad Peter made the land contingent on you remaining sole master. It's better."

"I'll take that as a compliment."

"You're right. I don't thank you enough. I don't thank Betty either."

"Buy flowers. Go home and kiss her."

"Think I will."

"Two more quick questions. You usually lead hilltoppers. I don't see what's behind me but you do. I hear Fontaine used to stop at least once during a hunt."

"He did."

"I assumed this was to go to the bathroom. Now I think maybe not."

"What do you mean?"

"Well, did you ever see him go to the bathroom? Not that you're looking but sometimes you men will stop and hold one another's horses."

"No. I never saw him. I'd see him veer off and then he'd be back with us within fifteen minutes. Sometimes took longer if we were on a hot run."

"Two thoughts occur to me. He always found the field. He knew hunting. He knew territory. He knew the shortcuts and he knew not to foul the line of scent. Is it possible he stopped for an assignation?"

"Pretty short one."

"That would appeal to him."

"Well—I guess, but wouldn't we see a woman leave, also?"

"Not if she were a whip."

He winced. "Pretty damned irresponsible."

"As I said. Done is done. It's a theory, not a fact, but my mind is turning over everything. If he wasn't stopping to go to the bathroom, he had to be doing something he didn't want the rest of us to see."

"Tell you what. Let me ask the men. Maybe someone did see him."

"Good. It's easier for you to ask than for me. The next question is, when do you want to call a general membership meeting to announce Peter's bequest? If we don't do this, it will leak out. I'll be besieged with calls. You'll be besieged with calls." She poked his biceps. "Bet you rue the day you were elected president."

"Sometimes. Got a calendar?"

She flipped down the glove compartment. A calendar was fastened to the inside. "How's that for service."

He put on his reading glasses, the black heavy frames, square, so ugly they bordered on fashionable. "Friday. I'll get the phone tree started. Or we could just meet after hunting Saturday." He stopped himself. "No, horses will be tied to the trailers. Everyone will be thinking about their horses and about food. Friday. It's awfully short notice but I bet we'll get a good turnout—all things considered. Time?"

"Six. Let's get them right after work. Ask Betty to organize coffee—maybe some cookies or something."

"Okay. Whoo, coming down now. You know I've put over a hundred twenty thousand miles on that old Chevy Blazer." He nodded toward his smallish four-wheel-drive vehicle parked next to Sister's car. "Still runs like a top and no rust. When the engine finally dies I think I'll just pop in a rebuilt one."

"I think you should donate it to the club. We'll auction it off as Wonder Wheels." Her voice rose in imitation of a salesman.

"We'll make a fortune." He leaned over, kissing her on the cheek, then opened the door. "Course, you could bronze it and use it as sculpture."

Driving back home, Sister remembered Peter had also left the club his 1974 badass pickup with the 454-cubic-inch engine in it. Another old Chevy.

She listened to Rachmaninoff's Symphony in E-flat on the way home.

CHAPTER 54

Understanding one's emotions isn't the same as conquering one's physical desires. Every day Cody Franklin fought her profound thirst for alcohol, specifically tequila. The hours, the tears, the laying bare of frailties during her intensive week of rehab and subsequent therapy couldn't prepare her or anyone for the body's craving.

She could do without cocaine, marijuana, skin-popping heroin. But to spend the rest of her life without a drop of liquor seemed a cruel sentence. She'd dream of standing at a neon-lit bar, all cool aluminum washed in blue light. The bartender, Dionysus in disguise, would slide a glass of straight tequila to her. Margaritas were for wimps. Tequila sunrises were for trendies. Straight tequila on the rocks. She'd wake up sweating, mouth dry, hands shaking. Then she'd haul herself out of bed, pull a seltzer water out of the fridge, and drink. But she craved tequila.

One day at a time. Like a mantra she'd roll that phrase over and over in her head until it made no sense at all but sounded soothing.

She realized that the first day an alcoholic takes a drink, gets hooked, is the day emotional development stops. By her own reckoning she was eighteen years old. She'd smoked some weed before that, junior high school, popped the top of a beer can, but she started methodically drinking at eighteen, her first year in college.

She also realized that she was self-centered. Like many young people she assumed other people thought like her. One of the good things to come out of the rehab was the knowledge that just wasn't so. Other people were other people. She was making an effort to see the world through other eyes, making an effort to grow up at last.

She gave herself a pep talk as she left Real Estate Virginia. Turned down again, she trudged through the snow. She knew she couldn't make a career out of training horses. She was good but there were plenty better. She could exercise a horse, she could give a green horse confidence, but she couldn't put the spit and polish on a horse to go into the showring. She could bring along a sane foxhunter but that was a small market and people still believed they could find the perfect foxhunter for $5,000. Those days were long gone but no one would ever accuse a Virginian of keeping up with the times. Indeed, they prided themselves on not keeping up with the times. The times were for the rabble. Virginians were eternal and eternally above such silliness.

The cold air made her nose run. Great. If anyone saw her they'd say she was on coke again. She crossed the downtown mall, heading for the parking lot where her wheezing car awaited her.

She passed the side street where Fontaine's office was, a three-story Federal brick building painted beige with burgundy shutters. On a whim she turned down the street, walked up the steps, freshly shoveled and swept of snow. Inside, the office door was open. Martha Howard sat at her desk, landscaping plans unfurled.

"Hi, Martha. How are you doing? I was in the neighborhood."

"Come on in." Martha stood up. She had guessed at Fontaine's relationship with Cody but didn't pry. It was none of her business.

"It's strange—without him here."

"Yes. Very. Would you like coffee or tea? How about a soft drink?"

"Coffee. I'm chilled and I don't know why. I walked here from Real Estate Virginia. It's not that far."

"First bitter of the winter. Always takes me that way, too." Martha poured coffee in a mug with a horse's tail as the handle. "One or two?"

"Two and milk, please."

Martha delivered the coffee, then sat down with Cody on the sofa. "How are you doing?"

"Okay. And you?"

"A lot of changes. It's hard to believe Fontaine is really gone. Right now it seems like he's on vacation. Ireland. He loved Ireland better than any place. He had more energy . . ." Martha's voice trailed off. She rose, poured herself a coffee, reached into the white cabinet, and brought out a box of cookies. She sat back down and they both nibbled on the dark-chocolate-covered cookies. "I always thought that women had more energy than men and in the main I think they do but Fontaine was in a class by himself. Has the sheriff grilled you yet?"

"Yes. I don't think they know any more than when they first started questioning people."

"Maybe. I suppose it's too early to tell. People think Crawford did it. He hated Fontaine. He was missing for about fifteen or twenty minutes. Bad timing. He didn't kill him, though."

"He could have paid someone else."

Martha laughed, an unexpected reaction to Cody. "Never. Crawford is too smart to ever let emotions foul up his life. If he were caught, he'd be dragged through a court of law. . . . Not Crawford. Too cold-blooded and that was not a cold-blooded murder."

"I never thought of that." Cody wrapped both hands around the coffee mug to warm herself. "What are you going to do?"

"About Crawford?"

"Well, I wasn't thinking about that. I meant here. What will happen to the business?"

"I think Sorrel will sell it. Right now she's in no shape to make a major decision and I told her I'd finish up the jobs outstanding. If I had the money, I'd buy it. Fontaine was hardly regular in his work habits. He was good at bidding jobs and I learned a lot from him but a strong work ethic was not part of his makeup. At the risk of bragging, I kept this business on track. I love the creative part of this. Love design. I know I could make a success of this."

"Crawford would buy it for you. He'll do anything to get you back."

"Is that your opinion?"

Cody, not the most socially conscious creature, said, "Yes. Other people think that, too, but I guess it's hard to trust someone after they've—well—I'm kind of going through that myself only I was the one who screwed around."

Martha lowered her eyes for an instant. "What are you going to do?"

"About Doug?"

"No. About your life."

"I don't know. No one will hire me. I guess they'd hire me to dig ditches. Places want drug tests now. I don't mind that." She sighed. "What I mind is everyone peering at me as though I'm under a microscope. I think half of the people want me to fall on my face and the other half don't."

"Life." Martha smiled, a tinge of sadness in her face.

"I didn't think it would be this hard. The receptionist at Real Estate Virginia, Marcy Talmadge, took my résumé and blew me off. I remember that sorry bitch from high school." She ate another cookie in defiance.

"No one forgets anything around here. It's the reverse of California."

"Maybe I should move there."

"No." Martha quickly added, "I mean, it's beautiful. I can't make a decision like that for you but I think there are so many lost people there." She measured her words. "What did Fontaine mean to you?"

"Me?" A look of pure surprise crossed her beautiful features.

"You."

"Fun. Never knew what he'd do next. And he was generous."

"To pretty girls." She stopped, thought, then added, "Actually, he was generous to most people. He had a way about him. He lived for the moment. He never thought about the consequences of his actions. I wish I could be more, uh—present—without getting into the trouble he did. " She exhaled. "I never leave the house without an umbrella, Handi-Wipes, and a box of Band-Aids."

"That's probably why Fontaine liked you so much. Opposites attract."

"I don't know. I always thought he hired me to get back at Crawford, discovered I was good at managing the office, the clients, reading blueprints, scheduling jobs and workers, and counted himself lucky."

"He was lucky. Until the end. Say, Martha, I meant it. Don't you think Crawford would buy this business for you?"

"I don't know. I'd hate to be beholden to him."

"What if you worked out some kind of buyout over time? I mean if you two don't get back together."

Martha appraised Cody. "It's a possibility."

"Because if you don't go out and bid new landscaping jobs, you'll fall behind. You can't wait until the company is legally yours."

"Isn't it amazing how your mind works when you stop drinking?"

"I've wasted a lot of time."

"Think how you'd feel if you dried out at sixty-two. You haven't wasted all that much. Besides this will give you a checkered past, which will make you more fascinating to the stick-in-the-muds. Plenty of those around here." Martha picked up a napkin, placing it under her coffee mug. "Do you want to work here?"

"Yes."

Martha squared her shoulders; her voice was warm but authoritative. "You know, I believe we could work together but I have to know something. Tell me straight. Did you sleep with Fontaine?"

"Yes, but didn't everyone?"

"I didn't."

"My mother didn't." Cody laughed.

"What was the attraction? I'd think to someone your age he'd look, well, old."

"Yeah, a little. He taught me stuff. How to dress and what to drink. Not that I'll need that anymore. He paid attention to me and he'd give me money sometimes. If I'd fall behind on the rent or get messed up . . . he took care of things."

"You didn't feel that you betrayed Sorrel?"

"No. He betrayed Sorrel. I was along for the ride." A trace of bitterness, a whiff, lingered in the air.

"Did you sleep with him while you were with Doug?"

"Doug harped on me. Nagged. Once he smashed my bottle of tequila, you know, the kind with the worm in it." She drew in a deep breath. "I cheated on him. Hell, I cheated on everyone."

"There's enough money in the till for me to hire you for four months. Not a lot but better than the last job you had. Maybe we can keep this company going. Start Monday?"

"Deal." Cody held out her hand.

Martha shook it. "Deal." She smiled. "Think Sister will cancel tomorrow?"

"No. Takes a hurricane or blizzard to stop her. She'll call this snow a 'dusting.' "

They both laughed.

CHAPTER 55

Deep in the wood a crisscrossing of mountain lion and coyote tracks attracted Inky's attention. She'd left her own delicate prints in the snow, a tighter track than the red fox's. As this was her first snow she hadn't realized how tired she would get. She abandoned the idea of dropping down into the cornfields. She circled behind a cairn. A mouse had to be in there somewhere. She was right.

Nibbling on her breakfast, she heard the horn far away. Hounds could move better in the snow than she could, so she started for home, a short quarter mile away.

A soft hoot stopped her. *"Inky. Coyote coming this way and the hounds are on him."*

"I'll hurry." She talked as she ran, Athena flying slowly overhead. *"Did you have a good night?"*

"When the weather's bad I hunt the barns. Eight mice."

Impressed, Inky said, *"I'm satisfied with one."* She reached her den, sitting down outside it. *"This stuff makes me tired."*

"Don't venture far from your den in deep snow, Inky. It can be fatal. Sometimes the snow will get an icy crust on top. That's not so bad but you can slip and slide halfway to China." She chortled. *"Wings are a big advantage."*

"I'll let you know when I sprout some."

The horn sounded a bit closer, maybe two miles away.

"They cast behind Foxglove Farm." Athena perched on a low limb, her head turned nearly upside down. *"Didn't take*

281

long to pick up the coyote. They run straight as a die. You'd best be careful of them. They'll eat your game and run you out, too. Right now there's enough for everybody but during a famine the coyote will be your enemy. Never forget that. Not so good for the hounds either."

"I'd think it would be so easy. They stay on the scent and just run along." Inky blinked as Athena shook some snow off the branch and the snow fell in her eyes.

"A good hound figures things out. If you zig and zag and circle back, a good hound thinks about it, casts himself or herself until picking up your scent again. If all hounds do is run coyote, then all they need to be is fast. They don't have to solve problems. Sister fears the coyote. If he runs you foxes out, then generations of breeding for special characteristics in hounds will go down the drain. People will breed for nose, drive, and speed. They won't need brainy hounds." Athena noted Inky's crestfallen face. "Don't fret. There aren't that many coyotes here yet and as I said, it won't be a problem until there's a shortage of food. Besides, when Mr. Coyote starts snatching the house pets from suburban manicured yards, you'll hear a fuss. Next thing you know the laws will change and folks will be out there hunting coyote with guns. That, too, presents problems. I tell you, Inky, the first weekend of deer season there are more guns out here than there were at Gettysburg."

"What's Gettysburg?"

"Human foolishness. I'll tell you about that some other time. When the snow melts why don't you store up corn, oats, whatever, just in case we get a big storm. Squirrels have a point, you know."

"Thank you. I will."

The horn was within a mile of them now. They looked over at a rocky foothill to the Blue Ridge Mountains shining in the distance, the very edge of the Foxglove Farm territory. The coyote was trotting along the top of the boulders of the foothill.

"Is he in danger?" Inky asked.

"No. A coyote runs only as fast as he needs to run. When he's ready he'll vanish. Although he'd better not let Cora or Dragon get too close. They are very fast hounds. They're way back, though. Hear them now?"

And the faint music of the hounds drifted toward them.

Inky listened intently. *"Will the coyote kill me?"*

Athena swiveled her head back to focus on Inky. *"Don't give him a reason. Don't challenge him. You'll be all right. You have more to fear from St. Just now than from coyotes."*

"Exactly how did Target kill his mate?"

"Hubris. Conceit. Two summers ago, the summer of the grasshoppers, Target was sunbathing on Whiskey Ridge and she dive-bombed him. He leapt up and caught her. Wasn't asleep, you see. She brought it on herself."

Inky's beautiful eyes seemed even more lustrous as she sat in the snow. *"Athena, do you know everything?"*

She laughed. *"No, my, my, no, but I watch, I listen, and I learn. If you listen to older animals and watch everyone around you, you learn from their experiences, too. You can even learn from humans."*

"Really?"

"They're a case study. You see they've removed themselves from the rest of us and they're suffering. They're losing practical intelligence. Just one example: Humans are fouling their own nest. Every bird, every den dweller knows you can't do that. But they are. I don't mind that they'll pay for it. I mind that we'll pay for it with them."

"All of them?"

"Not all of them. Some are still close to us. But I fear their knowledge will be discounted by the city dwellers. I fear in another generation or two it will be lost and then the earth will shudder."

"I hope not." Inky felt frightened, for she respected the power of the earth.

"I hope not, too, little one, but they grow more and more arrogant. I tell you a common house cat—and I do not esteem cats, most especially that smart-ass, Golly—but even Golly has more wisdom than humans."

"Even Sister?"

"Sister is one of us. Peter Wheeler was, too, and Shaker and Doug. They live within Nature's rhythms and despite human frailty they are respectful. But Peter has gone back to earth. And what of the young ones? I just don't know." Athena glanced back at the boulders. The coyote had left and she saw the silhouette of the pack, in a line, crossing the rocks. *"There's good hound work for you."*

"It's pretty, isn't it?" Inky smiled. *"Athena, when the snows started I was at the hound graveyard. Sister and Raleigh were there and she was hurt. She was mourning Archie and the human dead, too. And she said she was going to lay a trap on Thanksgiving hunt. She didn't say what but when the snow melts I'll tell Aunt Netty and Mother and Father. I don't know what we can do but we can be out and ready."*

"I'll stay up on Thanksgiving, then. I wonder what she'll do?" Athena sighed, her plump chest pushing out, revealing the light-colored feathers under the long silky ones. *"I'm going home to bed. I suppose Babs is there."* Babs was the screech owl in the next tree. *"She's a dear friend, you know, but that dreadful voice."* Athena shook her head then lifted off as Inky turned and scooted into her den.

CHAPTER 56

A sudden wind swirled snow in Lafayette's eyes, up into Sister's. Shaker, just ahead, struggled down a steep deer trail snaking to Edmond's Creek. The coyote trotted along the rocks, then bounced down to the bottom of them and into the creek. He should have been easy to track but the hounds couldn't find scent and Shaker couldn't find tracks.

By the time Lafayette reached the bottom of the incline, Shaker reached the other side of the creek.

Lafayette called to Shaker's horse. *"A storm's coming up fast."*

"What'll I do?" Keepsake, being tried out by Shaker and a bit green, worried.

"There's nothing you can do. They won't smell it until it's almost upon them or until they see the clouds piling up in the west. Shaker will get you home; don't worry."

Sister patted Lafayette's neck. The weather kept everyone away, including the Franklins, who couldn't get the trailer down the driveway since Bobby didn't have a snowplow. The wind piled up drifts, which though not large were large enough to risk getting stuck.

She loved staff hunts. Not that she didn't enjoy her field—she did. But those days when she didn't have to shepherd people, when she could just fly or sit and listen to hounds turn back to her, those days made life worth living.

Standing out like a resplendent cardinal in the snow, Doug

waited upcreek for the hounds to find. He, too, checked for tracks. When Shaker looked his way Doug shook his head. The huntsman rode downcreek, Sister shadowing him on the opposite bank, portions of which were steep.

"Nothing." Shaker shook his head.

"Me, too."

"Right under our noses." Cora lifted her eyes back to the boulders. She felt he was hiding there but how he escaped detection she couldn't say. *"Let's go back up."*

"I don't think he'll allow it," Dasher said. *"And if they don't smell the storm, we'll have more to worry about than the coyote."*

The barren trees began to bend and sway. Doug noticed the scudding clouds first. He pointed to the western sky. Both older people glanced up.

"Damn, those clouds are rolling in fast," Shaker exclaimed.

They had hacked to Foxglove to cast hounds. From the kennels Foxglove was two miles on the trails. At the point where they now stood they were halfway between both farms.

"Makes sense to head home." She smiled at her hounds. "I'm proud of all of you."

"He's in the rocks." Cora wanted to circle back.

"Good girl." Sister praised her as she turned Lafayette on the narrow path, walking back to the creek crossing. Once on the other side the three humans walked through the forest, Shaker and Sister up front and Doug in the rear.

They hadn't ridden a half mile when the wind began to whistle. Heavy frock coats, a vest, shirt, and silk underwear kept their upper bodies warm, but their legs began to feel it. Each had learned the trick of slipping a flat heat pack in the toe of their boot, which helped keep their toes from freezing. There was no help for one's hands, since a rider must feel the horse's mouth.

Sister wore silk liners under her string gloves but her hands ached in the cold. She didn't complain about it, nor did Shaker and Doug. Came with the territory.

Their ears began to sting. Snow blew off the conifers. As if the heavens unzipped, all at once the snow fell, fat flakes falling quickly. Within minutes their helmets, shoulders, and backs were covered in snow. The hounds' backs began to turn white.

"If we cut down into the ravine, we'll be out of the wind," Shaker suggested. "It might take a little longer, as it's rough going, but this wind—" He raised his voice to be heard above the roar.

"Worth a try. Damn, how did this thing come up so fast?"

They picked their way down the folds of the ravine, holly bushes and mountain laurel sharing the banks with hardy firs. Once down in the bottom they followed the creek westward.

"I can't hear myself think." Sister bent low to avoid a branch.

Doug looked at the edge of the ravine. The snow spilled over the top like a white-powdered waterfall.

The creek widened into a roundish shallow frozen pool where a small tributary fed into it, ice encrusting the creek bank edges. They halted to allow hounds and horses to drink, as the tributary was still running strong. The water emerged from the other side of the pond, but the ice was closing in fast.

"Funny how you get thirsty when it's cold. Wouldn't think so." Dragon gulped the icy water.

"I'd like bacon-bit kibble right now." Dasher sighed, taking a few steps into the deeper end of the pool. He'd pushed through the ice crust at the edge of the pond. He felt something odd among the pebbles, metal. He dug at it, moving it closer to the other hounds.

"Whatcha got?" a large tricolor asked him.

"I don't know but I'm not giving it to you." Dasher reached down in the water, picking up the object with his mouth.

"I'd let you play with my toy." Dragon came over.

Dasher didn't respond or he would have dropped his prize.

Doug dismounted. "Dasher, that's really special. Let me keep it for you."

The handsome young hound turned his head away from Doug. Dragon bumped him to see if he could get him to drop the toy.

Sister said, "Dasher, what a good hound."

He turned around to face her, then slowly emerged from the pool, looking crossly at any hound that looked at him. He would surrender his find to Sister but they'd better leave him alone.

She dismounted also, reaching for the gun that he gave her. "Good hound. Good hound."

The gun, cold and wet, soaked through her string gloves. "Thirty-eight." She shook it, then slipped it inside the large game pocket inside her coat. "I've got a funny feeling about this."

"Yeah, I do, too," Shaker agreed.

CHAPTER 57

The storm raged for one full day. Power cut out. Those that had them switched over to generators, careful to turn off the main switch at their breaker boxes or the poor sod trying to restore power would have a most unpleasant sensation.

The transportation department of the state, playing the averages, which it had to do, didn't have enough snowplows to open the main arteries, much less the back roads. People dug out as best they could or sat home, eating canned soup off

Sterno stoves. The lucky ones who had gas stoves could cook real meals.

Then as quickly as the freak storm had hit, the temperatures rose into the sixties, the sky beamed heavenly blue, snow melting everywhere. The sound of water running into downspouts, across roads, under culverts, into creeks and rivers drowned out other sounds. It was as though the earth were melting. Creeks rose to the top of their banks, overflowing in low-lying areas.

As the snows melted the grass, still green underneath, deepened to a brighter green; the leafless trees seemed to stand out against the color.

Since Crawford Howard owned a Hummer, which suited him better than his Mercedes, he merrily drove everywhere. He surprised the Vanns by bringing them food, as they lived at the edge of the county down a twisting back road. He even delivered ten bags of kibble to the kennel in case chow was low. After a morning of good deeds he emerged from his mudbespattered behemoth, which he parked in front of Mountain Landscapes. Since Martha had an apartment downtown she could walk to work. With masses of roses in his left arm, he rapped on the door with his right hand.

"Come in."

He opened the door. "A rose by any other name is Martha."

"You must have bought out the store—or did you buy the store?" She laughed, rising from the drafting table. "I'd better get a tub."

"Brought that, too." He hurried outside, returning with a large round black bowl.

"Oh, they'll be stunning in that." Martha took the bowl, filled it with water in the small kitchen in the office, then placed the roses inside, careful to have a few falling over the side. She placed the arrangement in the middle of the coffee table. "There."

He sat on the leather sofa. "Quite a storm."

"I love watching the weatherman on Channel Twenty-nine. Even with all the sophisticated radar, satellite photos—they still don't know what the weather will do. Especially here next to the mountains."

"Hungry?"

"That means you are."

"How about a cold Coke?" He went outside again and this time returned with a Harrods hamper basket filled with exquisite sandwiches; cheeses, including Stilton; crackers; fruits; chocolate-covered strawberries; small delicious shortbreads. He carried this largesse with two hands, it was so heavy.

Under his arm he pinned a checkerboard tablecloth, which he now spread on the floor. "Picnic. Wine for you?"

"Oh." She surveyed the endless array of treats he kept pulling out of the basket. "I'll have a Coke with you. Let's save the wine."

"Goodo."

As they ate and chatted, Crawford reported on his heroic exploits delivering food, whose vehicles were stuck, the Fishers' collapsed shed roof.

She remarked that downtown didn't lose power and she enjoyed watching the snow fall over the rooftops. The Episcopal church steeple was wrapped in white. This was her favorite view from her bedroom window, Saint Luke's, and for a few hours the snow fell so heavily she couldn't even see that.

After laughter and chat he leaned toward her. "Martha, do you think people can change?"

"Of course I do."

"Do you feel that I have changed?"

"In some ways."

"How?"

"I think you've learned that younger isn't necessarily better." She suppressed a smile.

He blushed. "Well, yes, but I was hoping you'd see that I've become more sensitive, more responsive to others."

"Crawford, you are trying." She wanted to encourage him but he'd always want his way. The bully was never far from the surface.

"And I'll keep trying. I've learned from my mistakes. I want to make amends."

"I appreciate that."

"I want to marry you all over again."

A long pause followed until Martha leaned over the fragrant chocolate-covered strawberries and gently kissed him. "Let me think about it. You know I love you. I never stopped loving you but I'm afraid."

"I promise I will never do anything like that again. Only you."

"Give me some time." She kissed him again.

"I'll do anything, Martha. Anything." He kissed her passionately.

"Well, I have a task for you if that's true. What I learned when we divorced was that no one wanted to hire me. The work we did together didn't count on a résumé. I could have starved. And you know, Crawford, you're very tough in business and I thought I was old business." She kissed him again, then continued. "I was burned. Not just by you but by people I thought were my friends. I found out exactly how I was regarded socially. So I was not high on anyone's employment list nor on the dinner-party circuit. Devastating as it was, it was valuable to me. If I should go back to you I want to work. Even if I don't make what you consider money, it will mean the world to me and I think it will make me more interesting to you."

"You're fascinating even in your sleep."

She lowered her eyes. "Thank you, but do you understand? If you got tired of me—"

"I won't," he interrupted, his eyes intense.

She held up her hand. "Okay, but for my peace of mind. Do you agree to my working?"

"Yes, as long as you can take vacations when I do."

"Then I need my own business." She sounded much calmer than she felt.

"That's not unreasonable."

"I'd like to buy this company. I can make it work and I've learned how to bid jobs."

He exhaled through his nostrils. "Will she sell?"

"I think she will. She'll need the money. You know how he was."

"Yes," Crawford replied simply.

Another pause ensued while he thoughtfully ate a strawberry. "I never really thought about what you must have gone through. I thought about it in emotional terms but not—I've been the captain of the ship. I can't imagine what it was like to look for work and I wish you had told me."

"You were occupied." She said it without rancor.

"What I was was a fool." He put down the stem end of the strawberry. "I'm sorry. I'm sorry for everything. I agree to your terms but it might be prudent if you approached Sorrel."

She threw her arms around him. "You've made me so happy. You don't know how happy you've made me."

"Does this mean you'll marry me?"

"Yes."

CHAPTER 58

"We could realize an annual income of $24,000 minimum. If we spent what needs to be done to rehabilitate the place, probably $40,000, then we could realize an annual income of close to $48,000, since we could charge $4,000 a month." Georgia Vann, treasurer, spoke. She had taken the precaution of handing out these figures along with the bids for repairs at the beginning of the ad hoc meeting to announce Peter Wheeler's generosity.

"Why can't we hire someone to clear trails and build jumps year-round and house them there? They could make the repairs and it would save some money." Betty Franklin was trying to be helpful.

"When would they have time? I mean, if they were properly doing their job for the hunt club? It's better to hire professional roofers and painters. Look at what we've been through at the shop, hon," Bobby, seated at a long table facing the membership, reminded his wife.

"You're right."

"Is she always that agreeable?" a male member called out.

"My Princess, sure." Bobby laughed and the others laughed with him.

Peter's gift, an antidote to Fontaine's murder, had raised everyone's spirits.

"Would the renter have to be a hunt club member?" Cody asked, wishing she had the money to rent it.

"We never thought of that," Bobby responded, "but unless someone raises an objection I don't see why membership would be a requirement so long as the renter accepts this is a long-standing fixture and will be hunted regularly."

Walter stood up. "I would be willing to rent the place right now. I would also be willing to coordinate all repairs if the hunt club will pay for them. Naturally, I'll keep up the grounds. And I'd pay $3,000 a month so long as I have full use of the barns and all outbuildings."

A brief silence followed; then everyone talked at once.

Bobby banged down the gavel. "Does anyone wish to match Walter's offer?"

Crawford stood up. "It's a good solution for both parties. I move that we accept Dr. Lungrun's proposal. The rent to stay at $3,000 per month for a five-year period, at which time the lease can be renegotiated."

"I second the motion." Martha beamed at Crawford.

"Discussion?" Bobby asked. When none was forthcoming he continued: "All in favor, say aye."

"Aye," came the chorus.

"All opposed say nay."

One lone nay came from Cody.

"What's that about?" her father asked.

"Just that I wish I had the money to rent it. I'm not really opposed."

"All right, then." Bobby smiled at her. "Motion carries. Is there other business to be discussed?"

Sister, who sat in the corner during business meetings, called out, "New doors for the kennel."

Bobby scanned his list. "Forgot that. We need new interior doors. As you know, wooden ones last two years, if that. The tin-covered ones last about five years and our five years are up. If you'll flip over your sheet you'll see Georgia has itemized expenses and bids."

As the discussion about replacing doors droned on, Jennifer slipped into the meeting. Still carrying her schoolbooks, she sat next to her mother.

"How was practice?" Betty strongly supported Jennifer's field hockey efforts.

"Okay." Jennifer whispered, "Mom, Dean Offendahl got busted at school for drugs. He says I've been buying from him but I haven't." Betty shot her a dark look and Jennifer hurriedly added, "He's pissed that I don't hang with him anymore. Honest."

"We'll talk about this later," Betty whispered back. Inside she wondered if there'd ever be an end to this. If she'd ever trust Jennifer again.

Finally all the loose ends were tied up, the meeting was adjourned, and the members headed for the bar. Jefferson Hunt had no clubhouse. Meetings and events rotated among member's homes and large meetings such as this one were held at a new country club, Dueling Grounds, built on the old dueling grounds. Since the club was competing with older, more prestigious clubs it offered better facilities and encouraged people to come in and see what was available.

The bar, paneled with wormy chestnut, old hunt prints on the wall, was inviting.

As was the custom in Virginia, paid staff did not attend membership meetings. Shaker and Doug didn't mind, as neither man had much tolerance for the windiness that accompanies such gatherings.

"Sister." Walter leaned over to speak to her. "I'll take good care of Peter's home."

She smiled up at him. "You'll fill up that barn in no time. Have you ever noticed people start with one horse and wind up with a herd? I think it's some kind of progressive disease. You might want to do research on it."

He laughed. "All right."

She lowered her voice, which, considering the noise, wasn't

necessary. "Thank you again for dropping by the other day. Peter was a dear friend. I appreciated your sympathy."

"He saved me after Dad . . . died. I wish I'd known him as long as you did. He used to call you his movie star."

"He did?"

Before they could continue, Georgia Vann joined them and the conversation steered toward Thanksgiving hunt breakfast. The club needed to borrow utensils.

Crawford avoided Bobby, who did likewise. He told everyone that he and Martha were engaged. To celebrate his good fortune he bought a round of drinks for everyone.

Cody and Jennifer had Perrier as Jennifer told her tale of woe to her sister.

Sarcasm dripping, Cody said, "I'm so glad you're preparing Mom and me but what's the deal?"

"No deal." Jennifer shrugged.

"You might as well tell me now because I'll find out later and then, li'l Sis, I'll really be mad. Like I don't care how long you cry you ain't gettin' no help from me." She sounded like a country-and-western song, which was her intent.

"He'll say I slept with him."

"Did you?"

"Uh-huh."

"For drugs?"

Jennifer reddened. "Not exactly. I liked him. How was I to know he'd turn into such a butthead. When I stopped screwing up and screwing him, he—" She shrugged. "Getting even."

"Mom and Dad are going to be really embarrassed." She thought a moment. "Can't you talk him out of it?"

"How? He got busted in the locker room selling a gram of coke. I can't get him out of it."

"Does he still want to go to bed with you?"

"Yeah." She shrugged again.

"I'm not suggesting you comply but—" She shook her

head, trying to come up with solutions. "Has he named other people?"

"Oh yeah. By the time he's done half of Lee High will be tied and fried. Barbecue."

"His dad's a lawyer. I suppose that will help him but it won't help you or anyone else." She took in a deep breath. "Let's talk to Walter. He's a doctor. He's smart. Maybe he'll help us. If nothing else he can testify that you're making every effort to keep clean." She put her hand under Jennifer's elbow, heading her in the direction of Walter.

"There's one other thing. Dean knows I slept with Fontaine."

Cody went white. "You idiot."

CHAPTER 59

The sting of not being chosen to be joint-master faded as Crawford focused on Martha. Winning her back meant a great deal personally and socially.

This euphoria somewhat dissipated when Ben Sidell walked through the office door to announce that the .38 found in the ravine was registered to Crawford Howard.

"Are you accusing me of killing Fontaine Buruss?" Crawford sputtered.

Calmly, deliberately, the sheriff replied, "I am informing you that a thirty-eight registered to you, purchased last June, was the gun that killed Fontaine Buruss."

Rising from his chair, Crawford said, "I didn't even know the gun was missing."

"Where do you usually keep it?" Without being invited to

do so, Ben sat down in a chair by the coffee table. He opened his notepad.

"In my trailer."

"What trailer?"

"My horse trailer."

"Why would you keep a thirty-eight in your horse trailer? I thought foxhunters didn't shoot foxes."

Walking around his desk and leaning against it, facing the sheriff, Crawford, quickly in control of himself, replied, "In case I find a wounded animal. In case there's an accident in the field. You know, a horse breaks a leg."

"I see. Then why was the gun in your trailer and not on your person? I'd think you'd notice its disappearance promptly." His tone was even, his voice deep.

Embarrassed, Crawford folded arms across his chest. "I anticipated being asked to carry the gun but when I wasn't, I put it in the medicine chest in my trailer."

"Why would you be asked to carry a gun?"

"One or two staff people usually carry a thirty-eight under their coat or on the small of their back. Just in case."

"So you bought the gun last June—just in case."

Crawford's voice rose. "I thought I would be asked to become joint-master. My rival, as you know, since you've questioned everyone, was Fontaine Buruss. Jane Arnold was to have made her decision at opening hunt. However, the death, the murder of Fontaine, convinced her to delay that decision until next season."

"You're disappointed?"

"Hell, yes, I'm disappointed but not enough to remove my rival."

"Why couldn't you both serve?"

"It would have never worked."

"Why not?"

"Fontaine was a lightweight. A bullshitter. What he wanted to do was seduce women."

"I was under the impression he was successful without being joint-master."

"Sheriff, this is Virginia. We're both outsiders. It took me a while to realize that M.F.H. behind one's name ranks right up there with F.F.V. Of course, if you have both you have everything." He caustically winked.

"Tell me again of your whereabouts during opening hunt. You were unaccounted for for twenty minutes."

"We went over that."

"Refresh my memory." Ben smiled at him, a cold glint in his eye.

"My horse went lame. I turned back. When I reached the small creek, Tinker's Branch, I was afraid Czapaka would jump it and I didn't want him to do that if he was lame. I don't know why it didn't occur to me at first but I picked up his front feet and found a stone. I removed the stone, walked him a bit with me off. He was sound. So I got up and rejoined the group."

"And no one saw you?"

"No. Not that I know of, anyway."

"Crawford Howard, I am booking you under suspicion of the murder of Fontaine Buruss. You have the right to remain silent. . . ."

CHAPTER 60

Crawford Howard strolled out of the county jail within four hours thanks to his lawyer, the best money could buy. The bail, set at two hundred thousand dollars, was paid with Crawford waggling his finger at the bailiff saying that the money would be back in his pocket within the month.

No doubt the lawyer was thinking the same thing.

That same afternoon Dean Offendahl named every student at Lee High School who had ever bought drugs with him or done drugs with him. His father had worked out an arrangement whereby if Dean cooperated with the courts he would not be sent to a juvenile detention center.

He also had to name anyone else he knew that sold drugs. Fontaine Buruss's name was on that list.

As this was immediately before Thanksgiving break, Mr. Offendahl hoped the worst of the gossip would be dissipated by the holiday.

During this time Sister Jane set out small heaps of corn throughout the fixture that would be hunted on Thanksgiving. She also walked deep into the ravine, patiently laying corn and bits of hot dog.

CHAPTER 61

Raising children, not an occupation for the faint of heart, baffled Bobby Franklin. He worked hard, paid the bills, supplied discipline when necessary, spent time with the girls. When they were younger Bobby carted them to horse shows, grooming, cleaning tack, applying that last-minute slap on their boots with a towel when they were mounted. He listened to them rant about unfair judges, sometimes agreeing, sometimes not. He observed them bite their lips so as not to cry when they lost. They also learned to win without undue celebration, as befits a lady.

Neither kid impressed her teachers with intellectual prowess but the physical education teachers thought them both wonderful. He feared the onslaught of adolescence but they sailed along. When Cody began to falter at sixteen he didn't notice at first. She still competed in horse shows. She wasn't surly, just diffident. He thought this remoteness a phase. He didn't recognize that she was struggling until she was in her sophomore year of college. Wrecking her ancient Jeep was the first sign; a report card below the line was the second.

Betty sensed it long before he did. He wondered now if he'd done the right thing. He'd hated his father sticking his nose in his business, probing him about girls, drinking, parties, his future. He thought he was giving his girls room. Sitting before the tiled fireplace, Betty in the wing chair to his right, both daughters on the sofa before him, he had occasion to repent of his laxness. Mr. Offendahl kept the story of drugs at Lee High out of the paper but he couldn't cut out people's tongues. Neither Betty nor Bobby was surprised when their phone rang off the hook. Jennifer, horrified, slunk to her room, refusing to come out, declaring she would never go to school again, her life was ruined, et cetera. . . .

Cody, upset but levelheaded, drove over the minute her mother called this Tuesday night. Jennifer, dragged from her room, curled up on the sofa, rested against her big sister, arm around her.

"What I'm trying to understand is why neither of you talked to your mother or me. I can't change what happened. You can't. We're all going to have to live with this for the rest of our lives."

"I'm getting out. Send me to school somewhere else," Jennifer begged.

"No." Betty stepped in. "The stories will catch up with you no matter where you go. You'll face the music now and put it behind you."

"I have no life." Jennifer's chin wobbled.

"Rada." Cody squeezed her. Rada meant Royal Academy of Dramatic Arts, a phrase the kids used when anyone was being overly dramatic.

"It's true." Jennifer flared. "My life is ruined! You at least have Doug."

"I have to live with my past the same as you. Stop this damned whining, Jen."

"Girls." Betty's voice was low, redolent with authority.

The two shut up.

Bobby spoke. "I'm here to apologize to you. I spent too much time running the business. I know that now. If I'd been paying more attention I might have noticed, I hope, anyway. But I'm here now and we're going to get this straightened out. We can't run to rehab every time something goes wrong, and I can't afford it anyway."

"Dad, I'm paying my bills." Cody felt guilty that she'd wasted her father's money in the past.

"For which we're grateful," Betty replied. "But let's get to the bottom of this. Your father and I aren't perfect parents. We thought by sharing riding with you that we were together, a family together, but we missed emotional clues. You've both told us that you drank because everyone else was drinking. I'm taking the words 'everyone else' with a grain of salt. However, we were young once. We remember the pressure to fit in, to be part of a group. I even understand the drugs. It can't be that much different from drinking. Someone says, 'Here, this will make you feel good,' and you do it. What I can't understand is Dean Offendahl's allegations. Jennifer, you've locked your door and cried in your room for over forty-eight hours. I assume there's no liquid left in your system." A wry smile crossed her full lips. "So let's get this out and over with. Why?"

"I won't go to bed with him anymore."

"She's right." Cody backed her.

"You shouldn't have gone to bed with him in the first place." Bobby smacked the arm of his chair.

Betty shot him a dirty look. "That won't help." She returned her gaze to Jennifer. "Let's use the defense 'diminished judgment.' I believe that. I even understand sleeping with a boy in high school. It happens."

"Did you?" Jennifer hoped her mother had, of course.

"No."

"I did." Cody smiled at Jennifer. "Not my best move."

"I want to know what Fontaine Buruss had to do with this." Bobby kept calm although if Fontaine were alive he'd kill him.

Cody spoke first, partly to spare Jennifer and partly to give her time to organize her thoughts. "I needed money so I offered to ride Keepsake, the new horse Fontaine was trying. He'd come around the barn when I was working the horse and hey, he was sexy." Noting the raised eyebrows of her father, she murmured, "Dad, he was."

"He was." Betty corroborated her daughter's judgment.

"We did drugs. He'd give me extra money if I'd braid, a lot extra, really. He bought me new breeches, a saddle. Big stuff. I liked him but I didn't love him and after a while I realized I was just another bird. Flying in and out. I also realized I was pretty messed up and I missed Doug. Dad, I know you aren't crazy about Doug—"

Bobby cut in. "He's a fine young man. My concerns were social and I was wrong. I was wrong and I'm sorry."

Her father's repentance touched Cody. She wasn't accustomed to Bobby admitting error. "It's okay, Dad. We'll put that behind us, too."

"Didn't you think about Sorrel?" Betty asked.

"No. Mom, when you're doing drugs you don't think about anybody but yourself. Besides, he'd cheated on her so many times I didn't see that one more affair was going to break her heart. He made the marriage vow; I didn't." She held out her palms upturned. "But I was wrong. I'm telling you what I thought at the time. People can rationalize anything, can't they?"

"World War Two proved that beyond a doubt." Bobby put his fingertips together. "What happened when you left Fontaine? Or did you leave Fontaine?"

"Nothing." Cody shrugged. "It wasn't a blowup. It's not like we were in love or even that emotional. We had fun. That's the best way to describe it. I had Jennifer drop me at the bar—" She thought a moment. "Maybe that second Saturday in October, I think. Anyway, Doug was there and I wanted him back. If he'd have me. Maybe I needed Fontaine to really love Doug. God, it's messy." She sighed. "I needed help. I still need help. I think I'll be going to AA and NA meetings and drug recovery meetings for the rest of my life. I don't think I can do it alone and"—she wanted to make her parents feel better—"you can only do so much. It takes a drunk to understand a drunk."

"Then how did Jennifer get into this mess with Fontaine?" Betty was more worried than she let on.

"I'd go over to the barn to help Cody." Jennifer sat up. "He'd be around, laughing, joking. He'd let me work Gunpowder. What a neat horse. He'd let me snort a line or two."

"But how did Dean Offendahl know this? I'm missing something." Betty bore down.

"I'd collect money from Dean and some of the others and buy coke from Fontaine. He had good coke. I didn't take Dean over there."

"But you told him who was selling you the drugs?" Bobby rested his chin on his fingertips.

"Bragging, in passing—how did you tell him?" Betty pressed.

"Kind of, uh—threw it off."

"Why is he saying you slept with Fontaine?"

"Mom, he's making that up. He's trying to get people's attention off of him. He thinks this is going to hurt me."

Clearly Dean's stories about Jennifer sleeping with Fontaine are what truly upset the young woman. It's one thing to sleep with a boy your own age but at seventeen to sleep with a man of Fontaine's years, that grossed out her classmates.

"I guess it did. You've been in your room for two days," her mother curtly replied.

"It's pretty rad." Cody defended Jennifer.

"Radical? I think it's close to the mark. I'm still taking the 'diminished judgment' tack and if Jennifer was over there at Fontaine's stable, the coke was pure or good or whatever it is, she gets high, he gets high, it's not an impossible thought no matter how disgusting it is to me. And not so much that I'm disgusted with you, Jennifer, although I'm not proud. I'm disgusted with Fontaine. He took advantage of you, both of you." Betty's eyes blazed.

"I'm over twenty-one," Cody flatly said. "I knew what I was doing."

"I don't think you did but I think he knew *exactly* what he was doing. Getting beautiful girls ripshit—isn't that the word, ripshit—and then taking you to bed. Goddammit, I wish I'd shot him, the sorry son of a bitch!" Bobby jumped up from his chair, pacing in front of the fireplace. "But the fact remains that he is dead. And I expect Sheriff Sidell will cruise around to us soon enough."

"Why?" Jennifer thought this was strange.

"Because either of you could have killed him in a rage—from a sheriff's point of view. You do drugs, you leave him or maybe he leaves you. Who knows how that will fall out. You're angry on two counts: He dumped you and no more drugs."

"That's not true!" Jennifer shouted.

"I didn't say it was." Her father coolly studied her. "But I'm trying to see this with a sheriff's eyes. Right now neither of you looks too good."

"Jennifer wouldn't kill anybody," Cody passionately replied. "You know that. She made a mistake."

"Did you know?" Betty's heart was pounding inside and she didn't know why. She was more afraid than when she'd fetched Doug from the bear.

"Not until the end." Cody lowered her voice. "I just never thought Fontaine would do something like that."

"You went to bed with him. Presumably you knew what kind of man he was." Bobby's sympathy was running thin.

"I'm older than Jennifer. Going to bed with an underage girl is statutory rape, isn't it? I never thought he'd do something like that."

"He knew he was safe." Bobby grabbed the mantelpiece. "He knew neither one of you would ever tell because he was your candy man. He could do whatever he wanted and he did."

"Dad, he was never ugly. He was fun." Jennifer thought she was relieving her father's distress. "He wasn't a mean kind of guy."

"Let's set motivation aside." Betty returned to her original question to Cody. "What did you do when you knew, and how did you know about Jennifer and Fontaine?"

"At first I half suspected but like I said, I couldn't believe he'd do something like that. When Jennifer skipped school that one day and came to me, I asked her. She said yes."

"And?" Betty stared at her.

"I told her to stop."

"Did you?" Betty focused on Jennifer.

"Yeah. I went to rehab. I never got the chance to go back, I guess. I mean I didn't even talk to him until opening hunt. Hi. That was it. So yeah, I stopped."

"Do you think Fontaine bribed your little sister with drugs to get even with you?" Bobby felt sick to his stomach.

As distressed as her father, Cody replied, "I don't know. I don't think so but then again I didn't think he'd seduce Jennifer in the first place. He could have done it to get back at me. Anything's possible."

"Did you tell him to stop?"

Cody exhaled. "Mom, I went over to his stable to pick up my tack. I didn't want to ride for him anymore. I wanted to put everything in my place, since I was going into rehab. He drove in just as I was driving out. He rolled down the window of his Jag and I told him to stay away from Jennifer."

"What did he do?" Bobby stepped away from the fireplace toward Cody.

"Nothing. He rolled his window back up." She shrugged. "Nothing."

Jennifer, crying again, asked, "Does this mean I can't go to Thanksgiving hunt?"

Bobby and Betty looked at each other and then at Jennifer.

"No." Bobby said. "It doesn't mean that. We're better off doing the things we usually do. It's worse to hide."

"People will laugh at me." Jennifer sniffled.

"Get it over with." Cody didn't relish the spectacle either. "Let them laugh and get it out of their systems. After a while they'll be bored with it."

"I can't go back to school."

"You can and you will. Ignore Dean Offendahl. His father was an ass to protect him. The only way you learn about life is to pay for your mistakes. If you don't pay, believe me, there's a much bigger bill waiting for you down the road. Pay up, Jennifer. Hold your head up and just keep walking."

"That's easy for you to say, Dad," she sniped.

"Not so easy. Crawford Howard came into the shop and called you two coke whores," he fired right back at her. "And you aren't the only person in the world, Jennifer Franklin. I've got feelings, too. So does your mother. We're in this together; let's think together."

"He called us that?" Cody was outraged.

"If that asshole says one word to me in the hunt field, there

will be two murders. I'll commit mine right in front of God
and everybody!" Bobby exploded.

CHAPTER 62

Being no fool, Crawford Howard hired a public relations spe-
cialist from New York City. Since his .38 was the weapon
used in the commission of a crime, since he was booked on
suspicion of murder and released on bail, he needed damage
control.

Jonathan Sweiss arranged special interviews with the local
television station, the local newspaper, and the Richmond paper as well.

Crawford, being a man of the world, was not surprised
when Jonathan didn't ask if he really had killed Fontaine Buruss. Jonathan didn't care. He was hired to perform a service
and this he did.

In each of the interviews, Crawford explained that he did
not like Fontaine, a personality conflict as well as a conflict of
modus operandi. Differences between them had escalated
during the past six weeks. Crawford expressed no regret at
Fontaine's death because he said that would be false but he
vehemently declared he did not kill the man, he would not kill
any man unless in self-defense.

Martha stood by him, the ordeal bringing them closer
together.

The social consequences were immediate. Fontaine's friends
dropped them both from their lists whereas everyone else

picked them up. The thrill of having a possible murderer in their midst proved enticing to many a jaded hostess.

After all this he called Sister Jane, ready for a fight. He was going to argue that he paid his dues and therefore he should be able to hunt no matter what people thought. Hunting was about sport not about what people thought, did, wore, et cetera. . . . He was stoked.

After hellos he stated, "I intend to hunt Thanksgiving. I know some people in the hunt field think I'm a murderer but—"

Coolly she interrupted before he got rolling. "Crawford, the laws of the land are innocent until proven guilty. You've been charged but you haven't been convicted. I'll see you at Whiskey Ridge on Thursday."

He hung up the phone pleased with her response. Later it dawned on him that she would have to answer for allowing him to hunt. He wasn't making her life any easier but still he was determined not to slink away. The difficulties of being a master were slowly percolating in his brain. Maybe you couldn't run a hunt club like a business.

CHAPTER 63

The small piles of corn brought out birds, woodchucks, deer as well as foxes.

Aunt Netty merrily nibbled away, ignoring the beautiful little bluebird swooping down next to her. The bird would grab a mouthful, then fly up to a tree branch. No matter how mellow Netty appeared to be, no reason to take chances.

The sides of the ravine loomed up; a few shady crevices had thin lines of snow stark against the dark gray rocks. The ravine remained cool.

Inky picked her way down the sloping southern edge.

Aunt Netty, her sleek head deep red now that her winter coat was in, called out, *"Hello."*

Inky bounded next to her. *"Isn't this wonderful?"* She ate a big mouthful of rich yellow corn.

"Sister's laid a trail. We might as well enjoy it. It's miles of trail. She's been working on it for days. She's even got corn under the hanging tree."

"Does she normally do this before the biggest hunts?"

"No. Sister only puts out food when weather's bad—like during the blizzards or during a terrible drought. She feels that we have to hunt for our food or we'll get soft. I expect she's right." Netty munched more corn, careful not to drop any.

"I wonder what she's going to do? A light frost tonight will ensure that our scent is everywhere. Mom and Dad will be out. I guess you all will be out."

"Uncle Yancy will eat and go to bed. He said he did his duty on opening hunt." Aunt Netty smiled. *"I don't know who will stay out but if they do retire, scent should be good for a while anyway. Given reports from the other foxes, I expect Sister made a loop of about four miles."*

"She won't run people through here." Inky appreciated the ravine's inhospitable character for galloping.

"Maybe not but she's got something on her mind." Netty pointed to an envelope inside a plastic baggie tacked to a tree by the pool at the creek crossing.

"Trying to catch Reynard's killer."

Netty smiled. *"Well, she's trying to catch Fontaine's killer but it amounts to the same thing, same person. You know there are a lot of hiding places in here. I'm going to be down here. I won't run tomorrow. There are enough other foxes to do that. I want to be fresh to see what happens down here and to be ready for anything. What are your plans?"*

"I was going to wait on the back side of Hangman's Ridge, then go down toward the kennels."

"Let me make a suggestion. Stay here in the ravine. Let me show you the dens. One or two are occupied by groundhogs but those are near the top of the ravine. You may have need of them and then again you may not. I suggest you not participate tomorrow either. When you hear hounds coming this way—and some will—climb a tree so that you can see everything. Between both of us we ought to figure out what's going on."

"Won't hounds pick up my scent and wind up under the tree?"

"With any luck, the hunted fox, most probably Target at this point, will run through this crossing and up toward the rocks. He can easily lose hounds there. If, for some reason, that doesn't happen, sit tight."

"That will bring down the huntsman." Inky thought a moment. "Huntsman and probably a whip." She shook her head. "Won't work. That will foul up the plan. Even though we don't know what the plan is I'm sure it doesn't call for two foxes in the ravine."

"Crush up pokeweed stalks and throw them around. That will foul scent."

"Maybe. Cora won't be fooled for long. I think what I'd better do is sleep here tonight in one of these dens. In the morning I'll walk in the middle of the creek until I find a tree close enough I can jump to. I don't mind sitting up there for a few hours, especially with all this corn to eat before I get up there."

"Why don't you take that den there." Netty indicated a den on the east side of the ravine not far from the pool. *"I'll take this one on the west side. I've investigated them. Lots of exits."*

"Until tomorrow, then." Inky headed toward the den.

CHAPTER 64

Foxhunters adore Thanksgiving hunt. The light-to-medium frosts of the night before promise a silvery morning, scent sticking to the ground. Low gray clouds hold hope of long, long runs but even if the day dawns bright and clear as a baby's smile, the cool temperatures and the late November frost ensure a bit of a good run no matter what.

Hunters prepare their dinner the night before, as much of it as they can. If no one is home to watch the turkey, then the oven isn't turned on until the horses are turned out. Traditionally, foxhunters eat Thanksgiving dinner in the early evening. This most American of holidays, the most uncommercial of holidays, rings out with toasts to high fences, good hounds, great runs, and much laughter over who parted company from their horse.

Since Thanksgiving is a High Holy Day, horses must be braided. Those who played football, those whose jammed fingers invited pain, those upon whom arthritis visited, cursed as they wrapped the tiny braids with even tinier rubber bands, weaving yarn on those same braids.

Doug, as first whipper-in, was responsible for braiding staff horses. A quiet man, he couldn't help but boast about his tight braids. Doug's idea of a boast was to say, "They stay put."

Lafayette, Rickyroo, and Gunpowder, for Shaker would be riding Fontaine's big gray, gleamed so brightly that Sister laughingly suggested she needed sunglasses just to mount her horse.

Hounds, always excited before a hunt, sensed the additional emotions of a star hunt.

Dragon bragged, *"I got a fox for opening hunt. I'll get one for Thanksgiving."*

Dasher sniffed at his brother. *"You picked up a shot fox. I'd hardly brag about that."*

Dragon turned his back on him.

Shaker backed the hound van into the draw run. Double sliding gates ensured that he could back in, then roll the gates to each side of the van. Shaker, an organized man, left little to chance. He prided himself on never being late to a hunt.

Since the first cast would be at Whiskey Ridge he had only to pull out of the farm and turn right as the state road curled around Hangman's Ridge. Two miles later, at the end of the long low land between the two ridges, he'd turn left and go to the back side of Whiskey Ridge. He particularly liked to cast at the base of the ridge or at the abandoned tobacco shed but the field liked a pretty view, so they generally started at the top, working their way down in no time. Often the fox would cross the road, a lightly traveled road, but any road strikes fear into the heart of a huntsman. He was careful to post a whip on the road to ask cars to slow down if hounds were running in that direction. Once across the road it was anybody's guess. But then foxes, being the marvelous creatures that they are, could just as easily bolt down the other side of the ridge, heading for the flattish lands even farther east. Whereas the land between Hangman's Ridge and Whiskey Ridge was rich and traversed by a strong creek, the lands to the east of Whiskey Ridge rolled into the Hessian River, named for the mercenaries of King George who bivouacked there during the Revolutionary War. This river eventually fed into the James River.

Jefferson Hunt territory proved a test of hounds and staff. The soils changed dramatically from the riverbeds to the rock outcroppings. Rich fertile valleys gave way to flinty soils. Lovely galloping country spiraled down into ravines or up into those same rock outcroppings. Every good hunt breeds hounds specifically for their territory.

A place where the land is flat or rolling, good soils, can use fast hounds with good noses. A wide-open place, like Nevada, needs hounds with blazing speed. Hounds don't need to hunt as closely together as they would back east.

The Jefferson territory demanded an all-round hound, a bit like the German shorthaired pointer, which is an all-round hunting dog. The Jefferson hound needed great nose, great drive, and great cry because light voices would be lost in the heavy forests. Speed was not essential. So the hounds were big, strong-boned, quite impressive, and fast enough to hurtle through the flatlands but not blindingly fast like the packs at Middleburg Hunt, Piedmont Hunt, and Orange County Hunt. Jefferson Hunt hounds were a balanced mix of crossbred and American hounds. Sister kept four Penn-Marydel hounds for those days when scent was abominable. The Penn-Marydels never, ever failed her. Being Virginia-born and -bred, Sister Jane loved a big hound. She thought of the Penn-Marydel as a Maryland or Pennsylvania hound and like any Virginian she felt keen competitiveness with those states but most especially Maryland. This hunting rivalry stretched back before the Revolutionary War, each state straining to outdo the other, thereby ensuring that the New World would develop fantastic hounds.

But in her heart of hearts, Sister knew the Penn-Marydel was a fine hound. The ears were set lower on the head. While they had speed, they kept their noses to the ground longer, which might make them seem slow but the other side of the coin was that a fast pack could overrun the line. So she kept two couple and was glad to have them but if a person asked what kind of hounds she hunted, she replied, "American and crossbred." The crossbred was a mix of American and English blood.

Hounds panted inside the van, not from heat but from anticipation.

Shaker shut the back door, rolled back the sliding doors, drove the van out, stopped it, rolled the gates back shut. Ahead of him, Doug waited with the small horse van. Sister, in her best habit, her shadbelly, sat next to him.

Thanksgiving brought out the best in everyone. It had none of the jitters of opening hunt. By now, staff knew how the pack was working or not working, as the case may be. Plus, at the end of the hunt, there was that glorious dinner with one's family and friends crowded around the table. Mince pie. The very words could send Sister into a swoon.

Every time she thought of her trap, her heart pounded. Would it work? She didn't know what she would do if she did catch the killer. She had substituted her .38 for her .22 loaded with ratshot. The holster hung on the right rear side of her saddle. No one would know she'd switched guns.

Shaker flashed his lights behind them, indicating he was ready.

"You don't mind that I put Keepsake on for Cody?"

"No. He needs the work and she's the best for it. If he can whip, he's more valuable. He can do everything but lead the field. Sorrel might be able to get more money."

"I thought she donated both horses to the hunt."

"She did but I'm waiting to see what her financial condition is—I'll sell the horses to help if she needs it." The van pulled out of the farm road onto the state road. "I heard that Crawford made an offer on the business. Nerve."

"Especially if he killed Fontaine," Doug replied.

"Do you think he did?"

"I don't know."

Other trailers and vans rumbled along ahead of them. Doug checked the rearview mirror; more were coming up behind. In the distance in the opposite direction, trailers were turning onto the Whiskey Ridge Road.

"Going to be a hell of a turnout." He grinned.

"Oh yeah, they're waiting for another murder. Probably hoping it's me because I'll be in front and everyone will get a good viewing. I wonder if they'll tallyho?" she sang out.

"How about 'Gone to ground'?"

They both howled with laughter, a bad situation bringing out the best in them.

Doug flicked on his left turn signal, waited for the Franklins to turn in from the opposite direction.

"You know what crosses my mind? Odd. Remember when we saw the Reaper or the Angel of Death or whatever it was?" Doug nodded that he remembered. "You were on the other side of Hangman's Ridge, picking up hounds. Well, I wonder if Fontaine saw it, too. I wonder where he was."

"He did. Maybe." Doug's eyes widened. "I hadn't thought of that. I saw him drive by. That is too weird."

"Do you think we're next or can you see Death and he doesn't take you?"

"You're giving me goose bumps."

"If I had any sense, I'd be afraid but I'm not. I'm more afraid of how I will face death than I am of death itself but I'll fight. Not ready to go. I don't know what the hell we saw that sunset. Plus there's a black fox out there—as shiny as coal." She surveyed the sea of trailers and vans as they cruised into the meadow at the base of Whiskey Ridge. "Jesus, Mary, and Joseph."

"Think of the cap fees," he gleefully remarked, since those people visiting the hunt had to pay a fifty-dollar fee to go out.

The cap fees helped defray the hound costs, which averaged about eighteen to twenty thousand dollars a year.

As Doug cut the motor and they disembarked, people doffed their hats, calling out, "Good morning, Master."

As tradition dictated, the master nodded in return or, if carrying her whip, would hold it high.

"Doug, I need to touch base with Shaker for one minute. Be right back. Oh, your stock tie pin is crooked. Get Cody to fix it for you." She noticed Cody walking over to help Doug unload the horses.

"Morning, Master."

"Morning, Cody." Sister hurried to Shaker, who parked a bit off from the crowd.

"I count one hundred and eleven rigs." Shaker bent over to rub an old towel on his boots.

"I keep telling you, the secret is to use panty hose. Better shine."

"I'm not going into a drugstore to buy panty hose."

"That's right," Sister mocked him. "Someone will think you're a drag queen and you'd be so pretty, too."

"Yes, Master." He bowed in mock obedience.

"Shaker, I want you to do something today. Should the pack split, stay with the larger body even if the smaller is in better cry."

His eyes narrowed. "Better not split."

"Not if the whips are on. Doug up front, of course. Betty on the left. How about Cody on the right. I'm keeping Jennifer in the field. The Franklins have to just get through this as best they can. Or more to the point, Jennifer has to face it down."

"Makes me glad I never had children," Shaker grumbled.

"Don't say that, brother. Children are a gift from God even when you'd like to brain them," Sister quietly but emphatically told him.

"I'm sorry." He had forgotten that Walter Lungrun was Raymond's natural son. Relationships baffled Shaker. Walter's parentage made him think of Ray Junior. He'd known Junior and liked the boy. He liked the father less. He knew about

Walter because once in a confessional moment, a tortured moment after Junior's death, Ray sobbed out the whole story. Shaker didn't think Walter knew who his real father was and he was certain Sister knew nothing about her husband's affair and subsequent child. He wondered if she would find out. He felt he could never tell her. She'd lived this long without knowing. Why disturb her?

She put her arm around his neck. "Don't worry about it. I remember the good times. Like the Thanksgiving hunt when Junior was ten and he viewed. He stood in his stirrups and was so excited he couldn't speak. His pony took off and he fell flat on his back, got up, and finally said, "Holloa.""

"Tough little brat. Like his momma." He watched Crawford pull in with his brand-new Dodge dually pulling his brand-new aluminum four-horse trailer with every convenience known to man or beast. "Can't believe that man is showing his face."

"Better his face than his ass."

Staff, mounted, surrounded the hounds. Sister rode through the trailers, welcoming people. Her presence made them move along a bit faster. Georgia Vann had forgotten her hair net. She bounded from trailer to trailer until she found a woman carrying an extra.

Finally, everyone was up.

Lafayette remarked to Oreo, carrying Bobby, *"On time. A bleeding miracle."*

"O-o-o," Oreo grunted. *"He's put on more weight."*

"Might want to loosen your horse's girth," a rider said.

"Might want to loosen his," Betty called out as she sat by the hounds.

"I want everyone to know that I'm above all this," Bobby joked, glad that people were willing to let his daughters work out their own problems. He felt a little extrasensitive today so the joking made him feel better. People weren't laughing behind his back but he noticed that few would talk to Crawford or stand near him as Sister addressed them.

"Happy Thanksgiving. Thank you all for coming out and we hope the foxes will come out also. As you know, we lost a faithful supporter, a generous man, and one of my best friends. I hope Peter Wheeler, young again and strong, is mounted on Benny, his big chestnut, and they're both looking down at us, wishing us well." She paused a moment. "Huntsman."

His cap in his hand, he nodded to the master. Putting his cap on his head, he asked the hounds, "Ready, children?"

"Yes!" they spoke in unison.

"Come along, then." He quietly encouraged them, turning his horse toward the top of Whiskey Ridge for the scenic first cast.

"Jennifer." Sister motioned for the girl to ride up. "Keep an eye on Crawford, will you? Talk to me after the hunt."

"Yes, Master." Jennifer pulled back, waiting for a few first-flight members to pass her. Then she fell in behind Crawford and Martha. She wasn't sure what Sister wanted but she was pleased to be given a special mission. At least Sister liked her and trusted her with responsibility.

The top of Whiskey Ridge was rounder then Hangman's Ridge off in the distance, the giant black oak stark against the silvery rising mists. The sides of Whiskey Ridge feathered and softened down to the creek bed, a small valley on the west side. The grade was even smoother on the east side; the Hessian River was visible across the rolling terrain, a cauldron of mist hanging over the snaking river.

Frost silvered each blade of grass, each leaf, the exposed roots of the old trees.

Shaker, voice low but filled with excitement, leaned down. "He's out there. Get 'im. Get 'im."

"Yay!" The hounds dashed away from the huntsman. Noses to the ground, sterns upright, they wanted a smashing Thanksgiving hunt.

Down on the east side of the ridge Uncle Yancy picked up a trot. He heard hounds above him and felt no need to provide them with a chase. He recalled seeing Patsy out before dawn, so just to be sure he swerved from a direct path to his den, crossed Patsy's scent, and then scampered the half mile to his cozy home.

Up on the ridge Sister hung back about fifty yards from her hounds. Since she wasn't sure what direction they'd finally take she sat tight.

Dasher's tail looked like a clock pendulum, back and forth. Finally, he spoke. *"Check this out."*

Cora and Diana came over. *"Faint but good. Let's see where it leads."*

Within minutes the hounds coursed down the eastern slope of the ridge, reached the grassy bottom streaking across the well-maintained hay fields, a beautiful sight for the field to behold, since the pack was running well together, Cora in the lead, Diana securely in the middle.

Although the grade was gentle, one rider, frantically clutching her martingale, flipped ass over teakettle when the martingale snapped. Georgia Vann, on mop-up duty, stopped to make certain the lady was breathing.

"All right?"

"Yes."

"Do you want to push on?"

"I think I'll go back to the trailer. I hate to ride without a martingale." She led her horse back up the hill and the poor fellow was severely disappointed—all his friends galloping toward the Hessian River in the distance.

At the end of the expansive hay field, a narrow row of trees bordering a sunken farm road presented an interesting obstacle. The old stone fence on the other side of the towering lindens was only two and a half feet high but the drop on the other side would scare the bejesus out of a few people.

"Yee-haw!" Lafayette snorted, sailing over. He loved a

drop jump because he was in the air so long. Horse hang time was how he thought of it.

Sister kept her center of gravity right over Lafayette's center. They landed in the soft earth of the lane, then scrambled up the small embankment on the other side into a field planted with winter wheat. She skirted the field, hearing the screams behind her of those who made the drop and those who didn't. She turned her head just in time to see Lottie Fisher pop out of her tack and wind up hugging her horse's neck. It was funny although at that precise moment Lottie didn't think so.

The hounds moved faster now as scent became stronger. They reached the place where Uncle Yancy had crossed Patsy's scent. Milling about for a few minutes Dragon bellowed.

Not trusting him, Cora hurried next to him before he could take off. She put her nose down. *"It's good. Let's go."*

They turned at a right angle, heading northeast now into the pine plantation owned by the Fishers. Paths were wide, easy to maneuver. At the end of the twenty-year-old loblolly pines, they hopped over an upright in an old fence line. Sister had built that jump with Ray Senior using sturdy locust trees felled in a storm. Fifteen years later the jump stood strong.

Everyone made it over the upright. Three strides from that another jump faced them as they moved into a cornfield, stalks uncut. This simple jump of truck tires suspended on a cable gave half the field a problem and they had to wait for Bobby Franklin and the hilltoppers to go through the gate. Once through they bade Bobby good-bye, hurrying to catch up with the field, now at the far end of the cornfield, pushing into a second cornfield separated by an expensive, impressive zig-zag or snake fence. Sister and Lafayette arched over the point where two sides crossed together. They landed smack in the standing corn. She ran down a row, hounds in front of her and to the side of her now in full cry. They'd picked up Patsy. She was running about a quarter of a mile ahead and being shadowed by St. Just. St. Just, unbeknownst to him, was being shadowed by Athena.

At the end of this cornfield a fence bordered a rocky creek. It, too, was a zigzag. Sister jumped that and one stride later clattered across the creek with inviting low banks. On the other side the hounds turned west. They ran, then lost the scent.

Patsy dashed into the creek, ran two hundred yards, then crossed back into the cornfield by tiptoeing across a log fallen over the farm road. She figured this would keep her scent high and she was right.

Even when Cora figured out where the red vixen had exited the creek she couldn't get high enough to smell the top of the downed sycamore.

The check lasted five minutes, which helped the field. Sister counted heads. She'd started with sixty-nine and was down to sixty-two. Jennifer stayed just behind Crawford and Martha. Sister winked at her.

People reached down, feeling their girths. A few tightened them. Many reached for their flasks. Nothing like refreshment or what some members called Dutch courage.

"I've got a line all right but it's a different fox," Diana remarked to her steadier brother, Dasher.

The rest of the pack trotted over to her. They checked it out.

"I can't pick up Patsy. She's slipped us somehow, so we might as well go on this. Target, I'd say." Cora thought a moment. *"Just so you young ones know, it's always better to stay on the hunted fox but Patsy's given us the slip, so—it's Thanksgiving hunt; let's put on a show."*

"Follow me," St. Just cawed overhead.

"Keep your nose to the ground. I'll keep an eye on St. Just," Cora commanded them.

"He hates Target. We can trust him," Dragon said.

"Oh yes, and he'll run us all into an oncoming truck as long as it takes Target, too. Trust your senses and me before

you trust him," Cora loudly told all of them. *"Now come on. Scent is holding."*

Hounds moved along the creek, then drifted away into woods through some thick underbrush while Sister and the field kept on the edges, crowding along a deer trail.

Sister could see Betty, since leaves had fallen off the trees in the blizzard. Betty moved along; Outlaw's ears pricked forward, since he could hear the hounds better than she. She let him pick the way.

Hounds burst out of the thicket, hustled along the deer path, then loped into a neatly clipped hay field, a stupendous one hundred acres of rolling land.

The temperature rose slightly; the tops of the grass blades swayed, the frost turning to water, the wind gentle but insistent from the west.

Hounds, in full cry, stretching out to their full length, flew across those one hundred acres in the blink of an eye. Cody was on the right border of the field; her mother was on the left; Doug was ahead, where the edge of the beautiful fields rolled into another farm road, cutover acres on the other side. Shaker stayed with his hounds, a wide grin on his face, his seat relaxed in the saddle. He could have been sitting in a rocking chair.

Target, just out of sight, headed straight through the cutover acres, making certain to make use of any toppled timbers. He knew the hounds could move through them easily but the debris would slow the field.

By the time Sister, first flight, and then Bobby with the hilltoppers picked their way through the cutover acres, Target curved back, running parallel to the fence line along the hay fields. Halfway down the fence line he climbed up on the top rail and sped along, jumping down at the corner, where he swerved across the creek-bottom fields, crossed the paved highway, and lightly trotted halfway up Hangman's Ridge, where he surveyed the panorama from a monumental boulder jutting out from the ridge.

Cora led the way. Doug pulled up at the highway to slow traffic. As soon as Betty saw him she waved him on, for it was important for Doug to stay in front of the hounds. She took over the traffic cop job. Next came Shaker, the bulk of the pack before him, moving together in good order and on the scent, slowed somewhat by Target's tricks, especially his jaunt along the fence. But Cora, wise, kept her nose to the ground until she found the spot where he'd launched off the fence.

One hundred and fifty yards behind Shaker rode Sister, Lafayette's big stride effortlessly eating up the acres. The trailing ribbons on Sister's cap danced in the breeze; her patent-leather-topped boots caught the light that pierced through the lifting silvery haze. Immediately behind her rode Martha Howard, a surprise to her as well as others as she moved right by them, but Martha, adrenaline banishing her normal fears, just this once wanted to ride in the master's pocket. Behind her the others spread out, Crawford not far behind, since Czapaka, although not the fastest horse, had a big, comfortable stride. Jennifer was immediately behind Crawford. Walter Lungrun, relying on athletic ability more than skill, was behind them. The remainder of the field was spread out.

They jumped the post and rail near the highway, looked left and right, then sped across, jumped the double coops into the bottomlands, striking straight for Hangman's Ridge.

By now the field had covered two and a half miles. Horses and humans were limbered up.

Target admired the sight before him. Then, mindful of Cora's speed and that of the insufferable Dragon, he hopped off the boulder, cut down the side of the ridge, crossed the silvery hay field on the back side, dashing into the woods, making sure to scramble over Fontaine's coop.

Once in the woods he put on the afterburners, streaking

toward the tip of the ravine. He'd covered another mile in less than five minutes over uneven terrain. As he looked down into the ravine he considered how best to trouble the hounds.

Comet walked out of the woods. *"Target, are you heading down?"*

Target thought if the young gray had been human he would have rolled up a cigarette pack in his T-shirt sleeve. *"Yes. You?"*

"Thought I'd walk along the edge here and duck into those rocks at the end. I've been eating the corn trail. I didn't expect hounds to get here so fast." He indicated the large rock outcropping with the ledge looming out of sight at the far end of the ravine. Holly bushes and mountain laurel covered the folds of land leading water down to the creek below. Enormous oaks, hickories, and walnuts, spared from logging by their inaccessible location, gave the place a magical air. Chinquapins dotted the upper rim, their bundles resembling baby chestnuts, a light spiky green.

"Let's make them crazy." Target grinned. *"See that den there?"* He headed over to an abandoned groundhog den. *"Let's go in together. I'll take the exit just under the edge of the ravine and you leave by the path heading back toward the hog's back. The death jump."* Target added, *"They'll split for sure. That will make the whips work up a sweat. Ha. Sister laid the corn trail and she intends for the pack to split. A painful thing for a master, so you know it's—vital."*

Eagerly both males zipped into the groundhog den, moving through the central living quarters.

Target sniffed. *"Groundhogs have no sense of aesthetics."*

Comet didn't reply. He thought the old den was fine although he'd have to pull out the old grass left behind.

At the fork underground, Target went left and Comet turned right.

"Good luck," Comet called as he wriggled out into the pale sunlight, filtering through low clouds.

"Ditto," the big red called back from the tunnel, his voice echoing. He emerged just under a pin oak, half of its roots clinging to the rim of the ravine, the other half securely in deep ground. Down he slithered, heading toward the creek. Comet, having the easier path but the more dangerous open one, ran hard to the hog's back, flattened and crawled under, making sure to leave lots of scent under the jump, then he crawled out, barreled across the high meadow, ducked under the three-board fence at the back side to scramble over the moss-covered rock. Then, feeling devilish, instead of dipping into a den just below the flat rocks he made a big semicircle back into the same high meadow and headed across to the western woods on the other side, blew through those, entering the hay fields leading toward the kennels. He screeched to a halt at the kennel.

"Hey!"

Those hounds left behind, gyps in heat and puppies, lifted their ears. *"What are you doing here?"*

"You can't get me." He lifted back his head and laughed.

"Just you wait, Comet. Pride goeth before a fall," a pretty tricolor hound warned.

Raleigh—sneaking up behind Comet, Golly behind him— would have pounced except that Rooster, overexcited at the prospect of game larger than a rabbit, bounded past the shrewder animals.

Comet heard him, spun around, knew he had a split second, and he leapt sideways, narrowly escaping Rooster's snapping jaws. He shot toward the chicken yard, a makeshift arrangement, as Sister hadn't time to put chicken wire up over the top, a precaution against hawks, who were hell on chickens.

Comet climbed up over the wire on the side, dropping smack into the middle of Peter's chickens.

"Fox! Fox! We'll all be killed," the chickens screamed, running around. The smarter ones hid under the henhouse.

Raleigh growled at Rooster, then ran over to the chicken coop.

Golly, ahead of the Doberman, climbed up the chicken wire. *"You get out of there!"*

Raleigh hollered, *"Golly, don't go in there!"*

Golly glanced down. Comet's open jaws awaited. *"You've got a point there, Raleigh."*

Rooster, frenzied, was digging, trying to get under the fence.

"Leave it!" Raleigh commanded. *"You won't get in in time and the chickens, if any live, will get out."* Turning his attention to Comet, equally as trapped as the chickens, Raleigh reasoned with him. *"If you kill those chickens, Sister will have a fit. Now let's work together. You need to get out."*

"I don't trust him," Comet snarled at Rooster.

Golly wasn't sure Rooster could be controlled under the circumstances. Back on the ground she leaned into Raleigh, who understood her wordless thoughts.

In the distance they heard hounds; then they heard silence.

Comet knew hounds would find scent soon enough but they weren't where he thought they'd have to cast again. *"I need to get out of here before the pack is here."*

"You're in dangerous territory even if you do get out. Your one hope is to go under the porch."

"You can't let him go! You can't." Rooster was beside himself.

"I have an idea." Golly spoke to Comet: *"Stay here. We can't get in. The hounds can't get in. If you don't kill one chicken, Sister will put hounds up and us, too. She'll let you go. It's better than taking a chance with Rooster."*

"No!" Rooster spun in circles of frustration.

"Calm down." Raleigh's deep throaty growl meant business. *"You can hunt rabbits all you want but leave the fox alone."*

"But I'm a harrier. I can hunt foxes as well as those damned foxhounds."

"I don't doubt that but you're not supposed to hunt foxes and besides, where would you be if Sister hadn't brought you home? She doesn't want any fox killed. This is no way to reward her. Peter would be upset if he knew you offended Sister."

Rooster, anguished, lay down, putting both paws over his eyes. He moaned.

"Your word?"

"Yes." Comet, full of corn, wouldn't have killed a chicken anyway, but no point in spoiling his image.

Raleigh stood over the harrier. *"I'm bigger, I'm stronger, and if you even twitch, I will tear you up."*

"And I'll scratch your eyes out." Golly puffed up to three times her size. Then she hissed at Comet. *"You, too. Worthless carcass!"* She was brave but sitting under Raleigh's chest she was especially brave.

The gyps in heat, the household animals, and Comet listened as cry picked up, then stopped again.

"I thought they'd be halfway here by now," Comet commented. *"I wonder what's going on?"*

Back at the edge of the woods, the hounds hit a hot pocket, one of those swirls of air sometimes ten or more degrees hotter than the air around it. The scent, already over their heads, scattered. As the hounds cast themselves St. Just flew low overhead. He circled, then flew down just above their heads.

"Target's in the ravine. Comet split off from him. You'll have a split pack if you aren't careful."

Dragon, ready to roll, shouted to Cora, *"Let's follow the raven."*

"No. We pick up scent properly. We aren't gallivanting across the county because of one raven's revenge. Put your nose to the ground and get to work. Now!"

The check, that pause in hunting where hounds must again find scent, although unexpected, was near the ravine, a half mile away if one could move in a straight line, which one couldn't.

Sister leaned over to Martha. "Will you take the field? I'm feeling punk."

Thrilled to be given such responsibility, acting field master, Martha gushed, "I'd be glad to. Would you like someone to go back with you?"

"You know, I think if I walk back I'll be fine and if I feel better I'll find you. I must have eaten something that doesn't agree with me." Standing in her stirrups, Sister said, "Stay with Martha." Then she rode across the meadow as though heading home. To her surprise, Walter Lungrun followed her.

"Ma'am, are you all right?"

"Upset stomach. I'll be fine."

"I'll escort you home. We're close enough to go back to your place, don't you think?"

"You rejoin the field. I'll be fine, thank you."

He hesitated. "It won't take long. I can find them."

It occurred to her that Walter might have killed Fontaine to revenge his father. She thought he was too smart to risk his career, his own life . . . but that didn't mean he couldn't have done it. Find a motive and you find the murderer. A thin ripple of fear shot through her. She shook it off. Even if he did have reason, she didn't think he could ride well enough or knew enough about scent to lay a good drag. She was fluttery inside.

"I'm the master and I'm telling you to rejoin the field."

"Yes, Master." He obediently turned Clemson back toward the field, which was still waiting for hounds to find the line.

Sister walked across the creek meadows to the base of Hangman's Ridge. She followed the base of the ridge until she was out of sight. She heard hounds strike again, moving across the creek meadows toward the woods. Once into the woods she turned back, squeezed Lafayette into a canter, skirted the meadow, jumping in at a stiff coop—three feet nine inches—used only by staff. This dropped her closer to the ravine. She dismounted, leading Lafayette to a sheltered overhang. Tying him to a low limb, she patted his neck. "Stay here, buddy, and stay silent."

"Yes, but don't leave me for long. It's too good a day," he pleaded.

She rubbed his head. "Silent, dear friend." Then she used whatever cover she could find and slowly worked her way toward the rock outcroppings. She reached them in five minutes, slipping a few times. At the outcroppings she dropped down to the ledge, partially protected from view by holly bushes at the edge plus the low full limb of a fir tree. There she waited.

She heard hounds at the other edge of the ravine, the sound funneling down, then lifting up to her. She heard another check, another find, and she heard the pack split, the bulk moving away from her, a splinter group heading down into the ravine. Below her she saw Target, fat, glossy red, trotting down to the creek. Then he walked through the creek, crossing a bit above the rocky crossing where the envelope was tacked to the tree. To her amazement, Aunt Netty popped out of her den and Inky called from the tree she was perching in.

Target paused, barked something to Netty, then hearing the splinter group close in, he hurried up toward the rock outcroppings as Netty ducked back into the den, her nose still visible.

Low into the ravine flew St. Just, dive-bombing Target. And behind St. Just, closing fast was Dragon, three couple of young hounds racing with him.

"Kill him. Kill him," St. Just screamed.

Hoofbeats thundered behind the rock outcropping. Sister shrank farther in, flat now against the rock. She prayed Lafayette, beautifully gray, wouldn't catch the eye of the whip above her and he wouldn't whinny to the horse. He didn't.

Down into the ravine the whip rode and it wasn't until she saw Keepsake that Sister knew it was Cody.

"What a gifted rider," she thought to herself as Cody cracked her whip, trying to turn back Dragon.

St. Just dive-bombed Target again, so intent on his mission, the blue-black bird didn't hear Athena overhead. She waited for St. Just to reach the bottom of his dive. Then with open talons she streamed down, raking the raven across the back.

Sister had never seen anything like it. The two birds climbed into the air and St. Just screamed at Athena, who silently flew to a high tree branch. St. Just swooped past her, then dove for Target again, who was climbing up toward the rock outcropping. Athena opened her wide wingspan, lifted off, again striking the raven, this time with her claws balled up. Black feathers flew and St. Just pulled off Target to face the huge owl. St. Just's only weapon against his foe was speed. Athena's size, wisdom, and famed ferocity ensured that only a fool would tangle with her.

By the time St. Just pulled away, turned in the air to strike again at the red fox, Target had reached the rock outcroppings, climbing to the ledge.

He froze when he saw Sister, then boldly ran right between her legs, ducking into the den behind her.

St. Just flew toward the den, squawking loudly. Cody, down at the creek crossing, would have seen Sister if she'd looked up but instead she was whipping off hounds and finally went to the ratshot to stop Dragon.

She fired.

"Ouch!" he yelped.

"Leave it!" She commanded. "Hold up," she yelled at the other hounds, who were scared now.

Sister admired Cody's whipping ability just as St. Just flew right in her face, screaming about Target. Athena struck again, knocking the raven sideways in the air. She scared Sister, who grabbed the fir limb.

Down below, Cody saw the envelope. She dismounted, holding the reins. She dropped the reins to reach the envelope.

As she did, Aunt Netty, who'd figured out the truth, stuck her head out of the den and taunted, *"Nah-nah-nah-nah-nah!"*

Dragon, butt full of ratshot, bolted toward the den. The others followed and Keepsake, green, spooked. He tore up the ravine.

Cody, hands shaking, whip draped around her neck, knew she couldn't get him back. Then she heard Lafayette whinny.

"Come stand with me!" the gray called from his hiding place.

Keepsake, scared at the hounds bolting, scared that he would really be in trouble for leaving, picked his way up to Lafayette. By the time he reached the seasoned master's horse he was lathered.

So was Cody as she read the letter. "I know who you are. Give yourself up and make it easy on everybody, yourself included."

She slipped the letter into her frock coat pocket, looked around. She didn't see Sister but she caught sight of Keepsake. She began climbing the ravine to reach her horse.

The hounds dug outside Netty's hiding place but she was safe in the back with lots of ways out. She laughed at them.

Inky stayed put in the tree. St. Just, bruised, repaired to the top of a walnut. Athena sat opposite him just in case. She watched Cody finally reach Keepsake, where she saw Lafayette. Defeated, she waited for Sister.

Sister reached the rim of the ravine, picking her way around to the horses. Cody led out Lafayette, handing him to a woman she had been trained to obey since childhood.

"Why?"

Tears rolling down her face, Cody simply answered, "Jennifer. Even after rehab he'd give her drugs."

"Oh, Cody, there had to be another way."

"I hated him."

Knowing that hate, like love, can't be explained neatly away, that passion defies all logic, she put her hand on Cody's shoulder. "Come on."

"I'm sorry."

"I know." Sister swung up in the saddle.

"I'm not sorry I killed him. I'm sorry I dragged everyone into it." A flash of panic hit. "Is there no way out?"

"No." Sister turned to her as they reached the farm road in the woods. "Crawford shouldn't pay for your sin."

"He's so rich he'll get off."

"That's not the point. You have to turn yourself in." Sister inhaled. "In a way I can understand why you killed Fontaine. You believed Jennifer wasn't strong enough to resist him. You were wrong but I understand. But to kill a healthy red fox and to use the hunt for your revenge . . . Cody, that was beneath contempt."

Although Cody could have fired ratshot straight into Sister's face the thought didn't occur to her. She'd acted impulsively once, fueled by love for her sister and hate for Fontaine. Her mind worked clearly enough now, even if her moral sense remained tilted. She hung her head, saying nothing.

Sister cupped her hands. "Come to me." She yelled for her hounds, who, tricked by Aunt Netty, ran up out of the ravine. Knowing they'd been bad, once in sight of Sister, they crawled on their bellies. "I'm ashamed of you. Now come on." She reprimanded them, which was worse than any ratshot from a whip, for the hounds loved Sister.

Each woman rode back with a heavy heart: Sister, distressed that a young life was wasted as well as a man's life taken away, no matter his irresponsible behavior. Cody, burdened with shame and fear, fought her tears.

In front of them they heard the hounds heading toward the kennel. Well, Cody would give herself up but they might as well hunt their way back.

They flew over the jumps, galloped across the upper meadow and then through the woods into the creek meadows, around Hangman's Ridge, reaching the chicken coop in about fifteen minutes of hard riding, the three couple of hounds behind them.

Shaker, on the ground, stood outside the chicken coop. The entire field, mounted, watched with amusement. Doug and Betty had come in from their posts as Shaker blew them in.

"Sister!" Shaker called out. "You okay?"

"Yes. Are you hunting chickens now, Shaker Crown?"

"Look here." He pointed and Comet stuck his head out from the chicken coop.

"Well, I'll be."

Golly, in a tree, bragged, *"He's afraid of me!"*

Raleigh ignored this. *"I promised he'd be safe."*

"This is a first." She smiled, dismounting. "Well, folks, you'll long remember this day. Shaker, take the hounds back to the kennel. And let's lock up Rooster in the tack room. Folks, we've put foxes to ground today but we've never put one to a chicken coop, so I think we'll call it a day. Thank you for hunting with us."

People raised their caps, others reached down, touching Sister's shoulder. Betty noticed the greenish-white cast to her older daughter's face.

Sister smiled up at Cody. "Ride on back to the trailers with your family. I expect you to call Ben Sidell."

Cody nodded yes.

As everyone left and Sister, Doug, and Shaker got the hounds in, praising them lavishly, they marveled over the day's hunt.

"If we ignore the chicken coop, he'll climb out and leave," Sister advised.

"Funny he hasn't killed any chickens," Doug remarked.

"Guess he's full," she replied, not revealing that she'd put out enough corn to feed a regiment of foxes. "But to be sure I'll put out corn." She left Doug to care for the horses. She opened the door to the chicken coop, warily eyeing Comet. "Here. Go when you're ready." She admired him, for he was a handsome gray. "You know, fellow, anyone who says grays aren't fun to chase doesn't know foxes."

"Thank you."

"Get that fox outta here," the chickens complained bitterly from under the chicken coop.

"Actually, why don't I hold open the door." She did and Comet scooted right out.

"You're a good dog," he called to Raleigh in passing.

Golly backed down the tree and Rooster howled from the tack room, deep distressed howls.

Taking a deep breath, Sister returned to the stable, where Doug was putting sweat sheets on the horses. "I'll go pick up the trailer later. Did Cody say when she would bring back Keepsake?"

"Tomorrow. I told her to take him home for tonight. Easier."

"Good." He whistled.

"Doug. Cody killed Fontaine." He stopped whistling as she continued. "She admitted it and she will turn herself in to Sheriff Sidell this evening. She's telling her parents and Jennifer now."

He rested his head on his hand, which was on Lafayette's neck; then he looked up. "I did it."

"No, you didn't."

"I did. I hated that she slept with him."

"Nice try."

"She confessed because she knew a black man wouldn't stand a chance. As a woman she can throw herself on the mercy of the court." He breathed hard.

She put her arms around him. "Honey, I'm sorry."

"I did it!"

"You're too smart to kill like that, Doug. I'm sorry she did it. I'm sorry for you, too. I don't know what will happen. With a good lawyer—" She released him. "Go to her. I'll finish the horses."

"Thanks," he whispered.

As he left, Sister checked the sweat sheets. She finally let Rooster out of the tack room.

Shaker came in from the kennel to discuss the hunt. She told him. "She could have lied and made it worse. But she didn't."

He shook his head. "Crazy. People do crazy things." He sat on a tack trunk. "Maybe it's better not to feel much."

"I don't know, Shaker. I just don't know. I liked Fontaine. I'm horrified he sold drugs and used drugs to seduce these girls. My God, it's sordid."

"Had a leak in his soul." He crossed his leg over his knee. "How'd you know?"

"Process of elimination. Had to be one of my whips or you, and I could see you all the time. But you are the only people who ride well enough to have pulled it off. That narrowed it down to Betty, Cody, and Doug. When Dean Offendahl started talking, then I figured it was probably Cody."

"Her mother?"

"Too stable."

"Jennifer."

"I don't think Jennifer could have executed the plan. She's a beautiful girl but she's a thirty-watt bulb in a hundred-watt socket."

"There is that. Doug?"

"Well, he had reason but in the end, character tells. He might have gotten into a fight with Fontaine once he knew the story but I don't think he knew the whole story until Dean spilled his guts. What a smarmy kid. He'll grow up to be just like his father. But Doug, he wouldn't kill a man for that even if he wanted to do it."

"Bobby?"

"Can't ride well enough to lay the drag, then fire through that ravine. Although Bobby could kill."

"I expect any of us could if we had to." Shaker sighed. "It's been quite a day."

"Yes. Thank you for a good hunt. Hounds did well."

"Not so well. Dragon took a few with him."

"My fault. I've been putting out corn for days. I needed to get Cody back into the ravine. I didn't know if it would work. Anyway, there were so many foxes out today it's a wonder the pack didn't split before then. I even saw a black fox up in a tree when I was in the ravine."

"I see her now and again. You could have told me about the corn."

"No. I had to do this alone. I'm sorry for her even if she did kill Fontaine. It will take me longer to forgive her for killing the fox—I know that sounds awful but it's truly how I feel. It's a Greek tragedy without the gods." She paused. "But then I suppose they are always with us."

"Oh, don't go into these weighty matters, Sister. Zeus. God. Allah. All the same to me."

"You're right. Well, how about fresh coffee? Come on up to the house."

"Thought you'd never ask."

The two old friends walked across the leaves, crunching underfoot. Raleigh, Rooster, and Golly raced around them. The chickens settled down again in their house.

As she made coffee she glanced at the photograph of Raymond, Ray Junior, and herself, in full regalia at the start of a hunt, years ago. It was the last year of Ray Junior's life. She thought to herself that she didn't know if the gods were always with us or not. She hoped they were or that something kind was out there but she felt, often, that the people she had loved in this life, her mother and father, her husband and son, and now Peter Wheeler, were with her. Love never dies, she told herself and a pain, deep and sharp, caught her breath. If only she could pass on what she had learned to young people. If only she could have stepped in and turned Cody away from the drugs, the downward slide. What love had been given her she wished to give to others. Most times they didn't much want it but hounds, horses, cats, and dogs did and they were a gift from the gods, too.

Back in Target's den, Target, Charlene, Patsy, Aunt Netty, and Uncle Yancy felt a satisfaction that Reynard's killer would pay the price.

After full discussion, including the help of the grays, especially Inky, the foxes dispersed to their separate dens.

When they were alone Charlene said, *"Sister thought like a fox."*

"I suppose." He sighed. *"But you know, I'm about as amused by humans as I care to be."*

SOME USEFUL TERMS

AWAY—A fox has "gone away" when he has left the covert. Hounds are "away" when they have left the covert on the line of the fox.

BRUSH—The fox's tail.

BURNING SCENT—Scent so strong or hot that hounds pursue the line without hesitation.

BYE DAY—A day not regularly on the fixture card.

CAP—The fee nonmembers pay to a hunt for that day's sport.

CARRY A GOOD HEAD—When hounds run well together to a good scent, a scent spread wide enough for the whole pack to feel it.

CARRY A LINE—When hounds follow the scent. This is also called "working a line."

CAST—Hounds spread out in search of scent. They may cast themselves or be cast by the huntsman.

CHARLIE—A term for a fox. A fox may also be called Reynard.

CHECK—When hounds lose the scent and stop. The field must wait quietly while the hounds search for scent.

COLORS—A distinguishing color—usually worn on the collar but sometimes on the facings of a coat—that identifies a hunt. Colors can be awarded only by the master and can be won only in the field.

CUB HUNTING—The informal hunting of young foxes in the late summer and early fall, before formal hunting. The main purpose is to enter young hounds into the pack. Until recently only the most knowledgeable members were invited to cub hunt since they would not interfere with young hounds.

COVERT—A patch of woods or bushes where a fox might hide. Pronounced *cover*.

CRY—How one hound tells another what is happening. The sound will differ according to the various stages of the chase. It's also called "giving tongue" and should occur when a hound is working a line.

DOG FOX—The male fox.

DOG HOUND—The male hound.

DOUBLE—A series of short, sharp notes blown on the horn to alert all that a fox is afoot. The "gone away" series of notes are a form of doubling the horn.

DRAFT—To acquire hounds from another hunt is to draft them.

DRAW—The plan by which a fox is hunted or searched for in a certain area, like a covert.

DRIVE—The desire to push the fox, to get up with the line. It's a very desirable trait in hounds, so long as they remain obedient.

DWELL—To hunt without getting foward. A hound that dwells is a bit of a putterer.

ENTER—Hounds are entered into the pack when they first hunt, usually during cubbing season.

FIELD—The group of people riding to hounds, exclusive of the master and hunt staff.

FIELD MASTER—The person appointed by the master to control the field. Often it is the master him- or herself.

FIXTURE—A card sent to all dues-paying members, stating when and where the hounds will meet. A fixture card properly received is an invitation to hunt. This means the card would be mailed or handed to you by the master.

GONE AWAY—The call on the horn when the fox leaves the covert.

GONE TO GROUND—A fox who has ducked into his den or some other refuge has gone to ground.

GOOD NIGHT—The traditional farewell to the master after the hunt, regardless of the time of day.

HILLTOPPER—A rider who follows the hunt but who does not jump. Hilltoppers are also called the "second field." The jumpers are called the "first flight."

HOICK—The huntsman's cheer to the hounds. It is derived from the Latin *hic haec hoc* which means "here."

HOLD HARD—To stop immediately.

HUNTSMAN—The person in charge of the hounds in the field and in the kennel.

KENNELMAN—A hunt staff member who feeds the hounds and cleans the kennels. In wealthy hunts there may be a number of kennelmen. In hunts with a modest budget, the huntsman or even the master cleans the kennels and feeds hounds.

LARK—To jump fences unnecessarily when hounds aren't running. Masters frown on this since it is often an invitation to an accident.

LIFT—To take the hounds from a lost scent in the hopes of finding a better scent farther on.

LINE—The scent trail of the fox.

LIVERY—The uniform worn by the professional members of the hunt staff. Usually it is scarlet, but blue, yellow, brown, or gray are also used. The recent dominance of scarlet has to do with people buying coats off the rack as opposed to having tailors cut them. (When anything is mass-produced the choices usually dwindle and such is the case with livery.)

MASK—The fox's head.

MEET—The site where the day's hunting begins.

MFH—The master of foxhounds; the individual in charge of the hunt: hiring, firing, landowner relations, opening territory (in large hunts this is the job of the hunt secretary), developing the pack of hounds, determining the first cast of each meet. As in any leadership position, the master is also the lightning rod for criticism. The master may hunt the hounds, although this is usually done by a professional huntsman, who is also responsible for the hounds in the field, at the kennels. A long relationship between a master and a huntsman allows the hunt to develop and grow.

NOSE—The scenting ability of a hound.

OVERRIDE—To press hounds too closely.

OVERRUN—When hounds shoot past the line of scent. Often the scent has been diverted or foiled by a clever fox.

RATCATCHER—The informal dress worn during cubbing season and bye days.

STERN—A hound's tail.

STIFF-NECKED FOX—One that runs in a straight line.

STRIKE HOUNDS—Those hounds who through keenness, nose, and often higher intelligence find the scent first and who press it.

TAIL HOUNDS—Those hounds running at the rear of the pack. This is not necessarily because they aren't keen; they may be older hounds.

TALLYHO—The cheer when the fox is viewed. Derived from the Norman *ty a hillaut*, thus coming into our language in 1066.

TONGUE—To vocally pursue the fox.

VIEW HALLOO (HALLOA)—The cry given by a staff member who views a fox. Staff may also say tallyho or tally back should the fox turn back. One reason a different cry may be used by staff, especially in territory where the huntsman can't see the staff, is that the field in their enthusiasm may cheer something other than a fox.

VIXEN—The female fox.

WALK—Puppies are "walked out" in the summer and fall of their first year. It's part of their education and a delight for puppies and staff.

WHIPPERS-IN—Also called whips, these are the staff members who assist the huntsman, who make sure the hounds "do right."